# Death in the Black Patch

ISBN: 978-1-932926-56-9
Library of Congress Control Number: 2016908240

Cover Design: Nikki O'Connell (www.nikkiodesign.com)

Printed in the United States.

Artemesia Publishing, LLC
9 Mockingbird Hill Rd
Tijeras, New Mexico 87059
info@artemesiapublishing.com
www.apbooks.net

# Death in the Black Patch

## By

## Bruce Wilson

Artemesia Publishing
Albuquerque, New Mexico
www.apbooks.net

# Acknowledgements

I would like to acknowledge Bill & Berdie Foy of Mayfield Kentucky for helping me find the details related to the incident on which this story is based.

I want to dedicate the book to my wife Mary and to thank her for her selfless assistance, advice and encouragement at each step along the way from first idea to finished manuscript.

*Tiger Father begets Tiger Son*
Ancient Chinese Proverb

*The Truth is in the Ending*
Anonymous

# Chapter 1

May, 1906
Lynnville, Kentucky

The fluid light from a dozen torches cast moving shadows against the trees and the barn, reflecting off the single glass window of a weathered house. A shirtless black man knelt in the dirt, cowering at the edge of what had been his freshly planted tobacco field. Howling, pleading with the angry, masked Riders as they drove their horses across every row, crushing the tender plants to pulp, he begged them not to hurt his family. The man's cries could be heard over the pounding of the hooves, the snorting horses and the gleeful shouting of the Riders. In the house behind him, looking through the window, his terrified wife tried to keep their children quiet. Her husband's cries ripped at her heart.

A single Rider rode up to the house, his torch held under the edge of the roof, and yelled at the kneeling farmer, "You tell your friends that this is what'll happen to hillbillies who don't think the same way we do! If you don't, we'll be back and we'll burn your damned house to the ground with your family inside."

The farmer's feeble, strangled cries were lost in the thunder of the horses as they stormed out of the yard, and the deathly shadows of the torches fled into the dark like ghosts.

\* \* \*

The sun was still below the horizon and the night's shadows lingered as Wes Wilson moved along the eastern tree line of his empty tobacco field. The muted aroma of new honeysuckle scented the morning breeze, and dew from the grass next to the field soaked his worn-out work boots and the cuffs of his overalls. His hound, Rufus, trailed along, stopping occasionally to sniff the air. Hearing a noise, Wes quickly looked back across the empty field toward the house, and his boot caught the edge of a rock, sending him down hard on his knees.

Wes clawed around in the grass and found the apple-sized stone. Clutching it in his hand, he lurched up and threw it wildly into the woods.

"Damned rocks!" he bellowed, forcing a flock of birds out of the trees.

Swearing under his breath, Wes leaned over and slapped the damp earth off his faded overalls. Wes was tall, his muscles hard and his skin dark from years of working on the land. He looked around and yelled for the dog. Then he stepped carefully over the mounded rows of earth, heading for the house. Even though his knees hurt and his mind wrestled with worries about tobacco prices and the monopoly, he still needed to eat something and get the boys out into the field. *I can't worry about sellin' tobacco if it ain't planted first*, he thought, limping toward the cluster of buildings he'd built himself.

From the kitchen, his wife, Zora, watched him cross the yard. Even in the dim light she could see the stress lines on his face as he scraped the mud off his boots and stepped up onto the porch.

"What was all that shoutin' about?" she asked, stepping through the open kitchen door.

"Nothin' much," he grumbled. "I fell down because I wasn't watchin' where I was goin'." He took the cup of coffee she handed him and looked back toward the field.

"You decide what you're gonna do?"

"No, I ain't yet," he growled, still upset about falling down. "But I'll tell you this: nobody's gonna tell me what to do with my crop or my farm or my family—nobody." He paused for a moment, failing in his attempt to calm down. "I built this place for all of us, and no damned Planters' Association or cheatin' Tobacco Trust buyer is gonna get away with takin' it from me."

Wincing a little at his words, Zora put her hand on his shoulder. "Well, you can think about all that later. Come on inside and have some breakfast. I got biscuits and bacon and more coffee. Then you can get out to the fields. The boys should be ready when you are." She walked ahead of him into the kitchen and tied an apron around her small waist. Zora was a strong woman, capable of doing much of the work around the farm, but she was also wise—she knew when to speak up and when to keep her mouth shut.

* * *

The tallest building on Wes's forty-acre farm wasn't the two-story, three-bedroom house he'd built fifty yards from the road. Nor was it the lofted barn that sheltered the mule, cow and farm tools. The structure that dominated the sky-line was, like every other farm in the region, his tobacco-drying barn. Nearly three stories tall, the slat-sided build-ing stood on the north side of the tobacco field. At present, it was empty, awaiting the dark green leaves that would hang from its rafters over the slow-burning oak chips after the coming fall's harvest.

None of the buildings on Wes's land had ever been painted. Wes had never had enough extra money to spend on paint—feeding his family and paying the mortgage took most every dollar he earned in a year. Once, ten years ago, he'd managed to whitewash the house, but the sun and rain had long since turned its color to a mottled gray.

The fields and drying barn represented the economic lifeblood of the farm, but the house was its heart. There was no parlor like in the grand homes up in the county seat at Mayfield, no indoor plumbing and barely enough room for beds for each of the six children. But the kitchen was large enough for a wood-burning stove and a table capable of seating the entire family. Of all the places to gather on the farm, the kitchen was the only one that seemed always to pulse with the energy of the poor, hardworking family.

Crossing the yard from the chicken coop to the house, Zora felt the first warming rays of the sun as they peeked through the trees and chased the chill from her neck. She could tell that the day was going to be a hot one, and she smiled. Stepping up onto the covered porch, she glanced over her shoulder and caught a glimpse of Wes's blue shirt as he disappeared around the corner of the barn on his way to the fields, and she wondered if this would be one of the good days.

She pushed open the door to the kitchen with her one free hand and bumped into her sixteen-year-old, middle son.

"Lord, Anthie, you nearly made me drop the eggs!"

"I gotta hurry, Ma," he mumbled. "I was just tryin' to catch up with Pa. He said we were gonna finish puttin' in the shoots today, and if I didn't want to get whupped I'd better get out to the field."

"Are you hungry? Did you have somethin' to eat?"

"Not yet, but I grabbed a few of the biscuits from last night. I'll be fine, but I gotta go now."

"Connie and John Stanley left before your pa," she yelled at his back, "so you'd better get movin'."

Pulling the strap of his baggy overalls over one shoulder and cradling some biscuits in his hand, he nudged the door open with his foot and rushed out onto the porch. Smiling at her son's clumsy efforts to carry his breakfast and hurry at the same time, Zora watched him race across the yard toward the barn. As she turned and put the handful of eggs on the table she thought, *The hens must be as tired as I am; there should be more eggs than this.* She stared at them for a moment, listening to the sounds of the old farmhouse as it began to warm up from the rising sun and the woodstove. *If Wes is already threatenin' a whuppin', then today is likely to be one of his bad days.* With a deep sigh, she turned from the table and from her thoughts and headed to the back of the house.

"You girls get up now!" she yelled up the stairwell. "We've got lots of work to do today!"

* * *

At midday, Zora sent eight-year-old Irene out to the field with food for Wes and the boys. Zora had spent the morning washing clothes out at the pump while her oldest daughter, Mary Lula, watched the baby, Ruth. In her twenty-five years of marriage to Wes, Zora had washed his clothes so many times that this chore and the countless others gave her plenty of time to think—about her husband, her children and the future.

With the afternoon to herself, Zora started hanging her wash on the lines Wes had put between the barn and the coop. Clothes got dirty on a farm, and if you didn't keep them clean, they'd wear out far too soon. Using wooden pins, she started hanging one garment after another and began to think about Wes. She loved her husband and she knew that he loved her and the children. Wes worked hard for the family—planting and harvesting the crops, fixing what was broken and teaching the boys how to be men. But her mind kept coming back to what worried her most.

Wes drank liquor, and sometimes when he came in after working all day she could tell by his slumped shoulders and cold, hard face that he was tired and troubled. On nights like that, she knew that after supper he'd sit on the old wooden bench out on the porch and start in on the jug. One time she'd asked him to stop drinking and he'd gotten very angry. Even though that had been many years ago, she was still afraid of him when he was drunk. So she'd learned to keep her thoughts to herself.

The other thing that bothered her was more troublesome. In the last few years, one large tobacco company out of North Carolina had bought out all of its competition. It had started cutting prices, causing the farmers to split into two groups—those like Wes, who needed to sell at any price, and those hoping that by holding out they could force the company to pay them a fair price. The conflict between the two groups, fueled by the company's actions, had led to trouble. Wes had told her once how those who'd sold their tobacco to the company in other parts of the state ended up having their plant beds salted or their barns burned. Zora didn't like trouble of any kind, but she especially didn't want any trouble like that to touch the family.

Zora heard Irene singing as she came around the barn and realized that it was time to get on with some of the other chores. There was a chicken to butcher and supper to make. These other things would still be there, but she couldn't worry about them now. There was too much work to do before Wes came back from the field.

* * *

As day turned into evening, Zora sat resting in one of her kitchen chairs, quietly singing a hymn. The barely noticed scents of frying chicken and boiling coffee that filled this corner of the house and the chatter of the younger children in the next room only added to her sense of peace. Zora had been raised by her grandparents, and they taught her to think for herself, to cherish family, to stand up for what was right and, above all, to be patient. Zora never knew her parents. She was only two years old when her pa died after being kicked in the head by a horse. A few days after that, Zora's ma disappeared. Everything Zora knew about being a woman and a mother she'd learned from her grandma.

When she heard Wes and the boys coming into the yard, Zora rose from the chair and stepped over to the stove.

"You boys wash up, or your ma will have my hide!" Wes yelled as he stomped onto the porch. "And don't forget to scrape the mud off your boots."

He barely opened the door to the kitchen and stuck his head through the small opening. He saw Zora standing at the woodstove, stirring a pot of beans. "Hey, woman, you got enough food to feed four hungry men? We've worked all day long, and we're nearly starved to death."

With a quick sigh of relief, Zora turned to see the broad smile on Wes's face. Feeling a great rush of tenderness for him, she matched it with one of her own and said in mock anger, "I sure do, but not one of you men is gettin' a single bite until you're washed up. Nobody as dirty as you is gonna get fed in my kitchen. So get on out of here, and come back when you're scrubbed."

Wes chuckled, stepped back onto the porch and shouted to the boys. "The cook at this place is angry as a mean dog. Last one at the table gets nothin' but beans!" He ran to the pump and began to roughhouse with his sons. In a very short time they had their hands and faces clean. They went up to the porch, kicked off their muddy boots, lined up youngest to oldest and went into the house to have supper.

After the boys kissed their ma on the cheek, they moved to their spots at the table. The sound of chairs scraping on the floor eventually stopped, and most everyone was finally seated. While Zora held little Ruthie on her lap and watched her family, her heart felt full of love and joy. Mary Lula set the plates and bowls of food on the table and slipped gracefully into her seat. Anthie started to reach for a piece of chicken, but a quick cough from his father stopped him. Realizing his mistake, he pulled his hand back, whispered a quick apology and bowed his head like the others.

"Lord, we ask you to bless our family, keep trouble from our door and give us health and happiness. If these ain't in your will, then give us the strength to handle what does happen." Quietly lifting his head, Wes looked around at each of his children and then at Zora. With a shallow sigh, he quietly added, "Amen."

It always seemed to Zora that it took much longer to prepare a meal than to eat it. In seconds, the serving bowls were empty and the plates were full. Everyone was eating and talking at the same time. Rocking the baby who held a biscuit of her own, Zora listened to the sounds of a happy family.

"We did a good bunch of work today, boys," Wes said, looking first at his oldest son, Connie. "But we gotta finish tomorrow. We can't leave the shoots in the plant bed. We gotta get 'em in the ground." Then he added, "But it seems to me we might have got a lot more done today if sleepy-head had showed up on time and kept his mind on the job."

"Aw, Pa, I wasn't that late," said Anthie, his mouth full of chicken. "I came out quick as I could."

"True enough, but your head was in the clouds most of the day." Smiling at Zora, he turned toward his son and asked, "Are you still thinkin' about that girl? What's her name?"

"Sudie Morris," he mumbled.

"Well, when we're workin', you need to keep your mind on the job and not on Sudie Morris. There'll be enough time for girls when the fields are planted."

"How much did you get done today?" Zora interrupted.

"All but the section down near the ditch. We can finish that tomorrow if we get movin' early enough." He glanced at Anthie with a smile and added, "If there's any daylight left after that, me and the boys'll clean out the mess in the barn. Seems like once we start plantin' shoots the rest of the place starts to fall apart."

Seeing that their plates were empty, Zora said, "If you children are finished, go ahead and clear your dishes. There's no reason for you to sit here squirmin' like a bunch of night crawlers."

As if they had been waiting for her invitation, all five of them stood and pushed back their chairs. They each grabbed plates and bowls and carried them to the counter. After the others left the kitchen, Irene moved slowly around the table, pushing each chair up to it. When she got around to Wes, she put her lips close to his ear and whispered, "Pa, when it's time for bed, will you tuck me in?"

"Sure, honey. You just let me know when you're ready, and I'll come up."

Giggling, she hugged him around the neck and rushed out of the kitchen, her curly brown hair bouncing on her shoulders. Zora shifted Ruth to the other side of her lap, looked up at Wes and said, "What do you think is goin' on with Anthie and the girl?"

"If she's the one who lives across the state line, he won't get to see her as often as he wants to, that's for sure. But if he wants to see her bad enough, he'll find a way. I'm not so old I don't remember how that works," he said with a grin. "I recall tryin' to find any way I could to see you at your granddaddy's, and he wasn't easy on me either."

"He sure wasn't." She sat quietly for a moment and then added, "But you kept comin' back and kept tryin' to convince him you were serious about me."

"I was, Zora. I still am." They looked at each other across the length of the table, enveloped in a sweet silence. The sounds from the rest of the house seemed muted. Even the baby was quiet. For a moment, Zora saw Wes as he was twenty-five years earlier—a young man in love—and wondered if he was seeing her the same way. A crash from the other room interrupted the silence, shocking her a little.

"Here," she said, handing him the baby. "Take Ruthie in there and see if you can find out what got broken. I'll clean up the kitchen and then maybe we can figure out how to get this family of ours settled down for the night."

Holding the baby in one arm, Wes put his other one around Zora and pulled her close to his side. He squeezed her to his chest and kissed the top of her head. He didn't say anything, nor did he let her go. He just held her tightly. Zora's heart stirred with a wonderful heat, and her face flushed. She slipped out of his arms and pushed him gently away. Looking up into his eyes through the moistness in her own, she said, "Sometimes you're still that young man, Wes, and I'm glad, real glad."

*This is one of the good days*, she prayed silently as she watched him leave the kitchen. She wiped off the large table and then took a few minutes to wash the dishes and put them up on the shelves. Pouring the remaining coffee into her cup, she opened the door and stepped onto the porch. The happy sounds from the house and the gentle breeze gave her a sense of peace as she looked out into the night. With one free hand she curled a wisp of hair behind her ear and smiled. Wes's tenderness and strength were both comforting and exciting. She'd loved him forever, and though their love was comfortable, the moments of excitement always seemed to surprise her. She'd wake up every morning hoping for days like this one. But she was always aware that a day could go bad and the sweet and tender moments would seem but memories.

As she turned to go back into the kitchen, a quick flash of light from the woods across the road caught her eye. She stared into the darkness, trying to see it again, but nothing was there. *Probably the moon reflecting in a dog's eye*, she thought and walked back into the house.

* * *

Hiding in the tree line fifty yards away, a lone man watched Zora enter the house. He took one more draw on the stub of his cigar, dropped it on the ground and crushed it out with his boot heel. Pulling himself up onto the back of his horse, he turned the beast into the open field behind the trees and headed off into the dark night.

# Chapter 2
Sunday Morning, May 6

An hour before sunup, Anthie stumbled out the door and headed toward the barn. The moon was partially hidden by some clouds and cast a soft light across the yard. The air was damp and the crickets were scratching out the same old song they always did. He had hardly slept all night, and like a man headed toward a firing squad, he took reluctant steps. When he reached the barn, he set the lantern down and used both hands to open the door just wide enough to get through.

He crossed the hard-packed dirt floor and opened the stall, squeezing in beside the cow. The sounds and smells enveloping him were familiar, but didn't bring him any pleasure. He could hear the skittering mice in the loft, and the odor of dung and hay and dust seemed to hang on him like a fog. Reluctantly, Anthie squatted down next to the cow and put the bucket under her udder. The beast shifted sideways and stomped her hooves a few times before finally settling down. Of all the chores Anthie had on the farm, milking the cow was the one he disliked most.

"Come on, cow, let go of your milk! I don't have all mornin' to spend out here with you." Rubbing his hands together to warm them, Anthie reached for her distended teats. Squeezing and pulling them the way his father had taught him, he directed the steady streams of warm milk into the bucket.

With his head resting on the cow's flank, Anthie contin-ued to squeeze and pull and worry. He had worked hard from sunup to sundown Saturday and went to bed right after supper, but all night long he tossed and turned. Even as tired as he was, sleep just wouldn't come. Whenever he'd closed his eyes, he'd thought about Sudie—how she looked, how she smiled and the sweet sound of her voice. Every time he came up with a plan to go see her, he'd think of all the reasons his folks would disagree with him. *Maybe I can borrow Uncle George's horse, or I could walk; it'll only take a couple of hours.* When he'd finally run out of ideas, he realized it was time to milk the cow.

"So here I am, cow," he groaned. "You're milked, I'm tired and I probably won't get to see my girl." He stood up, took the heavy pail out of the stall and closed the gate behind him as he headed toward the house.

* * *

By mid-morning, the hot sun had turned the air to sludge. The sagging branches on the trees provided little relief as Wes drove the wagon along the deeply rutted road. The clopping of the mule's hooves on the packed dirt and the bouncing wagon did little to lift Anthie's spirits. He didn't much like going to church anyway, and after his sleepless night, he was even less in the mood for hymn-singing and the endless preaching of the minister. There was nobody he could talk to about Sudie or how he felt. His father teased him, Connie had his own girl problems and his ma would only tell him to wait until he grew up. *I am grown up*, he thought. *I'm as tall as Pa is, and I'm nearly as strong as Connie.*

As soon as Wes pulled the brake on the wagon, the kids spilled out of the back like a busted bag of beans. Mary Lula came around to the front of the wagon and waited for her mother to hand down Ruthie. Connie, a twenty-year-old version of his pa, helped Zora down from her seat and then wandered toward the church building. Still not done with his chores, Anthie took an empty bucket out of the back and walked toward the well. After he'd filled it with water, he set it in front of the mule and then went to find Connie.

As Zora watched Wes hobble the mule, she noticed something had changed. The warm, loving man she'd woken up with had become distant, his face hard, his eyes dark. "Are you comin' in today?" she asked, but he didn't answer right away.

"Don't know," he finally said, his voice flat, distracted.

"All right, Wesley, I'll save you a seat," she said to his back as he walked away. She headed toward the whitewashed church, thinking, *It's always like this with Wes on Sundays. There's a distance between him and God. He's a good man but he ain't ever needed church.*

She lifted the hem of her long Sunday dress out of the dust as she covered the distance to the porch. Waving a fly away with her hand and with it her worries, she decided it was time to ask God about Wes. She walked into the building and up the center aisle to the pew where the family always sat. Sliding in, she left enough room for Wes on the aisle and sat down. Mary Lula was seated to her right, the baby in her lap. She glanced at her mother expectantly, but Zora just shrugged.

As the room began to fill, the preacher rose from his chair and stood silently behind his pulpit. Zora's children scooted into the pew from the side aisle, and Connie wisely sat between Irene and John Stanley, whose energy hadn't yet subsided. Anthie slumped into the last available spot. The noise level in the room dropped as mothers shushed their children and latecomers found places to sit. Even with the windows open, the room was warm. Rather than cooling the air, the sparse breeze carried dust and a few flies into the nearly silent building. The open space next to

Zora seemed to shout out Wes's absence.

The preacher's frayed coat sleeves slid down to his elbows as he raised his arms toward the ceiling. More by habit than by his direction, the congregation stood and picked up the tattered hymnbooks that were in the slots on the back of the pews.

"Let us sing praises to the Lord!" the old man said. "Everyone turn to 'Bringing in the Sheaves.'" Soon his reedy voice was joined by those of the people as they sang the familiar hymn. Most didn't need the books, but they held them out just the same.

Although she often found comfort in singing hymns, Zora was distracted by the empty space next to her, and the words of the song brought little solace. She sensed Mary Lula's tentative glances in her direction and felt her daughter's tension as well. Wes had seemed happy the past few days, and as hard as she tried, she couldn't figure out why he was so withdrawn this morning. He and the boys had made good progress in the fields; even Anthie had focused on doing a good job. There had been no talk about troubles with tobacco prices, and she was sure that Wes hadn't been drinking. A gentle nudge from Mary Lula interrupted her thoughts, and she realized she was still standing even though the song had ended. Hoping that no one had noticed, Zora sat down quickly, her cheeks reddened. The preacher began a loud prayer beseeching God to touch the hearts of the lost souls in the congregation. Anyone watching Zora would have thought she was praying, but her mind and heart weren't focused on God. She was worried about Wes.

While the preacher droned on with his prayer, Zora's uneasiness grew. She could hear nothing but the thoughts in her head. When Wes slipped into the seat next to her, she flinched as if she had been awakened from a nap. Her heart pounding, she turned toward him, hoping to see a

smile. But Wes wasn't smiling. He wasn't looking at her either. Even though his eyes were closed, Zora knew that he
wasn't praying. His face looked hard, cold, and the muscles
in his clenched jaw stood out like knots. A little frightened,
she reached out to hold his hand, seeking the warmth
and softness she knew lay below the hard calluses. At her
touch, he clenched his hands into fists, and she pulled back,
afraid of whatever was going on inside him. She couldn't
tell if it was anger or fear. She wanted to comfort him, to
put her arms around him and tell him everything would be
all right. She knew she should be praying for him, but she
couldn't control the thoughts that filled her head, let alone
talk to God. Instead, she sat in the pew, as close to him as
she dared, and soundlessly said his name over and over.

* * *

"Anthie, you take your ma home," said Wes as they stood
near the wagon. "I've got some things I need to do." Connie
had already helped his mother onto the wagon seat, and
the others were getting settled in the back. Zora turned toward her husband, hoping for an explanation, but Wes was
staring down the rutted road. After a moment, he turned
back toward his family.

"Go on, now, get on home," he said to Anthie, but he was
looking at Zora. "I'll be there later." His eyes were dark,
and the look of hardness hadn't left him. He stood in the
churchyard, rigid as a fence post, offering them no explanation, no comfort, waiting for them to start the five-mile trip
to the farm.

"Get, mule," said Anthie as he flicked the reins. The animal snorted and tugged, and the wagon pulled away. The
children in the back of the wagon watched their pa until
the trees blocked their view. No one spoke, but all of them
were distressed, wondering what was wrong. Zora sat erect,
staring straight ahead. Anthie thought he saw tears on her

cheeks reflecting the afternoon sun, but he wasn't sure. In the back of the wagon, Mary Lula held the baby close to her chest, while the others grew pensive, each wondering what had turned a good day into a troubled one.

* * *

Wes's broad shoulders sagged a little as he stood in the churchyard for a few minutes, watching his family leave. He paid no attention to the other families as they turned their wagons onto the dirt road. From the front door of the church, the skinny preacher watched Wes for a moment and then turned back inside. Wes shoved his hands into the pockets of his overalls, took a deep breath of the dusty air and walked out to the road. He paused once more before turning right and then walked toward the farm he'd seen during the ride to church. He didn't really want to talk to the man who lived there, but he knew he had to, that it was a matter of survival for himself and his family.

Wes had seen the black man standing at the edge of his tobacco field, or at least what had been his tobacco field. From the wagon seat, it had appeared to Wes that most of the five or so acres had been trampled. The newly set plants were no longer in neat rows, and the furrows themselves were beaten down nearly flat. Wes's first thought had been that a tornado had come through the farm. But there had been no storm, at least not one made of wind and rain and hail. As he plodded on toward the farm he knew that the storm had been men, men with masks. *Why would anyone destroy this man's crop?* he wondered. *He's just a sharecropper, and his little bit of tobacco won't make much difference in the problems between the farmer's Association and the Tobacco Company Trust.*

When he arrived at the lane that led to the farmhouse, Wes stopped. The man was no longer outside staring at the destruction, and his absence allowed Wes to get a closer look. There were only a few untouched plants, and these would never yield enough tobacco to sell. Wes looked both directions along the road and, seeing no one, looked toward the weather-beaten house. What he was doing was unacceptable and would have been frowned upon by everyone he knew. White men did not make calls on black men. The government might have ended slavery in the war, but they didn't end three hundred years of custom. Even if Wes didn't like the way these people were treated, he knew he had to at least act the same as his friends and his neighbors did toward them. Yet Wes needed to talk to the man and find out what had happened; he didn't care what anyone thought.

Wes turned from the destruction and walked up the sagging steps to the door of the house. After looking around again to see if he was being watched, he knocked twice on the door. He could feel his heart beating, but told himself it was because of the quick walk from the church. *That's probably why my hands are sweating too,* he thought. There was no response, so he reached to knock again, when the door opened and the dark face of a man a few years older than Wes peered out at him. The sunlight on the porch bled into the darkened room. In the gray shadow, Wes could see the man's hand clutching the barrel of an old shotgun.

"What you want?"

"I ain't here to cause you any trouble, mister. I'm a farmer just like you, but I need to ask you somethin'." Wes sensed the man's pent up anger.

"Ask me somethin' about what?"

"Let's talk out there in the yard. I don't wanna disturb your family." Wes's solemn face didn't reveal the hint of fear he felt about the gun.

The black man turned away from Wes for a moment. He leaned the gun against the wall, reached for his hat and stepped out onto the porch, closing the door behind him.

He glanced at Wes for only a second before he dropped his eyes, a custom he hated but one he knew was still expected. Wes turned from him and walked off the porch toward the field, stopping when he reached what was left of the first plowed row. When he turned and looked at the man's face, he saw someone who knew hard work and sorrow. For a moment Wes felt that the only difference between himself and the farmer was the color of their skin.

"I'm Wes Wilson. I've got a farm on the other side of Lynnville." Wes started to reach his hand forward to shake hands, but realizing it would be an awkward gesture for both of them, he quickly shoved it into his pocket.

"Jackson," said the man. He risked looking into Wes's eyes and, seeing no anger or arrogance, added, "Joseph Jackson."

With genuine curiosity and a good deal more respect than Jackson would have expected, Wes asked, "When did this happen, Jackson?"

"Night before last," Jackson said as he kicked at a clump of dirt and then sat down on his haunches. "Don't know what I'm gonna do."

"I've got to ask you this," said Wes, "and I mean no disrespect." He paused as he tried to come up with the right words. "Was it the Klan or the Association Night Riders?"

Jackson didn't respond right away. Wes even considered asking him again, but then Jackson mumbled, "Is there a difference?"

"Have any of the boys from the Association been around talkin' to you about your crop?"

Looking up at Wes, Jackson said, "Mr. Wilson, I'm not sure who I can trust anymore, so let me ask you a question first. Are you one of the Association boys? Or are you a hillbilly just like me?" Without waiting for an answer, Jackson scooped up some of the dirt from the mound in front of him and then stood up slowly. He held his cupped hands in front of Wes and then showed him. "See this salt? The Klan don't salt fields like this." He turned his hands over and let the dirt fall back to the ground. "It ain't right," he said. "I've got a family to take care of."

He stood silently, searching it seemed, for a way to start his story. "We ain't got a clock, but it must've been after midnight. I heard a dog howlin' down the road, but that ain't strange, so I didn't worry too much about it." Jackson started walking into the field and Wes followed.

"Then I heard somethin' like thunder way off to the west. I thought we were gonna get some rain and how good that'd be, things bein' so dry. So I rolled over and tried to go back to sleep. A few minutes later, that dog started up again, so I got up to take a look outside. That's when I saw 'em." Jackson turned and looked at Wes. Beneath the anger, Wes saw a deep sadness in the man's eyes and knew that as much as he'd wanted to fight back against his situation, Jackson also knew he didn't stand a chance.

"There was ten or twelve of 'em all on horses and they was carryin' torches. A couple of 'em had shotguns. The rest, though, were just millin' around out there in the yard." Jackson pointed to the space between his house and the road and then looked at Wes again. "All of 'em had masks on. I thought they were Klan, but then one of 'em, I guess he's the boss, asked me if I'd decided to join up. I asked him what he meant, and he said 'Are you stupid? I want to know if you're goin' to join the Association.' I told him that I didn't think they'd let me join up, me bein' a nigger and all." Jackson looked over at his house and then turned back to Wes. "Then the man said he didn't expect me to go to no meetin's but if I wanted to have a crop at all this year I'd better plan on puttin' my tobacco in with 'em. He said I'd better not have any ideas about sellin' to any Trust buyer."

Wes waited while Jackson stared off into the field.

"When I told him that I had a family and I owed money

and I had to sell to the tobacco company or I'd lose everythin', he got real mad. The boss started yellin' and tellin' the others to show me what happens to hillbillies who want to sell out to the bastards tryin' to drive the prices down." Jackson stopped for a moment and took a deep breath. "I couldn't stop what happened next, and I couldn't do nothin' to save my crop."

When he started again, his voice had changed, and Wes felt, rather than heard, the fear. "Then the two boys with the guns rode up to me and pointed them at me. They made me stand there and watch as the rest of 'em rode out into this field and started runnin' the horses into my tobacco as they tromped down everythin'. They hooped and yelled and carried on like it was fun. But they didn't miss hardly a plant. It only took 'em half an hour to destroy my life. When I thought it was over, a couple of 'em grabbed some bags of salt off the back of their horses. Then they took the bags out here into the field and split 'em open with knives and started throwin' the salt around like they were feedin' chickens. I begged 'em not to do it. And all the while I wanted to do somethin', to fight back, but I was afraid. They had guns and I was afraid for my family. All that work plowin' and plantin' the seed beds, all of it for nothin'.'"

When Jackson finished, he dropped to his knees, out of words and, it seemed to Wes, out of hope.

Wes didn't know what to say. In some dark part of his mind he'd hoped that the damage to Jackson's farm had been done by the Klan. That way, even if he felt bad for Jackson, he could rest a little easier knowing that the problem wasn't related to tobacco prices. But that clearly wasn't the case, and now Wes knew a man in the county who had been visited by the Association's Night Riders. The threat of a raid was suddenly real. If they could tear up a field this close to Lynnville, nothing could stop them from doing the same to his farm. He had some hard thinking to do, but he also needed to get home.

"Jackson, I'm sorry about what happened here. These are sad times, hard times, and I don't think they're goin' to get better for quite a while. But I've got to get on home to my family. Thanks for talkin' to me." Wes waited for some response from Jackson, but there was none, so he turned away and headed back out to the road. As he turned toward home, Wes looked back toward the house, but Jackson had already gone inside. Wes walked home, thinking about the Night Riders and Jackson and wondering what all of this meant for his own family.

* * *

The long ride home from church had given Zora plenty of time to think about Wes. At first, he'd seemed angry or even afraid. But the more she thought about it, she believed that neither of these was true. Zora couldn't figure out what was going on, but Wes's older brother George lived in the farm next to theirs, so she decided to talk to him. *Maybe he knows what's wrong with Wes,* she thought, *and maybe he can tell me why Wes seems so troubled.*

"Anthie, I want you to let me off at your Uncle George's. Then you take the rest of the family on home."

"All right, Ma," he said, "but why?"

"That's none of your business, son. Just do as I tell you."

Anthie drove the wagon onto the lane of his uncle's farm and pulled up in front of the house. He waited while Connie helped his mother down from the wagon, and when his brother climbed up onto the seat, Anthie turned the mule toward home. During the ride, he had been thinking about Sudie and decided to ask his ma about going down to the Morrises' farm when they got home. *But, if Pa ain't home yet and Ma's at Uncle George's, no one will miss the mule.* Whether or not his reasoning was sound, it worked for him. "Go mule," he said with a smile on his face.

* * *

Zora stepped up onto the porch and then turned back, watching the wagon pull out. She heard the door swing open behind her and looked back to see her sister-in-law. Malinda paused and then came out to stand beside her. She put her arm around Zora's shoulder, and they waited until the wagon turned onto the road.

"What a nice surprise, Zora," she said. "As close as we live, it seems we don't see one another nearly often enough. Come on inside. It's too warm out here. Can I get you a glass of water?"

"Yes, thank you," she said and stepped into the house. It wasn't much cooler inside, but at least it was out of the sun and away from the dust. After Zora brushed off her dress and removed her bonnet, she sat down at the table while Malinda headed to the kitchen for the water. Zora always enjoyed visiting with Malinda, but today she needed to talk to George. She hoped that he would know what was going on and maybe give her some information that would help.

"Here's your water," Malinda said as she handed the cup to Zora and sat in a chair across the table from her. "It surely is warm out there. It'd be real nice if we got a shower to cool things off." While Malinda chattered on, talking about the children, Zora nodded and smiled occasionally. She didn't want to be rude to Malinda, but she had to figure out a way to find out if George was around and if he'd be willing to talk to her.

"Are you all right?" Malinda said as she rose from her chair and came around the table. "You seem bothered about somethin'." She sat down next to Zora and took her hand. "What is it?"

"Oh, Malinda, I don't know what's wrong. That's the problem." Zora's words came in a rush. "I'm worried about Wes, and I thought if I came over here I could talk to George and maybe he'd know what's goin' on with him." She clutched Malinda's hand while tears slid down her cheeks. "There's somethin' the matter with Wes, and I don't know what to do for him. Is George here? Will he talk to me?"

Malinda put her free arm around Zora's waist and pulled her close. She held her tenderly for a moment, and then said, "Don't you be concerned, dear. I think George is out in the barn. I'll go fetch him, and we'll figure out what to do."

When Malinda scurried out the door to find her husband, Zora dabbed at the moistness in her eyes with the sleeve of her dress. She hadn't wanted to cry or lose control of her emotions, but her worries were clearly deeper than she'd thought. While Malinda went looking for George, Zora's fear that she'd said too much or maybe even the wrong things began to fill her mind. *Wes isn't going to like me talking to anyone about his problems. He's not going to like this one bit. I should just go on home, and we'll work this out ourselves.* She rose from the chair and looked around for her bonnet and spotted it lying on the table. She picked it up and quickly turned toward the door as George and Malinda came in from the barn.

"What's wrong with Wes? Is he sick?" bellowed George, a skinnier, taller version of his younger brother. He was breathing heavily and gripped his hat in one closed fist. Malinda stood behind her husband, her hands clasped in front of her chest.

"No, he's not sick. At least I don't think he is." Zora started to put her bonnet on, searching for words. "He must be worried about somethin'. I just thought you might know if there's anythin' botherin' him."

"I ain't talked to Wes for quite a while," said George.

Zora moved around them to the door. "I'm sorry I took you away from your work, George. I should just go on home. Don't go worryin' about us, we'll be fine. I'll have Wes come see you." Zora knew, though, that Wes wouldn't be coming over to see George, because she wasn't going to say anything to Wes about her visit. As she stepped off the porch and walked quickly into the yard, she ignored their mumbled replies. Her head down and her heart beating, Zora rushed up the lane to the road. *Oh, Lord. What have I done?*

\* \* \*

Anthie had been on the mule for nearly an hour when he caught the glint of the sun off of running water. He led the animal down the shallow bank and let it drink while he pulled off his shoes and socks. The cool water felt good on his feet as he sat in the soft grass on the bank of the little creek. Although he was anxious to get to Sudie's, he was still a bit afraid. He convinced himself that a short rest for the mule was a good idea for both of them.

Anthie wasn't afraid of seeing Sudie; he was just a little scared about facing her father. He'd only seen the man once before, and he'd never spoken to him. But today, he would have to meet the man face to face. The other thing he was worried about was that he was making an unannounced call on Sudie. He hadn't spoken to her since the picnic, and despite his luck today with the mule, there was really no way to tell her he was coming.

The mule snorted and interrupted Anthie's musings. It also convinced him that he'd stalled long enough and needed to get moving again. The Morris farm was only a few miles ahead, but Anthie had to watch his time if he was going to get back home before dark. Grabbing the mule's halter, he led it back up to the road and climbed onto the animal's back. He kicked the mule gently and got moving.

\* \* \*

While walking down the road toward home, Wes thought about Jackson and the man's troubles. He kept trying to convince himself that his own situation was different, that he didn't need to worry about a visit from the Night Riders. He knew that except for the color of their skin, he and Jackson were the same—farmers with families and with the need to sell their tobacco at the best price and to sell it in time to pay what they owed. Wes knew he had few choices, and each of them held considerable risk. He believed he couldn't win no matter which option he picked. Regardless, he knew that he had to keep a watch over his crop and do everything he could to protect it. *I will not let this happen to my family,* he thought. *No Night Rider is gonna destroy my crop.*

From her kitchen window, Zora watched Wes as he walked slowly toward the house. His hands were shoved deep into his pockets and his face was shaded by the brim of his hat. If he was angry, she thought, what she had to tell him would upset him even more. But she had to tell him before he found out on his own. When Wes stomped up onto the porch and came into the kitchen, slamming the door behind him, Zora saw the same face on him he'd had in church. Whatever he'd been doing, wherever he'd been had done nothing to relieve him of the burden she sensed he carried. She was afraid now, not of him, but for him. She saw the angry, mean side of her husband in his dark eyes and clenched jaws. When he finally spoke, her fears were confirmed.

"Go get my shotgun."

"Wes!"

"You heard me. Go get my damn shotgun and bring it out to the porch."

He turned away from her, reached up onto the shelf and brought down the whiskey jug. She watched him pull the cork and take a quick swallow. But she didn't move, couldn't move. The iciness of his voice had frozen her feet to the floor. Holding the whiskey jug by its neck ring, Wes carried it out the door and onto the porch. He slammed the door, and the noise was enough to get Zora moving. She walked quickly into the hallway toward the back of the house and pulled the heavy shotgun off of a high shelf near the back door. She checked to see if it was loaded and was relieved to discover that both barrels were empty. She took a box of shells off of the shelf and put it in the pocket of her apron. *Be strong*, she prayed to herself and walked back up the hall to the kitchen door. When she stepped outside, she found Wes sitting on the porch bench. He held the jug in his lap and stared off to the west, watching the sun drift toward the horizon. Zora walked over to him and leaned the shotgun against the wall. As her shadow fell over his face, he turned to her.

"Did you bring the shells?" he snarled.

Zora pulled the box from her apron pocket and set it in his lap next to the jug. She didn't speak, afraid of what he had to say, desperately wanting to ask him what was wrong. But she feared she'd stir up the anger she saw in his eyes. Since not knowing was even worse, she finally asked, "What's wrong?" and his answer came quickly, like a rushing summer rainstorm.

"The Night Riders are in the county and they're tearin' up tobacco. They wiped out a farm over near Cuba just because the man was gonna sell his crop to the Trust. They ran horses through his field and salted it when they were done." He stopped and took a drink. "Zora, he's just like me. He's a farmer with a family and crops and debts just like me. If they'd do it to him, what's to stop 'em from doin' it to us?"

Afraid of what he might say next, Zora waited.

"But I'll tell you this. Nobody is gonna force me to decide what I can or can't do with my own crop. Maybe some fellas can hold out. I can't, Zora, I won't." When he ran out of words, he lifted the jug and drank some more. He set it down on the bench and picked up the box of shells, opened it and took two of them out. He loaded both barrels and then stood up.

"I promise you this, Zora. I'll stay out here forever if I have to, but I'll be damned if anybody is gonna destroy my crop. I'll kill 'em first. I swear I will. I'm gonna protect what's mine. Nobody is gonna hurt me or my family or my farm or my . . . "

The whiskey had slowed the flow of words, but it hadn't made him any less angry. He gripped the shotgun tightly and began pacing back and forth on the porch. Zora stayed quiet and kept out of his way, watching him closely, waiting for a chance to speak. She didn't yet know what she'd say, but she knew she had to wait for the right time to speak. A moment later she said, "Anthie took the mule and went down to see Sudie."

\* \* \*

Anthie's first thought as he slid off the mule was that no one was home. Except for the light breeze blowing past his ears and the chirping of a few warblers, it was quiet. Tying the reins to the rail, he walked onto the porch and tapped lightly on the door. Anthie waited for a moment, hoping for some response, and when there was none, he stepped over to a window and peeked in through the muslin curtain. After knocking on the door for the third time and waiting even longer for someone to answer, he turned around and sat on the steps.

"There's no one home," he said to the mule. "Everybody stays home on Sunday afternoon, don't they? Where are they?" The mule didn't answer; it didn't even look up. It just kept nibbling on the grass. "You're a big help, you dumb mule."

He reached down and picked up some pebbles out of the dirt and tossed one of them at the mule's flank. The animal lifted its head and snorted at him. When he tossed a second one, the mule ignored him. Anthie must have sat there for an hour or more, pondering what to do. The sun was starting to go down, and he knew he should be heading home.

His head down and his mind churning, Anthie didn't see the Morrises' wagon turn off the road. When he heard the clopping hooves of their horse, he stood up and froze. Sudie's father was staring right at him, and he didn't look a bit happy.

"Hey, boy, who are you? What are you doin' here?" His voice was strong, and his stern look gave Anthie an icy chill. He was saved from having to come up with an answer when Sudie, a petite fourteen-year-old, popped up from the wagon box behind her father.

"It's Anthie, Pa, Anthie Wilson." Anxiously she pushed her way through her siblings in the back of the wagon and hopped off the back. She ran around to the front, but stopped short when her father spoke again.

"Sudie Mae, you stop right there." He looked from his daughter to the lanky, speechless boy standing in front of the horse. "You didn't answer my question. What are you doin' here?"

Searching for words, Anthie could only mutter a few mule-like sounds, and then the chill he'd felt a moment before turned to sweat. But when he looked at Sudie, her smile, tentative yet hopeful, gave him the words he'd been seeking.

"Sir, uh, Mr. Morris, I came all the way from Lynnville to pay a visit on your daughter, Sudie."

Morris started to say something else, when his wife jabbed him in the ribs with her elbow. He turned to her and she whispered something only he could hear. The muted conversation between husband and wife evidently ended in Mrs. Morris's favor, because he frowned at her and then turned to Anthie.

"Well, boy, it's mighty late for makin' a call," he said. "The sun'll be down in a bit, so you better make it quick, and the two of you stay up on the porch. You hear me?"

"Yes sir. We'll make it quick, I promise. And thank you, sir, uh, ma'am, thank you."

Sudie ran over to Anthie and stood stiffly in front of him. He looked down at her and then back up at her parents. When he dropped his gaze back to Sudie, she was smiling again. He still hadn't moved, so she took his hand and gently pulled him toward the house.

While Sudie and Anthie sat side by side on the porch, the children walked slowly up the steps, never taking their eyes off of their sister. Anthie didn't look at them or Sudie's parents; he just stared at his feet. As the two adults made their way up the steps, they, too, looked at Sudie and her caller. Just before he entered the house, Mr. Morris grumbled another warning about the lateness of the call and the need to stay on the porch.

When they were finally alone, Sudie reached over and held his hand. Still speechless, Anthie turned toward her. Earlier he'd been afraid to speak because he wasn't sure what Mr. Morris might do to him. Now he was afraid of not knowing what to say to this beautiful girl. All of the clever things he'd thought of during his sleepless night simply vanished from his mind. Even if he'd found the words, his throat was so tight no sound would come out, and his mouth was as dry as a week-old biscuit. But the words eventually came as he grew more relaxed. The two young people sat and talked as the sun disappeared, and they became washed by the light that spilled onto the porch from inside the house.

"Sudie?"

"Yes, Mama?"

"It's time for the young man to go, now. You need to say good-bye and come in the house before your daddy gets mad."

"All right, Mama," she said. "I'll be right there." Sudie heard her mother walk away from the window, and then she stood up quickly.

Anthie rose and stepped down into the yard, towering over her as she stood on the porch, facing him.

"I don't want to go," he said, "but I guess I'd better."

"I wish you didn't have to go. But I'm real glad you came. Don't be afraid of my daddy, though. He sounds mean, but he's really not."

"Sudie, I, uh . . . " Anthie looked into her eyes, not knowing what to say or how he truly felt.

"Me too, Anthie," she blurted out. Then she put her hands on his shoulders, leaned up and kissed him quickly on the cheek, spun around and ran into the house.

Anthie was stunned. He stood rooted to the ground, unable to move. He only stirred when the oil lamp inside the house was extinguished, and he was left standing in the dark. The boy looked up at the stars that were just beginning to show and walked over to his mule. He untied the reins from the porch rail and led the animal out to the road. The moon hadn't risen yet, so he walked the mule down the unfamiliar road until he could see better. He reached his hand up to the place on his cheek where Sudie had kissed him. He couldn't feel anything different with his fingers, but the skin felt warm underneath. His lips curled into an easy smile.

"I got me a girlfriend, mule," he said, still grinning, and walked on in the dark.

# Chapter 3
Sunday Night, May 6

Wes sat on the porch bench, staring out into the darkness; the shotgun lay across his lap, and the nearly empty jug rested at his feet. Not his anger at Anthie or his fear of what might have happened to him or even the energy he'd generated pacing along the edge of the porch had dulled the effects of the whiskey. Zora had talked him out of walking down the road to look for the boy, reasoning that it was still early enough for Anthie to find his way home. Wes had snapped at her and sent her into the house, but stayed on the porch, seething with a mixture of rage and fear.

*If anything happens to that boy, I'll kill him*, he thought. He rose unsteadily with the shotgun in his hands and staggered down into the yard. He stopped halfway to the barn and checked to see if the gun was loaded; it was. "Where the hell are you, boy?" he muttered.

* * *

The light from the rising moon hadn't yet reached the dark road between the trees where Anthie trudged along leading the mule. That little kiss from Sudie had put him in a trance, and the song of the crickets seemed to carry his daydreams along like a gentle stream. Yet, thanks to the mule, he was at least heading in the right direction.

Anthie's fantasizing was interrupted by a distant rumbling. The mule stiffened and its ears twitched. Anthie stopped in the middle of the road and looked up at the clear sky and saw nothing, but the ground began to shake, and he sensed that galloping horses were coming in his direction. He pulled on the reins of the mule and jerked it off the road and into a ditch behind a thick stand of trees. Then he stood next to a large oak and looked out into the dark night.

Whoever was coming had slowed down. The thundering was gone, replaced by the distinct sound of walking horses, snorting to clear the dust from their noses. Anthie wasn't sure how many riders there were, but he didn't have to wait long to find out. As he watched from behind the trees, a dozen riders came into view. Heavy rags had been tied around the hooves of each horse, which muffled the sound of their movement. They stopped in the middle of the road, and the night became quiet as the horses rested. The moonlight had just reached the tree line on the other side of the road, and Anthie could see that the riders were masked and carried guns. His curiosity quickly turned to fear when the mule snorted. He reached up and put his hand over the animal's snout, hoping that the men hadn't heard the sound.

"What's that? Sounds like another horse," said one of them as he pulled up not ten yards from where Anthie was hiding.

"What're you so spooked about, Charley," said another man. "We're ridin' horses, ain't we?" He began to laugh a little.

"Shut up, both of you, and no names," said another man gruffly. "We've got some serious work to do, and we don't have time for foolin' around. Everybody knows the plan, right?"

Some of the men responded, but most stayed quiet.

"Remember, I'll do all of the talkin'. You just spread out

and let him see your guns. Don't say or do anythin' unless I tell you to. Got it?" The leader waited for some kind of response and getting none, said, "Okay, then, check your masks and let's go. Keep it quiet." He turned his horse away from the group and headed down the road. Once they were all moving, he kicked his horse into a trot, and the gang followed.

Anthie stood frozen in fear. He could barely breathe, and his heart pounded harder than when Sudie had kissed him. When the mule finally shook Anthie's hand off of its snout and snorted again, the boy quickly led the animal out of the brush onto the road and pulled himself up onto its back. He stared down the road in the direction the riders had gone. All he could see was the dust from their horses. Kicking hard on the mule's side, he said, "Let's get home, mule."

Anthie was glad when the trotting mule slowed to a walk. Now he could think again about Sudie, but the encounter with the riders kept interrupting those sweet thoughts. Who were they and what were they gonna do?

Anthie knew he had a bigger problem—what was going to happen when he got home. *It's late and it's dark. I took the mule without Pa knowin' about it, and he's gonna be mad. He just don't understand.* The thoughts kept tumbling around in his head like a pot of boiling stew, and they didn't let up all the way back home. *Maybe I can tell him I was late because I ran into some bandits and had to hide on the side of the road. Pa can't blame me for bein' careful.* Having decided what to say, he nudged the mule in the flanks. The animal moved quickly toward the farm, much more eagerly than the boy on its back wanted him to.

Sitting on the bench in the shadow of the porch, Wes saw Anthie stop at the head of the lane and get down off the mule. Through his whiskey-weary eyes he followed the boy as he led the animal across the yard and into the barn. He lifted the jug to his lips and turned it upside down, but got only a small drop for his efforts and threw it into the yard. Anthie came out of the barn and headed for the house, his chin on his chest and his hands in his pockets. Wes rose unsteadily and leaned against the porch post, the shotgun cradled in his arms.

"Where the hell you been, boy?" he rasped.

Anthie stopped quickly, paralyzed by the anger in his pa's voice. He looked toward the porch, trying to find him, to see his face, but sensed from his pa's tone he was in deep trouble. No good excuse, no meaningful words would come out of his suddenly parched mouth. He took a step back, looking for an escape, but knew it was pointless. He had to say something.

"I, uh . . . " was all that came out of his mouth before Wes stumbled down the steps and, with all the force of his rage, hit Anthie across the face with the back of his open left hand, knocking the boy to the ground. Anthie ended up flat on his back, blood flowing from his split lip and his battered nose. He fought to get up, but Wes put his booted foot on the boy's chest. Trying hard to catch his breath, Anthie tried again to sit up, but his pa pushed him down and said, "Don't move," and stood over the boy, shaking with rage.

Anthie looked up, but all he could see in the moonlight was a dark silhouette. Wes's own chest was heaving, his body was rigid, and the shotgun was clenched in his right fist. He leaned down to his son, putting more weight on the boy's chest.

"Answer my question, boy," he snarled. "Where've you been, and you'd better not lie to me."

"Pa," he said, wiping his arm across his bleeding face, gasping for enough air to get the words out. Blood and snot ran out of his nose and down across his chin. He coughed once, turned his head and spit a glob onto the dirt and tried again to say something. "Pa, I can't breathe," he groaned and coughed again. He grabbed his father's ankle with both

hands and tried to push the foot off his body. Caught off
guard, Wes tottered back for a moment. Then, enraged by
his son's resistance, he reached down and grabbed him by
the collar of his shirt, pulling the boy's face up to his own.
Wes's bloodshot eyes bored into Anthie's as he squeezed
the collar tighter. Sweat dripped off his face, and he grunted through his clenched teeth, his body vibrating with anger. Anthie grabbed his father's wrist and held on.

"Pa, I'll tell you," he pleaded, "just let me catch my
breath." Anthie fought back tears as he struggled to force
air into his lungs. *I don't wanna cry,* he thought. *I can't cry,
I won't cry.* Believing it was his only chance, he let go of his
pa's arm and looked directly into Wes's eyes. "Please, Pa,"
he croaked.

Wes continued to stare deeply into his son's eyes, and
then he let go of the boy's shirt. Anthie fell back to the
ground and began coughing and gagging. He rolled over,
spitting blood and gasping for air. Wes remained standing
over Anthie, his posture no less threatening. He hadn't let
go of the gun.

Anthie sat up and swiped his sleeve across his mouth
and nose again. He stared down at the blood on his shirt
and then looked up at his pa. What he saw in his eyes gave
him no comfort. He had been whipped by him before, but
never beaten, never hit so hard that he'd drawn blood.
Something was very wrong; without hesitating, Anthie
blurted out the whole story.

"I went to Sudie's, Pa. I took the mule and went down to
the Morris farm. I didn't mean to be gone so long. All we
did was talk, and when it got dark I knew that I'd better get
home. I woulda been home sooner, but I had to hide from
some bandits or Klan, I'm not sure what they were." He
stopped to catch his breath, but before he could continue,
Wes interrupted him with a shout.

"What'd you say?"

"I said we just talked and it got dark—"

"No. What'd you say about the Klan?" Although his words were still slurred, Wes's voice was strong. He straddled his son, looking out into the darkness. "Where'd you see 'em?

"It was just this side of the line. I heard 'em comin' and pulled the mule off the road and hid in some brush."

"What were they doin'?" Wes shouted as he looked quickly toward the road then back at Anthie. "Did they see you?"

"No, they didn't see me. I was hidin' real good. But they stopped right in front of me. There were maybe ten or twelve of 'em wearin' masks and all of 'em were on horses. Some of 'em had guns. One of 'em, I guess he was the boss, talked about some kind of plan. He told all of 'em to be sure to show their guns. I don't know where they were goin', but they were up to no good. I was scared, Pa, really afraid." Anthie's story spilled out. His throat was dry and sore, and he could still taste the blood in his mouth.

Wes stepped away from Anthie and, like a hungry wolf, began circling him. "You listen to me and listen good. You disobeyed me and I'm gonna punish you. But I gotta think about what you just told me, so I don't have time to worry about you right now. Now get out of here."

Anthie stood as quickly as he could and ran to the pump. He splashed water on his face and arms, and then he turned and raced up the porch and into the house. Wes watched his son until he closed the door behind him. Then he turned and headed up the lane. He looked both directions on the road and listened, his ears searching for the sound of Riders. Satisfied that the night was quiet, he strode back to his seat on the porch, kicking the empty jug out of the way.

* * *

Zora wiped Anthie's bloody face with a cloth she'd dipped in cool water. She looked deeply into his sad eyes and, hugging him gently, told him to go up to bed. She returned to the window in time to see Wes step up onto the porch. She'd watched and heard the struggle in the yard and had wanted to run outside and protect her son. But she was afraid that getting into the middle of the conflict would only make things worse for the boy. Wes had punished his children before, but Zora had never seen him beat one of them. Anthie was a strong boy and would heal physically, but she wasn't sure if or how soon he would get over the emotional injury of his pa's anger. At least now she knew what was bothering her husband. *He's afraid,* she thought. *He's afraid of the Night Riders and what they might do to his tobacco, and he don't know what to do about it.* She believed deep in her heart that they could find a way out of this trouble, but realized now was not the time to confront Wes. That would have to wait until he was sober.

# Chapter 4
Monday, May 7

From his seat on the porch, Wes looked at the sky as it began to brighten over the top of the trees. He had spent the night thinking about the Night Riders and the fight with his son. He knew he had overreacted by hitting Anthie, but he was still mad at him. Yet, he had a much bigger problem than worrying about the boy's bloody nose. He'd be making a lot of trouble for the family if he sold his crop to the Tobacco Trust and didn't join the Association. Wes got up from the bench, picked up the shotgun and walked out to the tobacco. *It isn't much land,* he thought, *but for Black Patch tobacco it's plenty.* Now that the Night Riders were in the county and causing trouble for farmers like Jackson, he knew that the possibility of losing the crop was a huge problem. But this was his farm, and he would make the decision about selling his tobacco. It wasn't anybody else's concern how he handled his business. *If they're looking for trouble, they'll find plenty of it right here.*

Wes started walking between the rows, but was interrupted when Anthie closed the barn door. He turned and glared at his son. With just a quick glance at his pa, the sulking boy looked away and carried the full milk bucket straight to the house. Shaking his head, Wes wandered out into the field, still angry about Anthie's decision to take the mule without asking.

Zora was cooking breakfast and turned to meet Anthie as he came into the house. She waited until he'd set the milk bucket on the counter and then stepped in front of him. Placing her hands on his broadening chest, she looked up into his eyes and reached toward his damaged nose and lips.

"Don't, Ma, leave me alone." He started to move, but she stepped into his path. She put her hands on his bruised cheek and looked deeply into his eyes.

"You hush a minute and listen to me." She paused. "What happened between you and your pa wasn't really about you or what you did yesterday. You're hurtin' right now and you may not believe it, but so's your Pa. He knows what he did to you was wrong, but he was drunk and angry and worried about a whole lot more than whether or not you had permission to take the mule or go see Sudie."

"You're wrong, Ma. He wasn't gonna use the mule yesterday, and if I'd waited until he got home to ask him, it would've been too late to go. He's just mean. He didn't just whip me, he beat me, and he knew I wouldn't hit him back. He don't care about me and I sure don't care about him."

Anthie tried again to move around his ma, but she held onto his shirt. Knowing that her son needed tenderness rather than strong words, she gently shushed him.

"No, son, you're wrong. He cares about you more than you know. I know you're hurtin' and you're confused. Your face'll get better, but I'm worried about your heart. That's where the hurt goes deeper and takes longer to heal."

Zora let go of his shirt and patted him on the shoulder. His face looked hard in a way she'd not seen before. As he turned away from her and walked into the back of the house, she wondered how long it would take before he would see that his pa does care for him and for all of them. She walked out onto the porch and saw Wes far off at the back of the tobacco field. He was just standing there, staring at his crop. *Maybe the heat and sweat and sore muscles of hard work'll get his mind off the trouble.*

Zora went back into the house and up the stairs. It was time to get the children up and moving. "Connie, Mary Lula, you all get out of bed. The sun's almost up and it's time to get to work. Come on, now, everyone up. I'll have some biscuits and bacon ready in a bit." She went back to the kitchen to finish up the breakfast, and while she worked she wondered about her family's future. *We've been through tough times before and this is no different,* she hoped.

* * *

Wes sent John Stanley to the barn with instructions to muck out the stalls of the cow and the mule. Once he finished that chore, he was to get back out to the cornfield to help Connie and Irene. The corn was nearly knee high, but with last week's rain, the weeds had started to pop up, and Wes wanted the entire field cleared so the corn would have a better chance of survival.

Wes had saved the toughest chore for himself and Anthie. The tobacco shoots had been in the field less than a week, and the entire five acres needed to be looked over to see if there were any weeds or worms and to make sure that each of the young plants had a shot of water. Wes thought that the job would get Anthie's mind off of the girl and serve as a reasonable punishment for the things he'd done the day before.

The sun's torrid heat bore down on Anthie as he stood in the middle of the field. His nose was sore, his cheek swollen, and he was tired. All morning long he'd been walking up and down the rows of small plants, pouring a ladle full of water on each one and bending down, searching for weeds and worms. It was mindless work, so he had plenty of time to think about Sudie, but the images of her faded every time he thought about his pa. He'd never seen him so mean. Sometimes when he got drunk, he'd yell and swear, but most of the time he'd just get grumpy and end up falling asleep. Last night was different. Last night Anthie had been truly afraid, physically and emotionally afraid of his own pa.

As the sun climbed higher and the temperature rose along with it, Anthie kept working. *Pa thinks I'm gonna quit,* he thought, *but I'm not. I'll show him that I can work longer than he can. He shouldn't have hit me. All I did was take the mule without askin' and come home late. What's so bad about that? Connie's done stuff like that before and he never got beat for it. Pa hates me.* The idea saddened Anthie, and his eyes filled with tears. As the painful thought rolled around in his mind, his sadness turned to anger. *Well, then, I hate him too.*

At midday, Zora brought the leftover biscuits and bacon out to where the corn and tobacco fields joined. Everyone sat under the cool shade of the trees at the edge of the field and ate the meager lunch, except Anthie, who had wandered off by himself. She watched him go and then turned toward her husband. Wes was sitting with his back against a tree, his face shaded by the brim of his hat. She knew him well enough to see that he was still mad at the boy. She continued to stare at him, but he didn't look up. *Today is different than yesterday,* she thought, *and I wish I knew how to make it better.*

After a short rest, Wes got up and growled, "Let's get back to work. There's a lot to do and the day's not gettin' any longer."

On any other day, such a statement would have generated some moaning and complaining, but everyone knew the best response was to say nothing. Anthie was the first one into the rows, determined that his pa not find fault with his work. The few worms he discovered were crushed under his foot, much like he had felt the night before. Plant after plant, row after row, he pushed on, repeating to himself, "I hate him, I hate him."

When the sun dipped behind the tree line in the west, Wes picked up his tools and started toward the house. All of the others, except Anthie, followed their father. It had been a hard day, and they were tired and dirty and ready to quit. Wes never looked back as he entered the barn, leaned his hoe against the stall and walked out to the pump in the yard. Afraid to disturb their father, the others waited until he finished. When he walked away, they gathered around the tub and rinsed the sweat and dirt from their hands and arms and followed him into the house.

"Supper's almost ready," said Zora over her shoulder. "I'll have it on the table in a minute." Turning to face them, she watched as Wes slid into his chair and the children quietly found their own places.

"Where's Anthie?" she said. Getting no response, she looked hard at Wes and then turned to Connie. "Where's your brother?"

"I think he's still workin', Ma."

"Well, you go out and get him and tell him he'd better get in here if he wants to eat tonight." As Connie walked out the door, Zora glared at Wes. She said nothing more and continued setting the food on the table. No one reached for a fork or squirmed in his seat or said a word. Zora stood at the window, looking out into the growing dusk, trying to hide her anger. She still hadn't thought of the right words to convince Wes he'd been wrong when he'd hit Anthie.

When Connie returned and said that Anthie was still in the tobacco field, Zora told the others to start eating. She turned away from the table and walked outside. In the failing light, she saw her son at the far edge of the field. He was bent over some shoots, his back to her, and didn't see her walking through the rows toward him.

"Anthie, what are you doin', son? Supper's ready. Ain't

you comin' in?" Her words were soft and gentle. As she held out her hands to him, she saw that the dirt on his face was traced with tears.

A bit startled, he backed up a step, not letting her draw any closer. "No, Ma, I ain't comin' in. I got more work to do, and I don't wanna be around Pa."

"But Anthie, it's gettin' dark."

"I don't care. I can see good enough and I gotta finish. I'm not gonna give Pa anythin' more to be mad about." He reached down to pull a barely visible weed. Zora moved to touch his arm, but he brushed her away.

"Anthie, please son, don't be like this."

"Like what, Ma? Like someone who's been hit by his pa? Like someone who knows his pa hates him? Oh, I'll do the work and I'll be quiet about it, but as soon as I can leave here, I will. I hate Pa and I hate farmin'. I'm gonna do somethin' better with my life. Maybe I'll own a store like Uncle Mark. Maybe I'll join the army. I don't know what; but whatever I do, I'll be away from him and any farm."

"You don't mean that. You can't."

"I can and I do." With that he turned once again to the weeds, pulling at them and tossing them aside.

Zora watched him until he finished the row. At the end, he stood up and faced her. For just a moment, she saw how he'd aged. Without saying a word, he stalked away from the rows of tobacco. The look on his face and the set of his shoulders as he turned from her reminded Zora of Wes. She saw in her son the temper of her husband. She continued to watch him until he disappeared in the shadows of the trees along the road. She was worried about him—his pain, his confusion and even his growing interest in Sudie—but she wasn't concerned about his ability to take care of himself, even at night on the road. He was young, strong and smart.

When she opened the door, Zora saw that supper was over. Mary Lula was washing dishes, with Ruthie at her feet. Mary Lula turned to her ma and said she'd fix her a plate. Clearly her oldest daughter was no longer a child, but a young woman, sensitive to the tensions in relationships and, perhaps, wanting to shield her siblings.

"Thank you," was all Zora could say as she sat and waited for Mary Lula to finish the dishes. Ruthie toddled over to her mother, and Zora pulled the baby up into her lap. She hugged her and idly rubbed her back. *I'm a truly blessed woman.*

After wiping her hands dry, Mary Lula filled her mother's plate with beans, biscuits and a small slice of ham. She brought her a cup of coffee and sat down across from her. She reached across the table and took Zora's free hand. Looking into her mother's eyes she said, "I love you, Ma."

"I love you, too—"

"Please let me finish. I love you and I love Pa. I know there's somethin' goin' on that's troubling you both. I also know it's none of my business, but it hurts to see it happenin.'"

Zora could only nod. She knew that Mary Lula was telling her the truth. She was also silenced by her daughter's love, insight and growing maturity.

"So, Ma, I don't want you to worry about us. I'll make sure that the children get fed. We'll all keep doin' what we're supposed to do. Just help Pa deal with what's botherin' him."

She released her ma's hand, came around the table and kissed her cheek. Then she picked up Ruthie and slipped out of the kitchen. Zora sat in the quiet room, picking at the food on her plate and thinking about the things Mary Lula had said. She knew she couldn't sit at the table all night. She had to talk to Wes.

Zora rose from the chair and set her plate and cup on the counter. She smoothed the front of her cotton dress, pushed a lock of hair back behind her ear and took a deep breath. With only a hint of hesitation, she strode from the room toward the back of the house, looking for Wes. She found him sitting on the bed in the room they shared. His back was to her as he stared out the open window into the growing darkness. The only light in the room came from a candle in a dish on the top of a bureau her grandmother had given them when they got married. The soft light did nothing to hide the weariness she saw in him. Despite her quiet steps, he knew she had come into the room, and she stopped short when he spoke.

"Don't start in on me, Zora. I know what you're gonna say and I don't want to hear it." His voice was gruff, but lacked the strength she'd expected. She walked around the end of the bed and looked at him. He didn't turn to her, but continued to stare out the window. Zora wanted to touch him, to put her hand on his shoulder, but she truly didn't know if she should.

"Wesley, please," she whispered. "I know you've got a lot on your mind and you're worried about so many things. I just think—"

"Zora, I told you I don't want to hear it. Leave me alone."

"Wes, I know you don't want to hear this, especially from me, but I'm gonna say it anyway. As wrong as Anthie was to take the mule and to stay out late, you were very wrong to hit him. That was you reactin' to your own fear and takin' it out on your son. He deserved punishment, but he didn't deserve gettin' beat up by his own pa."

Wes's silence filled the room, so Zora continued.

"What's goin' on with the Night Riders is very trouble-some; I know that. But it has nothin' to do with our son. Wes, you've got to apologize to Anthie. He just don't under-stand."

Wes turned away from the window and looked at her. His eyes were bloodshot, his face blank, but he was listen-ing.

"I've spoken my piece," she said. "If you need to be mad at someone in the family, then be mad at me and not our children. I'm goin' to put the young ones to bed and then go out and sit on the porch for some fresh air." With that, she spun around and walked out of the room. She pulled the door shut behind her and left Wes sitting on the bed, thinking about how things had been between himself and his own father.

* * *

Wes was born the year his father came home from the war. John Henry Wilson had spent more than three years riding with the 12th Kentucky and, like most of his neighbors, had come home a deeply changed man. He'd fought battles in Tennessee, Mississippi and Alabama and had only two short furloughs in all that time. He'd seen men die; some of them were shot, others run through with a bayonet, still more blown to pieces. But most of them died simply because they got sick from the bad water in the crowded camps.

John Wilson didn't talk about the war except with those neighbors who'd shared the experience. Like many of them, he sometimes had nightmares and would wake up in the middle of the night screaming. But by the time Wes was ten or so, the dreams had become less frequent and less intense.

Like most young boys, Wes was fascinated by the idea of war and battles. When he wasn't helping on the farm and had a chance to play with his friends, they'd run around the hills and lanes, pretending that they were soldiers. They'd use wooden sticks for their swords and muskets. They'd take turns being Damn Yankees and would try to outdo one another in the gruesomeness of their deaths. Wes wanted to ask his pa about the war, but he sensed that his pa didn't want to talk about it. Wes didn't understand why his pa was reluctant, so he never asked until one evening, just a few years before his pa died. Wes had come out onto the porch of their farmhouse and found his pa sitting in a chair staring off into the distance. As he did on most nights, he was drinking whiskey. Wes sat down on the porch, not far from his pa, and turned to look up at him.

"Pa?"

"Yeah," he said softly.

"What was it like fightin' in the war?"

"Why do you want to know?"

"I dunno, I guess I was just wonderin' what it was like. What was it like to be in a charge? What was it like to shoot at Yankees?"

His pa didn't answer him right away. Several minutes went by before he turned toward his son and said, "War is a nasty business, son. You're too young to hear about it."

"But, Pa, I—"

"You heard me, son. You don't know what you're askin'. Now go along, get out of here and leave me alone for a while."

"Please, Pa, I was just wonderin' if you ever killed anyone."

"Damn it, Wes, I told you to get out of here!" he yelled, rising quickly from his chair.

Wes jumped from the porch and started to run off toward the pig pen. Before he'd gone a few yards, his pa yelled again.

"Wait a minute! Get back here."

Wes walked slowly back toward the porch, stopping a few feet away from his pa. Reluctantly, he looked up, wondering if he was going to be punished just for asking questions. Instead, his pa just stared down at him.

"I want you to stand right there and listen to what I say. I'm only goin' to talk about this one time, and I don't want you to ever ask me about it again. Do you understand?"

Wes stood absolutely still, fearing that even the smallest movement might set his father off. When he finally spoke, the words sounded like a gate hinge in desperate need of oiling. "Yes, Pa."

"Now you listen to me and you listen good. War is a terrible, awful thing. I know, because I fought in the war for almost four years. I saw men die, and the way they died was not like it is in books. Sometimes they got shot in the belly and their guts just spilled out on the ground. Sometimes a cannonball ripped their head off. I've seen men just disappear. One minute they're standin' next to you and the next minute they're gone. There's nothin' but a mist of blood floatin' in the air. You asked me if I killed anyone. Well, I did. I killed too many to remember the number of them, but I remember every one of their faces. I see their faces in my nightmares, and I hear their screams and their groans and their cries for their mamas."

Wes felt like he was going to throw up, but he was able to swallow the acid-like liquid back. He still hadn't moved from the spot in front of his pa.

"War stinks. When men die, their bladders and their bowels empty. When hundreds or thousands of men die, the smell is a thousand times worse. And that smell is the smell that is in all of my nightmares. What you see and hear and think and smell and do in war never goes away."

Still not moving, Wes began to cry. Tears filled his eyes and dripped down his cheeks. He could barely breathe as he watched his pa slump into the chair and lift the jug off the porch. He tipped it up, taking two huge gulps of the potent liquid and looked at his son.

"So there it is. That's what war and killin' is like. Now you try to forget about it. But know this: I can't forget about it. If I could I would, but I can't. I don't ever want you to ask me about this again. Never! Do you understand?"

"Yes, Pa," he whimpered.

"Now get. Leave me be."

Wes turned and walked slowly around to the side of the house where his pa couldn't see him. He dropped to his knees and retched up whatever was in his stomach. His belly and his bowels kept clenching even though there was nothing left to purge. Wes's throat was on fire and his head pounded. He crawled toward the pump, hoping that a drink of water would get rid of the awful taste in his mouth. Standing up, he dunked his head into the nearly full tub, soaking himself to his shoulders. When he came up for air, he cupped his hands and drank the soothing water. After he'd satisfied his thirst and rinsed the foul taste from his mouth, he stood and walked out into the field.

Even though his mouth and throat felt better, his head was still pounding. As he wandered among the drying corn stalks, his pa's words wouldn't leave him alone. *What you see and hear and think and smell and do in war never goes away.* Finally, out of sight of his pa and anyone else in the family, Wes fell on his face in the dust of the cornfield and wept. He sobbed nonstop for a quarter-hour. He'd gotten the answers to his questions, the questions he wished he'd never asked. Long after dark, Wes came into the house and crept to his bed. He lay down, but he didn't sleep all night.

In the few years left of his father's life, Wes never asked him again about the war. But he believed that the whippings he got when he'd done something wrong or the angry shouts and withering stares his father sent his way were more than just a man punishing his son. They were his pa's only way of dealing with pain that would never go away, never leave him alone.

When Wes was just thirteen, his pa killed himself with his shotgun.

* * *

Zora's challenge to Wes hung in the still air of their bedroom. Wes hadn't moved from his place on the bed in the hour since she'd walked out. Although his body had been motionless, his mind hadn't rested. The ever-present issue of the Night Riders had been overshadowed by thoughts of his father and of his son. As far as Anthie was concerned, Wes had decided he'd back off a bit on his punishment, that perhaps he'd worked him too hard. But he was not going to apologize to the boy. Anthie would have to learn that life wasn't easy and that there are consequences for doing the wrong thing. *He'll get over it,* thought Wes.

Remembering these things about his pa, on the other hand, had been more unsettling than helpful. Clouded by this dark history, Wes used to blame his pa's anger and drinking on the war. But now he wondered if the violence came from something else.

These thoughts troubled Wes, but he had more important, more immediate things to consider. He needed to talk to Zora's cousin Art, whose farm was northwest of Lynnville. He had to find out what Art's plans were for his own crop, and he needed to find out soon.

* * *

After a restless night, he rose before breakfast, took the mule out of the barn and walked it over to the porch. Zora had sent the children out of the kitchen, and they watched Wes as he placed a bridle over the mule's head. The filtered sun warmed their backs while the cool breeze from the west ruffled their hair where it stuck out under their hats. They stood still, their faces expressionless, waiting for him to speak. Wes took the padded blanket from Connie and put it on the mule's back, checked to see that it was snug and pulled himself up onto the animal.

"I want each of you to get your chores done by the time I get back from Cousin Art's. I don't care when you start, just be finished before supper."

He looked at Irene. "You find out what your ma wants done in the garden and you do it, hear?"

"Yes, Pa," she whispered.

"When you're done with that, you help John Stanley."

Turning to John Stanley, he said, "I want you to chop all the weeds out of the ditch along the road. When you're done, pile 'em up and burn 'em. I don't want any of them weeds gettin' into the tobacco." He paused for only a moment and then turned to Connie.

"That sow's been chewin' on the boards like she's tryin' to dig her way out. Take some of that old lumber and patch it up good and tight. We gotta keep her from gettin' out in your ma's garden."

Looking at the purple bruise on Anthie's face, he said, "I want you to finish up what you started yesterday. Weed, worm and water those last rows."

"I finished all of it last night, Pa." Anthie stared at him, his jaw set and his eyes hard.

"Then I want you to go find a quiet spot and spend the day thinkin' about what you saw on the road the other night. We'll talk when I get back, and I want as much detail as you can remember." Wes knew this would please Zora, and in return he'd learn more about the Night Riders.

He paused for a moment, "Now remember, all of you, get your chores done before I get back from Art's. Do all of you understand what I want done today?" He looked hard at each one of them in turn and then kicked the mule in the flanks and rode out onto the road and away from the farm.

Irene looked up at the boys, expecting them to say something, and when they didn't, she turned and skipped across the yard and went into the house. John Stanley grumbled something to himself as he followed his sister. Anthie didn't move from his spot for a moment. Then he walked to the well to get a drink of water. Standing in front of the tub with the ladle to his lips, he seemed lost in thought. He finally took a sip of the water and hung the ladle on the hook.

When Anthie walked into the kitchen, John Stanley and Irene were sitting at the table, putting butter on biscuits. Mary Lula asked him if he wanted some. He shook his head and said, "Where's Ma?"

"She's in her room. If you go in there, be sure to knock on the door."

Anthie walked to the back of the house, took off his hat and tapped gently on the door. "Ma, it's Anthie," he whispered. "Can I come in?"

"Wait just a moment, son."

A minute or so passed before Zora opened the door and smiled at her son. "Come on in."

Standing in front of his ma, Anthie realized he didn't know what to say.

"Anthie, what is it?"

"It's nothin', Ma. I guess I just needed to tell you what Pa wants me to do today. I'm not sure why, but he asked me to think about what I saw on the road Sunday night."

Zora stepped toward her son and hugged him tenderly. "Then you do exactly what he asked."

"But why would he do that, Ma?"

"Your pa has lots on his mind. It's important for him to know what you saw, and it'll help him make some important decisions."

"But why won't he say he's sorry? Why would he beat me and then give me an easy chore?" Anthie felt bad as soon as the question left his lips. "Never mind, Ma. I know you don't know what Pa's thinkin'. I'm goin' down by the creek to think about what Pa wants. Sorry I interrupted you."

"Don't fret none about it, son. Just remember that your pa loves you."

Without saying a word, Anthie turned and walked out of the room. He went back through the kitchen, past Mary Lula and the little kids and out the door. Putting his hat back on his head, he headed through the trees to the creek.

# Chapter 5
Late 1905

T he banging on the door of the old farmhouse reached through J.D. Hooper's numb ears, tugging at dark dreams, forcing him to open his sleep-crusted eyes. The early morning sunlight shining through grimy windows burned through the narrow slits. Barely able to lift his head from the greasy pillow, he pushed himself up from the straw-filled mattress and lurched toward the door.

"Come on, Hooper, open the door."

J.D. hawked and spit onto the floor, his head drumming pain, his mouth cotton dry. Cupping his hands over buzzing ears, he tried to block out the pounding and yelling, but it wouldn't stop.

"What the hell," he croaked, cringing as the racket stabbed at his brain. "Hold on, I'm comin'." Halfway to the door, he tripped over an empty whiskey jug.

"Open the door, Hooper. This is the sheriff and we've got business."

J.D. grabbed his shotgun from where it leaned against the wall. Clutching it by the barrel and using it like a crutch he staggered to the door and fumbled for the latch. He swung the door open and tried to focus on the two silhouetted figures standing on the porch. "What do you want?"

"J.D. Hooper," said the sheriff, "I'm here to officially advise you that you are in default of your mortgage loan with the Henry County Bank." Pointing to the bank president next to him, he continued. "As such, your farm is now in foreclosure and you are to be evicted immediately."

"Evicted how? What do you mean evicted?"

"I'm here to ensure that you leave the property and take only your personal things." The sheriff removed a watch from his pocket and said, "You have exactly five minutes, so you'd better get moving."

J.D. lifted the shotgun up across his chest and put his thumb on the hammer and pointed it at the sheriff. "I ain't leavin' my farm, sheriff, and not you or any thievin' banker can make me." J.D. looked to his right at the banker and never saw the sheriff swing his pistol around and slam it against the side of his face. The shotgun slipped to the porch as J.D. slumped against the door.

Within two hours, J.D. was arrested, taken to the judge's house, charged and convicted with misdemeanor assault and sentenced to ninety days in the Henry County jail.

* * *

Charley Randall was miserable. He'd been in jail less than a week but felt like he was serving a life sentence. His cell was small, the mattress on the iron cot was lumpy and full of biting bugs, and the food gave him a bellyache. He gagged every time he used the foul-smelling bucket in the corner and had pretty much decided that things couldn't get any worse. He was wrong.

The iron-barred door at the end of the cell block swung open and banged against the pitted brick wall. The crashing steel assaulted his ears and battered his brain. Over the jingling of the jailer's keys, he heard a familiar voice, lifted his head and turned to look down the narrow passageway between the cells. *That's all I need,* he thought.

"Quit pushin' me, damn it. I ain't no cow."

"Got a neighbor for ya, Charley!" yelled the jailer. "I think he's an old friend of yours." He opened the cell across from Charley's and nudged J.D. Hooper into the tiny space. "This, my good man, will be your home for a while. Get used to it and be nice, and you won't have to stay any longer than ninety days."

"Shut up and leave me alone," said J.D. as he flipped the turned-up mattress onto the springs of the bed and sat on the edge. He looked across at Charley and shook his head, clearly annoyed that he was in jail.

"It looks like you been in some kinda fight. What'd you do, try to wrestle with a mule or somethin'?" said Charley.

"It wasn't a mule. It was that damned sheriff. He whopped me on the jaw with the side of his pistol."

"Why?"

"Because he didn't think I shoulda been pointin' my shotgun at his big belly."

"Why're you in here, Charley? It wouldn't have anythin' to do with that missin' money down at the Baptist church, would it?"

"That's why I'm in here," he said, "but I didn't take no money from the church." Charley sat up on the edge of the mattress, put his elbows on his knees and looked over at J.D. "I was just in the wrong place at the wrong time." He tried to stretch his back to get the kinks out of it and let out a groan. "I'm innocent, but the judge won't let me tell my side of the story."

"Didn't you have no lawyer?"

"I can't afford a lawyer, J.D. I ain't had a coin in my hand since I lost my farm. I probably woulda been all right if Sally hadn't divorced me." He dropped his face into his hands and groaned again. "Damned woman didn't know when to keep her mouth shut. I'll bet she lied to the sheriff and told him I took the church money. It'd be just like her to do somethin' like that. She got everythin' I own except freedom, and now it looks like she's taken care of that too."

"How long you in for?"

"Until I can prove I'm innocent or after another eighty-five days, whichever comes first. Since I didn't take the money, and I don't have thirty-seven dollars and fifty-four cents, I guess I'll be here for another three months."

Charley stood up and walked the short distance to the front of the cell. He grasped onto the bars and rested his head between them. His head hurt and his eyes burned, but he looked across at J.D. and whispered, "I don't think I can make it another week, let alone three months."

"You can and you will," said J.D., pausing to look toward the front of the cell block. "At least until we break out of here." He grinned and watched as Charley opened his eyes. "What?" J.D. said. "Did you think I was gonna stay in here for three months?"

Charley pushed himself back from the bars, his brows furrowed. "What're you talkin' about?"

"I'm talkin' about findin' a way to get out of this jail. I ain't gonna stay in here while that crooked banker is out there gettin' rich off my farm." J.D.'s voice grew louder, his grin shifting to a scowl.

"I dunno, J.D., if we . . . if you break outta jail, they're gonna find you and send you to the state prison; and nobody gets outta there."

J.D. turned away from Charley and flopped onto his bed. He pulled the flat, smelly pillow up under his head, closed his eyes and said, "Leave me alone. I got some plannin' to do." Then he pulled his hat down over his cut and bruised face.

Charley waited to see if J.D. was going to say anything else, but when he started snoring, Charley let go of the bars and sat on his own bunk. *If I get involved with J.D., I'm gonna be in trouble forever,* he thought. *But if I can get through ninety days in here, I can leave this county and go someplace where no one knows me.*

But Charley made it through the whole ninety days; they both did. In time they'd gotten used to the routine, the bad food, and the smell of the bucket. The jailer told his friends that the two of them were never going to stay out of trouble and that they'd probably end up in the state prison someday. At the end of December 1905, they walked out of the jail and stood on the boardwalk.

"Good-bye, J.D.," said Charley as he stepped into the street.

"Where're you goin'?"

"I'm gettin' outta this town and this county before I get arrested again for somethin' I didn't do." Charley hitched up his pants and hung the flour sack containing his worldly goods on his shoulder.

"Wait a minute, Charley," said J.D. "I'll go with you."

Charley turned back to face him, confused by J.D.'s friendly tone. He couldn't remember ever hearing the man say anything that nice. "You don't even know where I'm goin.'"

"It don't matter; I need to get out of this county too. We might as well go together. What do you say?"

"I'm leavin' anyway, and if you're walkin' in the same direction I can't stop you."

"Okay," said J.D., "but I've gotta make one stop at the farm to pick up some of my things. Headin' west is as good as any other direction and my old place is on the way." J.D. walked up to Charley and waited for a response.

"Might as well," Charley said, turning west and kicking up dust in the road.

They walked out of town in silence for about an hour and turned off the main road toward J.D.'s farm.

"The place don't look so good, J.D."

"Course it don't. There ain't been anybody here for three months. It's not like I could hire someone to take care of it."

They walked up to the porch, and J.D. set his bag down.

"You wait here a minute while I go take care of some business."

Charley nodded and turned away, looking at the trashy yard and fallow fields. The barn door was hanging crooked, and there were large patches of weeds everywhere. He sat on the porch and wondered if his plan to let J.D. tag along was going to work out.

"Okay, let's go," said J.D. as he ran out the door.

Charley turned toward him and saw that the room behind the door was on fire. Smoke billowed through the window and the open door. "What'd you do that for?" he yelled.

"If I can't have this farm," J.D. shouted, "then nobody can."

Charley stood up and watched the fire for a moment and turned to see J.D. running down the lane toward the road.

"You gonna stick around and wait for the sheriff?" yelled J.D. over his shoulder. "Or are you gonna get outta the county like me?"

Looking once more at the growing fire, Charley gripped his flour sack and ran after J.D.

*  *  *

When J.D. and Charley arrived outside of Lynnville, their jug was empty and so were their pockets. They'd walked for weeks, working when they could and eating when they could afford it. It didn't take long before they stumbled across Ol' Man Smith's place and he took them in and gave them food. Soon after, they made a deal with him. He would give them a shack to live in if they'd keep him supplied with whiskey. All they needed now was work.

Most folks thought that they were from up in the Burley region around Henry County, and it was pretty clear to the Lynnville farmers that the two men knew plenty about tobacco. They made it through the winter doing odd jobs until one day they were approached by Art West about working for him. They were just about at the end of their money, so they started helping at his farm just in time for the three of them to get the seeds into the plant beds. They weren't going to get rich working for Art, but they wouldn't starve either. Art was pleased with their work and had even included them in the noon dinner on days they were working with him. Saving five or six meals a week allowed them to buy Ol' Man Smith's occasional jug. So now they had steady work. They'd also found a local farmer who had a still hidden back in his woods and who was more than happy to supply them with jugs of whiskey for the right price. Now they had enough money to eat and whiskey to drink. All they had to do was stay clear of the law.

# Chapter 6
Tuesday, May 8

Art was chopping weeds in the ditch when he saw Wes riding up the road; he stopped and leaned on the handle of the hoe, waiting for his cousin to draw closer. Art wasn't surprised that Wes was coming to see him; the cousins were best friends and often got together. Art looked up to Wes and trusted him. He was glad to have the opportunity to talk with Wes, since there were so many rumors going around about the Association and the Trust. Art smiled as his cousin climbed down off the mule, but the smile quickly faded when he saw the frown on his face. The two men shook hands and Wes said, "We need to talk."

Glancing back to see that Charley and J.D. were still busy chopping weeds at the back of the tobacco field, Art pointed to the shade tree at the edge of the ditch and said, "Let's sit where it's cool and I can keep watch on the hired hands."

Leading the mule, Wes followed Art, wondering how he'd start the conversation. He still didn't know what Art's position was on selling his crop, and he had to be careful not to put himself on the wrong side of the one man he could trust. Art, always a patient man, waited for Wes to begin.

"I'm wonderin' what to do with my crop this year," Wes said. "The Tobacco Trust's bought up all the little companies we used to deal with, and now they've got a monopoly.

That don't give us any choice of who to sell the crop to."

Art nodded his head. "I hear what you're sayin', Wes. We all got the same problem. I heard that they'll offer high prices to a few farmers at the beginnin' to stir up interest, and then the price'll keep goin' down until the farmers left at the end'll get less than it costs to grow their tobacco." He paused and added, "Not everybody knows how they operate, though."

"I sure don't wanna be one of them farmers. I got a mortgage to pay, and I'd like to make enough this year to buy a horse and some other things for my family." Wes rolled and lit a cigarette. "Another choice we have is to join the Association. I don't know much about what they have to offer. You heard anythin' about 'em?"

"I've been wonderin' what to do myself," said Art. "I've talked to a few fellas who've held back their crop with the Association. I've even been to a few meetin's and I ain't learned much so far. They don't say much until you've joined up, but I think they want us all to stay together and to promise not sell our crops to the Trust. They say that if we do that, it'll force the Trust to give everybody a fair price instead of just a few of us." Art looked toward the farmhands, then back at Wes. "But like you, if I don't sell my crop right away, I won't make it. Somethin' else I been thinkin' about is that some of those farmers in the Association have big fields and lots of money and I don't think they care much about the rest of us."

"I think you're right, cousin, but if I join the Association, I'll need my money as soon as my crops're ready to sell. Did you hear how long all of this might take or what we're supposed do in the meantime to pay our bills and feed our families?"

"Well, last week I was in your brother's store, and I overheard someone say that the Association is sayin' they'll get six cents a pound. I'd need to get a price like that just to survive. If the Association could get us that much with a guaranteed loan from the bank until this is settled, then it might be worth it to hold out and not sell to the Trust."

Wes dropped his cigarette butt on the ground and kicked some dirt over it. "Then maybe it's worth goin' to a meetin' to hear 'em out. Do you know when the next one is?'"

"I don't know, but I can find out. I'll do that and get word to you."

Wes's gaze drifted across the field, and he watched Charley and J.D. working on the weeds. Art waited for him to speak. "We got another serious problem, Art. We've got Night Riders in the county and they've been busy."

"I heard a rumor that they salted a field over near Cuba. Where else have they been?"

"Last Sunday after church I talked to the man in Cuba. I stopped at his house, and I walked around in what was left of his crop. He said they came late Friday night on horses. They tore up his whole field and salted it when they finished. He was outnumbered, unarmed, and, just like us, he had a family to protect. From what he told me, they didn't even give him a chance to join up. Those damned Night Riders are doin' more harm than good, especially if they're takin' away a man's only chance to feed his family." Wes paused again and then added, "Then Anthie saw a bunch of men on horses just this side of the state line late Sunday night."

Art watched Wes and listened patiently.

"He said there was a dozen of 'em, and he heard 'em talkin' about what they were gonna do to someone's crop. They were headed to Tennessee, he said, but that don't make no difference. I'm gonna talk with Anthie some more about it later today. I don't think he saw anyone he knows, and they didn't see him." Wes frowned. "I don't know what they'd have done if they'd caught him."

"That's not good, not good at all."

"I'm gonna start carryin' my pistol," said Wes.

This surprised Art, and even though he hadn't considered it for himself, he said, "I don't know if I will or not." He paused and then added, "But I'll sure think about it."

"Who do you think these fellas are and who pays 'em? Do you think they're part of the Association?"

"I hope not. If they are, how could we trust anythin' the Association has to say?" Art had plenty to think about now.

Eventually they'd said all they could about tobacco and the Association and moved on to other things. Wes talked some more about Anthie and his Sunday trip, leaving out the fight in the yard. Art told his cousin about Mollie's illness and how the kids were doing their best to help out. The conversation went on for a while, and neither of them noticed that J.D. had stopped working and was staring at them. The hired hand watched them for a few more minutes, turned back to his work and then dropped the stub of his cigar on the ground, crushing it with his boot.

*  *  *

Twelve-year-old John Stanley was standing waist-deep in the ditch, chopping weeds. After working a couple of hours, he was sticky with sweat and dirt and his hands were stained green by the weeds. He stopped chopping for a moment and took a drink of water from the pail he'd brought along. He looked down the ditch to the west and saw that he had a long way to go. *I better keep workin' if I wanna get done before Pa gets back.*

He picked up the hoe and got back to work. Chopping, pulling and throwing, he worked in a rhythm. Yard by yard he made progress, and when Irene showed up with his dinner he was ready to rest and have something to eat. He dropped the hoe, climbed out of the ditch and walked toward his sister.

"What'd you bring me?"

"I don't know. Ma just handed me the pail and told me to bring it out to you."

"Well, then, just give it to me and go on back to your own chores. I've got to eat and get back to work."

"You better, or you'll get a whippin'." She paused and then said with a smile, "I'd sure like to see that," and started running back the way she'd come.

He threw a clump of dirt in her direction, but she was too fast and too far away. *Girls,* he thought, *nothin' but trouble.* Lifting the cloth off the top of the pail, he saw that his ma had made him a sandwich of bread and ham. He knew he should wipe the green off of his hands before eating, but hunger won out over cleanliness. Washing the last of the sandwich down with another swallow of the water, he stepped back down into the ditch and in a short time was back in rhythm and making progress.

\* \* \*

Edwin T. Jones truly liked his job. He liked being out on his own, working for a big company and making good money for himself. He'd been a crop buyer for the American Tobacco Company for over five years, and three months ago he'd finally been given a territory all his own. In the past he'd always reported to another buyer, and as much as he liked the work, he didn't enjoy having to share the rewards of doing a good job with someone else. After he'd spent a year working in Calloway County, his boss had sent him a telegram assigning him to Graves County, Kentucky, one of the areas in the Black Patch that was a good source of dark-fired tobacco. Jones had been told that the farmers in Graves County hadn't been interested in organizing into associations like those in Calloway and other counties to the east, but he knew that was no longer true, and his job was going to be harder as a result. Nevertheless, he'd been given permission to entice a few farmers—"prime the pump" his boss in Lexington had said—by offering them higher prices they couldn't afford to turn down.

In the early days of this new assignment, his efforts in the northern part of the county had proved fruitless. Jones concluded that it was because the farmers up there hadn't yet planted their crops. So he held off for a few weeks and planned to head down to the Lynnville District, hoping to find one or two farmers with their crops in the field who were desperate for the money. That desperation, he thought, would be the key to delivering tobacco to the company and to making himself an indispensable and valued employee.

As he shaved in front of the mirror in his hotel room, he mentally went over his pitch. "Good morning, Mr. Williams," he'd say. "My name is Edwin T. Jones of the American Tobacco Company. It looks like you've got a fine start to a great crop, and my company is definitely interested in buying your tobacco when it's ready for harvest. You see, the American Tobacco Company is the largest producer of tobacco products in the world. Our President, Mr. James B. Duke, is a very successful businessman. He has important contacts with many politicians in Washington, D.C., and wants to be sure that America is the strongest country on the globe. He has recently succeeded in making an agreement with the Imperial Tobacco Company—that's the British—which allows us to make sure that all American tobacco products are produced by an American company. I can tell, sir, that you are a loyal American and sense that, if you are given a fair price, you would rather sell to us than to a foreign company." He stopped for a moment, smiling at himself in the mirror and then thought, *That is one fine sales pitch, if I do say so myself.*

Jones was convinced that most of the farmers in Kentucky were illiterate and, despite their rebellious history, were proud of being independent and American. Their only concerns were getting their crops planted, harvested and sold at a good price. They probably wouldn't understand the issues related to monopolies and world markets, but they would surely understand the money they would get if they sold their tobacco to him.

Wiping the remaining soap from his face and putting on some sweet-smelling lotion, he looked once more in the mirror and decided that today would be the day he'd make a buy. Jones believed that what a man wore and how he presented himself was as important as what he had to say. So, he always wore a clean shirt with a fresh collar every day. He brushed his suit and polished his riding boots each night before retiring. He made sure his tie was on straight and his hat set just so. Looking like a professional, he thought, and offering real money for his crop will convince at least one farmer to sell his crop to him today. He posed in front of the mirror once more, cocked his hat a little more to the right and walked out the door. *This is going to be a very successful day.*

He checked at the front desk for telegrams and then went out the front door and headed toward the livery stable around the corner. Mayfield was the county seat, so it had most of the services that people doing business in the county might need. There were several banks, lots of stores and even more lawyers. On his way to the livery, he passed the sheriff's office and jail and then turned into the alley heading straight to the stable. He'd boarded his horse, a blood red bay, the night before and told the proprietor he'd be leaving by nine o'clock in the morning. Jones wanted to be sure that the horse was fed, watered, brushed and saddled. In an effort to at least appear successful, he used an English riding saddle. The tack was far different from that used by most of the riders in this part of the country, but it was very similar to what he had seen in Lexington when he first came to Kentucky, and it truly made him feel powerful.

As promised, his animal was ready, so he paid the owner and mounted up. He rode out of the alley onto the main street and turned south. He figured that a leisurely ride to Lynnville, fifteen miles distant, would give him time for more practice on his speech.

* * *

After Wes left, Art walked across the field to check on Charley and J.D. He surveyed their work and saw they'd done well. At least he was getting full value for what he paid them. But until Clarence, who'd just turned ten, and seven-year-old Thressie could handle the more strenuous tasks of farming tobacco, they'd have to work for their mother. Art's wife, Mollie, was older than he was, and she spent most of her time with the two young ones—three-year-old Martha and three-month-old Benjamin. She was still struggling with the pain from her last delivery. Art didn't understand a lot about what women went through during childbirth, but he knew that she'd had a pretty rough time. He would do anything to make her feel more comfortable.

Art told the hands that as soon as they had finished the last two rows they could go. "Tomorrow we'll get at the weeds in the road ditch and then finish up the racks in the hangin' house. I'll have your pay ready when we finish." He asked them if they had any questions. Neither man seemed to have one, so he told them to come back early the next morning. As they turned back to their work, he paused, wondering what hired hands thought about the Night Riders, and then headed to the house.

"Pa! Pa!" laughed Clarence as he ran from the house toward Art. "You should see what Thressie did. It's funny." The boy grabbed Art's hand and pulled him toward the house.

"And what is it that my beautiful daughter has done that is so funny?"

A powder-white Thressie stood on the porch, her hands on her hips and a frown on her face. "You're mean, Clarence West!" She started crying and waited until Art came to her. "Pa, I didn't mean to. I was tryin' to help Ma, and it just slipped out of my hands."

"Don't cry, sweetheart," said Art as he stared at his ghost-like daughter. Getting down on his knees and taking her small hand in his, he said, "Don't you cry. Just tell me what slipped out of your hands."

"I was just tryin' to help, that's all," she said through her sobs. "Ma wasn't feelin' well, so I was gonna make some biscuits." Another round of tears interrupted her.

"She was tryin' to make some biscuits, and she dropped the flour sack. There's flour all over the kitchen floor, Pa. It's really a mess, and she looks funny."

"Well, son, since you seem to be enjoyin' this so much, I think that you should help me clean up the mess while your beautiful sister dusts the flour off of her dress and washes her hands and face at the pump. Don't you think that's a good idea?"

"That's not fair, Pa. I didn't do anythin'." The boy's laughter had quickly vanished, and a smile broke through the flour on Thressie's face.

Picking them both up in his arms and carrying them into the house, he said, "Let's go see about this mess and figure out what the three of us can do to clean it up."

There was a mess, all right, but it wasn't as bad as his son had described. He sent Thressie back outside to clean up, and he and Clarence had most of the flour salvaged and the rest swept up in just a few minutes. Art reminded his son about the pail of milk he'd dropped the day before and hugged his daughter, thanking her for thinking of her ma.

Mollie was lying on the bed, nursing the baby while the toddler slept at her side. She looked up at Art as he walked in and smiled, but by the crease in her brow and the beads of sweat on her temples, Art could see that she was tired. He bent over and kissed her cheek, gently touching the baby's head.

"What was that ruckus out in the kitchen?" she asked. "What have your son and your daughter done now?" Her brow was furrowed, but there was a smile on her lips.

Art filled her in on the kitchen adventure and then told her about Wes's visit. He shared his cousin's concerns about the Night Riders and what the two of them planned to do. Art and Mollie had talked a lot about their own dilemma recently. She wanted Art to join the Association because his stories of the troubles over in Calloway County frightened her.

"We're gonna go to a meetin' next week. Maybe that'll settle it for both of us. We just need to find out how joinin' up will help. There are a lot of things to consider, and we can't just do somethin' without thinkin' about all of them."

"I know that, but sometimes I get so scared."

"Don't worry. Wes is smart and I trust him. We'll figure this all out and everythin' will be all right. All you need to do is rest and get well. If you need help with the baby, you just ask. The children and I will take care of everything else. Now, you finish up what you have to do here. I'll get some supper goin' and we'll talk some more later." He smiled at her, kissed her again and then left the room. As he turned away, the smile faded. *I sure hope we can figure this out.*

* * *

On his ride home, Wes had a lot of time to think. He remembered Anthie had said that the Riders passed him headed south. That meant they were going into Tennessee. Anthie's girl lived in Tennessee and her pa was a tobacco farmer, so he likely had the same questions Wes and Art did. *Maybe,* Wes thought, *I could let Anthie go see Sudie either Saturday or Sunday, and while he's there he could have a talk with her pa. If Anthie can find out Morris's position on the Association, or even better, how he feels about the Night Riders, then we'd have a good chance of making the right decision. Anthie might be scared to talk with her pa, but he'll want to do what I ask if it'll make it easier to go down to Sudie's in the future.* Wes was sure he could get his son's cooperation and, at the same time, perhaps even give Zora the feeling that he'd forgiven the boy. He hadn't, and he was still angry about what Anthie had done. But if he could use the boy's interest in Sudie to his advantage and in the process get closer to a decision that would protect all of the family, it was a step he was willing to take.

* * *

After the long, hot ride to Lynnville, Jones was ready to give his bay a rest and get something to eat for himself. When he looped the reins to the rail in front of the general store, he noticed there was a hotel across the road. Between the tied-back lace curtains in one of the tall windows was a hand-painted sign offering "Good Eats Ten Cents." *But food will have to wait,* he thought. *First I must introduce myself to one of the local storekeepers and state my business in Lynnville.* He opened the front door and went into the store. A man standing behind the counter was busy writing in a ledger and turned toward him when the small bell rang over the door.

"Yes, sir, how may I help you?"

"Are you the proprietor, sir?" asked Jones.

"I am. My name is Mark Wilson."

"Then, sir, it is my pleasure to introduce myself to you. I am Edwin T. Jones of the American Tobacco Company. I was hoping you might let me water my horse at your trough while I visit the eatery across the road. I've had a pleasant ride down from Mayfield and would like to rest a bit before I go about my work."

"Welcome to Lynnville, Mr. Jones. Feel free to use the trough. I would suggest that if you do eat at the hotel, be sure to avoid the daily special. It is usually made from what wasn't very special yesterday and is likely even less so today."

"Thank you kindly, sir," replied Jones.

On his way back to the front of the store, Jones spotted a genuine British-style derby. He'd been looking for one, thinking it would be the crowning touch to his look as a professional; and, he thought, it wouldn't hurt his relationship with Mark Wilson if he bought something from him.

"May I try this on?"

"Of course," said Mark.

"I've always wanted one of these," said Jones as he gently lifted the derby from the shelf and placed it on his head. The hat slipped down over his ears and covered his eyebrows. Slightly embarrassed, he asked, "Might you have another in your stockroom? This one appears to be a bit large."

"I do indeed, Mr. Jones. Would you like me to bring it out?"

"Perhaps not at this moment, but I would definitely like to look at it another time," he said as he put the derby back on the shelf. Hoping to get out of the store before embarrassing himself further, he put his fedora on and thanked Wilson. Once outside, he walked his horse to the water trough at the south end of the store. When he was sure that the bay was secured to the rail of the porch, he crossed the road to the hotel. *Maybe Wilson will be able to direct me to a farmer or two who might be open to making a deal,* he thought. *That would be fine, just fine.*

But Mark Wilson knew exactly what Edwin T. Jones represented, and it was trouble.

After dinner, Jones left the hotel in Lynnville, wishing he'd listened to the storekeeper's advice. He'd chosen the daily special, which had sounded tasty, but now the meal was churning in his gut. While he ate dinner, he'd had a bit of luck. He overheard some men talking in the hotel dining room. One of the men said that several farmers on the Fairbanks road would be in desperate need for cash come harvest time. Jones thought that he might as well take advantage of the opportunity and make his first deal with one of these desperate farmers. He turned east and found himself on another narrow, wheel-rutted road and spotted a young boy of ten or twelve engaged in clearing weeds from the ditch. He thought he'd find out if the boy's father was available to talk.

Before he approached the boy, though, Jones sat on his horse, concealed by the shade of a stand of beech trees. It had been his practice to watch people, searching for things about them he could turn into compliments. This had worked well for him in the past, and he was confident it would work again today. Once he caught on to the boy's rhythm, he gently heeled the horse's flanks and moved closer.

"Excuse me, young man. You are certainly a fine craftsman in the art of weed chopping. Might I have the privilege of knowing your name?"

The boy turned and squinted up at Jones. He clearly hadn't understood Jones, and when he saw the man's fancy clothes and his big horse, he immediately grew cautious.

"I said, what's your name?"

"John Stanley Wilson, sir."

"Well, Mr. Wilson, your family certainly has a fine farm and what looks to be a healthy crop of tobacco. Since I assume that you, Mr. John Stanley Wilson, are not the owner of the farm, could you tell me who is?"

"It's my pa's farm."

"And what might his name be?"

The boy appeared to be either formulating an answer or simply didn't understand him, so Jones added, "Who's your pa, son? Is he home today?"

"His name is Wes Wilson, and he ain't home."

"Then I suppose I'll have to carry out the first stage of my negotiation with you, young man. Would that be all right?"

"Yeah, I suppose."

Jones reached into the pocket of his vest and said, "All right, then. If I was to give you this brand new, shiny, silver ten-cent piece, would you be so kind as to give my calling card to your father when he returns from running his errands?"

"Yes sir, I will."

"And would you also tell him that I will return mid-morning tomorrow to discuss an offer on his tobacco at a price I believe he'll be seriously interested in?"

"Well, sir, Mr. Jones, I'll take the coin and I'll try to tell him what you said. But if I don't get this chore done before he gets home, then he truly won't be interested in anything else I have to say."

With that, John Stanley reached up to Jones, took the coin and the card and stuffed them into the pocket of his overalls. He looked directly into the buyer's eyes and then turned abruptly to his weeding. He only knew that Jones was leaving because he heard the sound of the bay as it trotted down the road. By the time he could no longer hear the horse, he'd returned to his rhythm of chop, pull, throw and began dreaming about what he could do with his shiny new dime. But it didn't take him long to realize that he'd have to give the money to his pa. *If I don't and Mr. Jones asks Pa about it, then Pa will ask me why I didn't tell him. If I do give Pa the dime, then I won't get to spend it myself.* He finally decided that the only safe thing to do, especially since his pa was already mad about something, was to give him the card and the coin and see what happened.

* * *

About a quarter-mile from his farm, Wes saw the smoke from the burning weeds. *I'll give John Stanley some time to finish up and head home so he can get there before I do,* he thought as he got down off the mule and let it chew on a patch of grass at the side of the road. While he waited, he thought about the distance he'd created between himself, Zora and Anthie, and wondered if there was some way he could hide his growing anxiety from them. He rolled himself a cigarette and lit it with a wooden match and waited until he saw the smoke begin to fade away. Guessing that his son was on the way back to the house, he mounted the mule and rode toward home.

When he turned onto the lane, he saw John Stanley trudging toward the barn, the hoe across his shoulders like an ox yoke. A few steps behind her brother, Irene dragged the water bucket at her side. Their bodies were covered with dirt, and they looked tired.

"It looks like the two of you have been rollin' around in an ash pile," he said, smiling just a little. "Maybe I ought to throw you in the pond."

"Aw, Pa, we were burnin' weeds just like you told us to," said Irene. "We didn't roll in no ashes."

"Yeah, Pa," added John Stanley, "I got rid of all of the weeds, and Irene finally showed up when I started to burn 'em." He looked at his sister and added, "But she helped a little."

"That's good, then. Go and wash up and tell your ma I'll be in soon. I want to check out the sty and the garden after I put up the mule. Did anythin' else happen today while I was gone?"

"A man stopped by this afternoon to talk with you. He gave me somethin' to give you." John Stanley looked at his pa, wondering if there was any chance he could keep the dime. He saw a softening in his pa's eyes and knew that telling him anything but the whole truth would turn them hard again.

"Well, get cleaned up and we'll talk about it when I come in," said Wes. He pulled the mule into the barn as the youngsters headed to the pump. After putting the animal into the stall, he removed the blanket and the bridle, set a bucket of oats in front of the mule and closed the gate. *A man stopped by to talk with me,* he thought. *I wonder what that's all about.*

Wes saw that Irene hadn't done much in the garden, but maybe Zora didn't have anything for her to do. Wes had no concerns about Connie's farming skills. He knew that the boy could work hard, that he understood what it took to grow the crops and keep the place in working order. Wes also knew that Anthie didn't have the same skills or interest. *What's going to happen to that boy?* he wondered.

* * *

Zora had just started supper when John Stanley and Irene came into the kitchen. When she saw that they'd washed their faces and hands but had neglected their arms, she almost sent them back outside to wash again, but was distracted when Mary Lula came into the kitchen from the back of the house. Ruthie hung onto her apron with one hand and a large wooden spoon with the other. A quizzical look crossed Zora's face, and when she started to ask about the spoon, Mary Lula said, "Ruthie's been chasin' flies."

Zora smiled at her youngest and then stood next to Mary Lula. She turned to Irene, and they talked about the garden. When she asked John Stanley what he'd been doing, he muttered "weeds" and then left the room in a hurry. *He doesn't look upset,* she thought, *but he sure must have somethin' on his mind.*

Zora looked up as Wes stepped through the door. His eyes were not as dark, and his face seemed softer, more relaxed. But she knew from the set of his shoulders that he was still bothered. She waited for him to speak first, and when he did, her thoughts were confirmed.

"After supper, before I speak with the boys, we need to talk. I've got some news and a few ideas."

"All right," she said. "Will you be ready to eat soon? Supper's almost ready."

"Uh huh. I just want to change out of these muley clothes. Do we have coffee?"

"I just made a fresh pot. I'll pour you some."

Wes headed toward the bedroom, stopping only to touch Mary Lula on the shoulder and to kiss Ruthie on the top of her curly hair. "What's that you have there, little girl?"

Ruthie mumbled something that sounded like "flies," but Wes could only guess what she meant. Ruthie spun around and followed her pa as he walked down the short hall. Zora set the knife down and caught Ruthie before she'd gone a half-dozen steps. She picked her up and brought her back into the kitchen.

"Here, munch on this for a while," she said, handing her a small chunk of raw potato.

While Wes was buttoning up a clean shirt, John Stanley tapped lightly on the door. "Pa, can I come in?"

Wes looked up and nodded. Then he told him to close the door. "You said a man came by today askin' for me?"

"Yes, Pa, he said his name was..." the boy paused for a moment, trying to remember what the man had said. "He said his name was Edwin T. Jones. He told me to give you his card and to tell you he'd come by tomorrow." He blurted out the rest of what he had to say in a flurry of words. "He gave me this coin too, but I think I need to give it to you 'cause we need the money and I'd just prob'ly waste it anyway, so here it is." He placed the dime on the bed next to Wes and just stood there, with his chin on his chest.

"Hold on, son." Wes could barely conceal the smile that broke out on his face. "He gave you this dime and told you to give me a card?"

"Yes, Pa," he said, still staring at the floor.

"Well, why don't you give me his card and tell me the whole story." Wes sat on the bed and pulled his son down next to him. He took the calling card from John Stanley and looked at it. Despite what Jones might have thought about farmers and their literacy, Wes could read. What stood out and caught his attention were the bold black letters at the top of the card—The American Tobacco Company. He turned and looked at the boy.

"Tell me about this Mr. Jones."

For the next five minutes, John Stanley told his pa everything he could remember about the conversation and what the man looked like. He described the fancy clothes and the horse and told him how hard it was to understand Jones because of the odd words he used. He made sure to tell him that there was something about Jones that he didn't like.

"It was somethin' in his eyes, Pa. He was smilin' but it wasn't real."

"Thanks, son. You can go get ready for supper now." Wes suddenly felt anxious. His chest tightened as he considered the news. He stood up and walked into the kitchen, looking for Zora.

* * *

For most of the morning, Anthie had done what his pa had asked him to do. He found a cool spot under a tree and sat down to think about the men he'd seen on Sunday night. He tried to remember how many of them there had been, but couldn't be sure if there were ten or twelve. Only three of the men had spoken, and he hadn't recognized any of the voices. He couldn't even remember exactly what was said. It had been too dark to tell the color of the horses or recognize any piece of clothing. As he whittled sticks he kept searching his memory for something that might be helpful to his pa. But after a while, the gentle sound of the water flowing in the creek caused his thoughts to drift along with the ripples, and he started thinking about Sudie. He remembered how the setting sun highlighted her brown hair with gold streaks. He could still feel the warmth of her hand and the touch of her lips on his cheek. He remembered how good it had felt when she said his name. Before long, Anthie was snoring, propped up against the tree.

The screech of a raven flying through the woods startled him awake. His knife and whittling stick lay in the grass beside him. He sat for a moment looking up at the peaceful sky. *Sure would be nice to go back to sleep,* he thought, but he knew he needed to have something to tell his pa. He tried again to recall the event on the road, but he could remember no more than he already had. *I guess that's what I'll tell Pa. Ten or twelve masked men on horses, three of them spoke, one was the leader and he was angry. They were headin' into Tennessee and knew where they were goin'.*

His growling stomach reminded him that he'd slept through dinner. He slipped the knife into his pocket and kneeled down at the edge of the creek. He cupped his hands and drank some of the water and then splashed another handful in his face, hoping it would wake him up. Drying off with his shirt sleeve, he rose and headed home. *I hope this gets me off the hook with Pa,* he thought. *I hope he apologizes and that he's not drinkin'. If he is, I'm not stickin' around.*

Coming out of the woods, he looked across the field of tobacco and saw his pa leading the mule into the barn. He stopped and took a few steps back. Hiding in the shade, he decided to wait until his pa was inside. *He won't yell at me in front of Ma,* he thought. He watched John Stanley and Irene wash up at the pump and then go into the house. A few minutes later his pa did the same. *It doesn't look like he's drunk, but it's hard to tell from this far away.* He stood there for a few minutes, wanting to avoid what lay ahead.

He thought one more time about Sunday night, trying to remember the details, and then walked to the house.

When Anthie walked through the door into the kitchen, the smell of ham filled the air. His older sister was busy slicing the meat from the bone, and the sizzling sound it made as she placed it in the skillet made his stomach ache. When he reached into the pan to grab some of the meat, Mary Lula smacked him lightly on the back of his head.

"Can't you wait for supper?"

"No, I can't. I haven't had anythin' to eat since breakfast. I'm starvin'."

"Then grab a piece of bread instead. I baked it today. Be sure you wash up first."

"You ain't my ma."

"No, I ain't. But I am the cook, so wash up first."

He carved a piece of bread off of the loaf and turned to go back outside. But Mary Lula caught his shirt sleeve and handed him a good-sized chunk of ham. Then she smiled at him and said, "That ought to keep you 'til supper."

"Where's Pa?" he asked Mary Lula.

"He and Ma are outside, back of the barn. They're talkin' about something private, so don't you go out there."

"I'm not goin' anywhere near Pa until he wants me to."

* * *

Wes and Zora were standing near the woodpile at the back of the barn. She watched his face, looking for signs of trouble, as he told her what he'd learned at Art's.

"I expected Mollie to have trouble after the baby," she said. "She's nearly as old as me, and she had four other children with Mr. Arnold."

"You're probably right, but Art's a good man, and it makes no difference to him if she's older or was married before. He'll take care of her."

Wes hunkered down and pulled at a weed. Then he

looked up at Zora and said, "But there's more you need to know about what's goin' on in the county."

"What is goin' on, Wes?"

"Art told me about some of the Association meetin's he's been to. Accordin' to him, those fellas don't talk much about what they're doin' or what they're plannin' until you join up. He ain't done it yet, but I think he will soon. I told him I'd go with him to one of the meetin's next week, just so we could get more information. We figure the more we know, the smarter we'll be when it comes time to choose. And we're both gonna have to choose pretty soon."

"Are you thinkin' of joinin'?"

"I just don't know, Zora. I still need more information from Anthie." He paused and added, "I'm also gonna talk with a tobacco buyer tomorrow."

"When did you meet him?"

"I haven't yet. He gave his card to John Stanley this afternoon and told the boy he'd be back here tomorrow. Once I talk to him and go to the meetin' next week, I'll know exactly what my choices are."

"I sure hope you and Art take enough time to think things through before you decide on what you're gonna do."

"We will." He paused and then stood up. Facing his wife, he said, "But I've got an idea that just might help." Wes pulled his hat off, rolled it up and stuffed it into his back pocket. He took both of Zora's hands in his own and looked straight at her. He knew his idea was selfish, but that it would please her. "I'm gonna let Anthie go see Sudie on Saturday or Sunday."

"Oh, Wes." Her eyes smiled back at him.

"I'm gonna let him go see her if he does somethin' for me while he's there. I want him to talk to her pa and find out what the farmers down there are thinkin'. I want him to ask about buyers, the Association and if there's been any Night Riders."

"But, Wes, don't you think that's dangerous? What if her pa is a Night Rider?"

"I'm gonna have to trust my son to know when to ask the questions. I'm gonna talk to him after supper, and I won't send him without bein' sure he's ready."

They spent the next few minutes talking about tobacco and their limited choices. Zora got the feeling that Wes was less angry with Anthie and that he hoped the boy would appreciate the chance to see Sudie. She also saw this as the only apology he'd likely get from his pa.

* * *

After a calm supper, Zora and the girls picked up the dishes. Wes looked at Anthie and signaled that he should follow him outside. Anthie's throat felt suddenly tight and his mouth dry, but he didn't hesitate. He didn't know which of his pa's personalities he'd see out there: the one who'd beaten him on Sunday, or the one who'd given him a free day today. They stepped off the porch and walked to the end of the lane. Cautiously, Anthie stood back from his pa and waited, thinking, *I'm not gonna risk gettin' hit again.*

Wes took a moment to roll and light a cigarette. He took a drag on it, spit out a piece of tobacco and turned to his son. To Anthie, his pa's face looked softer, less angry.

"Before you tell me what you remember about Sunday night on the road, I want to fill you in on what's happenin' around here. You know how important tobacco is to our family." Anthie nodded, his eyes focused on his pa. "It costs a lot of money and a lot of work to get a good crop. We always need to get a good price for the tobacco so we can have the cash money we need to buy the things we can't grow in the fields and to pay for the farm. Over the last few years, the tobacco buyers have been droppin' the price they'll pay us, and the price now is less than it costs us to grow it. You understand this, son?"

"Yes, Pa, I understand."

"So that makes it hard for me and Art and other farmers to decide what to do. If we hold our crop back with the Association, we don't know how much money we might get or when we might get it. If we sell it to the tobacco company, we could get raided by the Night Riders. But while the crop is new in the ground, we have time to think and ask questions about what to do. That's why I need to know what you saw the other night. I want to know everythin' you remember." Wes reached across and put his hand on his son's shoulder.

Anthie tried not to move, waiting for his pa to speak. He swallowed once, licked his lips and started talking. Wes took his hand off Anthie's shoulder and listened.

"I thought about this all day, Pa. I must've gone over it a dozen times. I was scared, and it's hard for me to remember. After a while, it started to get confusin', so I quit. But what I remember for sure is that there were ten or twelve men, no boys or women. They were all on horses, and it looked like they'd tied rags around the horses' hooves. But it was too dark to tell what color the horses were or what the men were wearin'. They were headin' south, down the road toward the state line. At first they were ridin' fast, so I hid off the road behind some trees. Before they got to me, they slowed down and then stopped so close I had to keep the mule from snortin'. One of the men must've heard somethin', because he said 'What's that?' or somethin' like it. Then another man laughed at him and teased him. I think he said the other man's name."

"He said his name? What was it?"

"Sorry, Pa. I can't remember it." Anthie took a step back, not sure what his pa might do.

"Go ahead, son. Tell me the rest of it." Wes tried to keep his voice calm.

"Anyway, a third man, I think he was the leader, told

both of the others to shut up and to keep quiet. He asked everyone if they knew the plan and if they were ready. No one spoke up that I remember, so they rode the horses on down the road. I stayed quiet until I couldn't hear them anymore, and then I walked the mule onto the road and headed home."

"Did you see any of their faces?"

"No, Pa, they were wearin' masks. Most of them were like Klan hoods, but some of them just had bandanas covering their mouth and nose. Oh, yeah and everyone had a handgun. Some had shotguns, and I think I saw at least one rifle."

Wes asked him if he recognized any of the three voices he heard. Anthie thought about that for a moment and then said he didn't recognize any of them.

"Okay, thanks, son. I want you to keep thinking about this for the next couple of days. If you come up with anythin' more, don't wait, just come and tell me."

Anthie nodded, thinking his pa was finished with him. He started to head back to the house when Wes told him to wait.

"Yeah, Pa?"

"There's somethin' else I want you to do for me. I want you to go down to the Morrises' and see Sudie on Saturday or Sunday."

Anthie was stunned. He couldn't speak or move. One second he felt hopeful for a chance to see Sudie and the next confused as to why his pa was being so nice.

"While you're there I need you to talk to her pa. This is important, Anthie. I've got to get some more information about what's happenin' down there so I can decide what to do about our tobacco. I know this might be hard for you to do, but you've got to do it. I want you to spend some time with the girl. But the important thing is to ask her pa about prices, about the Association and about Night Riders."

"Do you really think I can do that, Pa? I only talked to him once, and he was pretty mad that I was even there. Besides, he thinks I'm just a boy."

"Maybe he was mad. But if you are respectful and take your time, he might see you're more than just a boy. He might see that you're smart and know what it means to be a man." He let that sink in a bit and then said, "The most important thing to find out is about the Night Riders, but you can't start out with that. You'll have to ask the simple questions first."

"Okay, Pa, but can we talk some more about this before I go down there? I don't wanna say the wrong things or come back without answers."

"We can. We still have all of our regular work to do, but if you want to talk about this, we will. Do you have any questions now, tonight?"

"I don't think so, Pa."

"Okay, then. Let's go back in and get some sleep." Once more, Wes looked at his son and noticed that his frown was gone and his smile was back. Anthie looked into his pa's face as well and saw lots of things, but anger wasn't one of them. Not knowing what to think, but feeling better than he had in a while, he wandered back to the porch with his pa and went into the house just as the moon found its way into the eastern sky.

Even after the conversation with Anthie, Wes remained restless. He grabbed the jug from the shelf and walked back out to the porch. *The plan should work,* he thought. But until he knew a whole lot more, he'd need to keep watch over the farm. He got little rest as he continued to consider his options and to worry about the possibility of danger.

# Chapter 7
Wednesday Morning, May 9

It was still dark when Wes woke up on the porch the next morning. He'd barely touched the jug of whiskey, but the taste was still in his mouth. What little light remained from the moon reflected off a huge cloud bank in the west. It was a little cooler than it had been in the past few days but not enough to bring on a storm. He saw the glow from the lantern in the barn and knew that Anthie was milking the cow. *It looks like it might rain,* he thought. *I'm gonna have to get the boys hoein' between the rows of tobacco today.*

He heard Anthie close the barn door and watched him carry the milk pail to the house. His mind shifted from the weather and back to what he learned from Anthie. He knew his son had worked hard trying to come up with more details, and he just wished the boy had been able to recall more. If Anthie could remember the name or even recognize one of the three voices he heard, Wes would know who rode with the Night Riders, and that would be valuable information.

He'd also spent a few sleepless hours wondering about Edwin T. Jones and the American Tobacco Company. Thinking about tobacco prices and the consequences of selling his crop to Jones had kept him awake long after Zora had begun her gentle snoring. Wes chuckled when he remembered John Stanley's rapid confession about the dime. A brand new silver ten-cent piece was more treasure than the boy had ever seen in one place. To have it in his own hand must have had him dreaming about how he could spend it on himself. Wes was proud of his youngest son and the decision he made to give up the dime. He also had a surprise in store for the boy. He was going to let him keep the coin, but only if he shared his wealth with Irene. She had, after all, helped him burn the weeds and finish his chores on time, and that had to be worth something. Sleep had finally come to him when he realized he'd know more after talking to the buyer.

* * *

Wednesday morning, Art and the farmhands had worked until noon and stopped only when Clarence brought out food and water for dinner. After they'd eaten, Art lay down in the grass and covered his face with his hat and decided to take a nap. J.D. and Charley took the opportunity to walk into the woods to have a smoke and a snort of whiskey. When they thought Art was asleep, they started talking, and the more they drank the louder they got. Art wasn't having much luck getting to sleep, and he was about to tell them to shut up when he heard something that caught his attention.

"That's the boss's cousin, you know," said Charley.

"Sure, I know, but it don't mean nothin' to me. If we're gonna hit his farm, we'll do what we're told."

"Yeah, I know, but ain't it risky? Especially since they're cousins?"

"Of course it is. That's why they pay us," said J.D.

Charley was quiet for a moment.

"Okay, J.D. So we go early next week, then?"

"Yeah, Tuesday or Wednesday night. Now, shut up and pass me the jug so I can have another drink before he wakes up."

Art lay still. He knew they were talking about Wes, and that meant the Night Riders were in Lynnville planning a raid on Wes's farm. That scared Art, and he realized that Wes would have to make a decision quickly. He stood up and yawned loudly. "You two fellas ready to get back to work?" he said, trying to sound calm.

Not looking back, he walked out to the row he'd been working, and they followed. In minutes, all three of them were digging at the crusty dirt with their hoes. Art's mind was clearly not on the work but on what he had to do next. He needed to ride out to Wes's right after supper and let him know what he heard. *We were looking for information,* he thought, *but we sure didn't expect this.*

* * *

Right after breakfast, Wes had asked Anthie if he'd re-membered any more about Sunday night. Anthie had scrunched up his face and thought for a bit and said he hadn't. Wes was pleased when his son said that he would keep thinking about it because he knew it was important. Although Wes believed that Anthie's response was prob-ably influenced by the boy's interest in seeing Sudie, he thought that his son also wanted to help the family. *Maybe there's hope for that boy yet.*

Dark clouds reigned over the county. It was evident that rain was brewing somewhere west of the farm. Wes gath-ered his sons on the porch and told them they would have to work fast. "We'll need to finish the whole field before the rain gets here." His sons hadn't disappointed him; they were making good progress, and Wes thought they'd easily be done by supper.

While he worked, Wes wondered what Jones might have to say. He knew that the man would want to talk about buy-ing his tobacco and would probably have a price; that was a given. But before he heard about a price, Wes wanted to get Jones talking about the things he was hearing from other farmers in the county. Were they refusing to talk to him?

Were they interested in what he'd pay? Answers to these questions would help Wes decide, and as soon as he had this information, he'd share it with Art.

Wes heard Connie and Anthie laughing and noticed they'd picked up the pace of their work. He turned around to watch them and saw that they were actually racing with one another, trying to see who could finish a row first. He wondered if they might be doing a poor job of digging, but he looked down each of their rows and saw that the work was as good as his own. They laughed again, and Wes noticed Connie looking back at him. *This isn't a race between the two of 'em,* he thought, *this is a race to beat me. Hunh,* he smiled, *I can't let 'em beat me; they'd never let me hear the end of it.* Wes took up his hoe, smiled at the boys and joined the race.

By noon they were more than half done. Both older boys had moved far ahead of their brother, and Wes had nearly caught up with him. John Stanley was covered with sweat, and the dust from the ground was turning that to mud. He looked tired, but Wes could see that he wasn't going to quit. They all needed a rest, and when Wes saw Irene turn the corner by the barn, carrying their dinner in her hands, he knew it was time for a break. He dropped his hoe and let out a shrieking whistle.

"Okay, boys!" he yelled, "It's dinnertime. Let's eat."

None of them needed any encouragement to stop. They dropped their tools and ran over to where Irene had begun setting down the food. Wes caught up with John Stanley and put his arm around the boy's shoulder. He gave him a little hug and asked, "You tired, son?"

"No, Pa, just hungry."

They sat down along the edge of the field, each with his back against a tree, and ate the sandwiches and drank the water without saying a word. Wes watched as Anthie and Connie never took their eyes off one another and began to take larger bites of the food, barely taking time to swallow before taking another one. John Stanley noticed as well and did the same. Pretty soon, all three were laughing, wolfing down their food and gulping the water. Within moments, they were on their feet and back out in the field, chopping at the dirt between the rows. Knowing he wouldn't be able to keep up with them this day, Wes just sat back and watched. Although he hadn't forgotten all the things that were on his mind, he at least felt good at that moment, and the smile that cracked his face felt even better.

* * *

As Jones made his way to the Wilson farm, he worked on his new plan. When he left his calling card with the boy the previous afternoon, he'd felt confident that the rest of his day would go well. It hadn't. He'd made his pitch to two more farmers; one had ignored him, acting like he wasn't even there. His encounter with the second one was frightening. The man had watched him as he left the road and rode toward the farmhouse. When Jones started to get down off his horse, he found himself looking down the barrel of a shotgun. That, in itself, was frightening. But when the farmer pulled back the hammer and aimed the gun at Jones's head, he nearly wet himself. It didn't take him long to spin the horse around and head back to town.

His heart had mostly settled down by the time he'd returned to Lynnville. He decided to stay at the hotel, and at supper, he'd tried to engage in conversation with some of the other hotel patrons, but they, too, seemed to know who he was and were less-than friendly. He'd finished eating, paid his bill and retired to his room. Fortunately, he had a flask of bourbon there, and he found it a lot friendlier than the farmers of the town. In less than an hour, he'd finished the flask and fallen asleep on the bed.

When Jones opened his eyes the next morning, he

opened the lace curtains and noticed that the sun was much higher than he'd expected. He had wanted to get an early start on this new day, but sitting on the edge of the bed in his now-wrinkled suit and un-shined shoes, he groaned. Even though his head hurt nearly as much as his pride, he decided he wasn't going to let a bunch of farmers beat him. He had more than one approach to winning them over and was convinced that he was much smarter than a dozen of them put together. After shaving and working the wrinkles out of his suit, he ate a modest breakfast in the hotel's small dining room. He also drank a lot of coffee, which usually gave him extra energy. On this morning, however, it simply made his headache worse. *Some fresh air might help,* he thought. *It'll give me some time to work on my presentation and maybe get a better sense of the townsfolk.*

So far he'd had no success in his new territory. He knew that his ultimate goal was to buy as much tobacco as he could at the lowest price it took. The idea of offering a higher price to one or two farmers and then driving the price down later had worked nearly everywhere it had been used. All he needed to do was to come up with a different way to sell the idea. By the time he headed to the small stable behind the hotel to pick up his horse, he was ready. He had an idea, and he knew it would work.

The clouds in the sky had taken some of the heat out of the air, and the ride along the country road was more comfortable than he'd expected. Jones had gone over his new approach to win over the farmers and was now ready to try it out on Wes Wilson.

* * *

Wes helped Irene gather up the mess from dinner and sent her back to the house. The boy's race to finish the hoeing was picking up speed. For now, John Stanley was keeping even, but Wes knew that the youngster would soon fall behind. Still, Wes believed that he wouldn't quit. Wes was about to join them when he spotted a rider coming down the road. As he watched the tall bay stop at the lane to his farm, he suspected it was Jones.

John Stanley looked up from his work and yelled, "That's him, Pa."

Wes leaned the hoe against the tree. Jones had spotted him and was waiting at the entrance to the yard. It wasn't patience that kept him there, however. Rufus was growling at the man and circling the nervous horse. Wes worked his way through the rows of tobacco and walked toward the buyer, fully aware that being seen with the man put him at risk.

"Good afternoon, sir. Would you be Mr. Wes Wilson?"

"That's me," Wes said and shooed the dog away. "What can I do for you?" Wes watched the man's eyes as he responded.

"My name is Edwin T. Jones, sir, and I represent the American Tobacco Company." He got down from the bay and stuck out his hand. "I was by here yesterday and advised your son, John Stanley—I believe that's what he said his name was—I advised him that I'd return to speak with you today. Did your son pass along the message?"

Wes took the man's hand, shook it and said, "He did," noticing that Jones's smile seemed forced and his eyes were empty of any truth.

"Then, sir, I have a few very interesting things I'd like to discuss with you about your tobacco crop. I must say as well that it appears to be a fine one and that your hired hands are working diligently to keep it that way."

Wes wondered why Jones didn't use regular words. *John Stanley was right,* he thought. *There's something suspicious about this fella.* "Let's go on up to the porch. I've got some questions I'd like to ask you before you tell me about these 'very interesting things.'"

Wes turned and headed for the house, and Jones followed, leading the horse behind him. He was pleased that Wilson was talking to him and very relieved when he didn't see a pistol in the man's belt. Wes pointed to the post, and Jones wrapped the reins around it once.

"Have a seat, Mr. Jones," said Wes, pointing to the bench. Wes leaned against the post, looking at his visitor. As much as he could, Wes wanted to control the direction of the conversation. He needed to find out what Jones knew about the Association and the Night Riders without telling him any more than he had to. Even though Jones used fancy words and rode a fine horse didn't mean he was smart or honest. In fact, in this part of the country, they might mean just the opposite.

"Mr. Jones, I'm interested in hearin' what you have to say, but before we start I have a few questions." Wes paused, expecting some kind of response. Getting only a nod from Jones, he continued, "First, have you gotten anyone in the county to sell you his tobacco?"

Jones looked directly into Wes's face. Although he believed that most of these farmers were uneducated, maybe even stupid, he also knew that some of them were not. He had to be careful with his answers if he wanted to draw Wilson in, get him to trust him and make the deal. He cleared his throat before he spoke.

"I have to tell you, sir, that it is not my normal practice to violate confidences. When I make a deal with an experienced farmer such as you, I keep that business between us." Jones told this lie as easily as he'd done scores of times before. "I'm sure you understand that. But I can tell you there have been a number of your fellow citizens who've heard what I have to say and who have indicated to me that they are very interested in my offer."

"I'm not askin' for names," said Wes. "Just tell me if you've made a deal with anyone."

Jones paused, trying to come up with an answer that would satisfy Wilson.

When Wes realized he wasn't going to get the answer he wanted, he said, "Let me ask my question another way. When you met with my 'fellow citizens,' as you called 'em, did they all want to hear what you had to say?" Wes tried to keep his voice calm. He didn't want Jones to leave before answering the rest of his questions.

Jones told his next lie even more easily than the first. "Mr. Wilson, everyone has been interested in hearing what I have to say. These are desperate times, and men want to be paid well for the product they've toiled to produce. I've been welcomed openly by the farmers of this county, and I've offered prices that are above the current market. Although no one has signed a contract, many of my clients have indicated that they would do so shortly."

Wes had his answer—no one had signed a contract.

As Jones spoke, Wes watched his eyes. Just like John Stanley had said, the man's eyes didn't match what his mouth was saying. He was lying. Wes guessed that some of his neighbors likely kicked Jones off of their farms after hearing his pitch. Others probably didn't even speak to him.

"That's very interestin', Mr. Jones. Have you heard any talk about the Planters' Protective Association?"

Once again, Jones tried to appear sincere as he thought about how to answer the question.

"Well, sir, there was a lot of talk about that sort of thing over in Christian County last year, and there have been rumors of an association up in Mayfield. I can't say I've heard any such thing going on in this district. Why do you ask?"

"I was just interested, that's all. Let me ask you another question. Did anyone say anythin' about Night Riders?" Wes knew that the question was a bold one. He'd wanted to catch Jones off guard, hoping he wouldn't have time to make up another lie.

Jones was surprised and knew he'd been backed into a corner. He had to be careful with his response since he didn't know if Wilson was afraid of the raiders or was one of them himself. His best chance, he thought, was to tell a half-truth. "I heard that there had been a raid of sorts near Cuba last week. But as far as I know, Graves County hasn't experienced any of the unfortunate events like they've seen east of here."

"You told my boy that you had an offer I might find interestin'."

Glad that the conversation had turned in his favor, Jones put on his best smile and rose from the bench. He clutched the lapels of his coat and began pacing back and forth in front of Wes. To Wes, he looked like a preacher building up to the powerful part of his sermon. When he finally spoke, he even sounded like a preacher.

"Mr. Wilson, as I said earlier, you have a fine crop of tobacco. It's probably the finest I've seen in my few days in Lynnville. And, even though we are months ahead of harvest and curing, my company has authorized me to offer an above-market price in advance of delivery."

Wes knew that his crop looked good, but he also knew that everyone's crop, just a week in the field, looked good. With every word Jones spoke, Wes trusted him less.

"Now, I know you are probably wondering why we would offer such a good price. Back when I was farming, I would have wondered the same thing. But there is logic behind our decision. We think that it is sound business to secure product early in the season. That way, we can be assured we'll have tobacco to meet our needs. We believe that the American Tobacco Company produces the finest finished tobacco products in the country, and it's all because we buy good cured tobacco from farmers such as you."

Wes wondered how long this speech would go on. He

had heard the same chatter every year he'd been farming on his own, and his father had told him similar stories
about his farming days. Wes was curious, though, about the
actual price.

"In any case, today I am prepared to offer you nine cents
per pound for your entire crop upon delivery to our warehouse in Hopkinsville." Jones stopped his pacing, folded his
arms across his chest and waited for Wes to respond. He
knew that the price he offered was probably higher than
any Wes had ever seen. He expected Wes to immediately
agree to the offer and was surprised and disappointed
when he didn't.

"Let me get this straight," said Wes, intrigued by the offer. "Even though last year's best price was six cents and
most of us got somethin' around four cents, you want to
pay me nine cents a pound."

Jones nodded, smiling smugly.

Already knowing what Jones's response would be, Wes
asked, "Why would your company do this?"

"As I mentioned a moment ago, we must secure a portion of our anticipated needs well in advance of our production schedule. That way, we are assured of meeting our
customers' demands. What you must understand, Mr. Wilson, is that this is a very, very short-time offer. I'm prepared
to discuss this same price with a few other farmers in the
area. The first one of you who signs a contract will get nine
cents a pound. The others might still get an above-market
price, but that depends on what the buyers in other parts
of the region have done." Jones paused, waiting for Wes
to react, but Wes was staring at Jones's face, particularly
his eyes. Jones began to grow uncomfortable, so he turned
away and added, "If you'll sign a contract with me today, I
will guarantee you a price of nine cents."

"I'll tell you what, Mr. Jones. I'll have to think about this
before I can agree. You've made an interestin' offer, but it's

gonna rain hard tonight, and I need to get out in that field and help my boys finish up. I appreciate your offer, but I'd like to think on this until next week."

"Although I certainly understand your need to consider all of the issues," Jones said, "you must understand that by next week the offer could be off the table. Others may not be as cautious as you are. Furthermore, at any time my company may instruct me to reduce the price. I believe this is a good offer and that you'd be wise to take it while you can. That way, you will know how much your tobacco will bring after delivery. Then you can enjoy the fruits of your labor and provide your family with the finer things I know you want them to have."

"I understand what you're sayin', but I still need to think about it. Why don't you come see me next week? If you don't show up, I'll know you've made a deal with someone else. Now I've got to get back to work." Wes stepped down into the yard. Jones followed him and, not wanting to give up, tried one more time.

"I will certainly keep you in mind, Mr. Wilson. However, if I am able to secure a contract with someone else, I'll likely not have time to come back and deal with you. Once the contract has been signed, most of the county will know about the price, and I will be busy making additional deals. I'm sure that you understand this. I appreciate your time and hope you will truly consider my offer."

Jones untied the reins from the porch post and mounted his horse. He was disappointed that Wilson hadn't agreed to sell his tobacco, but thought that after a few days of thinking about it he'd come around and make a decision in the company's favor. At least he hoped he would. As he rode up the lane and turned onto the road, he looked back and saw that Wilson was already headed back into his field. When he saw the growling dog headed his way, Jones nudged the horse's flanks and took off down the road as the first light drops of rain began to fall.

* * *

When Wes reached the boys, he saw that John Stanley had fallen back a full row. Connie and Anthie were within a yard of one another and had barely slowed down. The rain was falling in a fine mist and as welcome as it was, he hoped the downpour would hold off until they could finish chopping the rows. If they could keep going for another two hours and the rain stayed light, the entire field would get a good watering, and there would be little runoff. He picked up his hoe where he'd dropped it and got to work.

While he chopped, Wes thought about Jones and his offer. He began calculating how much money he'd get at nine cents a pound. The first total was so high he had to try again and then a third time to be sure of the numbers. Any way he figured it, he should end up with nearly three hundred dollars, and that was twice what he'd earned the previous year. Three hundred dollars would take care of his mortgage for the year, buy seed for next year's tobacco, corn and wheat and maybe even leave enough to finally get a horse.

But there were some problems that came with the nine cents a pound, and these troubled Wes. The first was Edwin T. Jones. Wes didn't like him. The man was shifty and a liar. His fancy clothes and words weren't enough to convince Wes that he was anything but a crook. Then there was the problem that taking such a price would create with the Association and, more importantly, the threat of the Night Riders. What bothered him was that taking the nine cents would likely turn his friends and his family against him. He'd end up with three hundred dollars, but no one would ever talk to him, sell to him, or trade with him. He'd have no choice but to sell his farm and move out of the county. He didn't want to do that, so, at least for the moment, he couldn't take Jones's offer no matter how good it sounded. He tried to keep his mind clear by focusing on the hoe, the dirt and catching up to his sons.

Over the next hour or so, the rain changed from a fog-like mist to steady rain. The wet dirt began to stick to the hoes and made it harder for them to keep their footing. By the time his older sons reached the last rows of the tobacco field, they were sliding more than chopping. John Stanley could barely hold onto the hoe, but he hadn't quit, and Wes, although he was stronger than his sons, was tired and ready to call it a day.

As the steady rain became a downpour, Wes finished his last row and then moved over to help John Stanley finish the one he was on. Anthie and Connie were sprawled out on the grass next to the trees. The rain was coming down so hard that all of them were soaked. What pleased Wes more than the finished task was that the boys were still laughing and that he could see the bright smiles that broke out on their muddy faces.

"We finished it, Pa!" yelled John Stanley.

"Yes we did, son. We surely did." Wes smiled at each of them.

"What do you say we get outta this rain and get somethin' to eat?"

# Chapter 8
Wednesday Evening, May 9

The trees sheltering the road gave Jones some relief from the shower, but as the storm grew stronger, the heavy leaves dripped water as fast as the rain fell. The gray sky and the chilling breeze did nothing to cheer up the tobacco buyer. All of his preparation and eloquence had failed to convince Wilson to sell his crop. He tried to figure out where things had gone wrong, but couldn't come up with any specific word or gesture that might have caused the discussion to turn in the wrong direction. *Wilson was smart,* he thought, *smarter than nearly every other farmer he'd met in the district. His questions were direct and well thought out.* That the man had controlled the entire encounter really annoyed him.

By the time Jones reached Lynnville, the rain had slowed to a mist, and the darkening sky loomed over the empty roads of the town. He rode his drenched horse directly to the stable, hoping to turn the job of caring for the bay over to the stable boy. But the boy wasn't there. Disappointed, Jones found an empty stall, removed the horse's tack and wiped her down with some rags he found on a bench along the wall. Taking a moment to straighten out his damp suit, he stepped outside. Jones knew that Mark Wilson's store was a place where people would gather to visit with one another, talk about what was going on in their lives and, most importantly, talk about business. If there were people in the store, he might just be able to salvage success from what had been an otherwise miserable day.

The bell jingled over the door as Jones entered the building. He saw the proprietor standing behind the counter at the back and smiled when he noticed there were four men sitting around the potbellied stove. Jones wasted no time in implementing his idea.

"Mr. Wilson, how are you, sir?" Jones strode confidently toward the counter, nodding to the crowd around the stove. "Quite the storm we're having, isn't it?"

"Ah, Mr. Jones," said Mark. "You seem pretty cheerful for a man who looks like he's been swimming in his clothes."

Jones heard no sarcasm in Wilson's voice. Keeping a smile painted on his face, he spoke loud enough for the other men to hear.

"I am cheerful, sir, despite the soaking I received in my ride through the rainy countryside. I have had a great day of business and wanted to share my success with someone involved in commerce, someone who would understand it from a businessman's point of view." Jones paused for a moment, hoping he'd gotten Wilson's attention with the flattery. "Today I met with a man who must be related to you in some fashion."

"Who'd you meet?" asked Mark.

"I visited with a Mr. Wes Wilson a few miles south of here. Since you and he share the same name, I thought that the two of you might be related. Am I correct in my assumption?"

"Wes is my older brother."

"Ah, great. Wonderful, actually. Then you'll be doubly pleased to hear that your brother is considering selling his entire crop of dark-fired tobacco to me." In a whisper meant to be heard by the men sitting around the stove, he added, "Nine cents per pound was simply too good a price to turn down." Jones left the words hanging in the air as he clutched the lapels of his suit coat, assuming his preacher pose.

*This is going to stir up all kinds of trouble for Wes,* Mark thought as he came around the counter and walked up to the buyer. Gently taking him by the elbow, Mark led Jones toward the door. Then, loud enough for everyone to hear him, he said, "Well, Mr. Jones, what you say is very interesting. Yet, knowing my brother Wes as well as anyone does, I'm quite surprised that he'd make such a commitment so early in the season. Wes usually takes longer than anyone else in these parts to make up his mind." Mark gently pushed Jones out the door onto the covered porch of the store. "Perhaps you misunderstood my brother's words, perhaps not. In any case, our custom in Lynnville is to keep such discussions confidential. I'll be sure to let Wes know that you've shared this information with me. I'm sure he'll be interested to know what you've said."

Jones wasn't pleased that he'd been ushered out of the store and even less so that Wilson had taken him away from his audience. But, he'd gotten the word out about the price he was offering and expected that by the next morning he'd be besieged by farmers wanting to sell their tobacco. *Another great idea put into action,* he thought as he walked across the road to the hotel.

Mark turned around and went back inside. He knew that at least three of the farmers sitting at the stove were members of the Association and that they would be troubled by the buyer's words. As he walked behind the counter, he brought out a jug of whiskey. "There's a man in love with his own voice," he said smiling. "He also seems to have a very active imagination if he thinks Wes would sell without thinking the whole thing over. I guess I'll have to talk to Wes and get the real story. Any of you fellas like a drink?"

The others seemed eager to talk about different things, but Mark kept steering the conversation back towards Jones. He needed to convince these men that Jones had been lying. Filling glasses with whiskey for each of the men, he leaned in toward them and did his best to clear

Wes's name. Warmed by the liquor and the stove, the men seemed to agree with Mark about Jones and soon their words became muffled by the driving rain on the roof of the store.

* * *

Throughout that afternoon, as he'd worked beside J.D. and Charley, all Art could think about was the new information about the raid and the fact that his two farmhands were Night Riders. At first, he wanted to fire them, hoping they'd leave the county for good. But the more he thought about it, he realized that getting rid of them could be dangerous for him and his family, since he didn't know if they'd make him the next target instead of his cousin. He also decided that even though he'd tell Wes what he'd heard, he wouldn't tell him where he heard it. *I gotta get this field weeded and then I can get rid of them two, and nobody will know.*

The workday was almost over, and shadows spread across the field when it started to rain. He sent the hands off, saying that the work would have to wait until the field dried. Then, when he was sure they were out of the area, he went into the house, told Mollie what he was doing and left. He didn't tell Mollie why he needed to ride over to see Wes. He just said that it was important and that he'd tell her all about it when he got back. She pleaded with him not to go and told him she wasn't feeling well. Art could still hear her sobbing in the back of the house as he'd gone to the barn, saddled his old horse and headed out in the rain to warn Wes.

Art's horse was a good animal, but the cold rain and the muddy road slowed her down considerably, and the trip took much longer than he wanted. The rain ran off his slicker, but had soaked his old felt hat until it looked like a rag on top of his head. As cold and miserable as this made him feel, he knew it was important to warn Wes. Waiting until tomorrow would be too late.

By the time he arrived at Wes's, he was cold and miserable. A trail of water followed him as he stepped onto the porch and knocked on the door. From the porch, he could hear footsteps, and when John Stanley's smiling face greeted him, he asked, "Is your pa home this evenin'?"

"Sure, he is." The boy turned back toward the table and said, "Pa, Cousin Art's come to see you!" He turned back to Art and said, "Do you wanna come inside?"

"I'm too wet, John Stanley. Could you just ask him to come out to the porch?"

When John Stanley turned back again, his pa was already out of his chair and walking to the door. He put his hand on the boy's shoulder and nudged him toward the table.

"You go back and finish your supper, son. I'll talk to him outside." Wes pulled the door open wider and stepped out onto the porch. He looked at his soaked cousin and then at the sad looking horse in the dark yard. "What're you doin' out on a night like this and so far from home? Is somethin' wrong with Mollie? Come on inside and dry off."

"No," said Art, "I gotta talk to you on the porch. I've got some news you need to hear, and then I need to get back home. Mollie's feelin' poorly, but she's all right. I just can't stay away long."

"Well, sit down and tell me the news that has you out so late."

Both men looked at Zora as she stepped out onto the porch. She handed a dry cloth to Art and asked him if he wanted to come inside. Art thanked her and dried his face. He started to say more, but was interrupted by Wes.

"Zora, we've got some important things to talk about. Now go on back inside." When she hesitated, Wes said, "Now."

The iciness in Wes's voice told her that this was not the

time to argue with him.

Art pushed the wet hair out of his face and cleared his throat. "I heard some fellas talkin', and they said that the Night Riders are gonna raid your place next week."

Wes was stunned, not sure he'd heard Art correctly. "What'd you say?"

"I said that there are Night Riders in Lynnville, Wes, and they're gonna raid your farm."

Wes had heard him clearly this time. "Who'd you hear this from?"

"I can't tell you, but they sounded serious. They said it was gonna happen next Tuesday or Wednesday." Art hated himself for avoiding Wes's question and not giving him the names. It was the first time he'd ever lied to Wes or held anything back from him, and it gave him a knot in his guts. But he had to protect himself and his own family and thought that this was the only way.

"But why would the Night Riders want to raid my farm? I ain't done or said anythin' that would give 'em a reason to do that. I'll be damned if anyone is gonna destroy my crop or my farm. I'll kill 'em first." He clenched his fists, the muscles in his arms pulsing, and he looked over toward his tobacco. "Who told you?" he demanded.

"I said I can't tell you, but trust me, they said it. We've got to find a way to change their minds. We have to figure out how to let the Association know that you're on their side." Art tried to ignore his demand.

"That's the problem, I ain't on their side!" Wes shouted. "I ain't on anyone's side but my own. Damn it, Art, this is my farm, and no one, not the Association or their damned Night Riders or even the tobacco company is gonna tell me how to run my life." He walked to the edge of the porch and banged his fist on the post and looked out to the field.

"I know, Wes, I know," Art said, feeling Wes's rage, trying to calm him down. "That's why we've gotta let 'em think that you're gonna join up." Wes turned toward him and Art continued. "Yesterday we talked about goin' to a meetin' together, and it seems to me that if they know you're gonna do that, they'll hold off the raid." He glanced at Wes to see if he was listening. "Have you told anyone you're gonna sell to the Trust?"

Wes knew he had to avoid the question because if he said too much about what Jones had told him, he could ruin the deal for himself. "I haven't decided a damned thing, Art. I don't know if I'm gonna hold out or sell. No matter what I pick, I lose somethin', and I'm not gonna lose without a fight."

"Let's don't talk about fightin' yet. We gotta find a way to let the Association know you're at least goin' to a meetin'. Then maybe that rumor will get back to who's in charge of the Night Riders." Art paused for a moment, wondering why Wes wouldn't answer his question. "What's important is to get the raid called off, and that'll give you more time to consider all the choices."

"That makes sense, but what doesn't make sense is that they wanna raid me. Why me?" Wes started pacing and his voice grew louder. "What have I said or done that makes me a target?"

As Wes turned, Art stood in front of him, his voice calm. "I thought about that on the way over. People respect you. They know that you're a good farmer. Most of 'em wanna do things the way you do. Maybe the Night Riders figure that raidin' you would send a message to the rest of 'em and scare 'em into joinin' up and holdin' back their tobacco."

"Well I'm afraid too, but I'm also mad as hell about this. If the damned Trust would give us a fair price for our crop, there wouldn't be any Association. The whole damned thing is a mess, and it's makin' me crazy. I feel like I'm fightin' everybody, and I'm doin' it alone."

Art thought a moment and said, "You're not alone, cousin. Wes, I gotta get back home. Mollie's not doin' well, and I need to be with her. What if I stop off at Mark's store on my way home? There's usually a couple of the Association fellas hangin' out there in the evenin's. I could tell Mark we were talkin' about goin' to the meetin' and say it loud enough so the others could hear. Then maybe the word'll get around. It's worth a try, ain't it?"

"I don't know, Art. I hate this. I hate other people tryin' to tell me how to run my own life." Wes stood at the edge of the porch, just out of the rain. He stared into the darkness and then turned back to face his cousin. "Maybe it's the only way to stop 'em." He paused and said, "Let's do it. You put the word out that we'll be at the meetin' next week. In the meantime, my boys and I'll be on guard every night until this is settled. Don't tell anyone that I'm gonna be watchin'. I don't want 'em to know that I know about the raid."

"All right, I'll do it." Art squeezed the water out of his hat again and put it back on his head. "We need to meet again before next week so we can talk more about what the Association is plannin'."

"Yeah, we do. How about we get together at Mark's on Saturday afternoon? If this rain keeps up, I'll have a mess or two in my fields to work on. So it can't be any sooner than in the afternoon."

"Okay," Art said. "I'll keep my ears open, and unless I hear somethin' new, I'll meet you at Mark's on Saturday."

Wes looked at Art, wondering why his cousin wouldn't tell him who mentioned the raid, trying to see something in his face that would convince him Art was telling the truth. "Thanks for comin' over to warn me," he said. "Give our best to Mollie."

"I'm sorry it was such bad news, Wes, but I knew you'd want to hear it. I just hope we can take care of this problem before somethin' happens."

The two friends shook hands, and then Art got on his horse. As the rain continued to fall, he rode off in the darkness. Wes watched him until he disappeared in the storm and then walked back into the house. *He's holdin' back somethin'.*

* * *

Up in his room at the hotel, Jones changed out of his soggy suit and muddy shoes. He was cold, and disappointed about the way his day had gone. He knew he needed to get back to Mayfield to check on telegrams from the company, but a trip to the county seat would have to wait until the rain stopped. As long as the storm continued, he couldn't be out visiting with any more Lynnville farmers. There was nothing left to do but get comfortable and wait until morning.

Downstairs, the lobby was empty except for a clerk who was standing behind the desk.

"Excuse me, sir, but I wonder if you could provide me with some whiskey," said Jones.

The clerk told him that Lynnville's laws didn't allow the sale of alcohol, but that he could probably come up with some whiskey by the next day. Jones gave him a silver dollar and told him that he looked forward to hearing from him in the morning. Then the clerk suggested that with another dollar, he might be convinced to give up his own few ounces of whiskey. Jones handed him a coin, and the man emptied the dregs from a jar under the counter into Jones's flask. At least now he knew if he was stuck in his room he could entertain himself, stay dry and get some rest.

* * *

It was dark and still raining when Art got down from the saddle and walked into Mark's store. Even though it was getting late, there were a few men in the store sitting with

Mark around the stove.

Mark looked over his shoulder as he heard the jingling bell. Seeing his cousin, he stood and greeted him warmly. "Art, what brings you into town on this stormy night?"

"I'm just on my way home from seein' Wes." He spoke directly to Mark, but was keenly aware of the other men sitting around the stove and knew this was the perfect opportunity to carry out their plan. "We talked about goin' to the Association meetin' next week. You know how Wes is, always wants to have all the information before he makes a decision."

"That sounds like my brother," said Mark. He'd spent the better part of an hour trying to discredit Jones's comments in order to protect Wes, and now Art's words would add credibility to what he'd been saying. "When you fellas come into town on Saturday, let's be sure to get together. We can talk about the special service out at Cuba church they got scheduled for a week from Sunday." Mark and Art both knew that the discussion on Saturday would really be about keeping Wes out of trouble.

"That's a good idea. We'll see you Saturday afternoon." Tipping his hat to the other men, Art turned toward the door. "I gotta get on home to Mollie. Tell Gertrude that she's about the same, but gettin' better."

"I will," said Mark. He walked Art to the door, gave him a quick look and a nod and watched him head down the road. When he lost sight of him in the dark and the rain, he turned back to the men. "See, I told you that Trust buyer was spinning a tale." He lifted up the jug and poured each of them another shot. He didn't say anything more, but hoped that at least the Association fellas would see that Jones was lying. The group talked for another quarter-hour and then broke up as each of the men headed home for supper.

\* \* \*

But three of the four men did not go directly home. Across the road, under the cover of the hotel's porch and sheltered from the rain, they huddled in the dark. Each of them was a member of the Association, but only one was involved with the Night Riders. This third man, a round, redheaded farmer, owned more acres of tobacco than anyone in the district and knew everything about the Lynnville Night Riders. He'd formed the group months earlier in order to put a little more pressure on the farmers, and even though he didn't ride with them on their raids, he directed their activities. The members of the Association knew about the raiders, but rarely spoke of the relationship between the two groups. Red waited patiently for the others to speak.

"What do you think is really goin' on with Wilson?" said the shortest of the three.

"That's a good question," replied the other, a tall, bearded man in overalls. "Right now I don't know what to believe. Why would that Jones fella go blabbin' about a price deal like that?"

"Yeah, why would he want anyone to know, especially when that price is so high? Nine cents! I've never seen a price that high in my thirty years of farmin'."

"You'll likely not see it again, I reckon," said the tall man.

"And it's only natural for Mark and Art to stand up for Wes, ain't it? They're right about one thing, though. Wes does take lots of time to decide what to do about anythin'. I remember the time when he was thinkin' about buyin' that old nag from Smith. Everyone knew the horse was on its last legs, even Wes, but he still took a couple of weeks to turn down Smith's offer."

"Let's get to what we know," said Red. "We all know that Wes is smart and he takes his time. And, we don't know much about this new Trust buyer. As far as we can tell, he hasn't bought a single pound in the county. This deal he's talking about with Wes could be true. It could also be a scheme on the part of Jones to get some of us to jump at nine cents. We need to let the other members know about what happened in the store tonight. But we also have to be careful not to say more than we heard."

"What do you mean, Red?" asked the short man.

"I mean that if we say Wes took the deal, even though we don't know that's true, then we could be setting Wes up for something he doesn't deserve. Or, if we say he's going to the meeting, even if we don't know that he really is going, we might be making some other kind of trouble."

"So, you think we should just mention what Jones said and what Mark and Art said and leave it at that?"

"That's exactly what I think. If Wes joins the Association, then a lot of the other holdouts will follow him. So let's hope he comes next week. We can't do any more tonight, but tomorrow we need to get the word out to all of the members."

The others nodded in agreement and, seeing that Red was finished with the conversation, said good-bye and mounted their horses. Red was going to go home as well, but he needed to make another stop first. He had to make sure that the raid schedule for Tuesday got put on hold. Getting Wes into the Association would go a long way toward defeating the Trust, and that, not the destruction of their neighbors' crops, was the real objective.

He watched his friends head off in different directions down the road and then mounted his own horse. He didn't much like the idea of getting wet or getting home any later, but he had to talk to the Night Rider captains before his day ended. He pulled up the collar of his slicker, pulled his hat down tight on his head and leaned into the rain as he kicked his horse into a trot.

\* \* \*

Wes sat back down to supper and finished his meal. Zora kept silent. She knew something was terribly wrong to get her cousin to come all the way down here in the rain. But Wes clearly wasn't ready to discuss what they'd talked about.

While he ate, Wes decided that keeping an eye on the crop and the farm overnight couldn't be put off any longer. He knew that it was time to get Connie and Anthie involved. That meant he had to say something to Zora and the boys about Jackson's situation and the news from Art. As Wes ate, he thought that now, more than ever, he needed to watch his crop day and night.

Wes had seen the results of a raid firsthand and couldn't help thinking about Jackson. Some nights he'd been so consumed with the images of the black farmer's destroyed field that he'd woken up sweating and gasping for air. A few hours ago, he thought that his problems, although troublesome, were at least manageable. But now, with a substantial offer from Jones on the table and a raid on the farm planned, he knew he was facing one of the most difficult things he'd ever confronted.

As the children finished eating, Wes asked Mary Lula to get the youngsters involved in cleaning up the kitchen. She nodded her head in agreement and then set about getting John Stanley and Irene working on the dishes. She put Ruthie in a chair next to the wash pan and handed her the wooden spoon. In the meantime, Wes told his older sons and Zora that he wanted to talk to them in the back of the house.

Zora pulled the door of the bedroom closed, and then Wes looked at each of them. He wanted to make sure that they were ready to listen to what he knew. So, he told them everything, from the visit to Jackson's farm to Art's discovery of a raid by the Night Riders and how he'd decided the best thing to do was to go to a meeting with Art and try to learn more. He told them that it was hard to know what was best for the family.

When he finished, he asked if anyone had a question. Anthie looked at his brother and his mother and then shook his head. The others remained silent, so Wes told them his plan.

"Here's what we're gonna do," said Wes. "The three of us are gonna start stayin' up all night. We've gotta keep watch on the crop and make sure that we ain't surprised by the Night Riders. I think the rain'll keep them away tonight, but I'll be out on the porch anyway. Startin' tomorrow night, though, we'll each spend three hours outside—on the porch, out by the barn, even in the field. We've got three guns. I'll keep the pistol with me all the time, day and night. Whoever's on watch will have the shotgun; it's the noisiest and it doesn't need to be aimed. We'll keep the rifle in the house. That way, whoever is not on watch will be able to get to it if he hears the shotgun go off. You all need to understand how important this is to keep our family safe and our crop in the field." He hesitated and looked around. "Don't be afraid to use the gun if you have to."

"What do you want me to do?" said Zora.

"I want you in the house," said Wes. "If all three of us happen to be outside, I know you can use the rifle, and we'll need your help. When I talk to Mary Lula later, I'm gonna tell her that she will be the one in charge of the house durin' the day. It's gonna be too wet out there for the next few days to get any work done, so I want her to keep the children inside the house or on the porch. She can sleep at night, and you can sleep durin' the day."

"Do you still want me to go down to the Morrises' on Saturday, Pa?"

"Yes, son, I do. Nothin's changed with that. Whatever you find out'll be helpful. Since I'll be goin' in to town to meet up with Mark and Art in the afternoon," he said as he looked at Connie, "that means you'll have to be around here all day. If things stay calm, maybe you can get over to the Wilkinses' to see Maud on Sunday afternoon."

"Okay, Pa."

"Now, we'll still have normal chores to do, and even though some of us will sleep durin' the day, we still need to get 'em done. I wish there was a better way to do this, but there's not. It's probably gonna take a miracle of some kind to get us out of this mess, Zora, so anytime you want to pray, you go ahead and do it."

Wes spent another ten minutes going over the details of the watch. Even though they were both familiar with the shotgun, he made sure that the boys understood how to load and fire the weapon. Once again he asked if there were any questions.

"It's a little scary, Pa," said Anthie, "but I ain't afraid."

"I know, son, but there ain't nothin' wrong with bein' afraid as long as you keep your eyes open and your mind clear. This ain't no time to be thinkin' about girls or any other thing except lookin' out for the Night Riders."

Knowing that Wes wouldn't think of praying, Zora knew there was no better time than right now to do just that. She took hold of his hand and Connie's and then told Anthie to grab his brother's and his pa's hands. In the same manner as Wes had done earlier, she looked directly at the faces of each of her men. Then she bowed her head and prayed.

"Lord, we are facin' a terrible enemy. We don't even know who he is, but you do. We ask that you keep us safe from harm and keep us watchful. You have provided for us and kept this family safe and happy for a long time, so now we are askin' you to send your Holy Spirit down to watch over us like he did for all of them Old Testament prophets. You are a great and powerful God, and we know that we gotta trust you to help us. Amen."

When she looked up and opened her eyes, she saw that

each of the others still had his head down. First Anthie and then Connie looked up at her. Wes muttered an Amen and then looked up as well. Zora signaled with her eyes that the boys should go on to bed. When the door shut behind Anthie, she turned to Wes.

"Wes, you know you can count on your children and you can count on me. But if you ever needed to learn that you can count on God, this is the time. Now, I gotta help Mary Lula in the kitchen." She paused and took a deep breath and whispered, "Wes, I love you." Zora saw something in Wes that was more than troubling, so she hugged her husband, held him close for a moment and then left the room.

Wes reached under the bed and pulled out an old cigar box. He opened it and picked up the .38 caliber Smith & Wesson revolver he'd bought nearly a dozen years earlier. He counted the shells in the cylinder and those in the bottom of the box. He made sure the cylinder was empty, and then he dry-fired the pistol three times. Convinced that it was working, he reloaded it and slipped it into his pocket. He stood up, opened the door, picked up the shotgun and walked toward the kitchen. He got the jug from the cupboard and headed out to the porch. As he passed Mary Lula standing at the wash pan, he asked her to come outside with him.

She wiped her wet hands with a flour sack towel and walked out onto the porch. Wes pointed her toward the bench and when she was seated, he kneeled down in front of her.

"I know you've probably already figured out what's goin' on around here, but I want to make sure that you know everythin'." He went on to fill her in on the problem and the plan and especially her role in all of it. When he finished, he gave her a hug and sent her back inside the house. He checked to see that the gun was loaded and then sat down on the bench and looked out into the dark, wet night.

Clouds of doubt were creating a storm in his head that was greater than the one he saw across his fields.

# Chapter 9
Thursday Morning, May 10

It rained steadily all night long, soaking the fields, filling the ponds and streams, turning the country road into a muddy bog. It washed the dust off of the shed, barns and chicken coop, making them smell clean and look new. Even though it was getting close to dawn, the thick clouds kept the sky dark and blocked out the usual pre-sunrise glow in the east.

The gentle, mind-numbing sound of the rain as it fell on the trees and the roof had lulled Wes into a deep sleep. The shotgun and the jug lay on the porch where they'd fallen. Wes was lying on the bench, his hands under his head, providing a makeshift pillow. Rufus was curled up nearby and woke only when Wes's snoring became louder than the drumming of the rain.

Over the few years Anthie'd been responsible for milking the cow, he'd developed a routine and learned, whether on purpose or by habit, when to wake up, which creaky steps on the stairs to avoid and how to gently close the door when he went out of the house. On this morning, he'd made it all the way to the kitchen without making a sound. But, when he stepped out onto the porch, the door slipped from his hand and banged against the door jamb. The noise scared Anthie. Rufus barked once and ran under the porch.

The sound jolted into Wes's slumber like an ax into a tree, shocking him awake. He sat upright, his arms searching for something to hold onto, his eyes foggy, unfocused. The muffled shout that rasped out of his throat was muddied by the whiskey in his belly. "Where's my gun?"

"Sorry, Pa," mumbled Anthie. "I didn't mean to wake you. The door slipped outta my hands." Anthie froze at the sound of his pa's voice. The bucket slipped from his hand to the porch, and its banging caused Wes to jump again.

"What?" Wes was clearly confused as he fumbled in the dark, trying to get his hands on the shotgun. He knocked over the empty jug, grabbed hold of the gun's barrel and tried to stand up. His first attempt failed, and he sat back down hard on the bench. He tried to rise again and only succeeded by leaning against the wall. Wes lifted the shotgun in front of his chest, the barrel aimed toward Anthie.

"I said I'm sorry. The door slipped."

"Damn it, boy, you coulda got yourself killed." Wes looked at his son and then down at the gun in his hand.

"I'm sorry, Pa." Fearing another beating, Anthie ran as fast as he could toward the barn. He opened the door and pulled it closed behind him. Then he sat down on the dirt floor to catch his breath. He waited until his heart slowed and then made his way over to the stall. He'd not forgotten what his pa had said the night before about the danger they faced and the need to be watchful. The warning had scared him and kept him from falling asleep for quite a while, but he'd eventually drifted off, knowing his pa was outside on guard. More than just afraid, Anthie was disappointed in his pa for falling asleep when he should've been protecting the family. *Why was he sleepin'? He told us we had to stay awake and watch for the Night Riders, but that was a lie. What if they'd come last night? We might've been killed.*

For most of the night, Wes had sat in the dark, brooding over the idea that the Night Riders wanted to raid his farm and about the offer from Jones. These two issues kept swirling around in his mind like a summer tornado. He didn't even know who to be angry with, or who was his friend or enemy. Everything seemed to be going wrong at the same time—Night Riders were going to ruin his crop if he decided to sell it to the Trust; if he didn't sell it, the bank might foreclose on his mortgage; and his trusted cousin Art wouldn't even tell him where he heard about the raid. *I think I'm goin' crazy*, he thought, *just like my pa did. But I'll be damned if I'm gonna do what he did and leave my family without a husband or a father. I'm not gonna give up, I'm gonna fight.* He shook his head. *I'm not gonna fall asleep on guard. Never again.* Then, looking toward the barn, the guilt he would never want to admit, especially to his son, draped over him like a smelly blanket.

* * *

In the small room on the second floor of the hotel in Lynnville, Jones lay asleep in the rumpled bed. His rain-dampened clothes were draped over the chair and small desk near the window. The empty flask, drained in his final moments of wakefulness the night before, was on the floor next to his muddy shoes. The night jar under the bed needed emptying, and its odor, mixed with the smell of wet clothes and sweat, gave the room an unhealthy stench.

As he'd sat on the bed the night before, Jones had taken turns sipping from the flask and complimenting himself on how well his idea had worked. He certainly hadn't liked being escorted out of the store by Wilson, but he was certain the other men had heard what he'd said about the tobacco price. For most of an hour, he'd sipped and smiled and planned how he would use this change in fortune to buy most of the tobacco in the district. Before falling asleep, he'd gotten up and written himself a note to remember to see the clerk about some more whiskey and to make one more stop at Wilson's store before he returned to Mayfield. When he'd finished the flask, he'd dropped it on the floor, turned toward the wall and passed out.

* * *

Outside Jones's hotel window, the rain continued to fall. In Lynnville, there was little activity near the muddy crossroads. Mark Wilson's store was closed up tight, and there were no lights showing through the windows of the nearby houses and stores. The glow from the blacksmith shop a few lots to the west of the store was the only sign that the town was surviving the rainstorm. Away from the town, surrounded by their drenched fields, the people living on the farms were getting up and doing the same chores that farmers had always done.

North of town, in the shack Ol' Man Smith let them use, Art's two farmhands were still trying to sleep. The old roof of the shack had a few leaks, and several of them were right over the crude, straw-filled sacks they used as mattresses. J.D. had pulled his slicker over his head so the rain that dripped down on him was being channeled to the floor. Charley wasn't as lucky. His bed lay underneath the bigger leaks, and there was just no getting away from the streams of water that poured through the roof. He'd also pulled a slicker over himself, but it was short and left his feet exposed. He tried to sleep, but he was wet and cold.

"This rain is gonna make me sick," he mumbled.

"Shut up, will ya?" growled J.D. under the slicker as he turned to face the wall. "I'm tryin' to sleep."

Charley shuffled under his cover, trying to find a dry spot. "My feet are cold. I'm hungry, and I could use another drink. Where'd you put the jug?"

"The jug's still empty, just like it was when you took the last snort. Now shut up, damn it, and leave me alone."

"We gotta find a better place to stay or get the old man to fix the roof. It ain't right that workin' men gotta sleep in the rain."

J.D. turned back toward Charley. He lifted his slicker just enough so he could see his partner and snarled, "Well, we ain't workin' today, that's for sure, and when we don't work, we don't get paid. Besides, where else in this lousy town are we gonna get a place to stay for free? So quit yappin' and go to sleep. We'll go into town later and see if there's somethin' we can do to pick up some money, maybe even enough to stay at the hotel. Then you'll be dry and I can get some damn sleep."

He let the slicker fall back over his face and more water ran onto the floor. Charley shuffled once more under his cover and mumbled, "I'm still hungry." *How the hell did I get in this mess,* he thought as he shivered and tried to pull his feet up under the cover. *I shoulda never let him follow me.*

Outside the shack, the rain continued to fall, and a cold, gray, wet dawn broke on the countryside.

* * *

After putting the coffeepot on the stove, Mark returned to the bedroom he shared with Gertrude, picked up his clothes and shoes and returned to the kitchen to get dressed. For most of the years he'd been married, he'd dressed more times in the kitchen than he had in the bedroom because Gertrude was a light sleeper. On those few occasions in the early years when he'd dropped a shoe or closed the wardrobe door too loudly, he'd suffered the scowl and bitter words she threw at him. On this day, however, the rain falling on the roof seemed to muffle the sounds of his feet on the creaky floor.

Leaving the house, Mark made his way through the wet grass along the side of the road. He thought about the things he wanted to do at the store that day and about how he might help his brother. He stepped up onto the small porch at the back of the store and unlocked the door. His thoughts went quickly to the dark morning a few weeks ago when he'd found the door open. He'd discovered that someone had taken his whiskey jug and some food, but hadn't damaged anything else. When he told the constable about it, the man had said he'd look into it. Shaking his head, knowing that he'd never see the missing items again, he walked into the back of the store. It took him only a few minutes to start a fire in the stove, get a pot of coffee going and open his safe. He took out what change he thought he'd need for the day, put it in the cash box and then closed and locked the safe.

Last night's incident with Jones bothered Mark. He was concerned about the kind of trouble the man could stir up. Mark could tell that he had no morals. Jones lied for his own gain and cared only about himself. He clearly wasn't worried about what might happen to any farmers who were raided by the Night Riders. If a farmer lost his crop, Jones would just move on to another part of the county where the Night Riders didn't exist. Mark knew about the raid in Cuba, and he'd heard rumors that something similar had happened down in Tennessee a few days after that. He also knew that, although unified in their distrust of the company, the farmers did not agree on how to deal with the problem of low prices, and this was beginning to create tension among them.

He poured himself a cup of fresh coffee and walked to the front of the store. Taking a sip of the hot brew, he looked out the window at the rain and the muddy cross-road and wondered if he'd have any customers today. The comforting sound of the shower and the popping of the blaze in the stove and the peacefulness of the empty store, however, were not enough to calm his fears about Wes. He loved his brother and owed him plenty for his loyalty and support when he was growing up. Mark had known early that he didn't want to be a farmer. On the day he told his mother about his decision, she cried, telling him that the Wilsons had always been farmers. Even his brother George had tried to get him to change his mind. But Wes was the only one who seemed to understand him. After he'd grown up and moved off of the farm and into town, it was Wes who helped him get settled. Then, when his store nearly burned to the ground three years ago, Wes was there to help.

Not long after those tragic days, he'd decided to rebuild the store on the same lot. He borrowed some money and added that to the little he'd gotten from the insurance company. Then he put all of it into erecting the triple-brick building that now housed Wilson's General Store. Although most of the citizens had feared that the fire signaled the end of Lynnville, Mark's efforts led many of them to rebuild as well, and now the community was thriving again. Even though the local doctor's house was destroyed, he rebuilt it and expanded it to include an examining room for his patients. The blacksmith managed to survive most of the destruction, but he replaced his roof with one made of tin-coated steel. East of the hotel, the feed store had been totally destroyed, but, inspired by Mark, the proprietor erected a safer, but smaller warehouse for his supplies.

Like nearly everyone in town, Mark owned a gun. He kept it out of sight under the counter in the back of his store. Only on occasion had he thought he might need to use it; he mainly kept it to protect his family. But now, more than ever, he thought it was important to keep it close at hand. Even though Lynnville had been a peaceful town, there had been difficult times. Mark had seen it all. Most of the difficulties, however, could be tied to the very things the town's preachers railed against every Sunday—greed, pride and the rest of the seven deadly sins. *There might be some truth to that,* Mark thought, remembering what had happened to him two years ago.

One Saturday night about nine o'clock, he'd been sweeping up after a busy day in the store, and someone started banging on the back door. At first Mark ignored the noise. When it continued, he went to the door and yelled that the store was closed. But the pounding kept on. Mark went to get his pistol and returned to the back of the store and eased the door open to see who was there. He was caught off guard when the man, John Canter, pushed the door into his face and knocked him onto the floor. He aimed his gun at Canter and pulled the trigger five times. Canter was hit once in the right side of his belly and stumbled back out the door. The gunshots coming from the general store brought many people out of their homes. Canter was taken away by the doctor, and most folks expected that his wound was mortal.

After a few days, however, Canter recovered. Everyone was convinced that Mark had acted in self-defense, since Canter had been drinking and was a known troublemaker who had shot and killed another man a year earlier. Rumors whirled around town how it took him five shots to hit Canter once. Mark had no choice but to go along with the teasing and the laughter. For a while, they called him Ol' Five Shot and Dead Eye and other, less pleasant names. In time the teasing ended and the shooting was largely forgotten by everyone but Mark. He'd never gotten along with Canter, but he always felt bad about shooting him.

Trouble seemed to settle down over the winter months. But now, with the Night Riders' raids and the tension building over tobacco prices, he thought that maybe Lynnville was headed for more trouble. He just hoped he could keep Wes and Art and other people he cared for out of harm's way.

Mark opened the front door and tossed the dregs of his coffee out into the rain. He looked up and down the road and saw that the town was still asleep. Refilling his cup, he walked to the counter in the back of the store, laughing at himself as he remembered being called "Ol' Five Shot."

* * *

On the Wilson farm, the work for the day had already started. Even as Jones snoozed in his hotel bed, as Mark sipped his coffee and reminisced and as the farmhands grumbled in their leaky shed, Wes and his boys were tackling the chores that could be done while it rained outside. Inside the house, Zora and the girls worked at cleaning and straightening.

While the family was finishing breakfast, Wes had grumbled out the list of things he wanted the boys to do, clearly still embarrassed and angry at himself. To the others, Wes's attitude seemed to come from the whiskey, but Anthie knew why his pa was mad, and he'd decided to stay clear of him as much as he could. He figured that doing what he was told and working hard would be safe. He still wanted to see Sudie on Saturday and to carry out his pa's assignment. So, when Wes told him that he was to work in the pigsty, he nodded and said he would.

Before their pa could change his mind, the boys put on their coats and ran out through the pouring rain. Inside the barn, John Stanley watched his older brothers, hoping they'd say something, wanting them to tell him why their pa was in such a bad mood that morning. Anthie and Connie exchanged knowing glances, but didn't say a word. John Stanley grabbed the old, dull, flat-nosed spade and a bucket and headed out into the rain toward the coop.

"What's goin' on with Pa, Anthie?" asked Connie as soon as his youngest brother was out of their hearing.

"I don't want to talk about it."

"C'mon, tell me. Somethin's goin' on, and I wanna know what it is."

Anthie stared at the tools stacked in the corner of the barn. He started to answer his brother and then stopped. He reached out and grabbed a rake, gripping it tightly, and then turned to face Connie. "When I went to milk the cow this mornin', Pa was passed out on the bench. He told us last night that we had to keep a lookout for the Night Riders, and he was sleepin'. He yelled at me and almost shot me with the gun. Why'd he do that? Why's he mad at me? I'm not the one who fell asleep."

Connie looked at his brother for a moment. "He's not mad at you. He's got a lot on his mind."

"That's no excuse for almost shootin' me, is it?" Ready for a fight, Anthie stared hard at Connie, almost wanting him to defend their pa. "He was wrong, Connie."

"You know how he is when he gets drunk. It's like he's blind or somethin'. I don't mean he can't see, but maybe he doesn't know what's goin' on around him."

"What if the Night Riders had come last night? They woulda found a drunk man with a gun." He took a quick breath. "I think he don't care what's goin' on around him."

They stood in silence for a little while and then Connie said, "We can't do nothin' to change him, Anthie. All we can do is make sure he don't hurt Ma or one of the kids. One of these days we'll be leavin' here, and then he'll have to take care of the farm by himself."

"I'm leavin' as soon as I can," Anthie mumbled. "And I ain't gonna be no farmer."

"You don't know what you're talkin' about. What else're you gonna do?"

"I don't know. Maybe I'll work for Uncle Mark. He don't have to get up early and milk a cow. He don't spend all day every day diggin' in the dirt and pullin' weeds and squishin' worms."

"What do you know about workin' in a store?"

"I'll learn," he said and added, "Leave me alone. I gotta get out to the pigsty before Pa comes out here, and I ain't gonna give him anymore reasons to be mad at me."

Anthie picked up his tools and left the barn. Connie watched him stride head-down through the rain and thought about his brother's stubbornness. Except for Uncle Mark, hadn't the Wilsons always been farmers? Anthie went to school like the rest of them, when they could and when there wasn't farm work to do, but he wasn't any smarter than anyone else. Connie knew he was going to be a farmer just like his pa and his Uncle George. That's what he knew how to do. He liked the work, and he knew that he was good at it. *As soon as I can, I'll get my own place and marry Maud,* he thought. *Then everything'll be just fine.* He was still gazing out the barn door when he saw his pa step off the porch and head his way. He quickly turned away and walked toward the cow's stall. He didn't want to be caught doing nothing.

* * *

So far this morning, Mark only had one customer—the banker had stopped by to pick up a box of pencils—and he'd spent the time straightening out the shelves. Mark believed that folks should be able to find anything they needed in his store. He also tried to supply them with the things they wanted, so he occasionally had new and different items for sale. He thought about heading into Mayfield to see what was on the shelves in the stores there, but he knew he'd need to wait until the rain ended and the roads dried up. He had just about finished working on the shelf of tin pots and pans when the bell over the door jingled.

"Good morning, gentlemen," he said to J.D. and Charley as they stepped quickly into the store. "What brings you into town on such a dreary day?"

"Mornin'," said Charley, trying to sound cheerful. Silent, J.D. sullenly looked at Mark, clearly uncomfortable with the storekeeper's cheerfulness.

Mark watched as the rainwater dripped off of their slickers onto his freshly swept floor.

"Can I help you find something?"

"No, sir," said Charley. "Actually, we were hopin' you

might have some work we could do for you today. We can't work out at Art West's place, and we don't get paid until tomorrow."

"Tell you what," said Mark. "Why don't you sit over here by the stove and have a cup of coffee first. You look like a couple of drowned cats, and pretty cold ones at that." He picked two cups off the shelf and poured boiling coffee into each of them. "If I can't find something for you to do, you might try over at the hotel. They sometimes need fellas to do odd jobs."

The farmhands walked to the stove, trailing water behind them. Taking the cups from Mark, they took tentative sips of the coffee, letting the steam warm their cold faces.

"About all I have that needs doin' is outside work, and it's a pretty miserable job. My pigsty is startin' to fill up with all of this rain, and I need a drain trench dug. I'd be willin' to pay a dollar to get that done."

"Would that be a dollar each?" asked J.D. Charley looked at the storekeeper, worried that J.D. might have offended him. He started to say something, but J.D. added, "We could sure use the work today. We're kinda hungry."

Mark had little interest in working in the rain and mud, and he certainly didn't want to wallow with his pigs. He noticed the worried look on Charley's face before he turned to J.D.

"You're name's J.D., right?"

"Yep."

"Tell you what, since my cousin says you all work hard and because it's so miserable outside today, I'll pay a dollar and a half for the job if you'll do it right away and get it done before noon." He looked at both men, trying to get a sense of their willingness.

Before Charley could get a word out, he was interrupted by J.D. "A dollar apiece would be better, but we'll do it for less. You'll pay us cash money, right?"

Mark didn't like J.D.'s attitude. "Of course, as soon as you've finished the job, I'll give you the money. There are some old shovels in the shed at the back of the store. The sty is between here and the house. I'd appreciate it if you'd work quietly, since my wife . . . well, just work as quietly as you can."

"We will, Mr. Wilson, and thank you, thank you very much," blurted Charley. Once they'd turned the corner and headed for the back of the store, J.D. slapped Charley on the back of his head.

"How come you talked so nice to him? You sounded like an old woman."

"You almost made him change his mind. We woulda done all right with a dollar." Charley knew he needed to calm J.D. down, so he added, "But you got us another half a buck. That's good."

"Yeah, I did."

They found the tools where Mark had said they'd be and walked through the rain to the pigsty. It was definitely flooded and although the pigs seemed satisfied with the situation, the men could see why Wilson wanted the trench dug. The fouled water was beginning to spill over the top and run toward the house. They saw that they'd need to make a cut on the road side of the sty in order to get the water moving in the direction of the ditch.

"Well, let's get this done," said Charley. "As bad as it smells, it's no worse than you after you've filled up with beans."

"Shut the hell up and start diggin' the trench. I'm gonna go over to the hotel and see if they've got somethin' we can do when we're done with this job."

"You'd better come right back. I ain't gonna do this all by myself."

"Don't worry, I'll be back." J.D. didn't even turn around as he walked across the muddy road to the hotel.

* * *

The night clerk stopped sweeping as he watched J.D. walk toward the hotel through the rain. He leaned the broom against the wall and put his hand in his pocket, checking again for the two silver dollars he'd gotten from the man in room five.

"Mornin'," he said as J.D. reached the porch.

"Mornin', Walter. Is this damn rain ever gonna quit?" J.D. took off his soaked hat and scraped his muddy feet on the recently swept porch.

"I suppose it'll have to stop sometime," he said as he looked at the mess J.D. had created. "If it ever does, I might be able to keep this porch clean."

"You got any ideas how me an' Charley can pick up some money? We won't be workin' today, and we don't get paid 'til tomorrow."

"Actually, I do," said Walter. "I was hopin' you'd come by this mornin'. I got a guest upstairs who ran out of whiskey last night, and he asked me to get him some. Is there any way you can help me?"

"It'll take some doin', but I think we can. Once we finish the job across the road, we'll have enough to get a big jug from—" he stopped before he gave away the name of his source, "—from this fella I know." J.D. quickly calculated how they could turn the six bits from Wilson into four or five dollars. "You go up and tell your guest that we'll have a jug for him in a couple of hours. Tell him it'll cost him five dollars. If he gives you the okay, get word to me. Once he's paid us, I'll give you a cut."

"Sounds good to me," said Walter. He saw no reason to tell J.D. that he'd already been paid for his part of the job. "I'll go right up. You wait here."

J.D. looked across the road and watched Charley digging the trench. He figured that the dollar-fifty from Wilson would buy the jug, which in turn would earn them five dollars. He only planned to give Walter fifty cents. That would leave him and Charley with over four dollars, which would easily get them through the day. He was still watching Charley through the rain when Walter returned.

"You got a deal," Walter said, "but the man plans to leave town by noon. Do you think you can get it before then?"

"It'll be tight, but I think we can. You tell him I want to meet with him. I want to hand him the jug and collect the money myself."

Walter nodded, shook hands with J.D., watched him hurry across the road and got back to his sweeping. Last night Walter had been down to his last few dollars before payday, but now he was wondering how he'd spend his unexpected fortune. He started whistling as he tried to clean up the wet mud J.D. had left on the porch.

At half past eleven, Charley shoveled the final clump of mud away from the top of the trench, and the smelly water rushed down into the ditch. Despite the still-falling rain, he was drenched with sweat. J.D. took the promised coins from Mark as the three men watched the pigsty drain. Mark went back to the store, and Charley carried the tools back to the shed.

"You get cleaned up and go tell Walter I'll be right back. I'm gonna get the whiskey. Then we'll go get the rest of our money." Without waiting for a response, J.D. ran across the road, past the hotel and down the road to the east.

The clock behind the counter at the hotel began chiming noon just as Jones came down the stairs into the lobby. Walter glanced at Charley and then walked toward Jones. The two men held a whispered conversation at the foot of the staircase. Charley was starting to fret, when J.D. came rushing in from the road, holding a rag-wrapped jug.

"Here are the fellas I told you about, Mr. Jones. Why don't you all go on into the dining room and take care of your business. I've got some matters to attend to, so I'll see you in a few minutes."

Jones led J.D. and Charley into the next room. The three men went to a table away from the window and sat down. J.D. kept the bundle in his lap. He glanced at Charley to make sure he stayed quiet and then turned to Jones.

"Do you have the money?"

"I do," he said, "but before we complete our transaction, I'd like to ask you gentlemen a question." Neither of the others spoke, so Jones continued. "I see that the two of you are quite resourceful. I also assume, because you are able to carry out tasks such as our current business, that you are capable of keeping confidences. Am I correct?"

"Yeah, so what?"

"Am I also correct in assuming that you have knowledge of the various activities that go on in this town, that you know the farmers and what they do and what they say?"

"We know a lot, but what're you gettin' at?" said J.D.

"What I'm getting at is this. I want to propose an arrangement between us. I am willing to pay you for certain information."

"What kind of information?"

Jones cleared his throat and looked at the two men. "I need to know if any of the farmers around here who haven't joined the Association are willing to talk to me about selling their tobacco. I will pay a reasonable fee for every piece of valuable information you bring me."

"How much?" asked Charley.

"That will, of course, depend on the quality of the information. If, for instance, you tell me the name of a farmer who has shown an interest in selling his tobacco to me instead of joining the Association, I'll give you a half-dollar. If he subsequently sells me his tobacco, I will pay you another half-dollar."

"Let me get this straight," said J.D. "You want us to give

you names of people we think might be talkin' about sellin' their crops, and then you'll pay us."

"That's right."

"What if they don't end up sellin' their tobacco to you?"

"Then you'll only get the first half of the money. So you see that you can't really lose in this arrangement."

Charley started to fidget and signaled J.D. that he wanted to say something.

"Can you give us a minute?" J.D. said to Jones. "We need to talk somethin' over."

"Of course. Why don't I go take care of my bill with the proprietor? I'll be back in a moment." Jones got up and went into the other room.

"I don't know about this," whispered Charley. "We're puttin' ourselves in a tight spot if we do this."

"How?"

"We'll be double-dealin'. We're already gettin' paid by the Night Riders to go on the raids to get farmers to not sell their tobacco to the Trust. And now we might be gettin' paid by a fella who works for the tobacco company to tell him about farmers who want to sell their crops. That puts us right in the middle of all of the trouble. We'd be workin' for both sides in this fight."

"Yeah, so what? We'd also be makin' more money than we have in a long time."

"I don't know, J.D. I'm worried we'll end up dead or back in jail, and I don't ever want to go back to jail. I mean, you burned down your own house. What if they find out about that?"

"Listen, Charley. If we can keep this to ourselves, we can earn enough money so that when the season's over, we can clear out of here. We can head to Memphis or St. Louis or anywhere we want to go, and no one'll ever find us."

"That sure sounds like a good idea, but I'm still scared."

"It don't cost us nothin' to take this man's deal. All we

gotta do is keep our ears open and give him names. That's the easy part. The hard part is that we've gotta keep this to ourselves."

Jones came back into the room, his slicker draped across his arm. He set his portmanteau on the floor and looked toward J.D. "Well, gentlemen, do we have a deal?"

"We do," said J.D.

"Then let's conclude our first arrangement. Here's the five dollars for the bundle. I'll be heading up to Mayfield in a bit, and I'll be gone until early next week. If upon my return, you can deliver some of the information about which we spoke a moment ago I'll pay you your fees."

J.D. handed the wrapped jug to Jones and put the handful of coins in his pocket. The three men shook hands, and then Jones put on his slicker, picked up his bag and walked out the door. Walter came into the dining room and walked up to the others. J.D. handed him a half-dollar, and then he and Charley left the hotel.

"Let's get back to the shack. We've got some thinkin' to do."

"That's for sure," said a worried Charley as the two men started off through the slackening rain toward their shack.

From the porch of Wilson's store, Jones watched as the two men rode off into the rain. Then he turned and went inside. He saw Wilson at the counter in the rear of the building and spoke to him for a moment. Jones waited by the counter until Mark returned with a box and handed it to him. He shook Mark's hand, handed him some money and walked out of the store.

*Now if I could only sell that other derby,* thought Mark, *I'd be a happy man.*

# Chapter 10
Thursday Afternoon, May 10

As the rain began to let up, Art was doing his best to fix dinner for his family. He was already tired from his morning chores, his children were hungry and his wife was sick, so it was up to him to take care of them. Without making too much of a mess, he'd managed to cut some side meat, make some biscuits and even heat up some corn he'd found in a Mason jar. There was plenty of water, so the children would have something to drink, and he could make coffee for himself. He put Clarence and Thressie to work setting the table, and they'd managed to complete the task without killing each other.

Art stared out the window into the door yard. *Seems like there's just no time to rest,* he thought. *There's always somethin' to worry about.* He was very concerned about Mollie's health—her raspy breathing and coughing and the fatigue that showed in her pallid face. He also worried about how her illness was affecting the children. At the same time, the problem about what to do with his crop kept nagging at him, and he couldn't forget about the pending raid on Wes's farm. It seemed to him that the only way to survive was to join up with the Association and hold back his tobacco. But he trusted Wes, and he knew he had to wait and see what more the two of them could learn at the meeting before he would make his decision.

When he finished setting the food on the table, he called the children in and told them to eat. He carried a bowl of corn soup into the bedroom and coaxed Mollie into eating most of it. They talked for a few minutes about the children, and when she finally fell asleep, he brought the bowl back to the kitchen. He sat down and listened to the young ones chatter, all the while thinking about how to solve the challenges that lay ahead.

* * *

By late afternoon, the storm had moved off to the east. The sun was shining, and all over the district people began to wander out of their homes. At the Wilson farm, Wes sat on his porch, the empty whiskey jug clutched in one hand. He pulled the brim of his hat down to keep the sun out of his eyes. Connie came out of the house, looked down at his pa and said, "I think I'm gonna go take a look and see if there's any damage in the fields."

Wes coughed and rose unsteadily from the bench. The jug slipped out of his lap and rolled into the mud. He followed his son off the porch and out of the yard.

While Zora watched them from the kitchen window, Mary Lula kept the younger children busy and out of their pa's way. Still angry and afraid, Anthie also steered clear of his pa and stayed in his room.

"It don't look too bad, Pa," said Connie as they stood in the muddy rows between the tobacco plants. The leaves were droopy but unbroken, and the water had mostly soaked into the ground rather than pool up.

Wes didn't respond, but walked on toward the ditch. Connie followed him, and recognizing his drunken stupor, decided to listen rather than talk. It was clear to him that his pa was drunk and not in a talking mood. The water in the ditch was running like a slow stream. John Stanley's weed chopping had made it easier for the water to move down the gentle slope to the west. Across the ditch, the road was muddy. Here and there, puddles formed between the wagon ruts.

"Gonna have to let all this dry out for a couple of days,"

mumbled Wes, his words mushy. "Let's go check the corn."

Staying clear of the young tobacco plants, they walked to the fields on the north side of the farm. A couple rows of the cornstalks were flattened, and maybe a tenth of the crop was under water. *It looks bad,* thought Wes, *but we could lose a little corn and still be all right.*

"We'll have to get out here tomorrow and drain off this water. Maybe we can save some of the corn."

"All right, Pa. You want me to go check the wheat?"

"No, I want to see it too. I'll go with you."

They spent most of the next hour walking around the fields, seeing what had survived. Wes sent Connie to check out the drying barn to see if there had been any damage. When they'd finished the survey, they had a good idea of what needed fixing and knew that they'd all be busy repairing the damage on Friday. Fortunately, there were only a few places where the standing water covered the crops and even fewer where the plants had been destroyed. *It coulda been a whole lot worse,* thought Wes, *but it's just one more thing I gotta worry about. If it ain't rain and flooded fields, it's the Association and the Trust and the damned Night Riders. I don't know how much more of this Zora's god thinks I can take, but I'm getting pretty tired of the whole thing.* He let Connie go ahead of him and then turned once more to look at his fields.

Back at the house, Zora and Mary Lula were working to put some order to the rooms that had been crowded the past day and a half—picking up, sweeping and moving the children around to keep them out of the way. After he'd been kicked out of three different rooms, John Stanley had had enough.

"Ma, can I go outside?" he yelled. "I'm tired of gettin' in the way!" He waited only a moment, and when he heard no response, he decided that it must be all right. He grabbed an empty jar from under the counter and ran out the door, heading for the ditch. He had a favorite spot down the road where the ditch was wider just past the fence line between their farm and his Uncle George's. There were usually a bunch of bull frogs there and an occasional snake. With all of the rain, he figured there might be some pollywogs, and he could always use another pet since Rufus didn't like to play much anymore.

The smiling boy raced down the muddy lane toward the road, happy to be out of the house again. He made a point to splash into every puddle, laughing as the water erupted into the air. Trying to make a hard turn to the left when he crossed the bridge to the road, he slid in the mud and near-ly went down. He regained his footing quickly and headed for the wide spot in the ditch. All of the energy he'd been forced to control for the past few days seemed to burst out of him.

He was nearly out of breath when he got to the wide spot. Bent over with his hands on his knees, he sucked air into his burning lungs and watched the water moving slowly through the ditch. It was at least eight feet wide at this point and nearly three feet deep, but the water only reached halfway up the bank. The excited boy stood up and looked both ways down the road, trying to decide the quickest way to get to the other side of the pond. *I could go back to our lane, cross over and come back along the field, or I could go on to Uncle George's lane and do the same thing.* He pondered his choices for a moment and then came up with a better idea. *Or I could just wade through the ditch. I'm wet and muddy anyway, so a little more wet and muddy won't hurt at all, and it'll be a whole lotta fun.*

Clutching the jar in his hand, he walked toward the ditch and stopped when his toes reached the edge. As he thought about how to start into the water, the muddy edge of the bank under his feet gave way. The jar flew out of his hand and ended up in the road behind him, and he fell backward, hitting his head on a rock. He saw stars behind his clenched eyes just before he blacked out and slid down the slimy ditch into the water.

\* \* \*

When Wes got back to the house, he left his muddy boots on the porch and went into the kitchen. Zora was standing at the sink, but he didn't look at her. Instead, he just took his other jug of whiskey off the shelf and went back outside. He wiped his hands on his damp overalls, pulled the cork out of the jug and tipped it to his mouth. The whiskey burned his lips and his throat, but he didn't seem to care. He slumped onto the bench and took another long pull on the jug.

Zora walked out of the open door and stood on the edge of the porch. She looked up at the clearing sky and shaded her eyes against the bright western sun. Turning to Wes, she put her hands on her hips and said, "Well?"

"Well, what," grumbled Wes, still not looking at her.

"Tell me about the fields. Is everythin' all right?"

"Hell no, everythin's not all right. The tobacco's okay, but we lost some of the corn, a whole lot of the wheat is flat, and we've got a half-acre pond where we don't need it."

"Can you save the wheat?"

"Maybe, if the rain stops and the sun keeps shinin'."

When Wes finally turned toward her, Zora could see how drunk and tired he was. His unshaved face was dirty and gray, his brow was wrinkled and his eyes were dull and red-streaked. But even through the mud she could see it was more than the rain damage and the fatigue that was weighing down on him.

"So, what's your plan?"

"Damn it, Zora!" he shouted. "Right now my only plan is to sit on my damn porch and get drunk. I got too much to think about to sit here and listen to you askin' me questions. Just go away and leave me the hell alone."

Zora glared at him and with tears of anger running down her cheeks she rushed back into the house, slamming the door behind her. Wes's only reaction was to lift the jug and take another drink. *I don't have time, I just need to think. Just too damned much goin' on,* he thought.

Inside the house, the children had heard their pa shout and their ma slam the door. They did what they always did when things got bad. They hid. As soon as her ma came inside, Mary Lula lifted Ruthie from the floor where she'd been playing and took her upstairs. Irene went into the room she shared with her sisters and crawled under the bed. Connie slipped out a window at the back of the house and walked off toward the cornfield. In his room, Anthie clenched his jaws and his fists and grew even angrier at his pa.

Zora watched her daughter's escape from the kitchen and knew that the others had disappeared as well. She walked to the counter and stared at the potatoes she'd been peeling. The tears continued to stream down her face as she picked up a small knife and went back to fixing supper. As she worked, she kept asking God to forgive her for wanting to use the knife on Wes. *I'm scared, Lord. It ain't like him to take it out on me or the children. We've been through hard times before and you always took care of us. He's drinkin' too much, and the liquor's only gonna make him madder than he already is and then he might hurt one of us again. Please, Lord, don't let that happen. Make him pass out or go to sleep.*

She stopped peeling for a moment and looked at the knife in her hand. *And don't let my anger get the better of me.* She paused and added, *Amen.*

She put the chopped potatoes into a pot of boiling water and checked to see how the chicken was doing in the oven of the woodstove. Satisfied that the chicken, potatoes and peas would be ready at the same time, she called for Mary

Lula and stood with her back to the sink. *It don't matter what he's goin' through and it makes no difference to me if he eats or not, but my children are gonna have a regular supper. They've been working hard and are afraid to even speak out loud because of him, and it ain't even their fault.*

"You called me, Ma?"

"I did," she said with a forced smile. "Tell everyone to get washed up. We're gonna have a regular supper tonight no matter what that . . . man wants or does. Everythin' should be ready in a few minutes, so get 'em all started."

"All right, Ma. Do you need any help in here?"

"No," she said softly. "You just get them children movin', and I'll take care of this."

Mary Lula headed upstairs to the bedrooms, hoping that everyone was where they usually went when her ma and pa started fighting. She saw that Ruthie was asleep in her crib and found Irene curled up under the bed.

"You come on out of there, sister," she said. "Everythin's all right. Ma wants you to get washed up for supper."

"I don't wanna come out. Pa's yellin'."

"It don't matter if you want to or not, you just need to do it. Pa's outside anyway, so there's nothin' to be scared of. Now come on out and get your face and hands washed. Be sure to brush off all of the dust that's in your hair, too."

Irene slid out from under the bed and stood up. She waited as her sister walked out of the room and then went to Mary Lula's small dresser. She lifted the delicate hand mirror from the top of the crude piece of furniture and looked at herself. Her hair was messy, and her cheeks were streaked with the trails of dust mixed with tears. She set the mirror down and walked over to the washbowl in the corner of the room. In a few minutes, her hair was nearly dustball free and her face looked reasonably clean.

Mary Lula tapped on the door of the boys' bedroom. "You all get washed up for supper. Ma says you got a few minutes."

"There ain't nobody in here but me," said Anthie, "and I ain't comin' down for supper."

"Where's Connie and John Stanley?"

"I don't know."

"I'll go find 'em, but you better get movin'." She found Connie standing at the edge of the field smoking a cigarette, but John Stanley was nowhere in sight.

"Where's John Stanley?"

"I don't know. I haven't seen him since you all were cleanin' the house."

"Well, you see if you can find him. Maybe he's in the barn. I'll go look in the house."

Connie walked to the barn, leaned inside and yelled. There was no reply. *He'll turn up. That rascal doesn't like to miss any of Ma's meals.* When he saw his pa on the porch, he turned away and headed for the back of the house. *No need to put myself in the line of fire.*

After searching the house for her brother, Mary Lula went back to the kitchen to see if she could help her ma.

"Ruthie's sleepin' and Irene's cleanin' up. I told the big boys what you wanted, but I can't find John Stanley."

"He's gotta be around somewhere. Did you look in the barn?"

"Connie's out there now."

"Well, that's probably where he is. You go on and wake up Ruthie. Supper'll be ready soon." Zora checked the potatoes and peas as they boiled on the stove. She set a pitcher of cool water on the table next to the plate of chicken and thought about telling Wes that it was time to eat. Then she remembered how he'd sworn at her, and she decided that if he wanted something to eat, he'd have to fix it himself. She walked to the end of the table and picked up the plate she'd set for him. *If he don't wanna listen to me, then he don't need to eat the food I cook.*

Even though Anthie had said he wasn't going to eat supper, his growling stomach reminded him that he was hungry. He sat up on the edge of the bed and slipped his feet into his shoes. Reluctantly, he rose and opened the door and made his way down the stairs to the kitchen. Connie and Irene were already sitting at the table, and Mary Lula was holding the baby as Zora stirred the pots on the stove.

"Where's John Stanley? Didn't you find him in the barn?"

"He wasn't out there, Ma," said Connie.

"Is he in his bed?" she asked, looking at Anthie.

"No, Ma, he ain't."

"Did anybody check to see if he was hidin' in the chicken coop or the sty?" When she got no response, she added, "He can't just disappear. You boys go outside and find him. Look everywhere, and when you find him you tell him to get back here pretty quick or he ain't gettin' anythin' to eat."

The boys got up from their chairs and headed out the door. Connie went back to the barn to take a closer look. Anthie strode toward the coop, wondering why his little brother would want to hide out in a place that smelled so bad. Wes watched his sons walk away and then said, "Where the hell are you two goin'?"

Anthie kept walking, but Connie turned and said, "We're lookin' for John Stanley, Pa. Nobody's seen him for a while, and Ma wants him to come eat."

"Why didn't anybody tell me it was time for supper?" he growled. But neither of his sons heard him. He tried to get up, but slumped back onto the bench.

Zora stepped onto the porch and glared at Wes. She yelled at the boys to keep looking and then turned back to her husband. Barely containing her rage, she snarled, "Are you gonna just stand there, or are you gonna go find your lost son? Nobody knows where he is, and while you're sittin' around drinkin', your boys are out lookin' for their brother. They're doin' what you oughta be doin'."

Wes pushed himself away from the wall. Trying to keep his balance, he stared back at his wife, searching for something to say back to her, to put her in her place, but nothing came. Instead, he began yelling at the boys.

"Look in the barn and the sty!"

"They're already doin' that, Wesley," Zora said, her voice filled with venom. She stepped off the porch into the mud and walked toward the tobacco field, looking for her son. "John Stanley Wilson, you get on home right now!" she shouted.

"You're all gettin' excited about nothin'," said Wes. "He's probably off playin' somewhere. I'll find him." When he tried to walk to the edge of the porch, he stumbled and nearly went down. Holding on to the support post, he weakly shouted out his son's name and then sat down on the edge of the porch.

Connie came running out of the barn and headed toward his mother. "He ain't in the barn, Ma. I'll go look in the corn field. Maybe he's over there."

"He ain't in the sty or the coop, Ma," shouted Anthie, coming up behind him. "I'm gonna see if he's at Uncle George's."

"What would he be doin' over there?" yelled Wes. "Don't waste your time doin' that. Did anyone look in the house? Anthie, you get back here!"

But Anthie was already running up the lane toward the road. He slowed when he got to the bridge, not wanting to slip on the wet timber. He looked to his right at first, checking to see if his brother was coming from the west, then he turned left and started running down the muddy road. When he got near the fence line that separated their farm from Uncle George's, he spotted a glass jar in the mud. *The frog pond, the one I showed him last year,* he thought, sliding to a stop. Anthie turned toward the ditch, walked to the edge and looked down into the water.

"Ma! Ma, come quick. I found him!"

John Stanley was lying on his back against the slope of the ditch. He'd slipped into the water up to his shoulders. Anthie lay down on the road and reached into the water, pulling his brother up by the collar of his shirt. Once he had a good grip on him, Anthie got up onto his knees and pulled his brother out of the ditch and onto the road. The boy was unconscious, and Anthie could see blood on the back of his head. He stood up and lifted his brother into his arms.

"Ma! He's hurt bad! His head's bleedin'!" he shouted again, carrying his brother's limp body back toward the lane. Anthie walked slowly, gently talking to his brother. "Everythin's gonna be all right. You'll be okay. Ma'll take care of you."

Zora got to the end of the lane just as Anthie turned into the farm. She stopped him just long enough to touch her youngest son's face and to see that he was breathing and then said, "Be careful with him, Anthie. Let's get him into the house."

Zora walked alongside Anthie while he carried his injured brother in his arms. She prayed as she held onto John Stanley's muddy foot. *Lord, take care of my boy. Don't let him die. I trust you, Lord, don't let him die.* As Anthie slogged on through the mud, she saw Connie running in from the field. He hurried up the lane toward them, clearly out of breath.

"Where'd you find him? Is he all right?"

Zora interrupted his questions and said, "I don't know how bad he's hurt, son, but I want you to listen to me. Are you listenin'?"

"Yes, Ma."

"You go get the mule and ride into town as fast as you can, you hear? I want you to go to the doctor's house. You tell him that your brother fell and hit his head. Tell him that he's bleedin' and breathin' but he's not awake. You get him to come out to the farm and don't leave there until he says he's comin'. Do you understand?"

"I understand, Ma."

"Then you get goin' and be careful."

Connie raced to the barn and ran inside. As Anthie and Zora reached the well, Wes stepped off the porch and stumbled toward them. He stretched out his arms and said, "Gimme my boy."

Before Zora could reply, Anthie said defiantly, his voice powerful, "No, Pa, I won't."

Wes took another step toward them, glaring at Anthie through his whiskey-red eyes. "Don't you talk to me that way, boy. I'll whup you if you don't do what I tell you."

"Wes, you stand back. Anthie, take your brother in and put him on my bed, you hear? Do it now, son."

"Stop right there," Wes growled. "Give me my boy!"

Zora stepped between her husband and her son. She quietly told Anthie to get moving and then turned to Wes.

"Now you listen to me, Wesley Wilson. Your son is hurt bad, and he needs a doctor. He don't need a drunken pa to carry him. You get out of my way, or so help me I'll knock you down myself."

Wes started to say more, but turned away, knowing that Zora was mad enough to do what she said. He staggered back to the porch, picked up the shotgun and sat down. He watched Connie ride the mule to the road and turn toward town. Zora stared down at him and shook her head. She started up the steps, but then stopped and looked at him again. This time, though, her face was softer. She leaned in and saw a rumor of fear.

"Look at me, Wes." She waited until his blurry eyes met hers. "This ain't your fault, any more than the other troubles are. But you need to be a father and take care of your family. You need to be a man right now, not a drunk." She searched his eyes, looking for something. Then she said, "Connie's goin' for the doctor, and I'm gonna go check on

John Stanley. You do whatever you need to do, but you'd better sober up quick."

She walked up the steps and into the house. Wes didn't move, couldn't move. He was paralyzed by Zora's words. He sat on the porch, looking out into his muddy yard and wondered what else could go wrong in his life.

Still holding the shotgun, he broke the gun open and removed the shells, putting them into his damp shirt pocket. His face was hot and his head was pounding. It hurt from the whiskey and too much thinking. He felt a wrenching, burning pain in his stomach. He set the gun down, got up and walked quickly to the outhouse. His steps were unsteady on the wet ground, and just as he reached the door of the outhouse, he slipped in the mud and went down on his knees and began heaving up the sour contents of his stomach. Gagging and coughing, he slapped at the muddy ground, taking out his anger on something that he couldn't hurt. He tried to spit out the ugly, burning taste in his mouth and then struggled to his feet, opened the door of the outhouse and stepped inside.

# Chapter 11
Friday, May 11

The rain clouds finally gave way to the bright sun. By Friday evening, all but the largest puddles on the roads had disappeared, and the mud had turned to a hard, dry crust that would become the dust spreading far and wide in the days that followed. Some of the water-damaged crops in the fields would recover, much to the relief of the farmers. Yet, their other losses would add to an already-difficult situation.

Late that night, a band of nearly twenty armed and masked horsemen rode hard toward the farm of a man they'd heard had agreed to sell his crop to the Tobacco Trust. The night was cool, and the bright moon lit the road. When the column reached the turnoff a mile from the farm, the leader slowed his horse and signaled a stop. The men remained quiet as he rode back along the line of horses.

"Light up your torches, and remember, no talkin' and no names." He repeated the instructions to every pair of Riders and watched as the light from the flames reflected off the water in the ditches along the road. "Don't do anythin' unless I give the order. Make sure your masks are on tight and that your guns are loaded." The nods and whispers of the men let him know that they understood and were ready. Hearing only the noise of the crickets and the hard breathing of the horses, he looked up at the moon and then back at his men. He raised his arm and signaled them forward.

It was well after midnight when they turned down the lane to the farm. They quietly surrounded the house and placed guards at the barn and other outbuildings. When he was certain that his Riders were in position, the leader rode his horse up to the porch until he was within a few yards of the door. Looking around to assure himself that everyone was in position, he took a rock out of his coat pocket and threw it at the door. The crash of it hitting the dry wood shattered the tranquil stillness of the night.

"Come out of the house, hillbilly!" he shouted. "Get on out here!" For a few moments, silence filled the air as the leader took out another rock and threw it at the window next to the door. The glass exploded and he yelled again. "Get on out here and make it quick!"

From his horse, he saw the light of a candle through the shards of glass. He watched as the flickering light was carried toward the front door.

"Who's out there? What do you want?" The voice sounded strong, but a little frightened.

"I'll be the one askin' the questions," yelled the raider. "Open your door and come outside." He threw his last rock at the door and shouted again, "Do it now."

The door opened slowly inward, and a tall, barefoot man in his nightshirt stepped out onto the porch. He held a small pistol in his right hand, but kept it at his side. He looked at the mounted men, saw that they were armed, and with as much resolve as he could, he said, "You all need to get off my land. This is my farm, and we don't want any trouble."

"You're already in trouble, and you better drop that gun or I'll shoot you where you stand."

The farmer heard the clicking sound of weapons being cocked. He stared directly at the man who'd been doing the talking and leaned down, setting the handgun at his feet. From inside, he heard his wife trying to keep his frightened children quiet. Her words were soft, but they were having little effect. He turned to the open door and said, "Get to the back of the house. I'll take care of this out here." Not hearing any movement, he added, "Go on now, you get on back there." He turned back to the Rider.

"What do you want?"

"We're here to keep you from sellin' your crop to the Trust. We know you've been talkin' to 'em, and we know you've already made a deal." He paused a moment to let the words sink in. "We ain't gonna let that happen."

The raider signaled to the two closest men, and they got down from their horses. They tossed the torches to the ground and grabbed the farmer by his arms then dragged him to the edge of his yard.

"Tie him to the tree," said the leader.

"I ain't done nothin'," groaned the struggling farmer.

The raiders got his arms around a tree and tied his hands with a coarse rope. One of them held a thorn branch he'd brought along while the other used a knife to cut open the back of the farmer's nightshirt. Whether from the cool air or the fear, he shivered and yanked at the bindings on his wrists. "What're you gonna do?"

"We're gonna make sure you don't sell your crop," whispered the man behind him. He signaled to the man with the branch, saying, "We're gonna teach you a lesson, hillbilly. We're gonna teach you not to turn against your neighbors."

Without warning, the raider struck the farmer's back with the stiff, thorny branch. The farmer cried out, and the man struck him again. From the house, the sound of the crying children was drowned by the screams of their mother. One of the mounted raiders rode to the porch to make sure the woman stayed inside. The raider with the branch struck a third time, and blood streamed down the naked man's back. His cries of pain echoed off the walls of his house and barn.

"Are you gonna sell your tobacco to the Trust?" asked the leader.

The man with the thorn branch swung and hit the farmer again. He cried out, and his wife screamed from the house.

"Unless you tell us you're not gonna sell, you won't have a crop. If you don't change your mind, we'll destroy your tobacco in the field and maybe even burn your barn. Now, are you gonna sell to the Trust?"

The bound and bleeding man groaned and slumped down onto the ground, the tree bark ripping at his cheek. He clenched his teeth as a spasm of pain hit him, and then he moaned out a barely audible "No."

The raider dropped the bloody branch and untied the farmer's wrists. He and the other Night Rider lifted him from the ground and walked him back to his porch. The torn remains of the farmer's nightshirt barely covered his nakedness as he struggled to stand on his own. The leader looked down at the frightened man and spoke again.

"Tell me again what you're gonna do with your tobacco."

The wounded farmer looked up toward the masked face of the raider. With as much dignity as he could gather, he said, "I ain't gonna sell it to the Trust."

"That's what I thought you were gonna say. Now get on back inside and think about how lucky you are that we didn't tear up your fields."

The farmer bent over to pick up his pistol and groaned as he stood back up. Suddenly, one of the mounted raiders fired his shotgun toward the house. The noise of the blast frightened the horses as the lead tore through the belly of the surprised farmer. He slumped down and the pistol slipped from his hand as his blood spread across the porch. His wife ran out to him and covered his body with her own. The copper smell of his blood overcame her, and she began screaming.

"You killed him. You killed my husband. Why?" She watched the raiders as they scrambled around the yard in confusion. "Killers!" she shouted. "You cowards murdered my husband!" The woman watched the backs of the raiders as they rode hard out of the yard.

In the dark, the new widow slumped over her husband's body and wept loudly. The crying children came slowly out of the open doorway and stood by their ma. They couldn't understand what had just happened, but they'd soon discover that their lives had changed forever.

# Chapter 12
Saturday Morning, May 12

As the sky began to brighten in the east, Mark Wilson stood on the front porch of his store, enjoying the cool air. Leaning on his broom, listening to the early morning sounds of the town, he was glad to have a few moments for himself. He could smell the coffee brewing on the stove inside and looked forward to the first taste of hot black liquid. Thursday's rain and mud had turned into Friday's dust, and he needed to finish sweeping his porch before the customers started showing up. Mark kicked at the last clumps of dirt on the lowest step and swept them off into the road. He turned to go back inside, but stopped when he heard a door slam somewhere.

He looked down the empty street and saw the constable making his way past the glowing furnace of the blacksmith shop, heading in his direction. Mark stood in the doorway, wondering what had motivated Dan Cleary to be out on the streets of Lynnville before sunrise. He waited until the large man reached the porch before greeting him.

"Mornin', Deputy. You're up awful early. Got time for a cup of coffee?"

"I sure am and I sure do," Cleary said after a moment. Frowning, he added, "But don't call me deputy. You know the sheriff don't like it."

"Well, come on inside anyway, Deputy." Mark intentionally used the title. "The coffee's about ready." He led Cleary into the store. "Have a seat and grab yourself a cup and pour one for me, while I put away my broom. That rain made a mess of everything, but it's what the farmers needed."

As Mark joined the constable at the stove, he noticed

that Dan hadn't touched the coffeepot. Instead, he was staring out the window as though lost in thought. Mark filled Cleary's cup, and the two said nothing as they sipped at the hot liquid. Mark knew better than to rush Cleary, knowing that the large man always took his time before speaking.

Cleary peered over the top of his cup at Mark, the steam from the coffee billowing around the brim of his hat. He took another sip and carefully placed the cup on the table next to the stove. Mark watched as he pulled the handkerchief from his back pocket and dabbed at his puffy lips.

"What's on your mind this mornin', Dan?"

"I got a call from the sheriff."

"And what did the lawman from Mayfield have to tell you that's so important he called early on a Saturday?"

Cleary was a little afraid of answering the storekeeper. He wasn't certain how the local farmers would respond to the news he had to share. The frank expression on Mark's face moved him to speak.

"The sheriff called to tell me there was a Night Rider raid last night. He said they killed a farmer. Shot him in the belly and killed him on his front porch in front of his wife and children."

Mark's gut clenched like he'd been kicked in the belly. "Was it—" He nearly said his brother's name. "Was it anybody we know?"

Cleary shook his head.

Mark's relief that the dead man wasn't Wes flooded through his chest. But he cared about his neighbors, and the thought of one of them being killed bothered him. He stood, almost throwing his questions at Cleary. "C'mon, Dan, where'd the raid happen? What else did the sheriff say?"

"He said he got a call from . . . that it happened over in Christian County. He said that the dead man's wife told him they showed up sometime after midnight and that the raiders whipped her husband before they shot him."

"The Night Riders murdered a farmer?" Mark's voice was soft, almost a whisper. "God help that poor woman and her children," he said. "But Christian County's over fifty miles from here. I hope we don't have any problems like that here in Lynnville." Mark couldn't stop thinking about Wes.

"The sheriff said he heard there might be trouble down here, that some tobacco buyer was sayin' he'd made a big deal in our district. He told me to keep my eyes and ears open and to let him know if there was any talk about raids." Dan sipped at his coffee and leaned back in the chair.

"So what else did he tell you? And have you heard anything about raids?" Mark demanded. He sat down and looked squarely into Cleary's eyes. This time when he spoke, he kept his voice steady.

"Dan," he paused, trying to calm down, "have you heard anything about raids around here?" He watched Cleary's face and saw his hesitation. He knew that the man had something more to say.

"I heard there was gonna be a raid, but that it got called off. I didn't hear any names, and I told the sheriff that I didn't know about any tobacco deals bein' made."

"So all you know is some poor farmer in Christian County got killed last night and that the sheriff is worried about trouble down here, right?"

"Yep, that's it. I thought you oughta know, since a lot of folks come into your store. Maybe you could listen to what they say, and if you hear about any raids, you could let me know."

"I'll do that, Dan. If I hear anything, I'll tell you." Mark wanted to get Cleary out of the store so he could think about all he'd heard. He stood up, hoping that Dan would get the hint, but the large man stayed in his chair. "Well, I gotta get ready for my customers, Dan. They'll be comin' in soon, and I need to be ready. You go ahead and finish your coffee, but I need to get busy. Thanks for comin' by to give me the news." Mark walked to the back of the store.

Cleary watched him go and then drank the last of the liquid from his cup. He set it back down on the table and stood up. "You let me know if you hear anythin'," he said. At the door, he looked back at Mark, hitched up his pants, straightened his hat and left the store.

* * *

Art was exhausted as he rose from the chair next to the bed and lifted the cooing baby from Mollie's arms. Holding the infant close to his chest, he crept out of the room, remembering to take a clean diaper from the top of the dresser. After coughing most of the night, Mollie had finally fallen asleep just before dawn, and Art didn't want to wake her. Leaving the door ajar so he could listen for her, he carried the baby into the front of the house and put the clean diaper on him. After wrapping Ben back up in his blanket, Art laid him on a padded chair and walked over to the window. He pulled the flour-sack curtain to the side and gazed at the sunlight peeking through the trees.

With little sleep over the past two days, he'd fixed meals, changed the baby, washed dishes and tended to Mollie's needs. There was simply too much to do, and he knew that it was his responsibility to take care of the family until she improved. At night, as he watched his wife sleep fitfully, he thought about the rest of his problems. He'd done what he could for Wes on Wednesday night and hoped things had settled down after his stop at Mark's store.

Now, looking out the window, he wondered if he'd still be able to meet with Wes and Mark in the afternoon. It was important, but so was Mollie's health. He decided he'd have to wait and see how she was doing before he'd leave her alone again. If she slept for the rest of the morning, he thought he'd probably be able to go into town. When he heard a sound from the back of the house, he picked the baby up from the chair and carried him into the bedroom.

* * *

Wes stood in the doorway of the upstairs room shared by his sons, watching Zora as she fussed with John Stanley's covers. She tucked and smoothed the blankets around her son, as if each wrinkle might be too much weight for him to bear.

"How're you feelin', son?"

"My head still hurts on the inside," he said, "and it itches where the doctor put in them stitches."

Zora gently grabbed his wrist as he reached his hand toward the back of his head. "He said the itchin' would go away when the stitches come out, so don't you go pickin' or scratchin' at 'em."

"When can I get up, Ma? I'm tired of bein' in this bed, and I wanna go outside."

Zora said, "Would you like it if your pa carried you out to the porch?"

"Would you, Pa? Would you take me downstairs?"

Wes looked down at his son. "Maybe it'd be better if you walked downstairs." He saw the frown growing on Zora's face and added, "I'll help you do that, and we'll see if you still get dizzy."

"Thanks, Pa."

Wes pulled the blankets off John Stanley, reached under the boy's arms and gently helped him stand. Concerned, Zora stood to the side and watched her son's face for any signs of discomfort as he placed his feet on the old wooden floor. But if he was in pain, it didn't show. She picked up the pillow and one of the blankets and followed Wes and John Stanley out of the room and down the stairs. Wes held his son up, one hand under the boy's arm and the other on his shoulder, as he cautiously navigated each step. All Zora could see was the wide smile of a happy boy.

When they reached the bottom of the stairs, Wes asked him if he still wanted to go out to the porch. John Stanley nodded and kept moving, pulling his pa with him. Zora stepped around the two of them and went quickly to the door. She held it open as they walked out onto the porch into the bright sunlight.

"Does the sun hurt your eyes?" she asked the boy.

"Only a little, Ma. I'll just keep 'em closed."

Wes helped his son sit down on the pillow and fussed with him a little, making sure he was comfortable and wouldn't fall over. Zora sat next to John Stanley on the bench and covered him with the blanket. She looked at Wes and smiled, and he responded with one of his own.

"I'll sit right here with you for a while," she said. "You enjoy the fresh air and watch your brothers work. You just tell me when you're ready to go back upstairs, and I'll help you."

The morning sun bathed the porch in bright sunlight, and even though his eyes were tightly closed, the boy was smiling and breathing in the fresh air. Wes relaxed a little and looked out at the yard.

"There's some stuff I need to get done before takin' off for town," he said to Zora. "Can you handle things here for a bit? If not, I'll stick around while you go fix this boy somethin' to eat." He paused and looked at his son. "What do you say, rascal? You want somethin' to eat?"

John Stanley looked through the narrow slits of his eyelids and smiled at his pa.

"Yes sir, Pa. I'm hungry."

"All right, then. Your ma'll fix up somethin', and I'll sit here with you. Maybe we can talk about them pollywogs you were in such a hurry to put in a jar."

Zora gave up her spot on the bench to Wes and went

into the house. She had a cautious smile on her face as she began putting some jam on a biscuit and pouring a cup of milk for her son. Zora grappled with the change in Wes. She hoped it was real, but she wasn't sure that it was. She whispered a prayer and walked out to the porch.

\* \* \*

Anthie leaned against the woodpile behind the barn, looking at the tobacco plants as they caught the morning sun. He felt satisfied that all the hard work they'd done before the rain came had paid off. After he'd milked the cow and brushed down the mule in anticipation of his trip to Sudie's, he went to look for a quiet spot to think about the things he was supposed to ask Mr. Morris. He'd need to talk with his pa one more time before he left. Then he heard Irene yelling his name and watched her run across the drying yard toward the edge of the tobacco field.

"Anthie, where are you? Pa wants to talk to you!" Her whiny shouting interrupted his thoughts.

"I'll be right there," he said mostly to himself as he pushed away from the split logs and headed around the barn to the house.

"How come you're wearin' your good clothes? It's Saturday. We ain't goin' to church today."

"Never mind, runt. It's none of your business."

"I'm not a runt! I'm gonna tell Ma you called me a runt."

Anthie didn't say any more as Irene darted ahead and ran up the porch into the house. He knew she'd complain to his ma, but he had too much on his mind to be concerned about what his ma might do. As he reached the house, he looked at Rufus lying in the sun at the edge of the porch and thought how easy a dog's life was. *All they gotta do is eat, sleep and chase rabbits. Sometimes I wish I'd been born a dog. Then I wouldn't be havin' to talk to Sudie's pa.* Before he walked into the kitchen, he smiled and thought, *But I'm glad I wasn't born a dog, because I get to see Sudie today, and she wouldn't be interested in no scruffy dog.*

Wes was sitting at the end of the table, drinking coffee and thinking about his plans for Anthie. He motioned for his son to sit next to him. Anthie felt uneasy being so close to his pa. The scab on his lip was too harsh a reminder of the beating he'd had, so he chose a seat across the table. With mock anger, Wes asked, "Did you call your sister a runt?" As Anthie tried to come up with a respectful reply, Wes grinned at him.

"Yeah, Pa, I did. I guess I shouldn't have done it."

"No, you shouldn't have, but don't worry about it now. We've got some more important things to talk about. You want some coffee?"

Surprised that pa was being nice and a little anxious to get going to Sudie's, he nodded. He waited while pa went to the stove and poured what remained in the coffeepot into a cup. Wes slid the cup across the table toward Anthie.

"Have you been thinkin' about today?" Wes asked.

"Yeah," he said, "but I just can't come up with a way to ask him the questions." The words rushed out of his mouth as he scooted his chair back a little. "He's probably not gonna be too happy to see me anyway, Pa, after I showed up last week without asking permission to see Sudie. I could tell he didn't like me too much. He sure didn't seem to want me around."

Wes chuckled and said, "Your great-grampa used to treat me the same way when I showed up at his farm tryin' to see your ma. It'll take a while, son."

"I know, Pa, but it ain't easy."

"I know it ain't, but today I need you to find out how he feels about these other things. I need to know what he's thinkin' and maybe even what he's gonna do. Do you understand?" Wes glared hard at his son, waiting for his response.

Anthie nodded and took a sip of coffee, looking away from his pa. Wes watched him for a moment and then said, "Listen to me, son. I've got some things I need to say and I want to make sure you hear them."

When he was certain he had Anthie's attention, Wes continued. "I know things around here have been rough for the past week. And I know you wish they coulda been different. But today I need you to be a man. I need you to think about how important these things are to your ma." He looked into his son's eyes and added, "Can you do this for your family?"

Anthie said he could, and Wes believed him. He waited until his son left the table, and then he rose, put on his hat and walked outside. He stood on the porch for a moment and glanced at the sleeping dog. Staring at the rows of young tobacco plants, he wondered how long he was going to have to deal with all the problems. Inside his head, a storm was raging, loud and violent and dangerous, and it was hard to think clearly.

While Wes had spent the night standing guard over his tobacco field, he'd felt weak and vulnerable. He needed the strength of his family and wanted them to trust him, to believe in him. Each time he got drunk, the mental storm became more twisted and the liquor gained control over his mind. He realized that if he was going to do what was expected of him—what he expected of himself—he was going to have to stay sober. Knowing that if he lost his family, he'd lose everything, Wes also had to find a way to hide his anger and anxiety so he could regain the respect of his children, especially Anthie.

But, even though he was fully aware of the risks and afraid that his worst nightmare might come true, Wes wasn't sure he could stop drinking.

\* \* \*

When Anthie got to the spot on the road where he'd seen the Night Riders the week before, he stopped and got down from the mule. He saw the tree where he'd hidden and had no problem remembering how afraid he'd been. He let the mule nibble on some of the fresh grass at the edge of the road and stepped behind the tree, hoping to recall something, anything that would help his pa. *If I could only remember that name,* he thought, *maybe that would be enough.* But his thoughts were as silent as the tree, and in the few minutes he stood there, nothing new came to him. He walked back up onto the road, mounted the mule and rode on.

Throughout the ride on the lumpy roads, Anthie tried to prepare himself for the discussion with Sudie's pa, but every time the mule navigated around a hole in the road or he heard a bird call, his thoughts turned to Sudie. *I hope she's glad to see me. I hope her pa's in a good mood. Will they even be at home?*

Anthie was relieved when he turned down the Morrises' lane and saw that all the children were outside. The younger girls were playing with a couple of puppies while the older ones, Sudie and her big sister, Hattie, were hanging wet clothes up to dry. Anthie's heart trembled, and a rash of goose bumps spread across his arms when he saw her. *Oh Lord,* he thought, *please make Sudie happy to see me.*

The worn out, sweaty mule came to a stop at the porch and snorted loudly, trying to clear the dust from its nostrils. Sudie glanced toward the house, and when she saw Anthie, she nearly dropped the shirt she was pinning to the line. She turned quickly to Hattie, giggled and then ran over and stood next to the mule.

Looking up at Anthie, she smiled. "I didn't know you were comin'. I'm so glad you did. Can you stay for a while?" The words rushed out of her mouth like a creek following a storm. He heard her speak but was so focused on her face and her smile that he couldn't reply. His own words were lost in the noise of the barking puppies and the screeching little girls; Sudie had to shout to be heard.

By this time, Sudie's ma had come to the front door to see what all the fuss was about. What she saw was a pack of yipping puppies and squealing girls, a snorting mule and two young people staring at each other. She looked over to see Hattie watching as well, and the two of them shared a smile.

"All right, girls, that's enough. Get them puppies away from the mule and get out of your sister's way. Go on now, get goin'." The youngsters tried to catch the puppies without success, so Sudie helped gather them up and, followed by the little ones, carried them around to the side of the house. Anthie tied the mule's reins to the porch and turned to Mrs. Morris.

"I hope it's okay if I came by today," he said. "I wanted to visit with Sudie."

Sudie came flying around the corner of the house like a delicate flower caught in a windstorm and stood close to Anthie. She looked at the scab on Anthie's lip, reached up and touched the fading yellow bruises on his cheek and then turned to her ma, trying to gauge her mood. When she saw the smile on her ma's face, she grinned and took Anthie's hand and led him over to the clothesline. Anthie was relieved, grateful for Sudie's strength.

"Hattie, can you help me in the kitchen? I need to . . . uh, I need your help doin' somethin' in here," Mrs. Morris said, turning and walking back into the house.

"I'm comin', Ma," Hattie said as she handed Anthie a couple of wooden pins. "Here," she said, "you'll need these." Then she smiled at her sister and ran toward the house.

Anthie was speechless, and he couldn't move from where his feet had become rooted to the ground. *It's happening again,* he thought. *Every time I stand next to her my brain and my voice stop workin'.* He held out the clothespins as if they were delicate treasures.

"You know how those work, don't you?"

"Huh?"

"I said you know how those work, don't you? The clothespins. You know how they work?"

Sudie laughed when he didn't respond. She saw the look of confusion on his face and was warmed by the effect she was having on him. Her own heart was fluttering, and yet she had no problem talking to him. In the half hour it took to finish hanging the clothes and bed sheets, she chattered like a bird. She told him about how they'd survived the rain, how cute the puppies were, how her ma had made a pie and that her pa and brother were down in Dresden getting supplies. Anthie was relieved and especially glad that Mr. Morris wasn't home. *Guess I'll have to face her pa sometime. Just not yet.*

Tossing the remaining pins into the clothes basket, she pulled him by the hand toward the porch. "Maybe we can have a picnic today. We can sit over there under the tree." She stopped and looked up at him. "Anthie, did you leave your tongue at home?"

"No," he said, "I . . . no, I didn't." He stood facing her, one hand in his pocket, the other clutching one of her smaller, fragile hands. He looked toward the house and then back at her. "Is your pa gonna be mad because I'm here? I don't wanna get him mad."

"I don't think he'll be mad. He was in a good mood when he left with Odie to go get supplies."

"That's good, 'cause I don't want him to chase me off when he gets back. Do you think your ma cares if I'm here?"

Sudie spent the next few minutes chattering away, trying to set his mind at ease. As she walked him out to the big tree, she convinced him that no matter what her folks thought or felt about him, she was glad he'd come to see her. Sudie stared straight into his eyes and sweetly said, "Anthie Wilson, I hope you can stay here all day."

"I can't stay here all day," he said, returning the smile, "but I'll be here until someone tells me to leave."

* * *

Charles Morris and his twelve-year-old son, Odie, rode their wagon into Dresden with a long list of supplies to pick up at the general store. The ride south from the farm had been uneventful, and Odie spent most of the time day-dreaming about what he might see in the county seat while his pa was focused on more important things.

The streets in Dresden were crowded with wagons and people. A lot of them had come because it was market day, and they, like Morris, needed supplies. He set the brake on the wagon and took the small bag of tobacco out of his shirt pocket, rolled himself a cigarette and lit it with a match he struck on the edge of the wagon seat. Odie stood in the back of the wagon, watching all the activity on the busy street. He was fascinated by the brick buildings and the fancy carriages.

"Pa, can I get out and walk around? I'm tired of bein' in the wagon. Can I?"

Morris took a drag from his cigarette and turned to his son. He thought about it a moment and then said, "Sure, but don't go far, and stay outside where I can see you."

"Thanks, Pa, I will," he said and climbed down off the back of the wagon. Looking both ways, he ran across the street and jumped onto the board sidewalk. He waited while a woman with a baby walked past him and then stood staring through the large glass window of a drugstore. He saw a cabinet that was filled with jars of candy, and his mouth watered just looking at the colors and shapes of the treats.

Morris was watching his son when his thoughts were interrupted by the sound of someone calling his name. He turned back toward the line of wagons and spotted one of the men from church. He raised his hand when he recognized him, and the man walked toward him.

"Good mornin', Charles."

"Mornin', Deacon. Sure is a busy day, ain't it."

"That it is," he said. "Seems like everyone decided to come into town today. If I didn't know better, I'd think it was time for the county fair." He paused a moment and asked, "Have you heard about the news from up in Christian County?"

"What news?"

"Everybody's talkin' about it. It seems that last night a tobacco farmer up there was killed by the Night Riders. According to the fella over at the newspaper, the man's wife said they whipped him and then gut-shot him. She said they wanted him to join up and hold back his crop, and even after he agreed to do it, they shot him." The deacon waited to make sure Morris understood and then added, "Left the woman a widow with five children."

Morris's face twitched, his jaw muscles clenched. "That's not good at all," he said. "This kind of thing is gettin' out of hand if the Riders are killin' someone who agrees to do what they want." He struggled with his thoughts for a moment and added, "I've got a wife and children of my own, and I sure hope nothin' like that happens down here."

"You're right about that. I hear that there's some Night Riders in the county, but so far there hasn't been any trouble that I'm aware of. Have you heard anything different?"

"No, I haven't, but I'm gonna have to do a lot of thinkin' about what to do."

The line of wagons had moved again, and the deacon said, "Looks like we can get back to work. I'd better get movin'. See you in church, Charles. Give my best to your wife." He tipped his hat and walked away.

Morris tried to absorb the news about the murder. *If that*

*kind of thing can happen, a man has to think real hard before he decides to go against the Association. It won't make any difference to that woman and her children what happens with the tobacco prices, no difference at all.* He looked across the street and saw that Odie was still gazing into the window of the drugstore. He released the wagon brake, clucked at his horse and moved the wagon closer to the store. *Killin' a man for doin' what they wanted him to do don't make any sense at all.*

* * *

Wes came outside to the bench after he walked John Stanley back up to his bedroom. He sat looking at the yard, listening to Zora working in the kitchen. He wanted to tell her about the storm inside his head because he thought she might understand and would maybe even comfort him, give him some sense of peace. But he was unwilling to let her see his weakness. *This is my problem, not hers,* he thought. He knew he needed to act as if he was strong and in control, even if he truly wasn't.

When Connie came around from the back of the house, Wes motioned for him to sit on the bench.

"I'm countin' on you to keep an eye on things today."

"I know, Pa. I will."

"I'd stay and help, but I need to go to a meetin' in town. I know your ma will be watchin' your brother, but I want you to check in on him a few times too. You oughta be able to see if he's really gettin' better or just tryin' not to work."

"I'll look in on him, Pa."

"I thought of another thing I want you to do today. Maybe you could do it out in the barn so you don't concern your ma." He paused, looking first at Connie and then over his shoulder. "I want you to take the shotgun out to the barn and make sure it's clean. With all of the rain and mud lately, it might need to be checked."

"Sure, Pa. I can do that. Do you want me to leave it out there?"

"No. Wait 'til your ma is upstairs with your brother and then put it back where it belongs."

"Pa, are you sure it's okay for me to go see Maud tomorrow? I could stick around here if you want me to."

"I'm sure. You just do this for me today, and I'll stay home with John Stanley tomorrow. Anthie can take your ma and sisters to church." He stood up and put his hand on Connie's shoulder. "I need to get goin'."

Wes waited until Connie left and then stepped up to the open door and asked Zora to come outside. After a moment, she walked onto the porch, wiping her hands on her apron. Wes looked up at her and then patted the empty spot on the bench.

"Sit down for a minute," he said.

Zora straightened her apron and sat silently next to Wes.

"I need to get goin', but I wanted to tell you somethin' before I left. The things that are goin' on around here—the things I been thinkin' about—are all important and need to be looked at."

"I know they are, Wes," Zora replied.

"I'm gonna figure out a way for us to get through all of this," he said, gazing out into the yard. "I'm gonna meet with Art and Mark this afternoon, and we're gonna come up with a plan that'll work for all of us. Mark may have some good ideas, too." He paused again and then sat up straighter. "I'm not sure when I'll get back, but I don't think it'll be much later than suppertime."

Zora was surprised about the meeting; she was also very pleased. *Maybe now that Wes'll have someone to share his frustration he can settle down. Lord knows he ain't doin' well on his own.* She looked over at her husband and said, "Wes, all I want you to do is take care of us and yourself. Be smart. Be careful. Pay attention to what's goin' on around you in town. We'll be fine here."

"I know you will. Connie's a good man. He knows what to do."

"He does." She looked at her husband and smiled. "Now you get goin', and I'll have somethin' nice for supper when you get back."

She stood up, hugged Wes tightly and then turned and went back inside the house. Wes watched her go and then started down the lane to the road. When he got to his brother's house, he and George talked for a while about the rain and John Stanley. Malinda stood next to her husband, listening intently. She promised to look in on Zora, but Wes said that everything was fine and that Connie would let them know if he needed any help.

Wes was anxious to get started into town, so he told George he'd have the horse back by sundown. Wes pulled himself up on the saddle and rode out to the road. *I'd sure like to have a horse of my own someday,* he thought. As he trotted past his own farm, he saw Zora standing on the porch, holding the baby, and he waved at her. She waved back at him and then walked into the house. Wes rode on toward Lynnville and his meeting with Mark and Art.

* * *

With Odie at his side, Charles Morris walked into the crowded general store and went right to the counter. He handed his list of supplies to the clerk and told his son to stay close.

"I don't want you wandering around and gettin' into any trouble. Besides, as soon as the supplies are ready, I want to get 'em loaded and head on home."

As much as Odie wanted to look at all the goods on the shelves, he could tell his pa was serious, so he stayed put. He followed his pa over to the back corner of the store, where a group of men were standing around, talking quietly. Several of them noticed Morris and nodded in recognition. Odie stayed behind his pa, trying to hear the discussion.

"Damn it, I know it didn't happen here," said one man, "but it still means trouble." There were murmurs of assent from the group and the man continued. "It don't make no sense for them fellas to kill somebody who's agreed to do what they want. It's just plain murder."

"Anybody know if the man that was killed was white?" asked a large man smoking a cigar.

"What does it matter?" said another.

"If he wasn't, maybe it was the Klan instead of the Night Riders." This caused another round of mumbling from the group.

"I heard he was white," said the first man, "and that they whipped him before they shot him."

"It seems to me we probably don't need to get all fired up about somethin' that happened so far away," Morris said, looking around the group. "Just because they're gettin' a little crazy up in Kentucky don't mean it'll happen here." As he spoke, Morris hoped that what he was thinking was true.

There was more mumbling from the group, but it stopped when the large man spoke again. "What about last Sunday night over in Henry County? Just because nobody got hurt don't mean we ain't havin' trouble down here." Several of the men seemed to agree. "So any of us who're growin' tobacco oughta be sure we know what the hell we're gonna do with our crops come harvest time." Whether the men standing around the stove took his comments as advice or as a warning, the words abruptly ended the conversation. Morris and the large man exchanged an unspoken, indecipherable look. Odie watched from his pa's side and reached up to hold onto his hand. Morris stood silently for a moment, realizing that he was wrong about the Night Riders only being in Kentucky; now they were in Tennessee.

"Mr. Morris, your goods are ready," said the clerk, interrupting his thoughts.

"Let's go, son. We need to get on home." Feeling a sudden urgency to get out of the store, Morris went to the counter, paid the clerk and then he and Odie headed outside to load up the wagon.

\* \* \*

For most of the morning, the constable, Dan Cleary, sat on the porch of the hotel. He talked to everyone who walked by or came into town on their wagons. He told them what happened in Christian County and then asked them questions about Night Riders and raids. The people of the district were used to Cleary's methods and knew he was just doing his job. But that didn't mean they told him anything useful. Not one of the people he talked to had heard of the shooting. The news made many of them uneasy and even a few of them afraid. None of them seemed to know of any Night Rider activity in the area.

By noon Dan decided to give up and headed back to his office. When he saw J.D. and Charley riding into town from the north, he stopped in the middle of the crossroad and waited for them. When they reached the spot where he was standing, they stopped their horses and waited for him to speak.

"You fellas got a minute?" he asked. "I got somethin' I wanna ask you."

"We're kind of busy," said J.D., looking away.

Charley didn't respond, but thought, *Please don't start any more trouble, J.D.*

"This won't take long. Let's go over here." He pointed back toward the hotel.

Charley's stomach churned as he climbed down from his saddle and walked with Cleary over to the porch. *This is not good,* he thought. *He must know what we're up to.*

J.D. didn't move, but watched the others walk away. Cleary looked back over his shoulder and stopped. He turned to face J.D. and said, "C'mon over here, J.D. This is important, and it includes you too."

J.D. stalled, waiting while a farmer drove his wagon by, and then rode over to the hotel. "What's so important that you gotta talk to us? We've got things to do."

"Have either of you heard about what happened over in Christian County last night?"

Neither of the men responded, but Charley looked worried.

"So you haven't heard about the Night Riders murdering a farmer in front of his family?"

"No," said Charley, clearly surprised at the news. J.D. remained silent, but both of them were nervous, hoping that Cleary wasn't trying to connect them to the raids.

"Apparently they paid a visit to the man, whipped him and then shot him dead. What I want to know is have either of you fellas heard about any Night Riders bein' in Lynnville?"

Before Charley could speak, J.D. said, "No sir, we ain't heard anythin' about raiders around here." He looked at his partner over Cleary's shoulder, the expression on his face signaling Charley to keep quiet. "If we hear anythin'," J.D. added, "we'll let you know."

Cleary looked at each of them and said, "You do that. You hear anythin' about raids, you come and tell me."

"One other thing," he paused, deliberating. "You two wouldn't be doin' any kind of whiskey business, would you?"

"What do you mean?" asked J.D. Charley anxiously watched Cleary's face.

"I mean you two aren't sellin' whiskey in town, are you? It's illegal, and anybody caught doin' it will end up in jail."

J.D. looked directly at Cleary. "We ain't doin' nothin' that'll put us in jail. We're law-abidin' citizens, Constable."

Not entirely convinced by J.D.'s claim, but unable to prove otherwise, Cleary walked off the porch and down the road. Charley started to say something, but J.D. told him to shut up. When Cleary finally disappeared into his house, J.D. spoke.

"Haven't you learned how to keep quiet around the law? Ain't we got enough trouble with that fella already?"

"Sorry, J.D., but I—"

"Just shut up and listen to me. You need to stop and think before you say anythin' to anybody. One of these days, your mouth is gonna get both of us in trouble. And when that day comes, I'm gonna be gone and you'll be the one sittin' in jail again." J.D. waited to see if Charley had any more to say. When he didn't, he added, "So let's do like we planned. You hang around here this afternoon and listen to folks. See if you can come up with any names for that Jones fella. I'll go over to the store and do the same thing. Whatever you do, Charley, just keep your mouth shut and listen."

Charley stared at J.D. for a few seconds and then nodded. *This double-dealin' is gonna be nothin' but trouble.*

# Chapter 13
Saturday Afternoon, May 12

By early afternoon, Mollie's health had improved. When she woke after sleeping for nearly six hours and announced she was starving, Art knew she'd be strong enough to take care of the children and he could go into town to meet with Wes and Mark. He promptly fixed her a big helping of eggs, biscuits and a large cup of milk. Several soft pillows supported her as she ate and talked with her children. Thressie was happy to sit next to her ma and brush her hair. Clarence decided that watching his ma smile was good enough.

"You're sure lookin' better than you did this mornin'," said Art.

"I feel a lot better, too. Thank you for takin' care of me. I don't know what I'd do without you."

"Mollie, I'll always take care of you—I love you." He paused. Touching her cheek, it felt to him like her fever was gone, and he noticed a healthy glow on her face. "I really need to run into town this afternoon. Wes and I have to talk some more about the crop."

"Can I go with you, Pa?" Clarence asked, standing close to his side.

"Not this time, son," said Art. "I need you to do some chores for me while I'm gone."

"Please, Pa, let me come with you," pleaded Clarence.

Art kneeled in front of his son and put his hands on the boy's shoulders. "I'm sorry, Clarence. I know you wanna come with me, but it's important that you stay here today. While I'm in town meetin' with Cousin Wes, I want you to be sure the chickens get fed and the cow has plenty of water. Can you handle that?"

"I guess so, Pa," he mumbled, clearly disappointed.

"Good. Then when I get home, I'll give you a surprise."

"Really, Pa?"

"Really. I'll bring you somethin' from town."

"What, Pa? What will you bring me?" he said, his face lighting up.

"If I told you what it was, then it wouldn't be a surprise, now, would it?"

"No, I guess not," he said.

"I'm gonna talk to your ma for a minute. I want you to get the horse and bring it up to the house." Eager to help his pa, Clarence left the room and headed to the barn. Art watched Mollie as she told Thressie a story. She looked up at him, her eyes bright again.

"How are you really feelin'?"

"I'm feelin' good. I'll be fine here with the children. Thressie's gonna help me, aren't you little girl?"

"Yes, Ma," she said, snuggling in next to her.

"So you get goin' and try to get back by supper. If I feel like it, I might even try to fix somethin' for all of us to eat."

Art bent down to kiss Mollie on the cheek. He rubbed Thressie's shoulder and then patted her gently on the head.

"You take care of your ma, and I'll be back by supper."

Art put the floppy hat on his head and watched his son lead the horse from the barn. He pulled himself up onto the saddle and looked down at the boy.

"All right, son, you're in charge while I'm gone. Be sure to do those two chores, and I'll see you at supper."

Clarence nodded at his pa, and Art turned the horse toward Lynnville and his meeting with Wes.

* * *

Anthie sat on the soft grass under a large tree, drinking in the sun, his back against the trunk and his long legs stretched out in front of him. Sudie had told him to stay put while she went to get them something to eat, and Anthie was happy to oblige her. He'd been daydreaming for a while when he saw her come out of the house, carrying a small basket. She was wearing a long white dress with puffy sleeves, and she'd tied white ribbons in her soft brown hair. *She looks like an angel,* he thought. As she walked toward the tree, she carried the basket in one hand and a pitcher of water with the other.

"Let me help you." Anthie stood and walked toward her. He touched her sleeve and awkwardly blurted out, "You look like an angel." Once the words were out of his mouth, he knew he couldn't take them back. *Oh Lord, I've gone and done it now,* he thought, but Sudie just smiled and handed him the pitcher.

"Thank you, Anthie. That's such a sweet thing to say. Please just sit back down."

Holding the pitcher, he looked around, trying to decide how he could sit down in the tall grass without spilling the water. Sudie held back a giggle as she watched the very tall boy's attempts at being graceful.

"I thought you might like to try some of Ma's fresh bread," she said as she kneeled down on the grass, her dress whispering. "I also brought a jar of peaches from last year. They're very sweet, just like you." She looked up at Anthie and smiled again when she saw the flushed look on his face.

"Anthie, are you all right?"

He looked away, his voice timid, "I'm sorry about what I said. I—"

"Oh no, don't be sorry. I like what you said. Nobody's ever said I look like an angel." She reached for Anthie's hand. "Here, why don't you let me have the pitcher?"

Sudie took two small cups from the basket and poured water into each of them and handed one to Anthie. While she busied herself with the bread and fruit, he watched her every move. The sleeves of the white dress went all the way to her wrists, but he could still see her small graceful hands. *She really is an angel,* he thought, stealing a swift glance at her face.

For the next hour, the two young people sat in the shade of the tree and talked while they nibbled on the food. The day was warm, and the gentle breeze from the west blew across the grass. They seemed to be in a world of their own and were surprised when they heard the wagon pull into the lane. Sudie's pa didn't see them, but Odie did, and he waved at them as the wagon rolled past the tree.

"Is he gonna be mad that I'm here?" said Anthie, his joy rapidly melting.

"I don't think so, but let's go see. Maybe you can help him unload the wagon."

Anthie stood and took hold of Sudie's small hand, helping her up from the grass. He tried to let go of it, but she held on tight. Sudie picked up the basket, and they walked toward the house.

"It's all right," she whispered.

Anthie thought, *He's gonna kill me.*

They reached the house just as Morris climbed down from the wagon seat.

"Good afternoon, sir. Can I help you unload the wagon?"

Morris frowned at Anthie, and then looked at his daughter. His face softened only a little as he shook his head and turned back to the boy.

"Odie'll show you where to put things. Sudie, you come on inside with me."

Sudie followed her pa into the house, and the two boys walked to the back of the wagon. Neither of them spoke as they placed several sacks and boxes onto the porch.

"The rest of this goes in the barn," Odie said, breaking the silence. "I'll move the wagon." He looked at Anthie and added, "I'm surprised you came back."

"Yeah, me too, and I'm surprised your pa's lettin' me stay."

"He don't much like anybody hangin' around Sudie or Hattie, but Ma keeps tellin' him that they're gonna leave someday."

"What do you mean, leave?" he asked.

"Oh, you know, get married or somethin' like that." Odie hid his smile and grabbed the horse's reins.

When they got back from the barn, Odie picked up the packages on the porch, opened the door and said, "You best wait outside for Sudie."

Anthie stepped onto the porch and sat in one of the chairs by an open window. He rested his head against the wall of the house and started to think about what Odie'd said about getting married, but his daydream was interrupted when he heard Mr. Morris talking through the window; his words were strong and clear.

"That's what I heard, Eddy. They whipped the man with a thorn branch and then shot him even after he said he'd join the Association."

"But why would they do that, especially in front of his wife and children?"

"I don't know. It don't make sense." He paused. "I'll tell you this, though. If them damned Night Riders are doin' that kind of thing up in Kentucky, what's to stop the ones we got around here from doin' the same thing?"

Anthie knew he shouldn't be listening, but worried that if he moved from the chair he might make a noise. He decided to stay put.

"I've been thinkin' about what to do with the tobacco," Morris continued. "There's a lot of pressure on all of us, and it's hard to know what to do. Prices are so low and Night Riders so unpredictable that it seems the only safe thing to do is to hold the crop back and hope the price goes up. I won't put the family in danger over money. Besides, we made enough extra on last year's corn and wheat to get us through for a while."

Eddy was quiet for a moment. "I agree with you, Charles. You've gotta join up before anythin' like that happens down here."

Anthie didn't want to be caught listening to Sudie's folks, so he crept away from the window, stepped off the porch and walked out into the yard. *Now I don't have to ask about prices, or the Night Riders or the Association,* he thought as he stood in the grass.

"Anthie, what're you doin' standin' out there in the yard?" said Sudie. "I brought some of Ma's pie. Let's go finish our picnic."

Anthie's face was pale and lacked the warmth Sudie had seen earlier. "What's wrong?" she said as they sat down on the grass.

"I guess I'm a little worried about your pa."

"Oh, don't worry about him. I already told you he's not that mean. Besides, I left him a big piece of pie in the kitchen. That'll make him happy. Let's just go eat and talk some more."

Anthie looked back toward the house for a moment and then turned to Sudie. As they sat under the tree, he let her do most of the talking. While she chattered like a tiny sparrow, he listened and nodded occasionally, but he kept thinking about the killing and all he'd heard.

Sudie was talking about her friends at church when Odie came walking toward them from the house. When he got to the tree, he said, "Sudie, Pa wants you two to come back to the house. He says he wants to talk to your friend."

*Oh Lord,* thought Anthie. *Did he know I was listening?*

"C'mon, Anthie. Let's go see what Pa wants." She stood and picked up the pie plates, and the three of them walked back to the house.

*I guess this is the last time I'll ever see Sudie,* he thought. *It may be the last time I breathe, if he wants to kill me.*

As they got to the porch, Morris came out of the house to meet them.

"Sudie, you and Odie go inside for a bit. I want to talk to young mister Wilson."

Odie went into the house, and Sudie looked at her pa. She wanted to ask him what was going on, but knew better than to question him. She turned to Anthie and gave him a comforting smile. Then she followed her brother.

Anthie froze, wondering what Sudie's pa was going to say. All alone and facing Mr. Morris, he felt like a rabbit caught in a trap, snared with no chance of escape.

"Tell me about your family, son." He led Anthie out into the yard.

"Sir?" said Anthie.

"Tell me about your family. What does your pa do? Where do you live?"

"Oh," he squeaked, no longer confused. "We're farmers just like you. We live about five miles south of Lynnville."

"Does your pa grow tobacco?"

"Yes sir, he does." His voice stronger now, more confident since Mr. Morris hadn't said anything about eavesdropping. "I think we've got about six acres, plus corn and wheat."

"I'd like to know what your pa is gonna do about his crop this year. I may be askin' somethin' you can't answer. Or maybe it's somethin' you won't answer since it's private business. But I'm interested in knowin' if your pa has decided to sell his crop or just hang onto it like so many folks are doin'."

Anthie relaxed a bit. "I'm not sure that my pa knows what he's gonna do yet. He is plannin' on goin' to a meetin' next week, but I'm pretty sure he ain't decided yet."

Morris pondered the boy's answer for a moment and

felt he'd likely learned all he would today. He looked at Anthie's face and then put his hand gently on the boy's shoulder. "Thanks, young man," he said and walked off toward his barn.

*Oh my Lord,* Anthie thought as he sucked in a huge breath of air and let it out slowly. He watched Morris disappear inside the barn and then looked toward the house and saw Sudie's smiling face staring at him through the window. She quickly disappeared and a moment later came running across the yard toward him.

"Is everythin' all right?"

"I think so," he said through a smile. "He just wanted to ask about my pa's tobacco. He didn't even get mad at me or nothin'."

"See, I told you he wasn't mean."

Sudie took his hand and walked him toward the tree. Anthie couldn't believe he'd been able to find out a lot of information for his pa without even asking a single question. Better yet, he got to spend the day with Sudie, and she still liked him. *I'm not ready to go home yet,* he thought. *I'm gonna stay right where I am.*

\* \* \*

"Why can't you just talk to them out here?" whined Gertrude.

"Will you please keep your voice down? We've got customers in here." Mark guided his wife toward the back of the store. "I told you that I need to talk to my brother and Art someplace where we won't be interrupted."

"But what's so secret that you can't talk to them in the store? I've got things to do at the house, and I don't want to waste my time standing around your store talking to a bunch of smelly farmers."

"Shush," Mark growled. "These farmers are the people who paid for your nice house. Now you just watch the store, sell them what they want and be nice." Mark untied his canvas apron, hooked it over her head, spun her around and tied it. Looking at her perpetual scowl, he said, "I won't be gone long. As soon as I'm done, you can go back to sittin' in your rocker."

"Don't you go sassin' me, Mark Wilson. I won't stand for it." Gertrude's face darkened as she walked to the front of the store to help a woman sorting through some bolts of cloth. Mark watched her march down the aisle, wondering why he'd ever married her. *I just hope she don't get someone so mad they stop comin' in here,* he thought as he slipped out the back door.

Wes and Art were waiting for him at the house. He opened the door, and they followed him inside. Except for the ticking clock on the fireplace mantle, the room was quiet. Mark looked at the large rocking chair by the window and cringed as he walked past it into the kitchen.

"You want some coffee?"

"No," said Wes, pulling a chair away from the table and sitting down.

"None for me either, Mark," added Art. "I'm full up with the stuff today. I need to get back home soon as I can anyway."

"Is Mollie any better?"

"Some, but I don't want her to get too tired."

"How long do you think it'll take for Gertrude to start a fight in the store?" asked Wes.

Mark turned to his brother, ready to defend his wife, but stopped short when he saw the broad smile that spread across Wes's face.

"Sorry, Mark. I was just havin' some fun." All of them laughed, and Wes said, "Sit down so we can talk and get you back to the store."

When his brother was seated, Wes laid his hands flat on the table and asked, "What's the news since Thursday?"

Mark looked across the table at each of them. "Cleary came by to see me first thing this mornin' and said the Night Riders killed a farmer over in Christian County last night."

"Killed a farmer?" said Wes, his mind reeling.

"Why would they do that?" added Art.

"Cleary said that he was whipped first and then killed with a shotgun. It happened in front of his wife and children."

"But did Cleary say why?" asked Wes. "Why would they kill somebody?"

"No, he didn't. They probably haven't got any information from his wife yet, and who knows if they even have any other witnesses." Mark clasped his hands in front of him and looked at his brother. "Maybe they killed him because he wouldn't join the Association." Again the ticking clock was the only sound in the room.

"This is not good news," said Wes. "If they're doin' this in Christian County, they could do it here."

"But we don't know that's why he got killed, do we?" said Art.

"What do you mean? What else could it be?"

"Well, maybe they shot him because he pulled a gun on 'em, or maybe because they wanted him dead for somethin' else."

"Either way, he's dead and the Riders killed him." Wes stared down at the table. "Christian County is too far away for the Riders to be from around here. It won't take long for the news of the killing to spread around town and right into the ears of the Night Riders in Lynnville. We gotta expect that they'll use this killing as an example to push more fellas to join up."

Art squirmed in his chair. He looked at the two brothers and said, "I ain't gonna risk gettin' killed over my tobacco. I got a sick wife and four kids, and I ain't gonna leave 'em to starve."

"What're you sayin'?" asked Wes.

"I'm sayin' that I ain't gonna get killed. If that means I gotta join up, then I guess I'll join up."

"But, that's what they want us to do. They wanna scare us into joinin'. Remember, we don't know why they shot him. You just said it coulda been for another reason."

"It could have, but I don't really think it was. I think they shot him because he wouldn't join."

"Look, fellas," Mark said. "We really don't know enough about this yet. Besides, there's more news. Thursday night, before Art got here, that Trust buyer came in braggin' about a deal he'd made with you, Wes. There were some Association fellas sittin' around the stove, and he made sure they heard what he said."

"I ain't made any deal!" shouted Wes. "Why would he say somethin' like that? He ain't gonna get away with lyin' about me. I'll kill him if I have to and stop all this madness."

Art stared hard at Wes. "You talked to a buyer? Why didn't you tell me that the last time we talked?"

"Sure, I talked to a buyer, but I didn't make any deal. It wasn't even worth talkin' about the other night."

Art was clearly upset by Wes's secret dealing with the Trust. He began to wonder what else his cousin hadn't told him but was brought back to the conversation when Mark interrupted.

"Hold on, you two. Let me finish. After I got rid of Jones, I told the other fellas that he was makin' no sense, that you wouldn't have made any deal. Then Art showed up and told me you two were plannin' to go to the meetin' next week. They heard what Art said, and I think they believed him more than they believed Jones."

Art stared at Wes, his jaws clenched tight. "You lied to me, Wes. Why didn't you tell me about this? We're family and supposed to be helpin' each other."

"I didn't tell you because I didn't make a damn deal, and I didn't lie to you," he said, clearly growing as angry as his cousin.

"Will you two please settle down for a minute? Let's look at what we know. First, the fellas who were in the store are all in the Association. Second, they heard Jones and Art and I think they believed Art, so they don't have any reason to be comin' after you."

"Yes, but they were plannin' to raid Wes's place," said Art, interrupting Mark.

"Even though they were plannin' to raid Wes, they have no reason to do it now since you two are goin' to the meetin'. They didn't kill anybody in that raid near Cuba last week, and we don't know for sure why the man in Christian County was killed. Those are the facts."

Wes looked over at Art. "Mark's right. We still don't know enough. At least I don't know enough, since you've already made your decision." His face darkened. "I gotta think about it some more. There's too much at stake to pick one or the other without really knowin' what's goin' on."

"Maybe you can hold out, but I don't think I can," replied Art. He shook his head and then looked at Wes. "But I'll wait until we've been to the meetin'. That's the best I can do, Wes."

"At least give me 'til then," said Wes. "We can talk about it after we leave the meetin'. Besides, Anthie's down in Tennessee today, talkin' to his girl's pa. He might have somethin' to add to all of this." Wes pushed the chair back from the table and stood. "Once I know what Anthie's learned, I'll let you know," he said, his voice cold. "Maybe we can meet day after tomorrow?"

Art rose from his chair. "Okay, let's meet here on Monday night. Would that be all right, Mark?"

"Yeah, but come after I close the store. I'd rather do it there than here at the house."

Wes extended his hand toward Art, hoping that his cousin would take it. When he did, the two men shook hands and quietly left the house. Mark rose from his chair and looked around the room. He made sure the chairs were pushed back against the table. *I hope she hasn't scared off all my customers,* he thought as he closed the door behind him and headed back to the store.

\* \* \*

All the way home, Wes's head was filled with the new information. He stopped by the creek, got down from the horse and splashed some of the cool water on his face. He looked down the road and rubbed his forehead, trying to still the growing pressure in his mind. *Sometimes it seems like I have no control. This ain't good,* he thought, *but I gotta pull myself together before I get home.* He breathed deeply and felt a bit calmer. As he rode past the farm, Wes saw Connie sitting on the porch with the shotgun across his lap. He waved at his son and went on to George's to return the horse. When he turned into the lane, he saw his oldest brother walking into his barn. *Might as well find out what he knows,* Wes thought, *and do it while Malinda ain't hangin' around.* He rode the horse up to the barn, slid out of the saddle and led the animal inside.

"You in here, George?"

"Over here, Wes," George said from the back of the barn.

Wes turned toward his brother's voice. "Thanks for lettin' me borrow your horse. It's a lot better ridin' on it than that old stiff-legged mule of mine."

"I don't know why you ain't got one of your own. It'd sure make your trips to town and church a lot easier."

"I'm thinking about it. I just can't afford one right now." He put the horse in its stall and removed the saddle and bridle. As he began to rub the sweat from the animal's back, he spoke. "Do you have time to talk?"

George walked over to the stall, wiping his hands on a rag. "Sure. What do you wanna talk about?"

"Art and I met at Mark's house, and our little brother told us about this fella who got shot by some Night Riders over in Christian County and died right in front of his family."

"I heard about a raid, but I didn't realize they killed the farmer."

"That's what Mark said. The constable told him they whipped the fella first and then shot him."

"That's not good, Wes. Do you know why they killed him?"

"We might find out in the next few days, but right now it looks like plain old murder."

Wes hung the sweaty rag over the rail of the stall and took the curry comb George handed him. He started to work on the horse and said, "Last week I talked to a nigger up near the church. The Riders tore up his whole field and then salted it." George shook his head slowly as Wes continued. "He didn't have more than a dozen plants left."

George pulled up a box and sat down in front of the stall as he watched Wes. "What else did you learn in town?"

Wes cleared his throat. "Well there's a Trust buyer in the county, and he's goin' around sayin' that I made a deal with him."

George looked directly at his brother. "So you talked to him?"

"I didn't make no deal with him, if that's what you mean." Wes's voice grew louder.

"Settle down, Wes. I meant no disrespect. I suppose a lot of farmers wanna know what kind of price he's offerin'. Did he mention a price?"

"He did, but the number ain't important. What's important is that he's tellin' folks I did somethin' that I never did. Now I'm likely in trouble with the Association. Art even said there'd been a raid planned on my farm."

"A raid planned on your farm?" George spit the words out. "Your farm, Wes? That's serious. They could hurt you and your family after what you just told me. Do you know what you're gonna do?"

"Nope, just keep my family safe and protect what's mine."

"Where did Art hear about the raid?"

"He heard it somewhere, but he won't tell me who said it." Even saying the words out loud, sharing them with George, didn't cool his anger at Art.

"That's not like Art to hold important information back, is it?"

"No it ain't, but he's workin somethin' out in his head, and he ain't tellin' me what it is. I don't like him keepin' secrets or us havin' trouble."

"Art has those two hired hands workin' on his farm, don't he? Maybe he heard it from them. I heard a rumor that Dan Cleary has to keep his eye on 'em 'cause he don't trust 'em."

"Art, Mark and I are gonna meet again Monday night. I might ask him then about those two fellas. Like I said, it seems like somethin' is botherin' him, so I wanna be real careful and not make him any madder than he already is."

George spoke up. "It could be Mollie and the children and the pressure of bein' a farmer and takin' care of all the other needs."

"No, it's somethin' more. He got real mad at me when he found out I talked with the buyer."

"Maybe he's worried about you, Wes. Heck, I'm even worried about you after what you just told me. Zora stopped by last Sunday, and she seemed upset. She talked with Malinda, and after a few words she said it was real important that she talk with me. But when I came in from the barn it seemed she'd changed her mind and was gettin' ready to leave. I could see tears in her eyes, so I know it must've had somethin' to do with you or the family." George watched Wes, remembering how sullen his younger brother could get when he was mad. "But I know if you need my help you'll ask."

Wes couldn't believe what he'd just heard. Zora had never mentioned her visit on Sunday. *Another secret,* he thought. He could feel the pressure building in his head, but he held back from asking more of George, thinking he'd deal with it later. Right now there was more he needed to know. Wes sat back on his stool hesitant about asking his next question.

"I'm wondering what you plan on doing with your crop, George."

George was quiet for a minute. He got up from the box and came into the stall. He took the comb from Wes and started working on the horse. Wes stepped back out of the way and looked at George and saw how old he'd gotten. He waited for his brother to speak.

"As much as we need the money, I think I'm gonna have to join up. I sure don't want to end up dead like that fella in Christian County, or run out of the county like the other farmer. Besides, Ma's gettin' older, and I don't want any-thin' to happen to her or Malinda or any of the children." He paused and looked at Wes. "I don't know, Wes. Joinin' up just seems like the safest thing to do."

"I know you gotta do what's right for you," Wes said, looking at his brother.

"I sure do," he said. Then he cleared his throat and wiped the sweat from his face. "Listen, Wes, I gotta know if you've really thought about what you're doin'." He shook his head and continued. "Not joinin' the Association is foolish. You or Zora or the children are gonna get hurt or even killed. Why don't you just let go of your stupid pride and be smart about this? Join up now."

"Why, you bastard!" shouted Wes, clenching his fists. "Didn't our pa always tell us to be men, to make our own decisions?" He moved close to George, his rage growing.

"You ain't never stopped tellin' me what to do. You keep on tryin' to be the big brother. Well, brother, I'll tell you this. I am a man and I make my own decisions without any help from you or Art or anyone else. You hear me?" Wes was ready to fight.

George calmly set the curry comb on a shelf and then turned away from Wes and walked out of the stall.

"Where're you goin'? We ain't done here," said Wes, his voice harsh, bitter.

"Oh, we're done, Wes. I just hope you don't do somethin' stupid." George was bothered by Wes's anger, but he still loved his brother.

Wes turned away from George and stalked out into the sun. Mad at George and even angrier with Zora, he walked across the field toward his own farm. The thoughts that people were keeping secrets from him and trying to tell him what to do echoed in his head.

* * *

Connie was still sitting on the porch when Wes walked up to the house.

"Is everythin' quiet, son?"

"Yeah, Pa. There's not much goin' on. Ma and the girls are out in the garden, and John Stanley is still up in bed." Connie stood up from the bench and leaned the shotgun against the wall. He started to walk toward his pa and then turned back to the gun, picked it up and broke it open. "Safer that way," he said.

"Anthie show up yet?"

"Not yet, but I guess he'll be home before supper." Connie stepped into the yard, his hands shoved deep into his pockets. He looked at Wes and asked, "Anythin' new goin' on in town?"

"Yeah, quite a bit, but we'll talk about it after supper when we're all together. You go see if you can help your ma.

I'm gonna go up and check on your brother."

Connie walked away toward the garden, and Wes went into the house and quietly made his way up the stairs to the boys' bedroom. John Stanley was lying in the bed, his head propped up against a pillow. The boy's eyes were closed, and it looked to Wes like he was sleeping. Wes slowly pushed the door open and stepped into the room. When the floor creaked, John Stanley opened his eyes and looked at his pa.

"Sorry, son. Were you sleepin'?"

"I dunno. I guess I was." He reached up and touched the stitches on his head. "These things sure itch, Pa. How long do I gotta keep 'em in?"

Wes walked over to the window and looked out toward the garden. He saw Connie talking to Zora while Mary Lula and the younger girls pulled weeds. He felt a cool breeze coming through the window as he turned his face toward his son.

"We'll let your ma decide that, but I expect it'll be about a week."

John Stanley closed his eyes and groaned. "When can I get out of bed, Pa? I'm tired of not doin' anythin'."

"Maybe you can tomorrow when everybody goes to church. I'll be stayin' home with you, so it'll depend on how you're feelin'. Are you dizzy or anythin'?"

"Only a little, I guess, but it's not so bad."

"Your ma will be up to check on you in a while." Wes stepped back from the window and walked out the door. *I need a drink,* he thought as he walked into the kitchen. "How could Zora think it'd be all right to go talk to George about our family?" he mumbled to himself. He reached up on the shelf to get the jug, but pulled his hand back when he heard his family coming toward the porch. Turning quickly away from the shelf, he sat down at the table. *That was close,* he thought, *too close.* Wes tried to control his breathing; nearly getting caught had frightened him. *If they don't see me drinkin', they won't know if I take a sip now and then.*

Mary Lula was first through the door. She was carrying Ruthie and pushing Irene with her free hand.

"Hi, Pa," she said and then nudged Irene again. "You heard Ma. Go on up and change your clothes."

The three girls left the kitchen just as Connie and Zora came in.

"How's John Stanley?" Zora asked, barely acknowledging Wes.

"He's doin' better, and he wants to get out of bed," Wes said. "I told him it'd depend on how he felt tomorrow." Wes watched Zora's face.

Connie poured himself a cup of milk, and Zora waited until he left the kitchen. "What did you find out in town? What'd Art and Mark have to say?"

"I found out a lot."

She waited for Wes to finish what he was saying, but he offered nothing more. "Can't you tell me somethin'?" she said, anxious for information.

"I'd rather wait, all right? I don't wanna have to repeat it all. Besides, I gotta get it straight in my head." His words were clipped, abrupt, and they clearly angered Zora.

Whatever her mood might have been when she came into the kitchen, Wes now knew it had changed. But he didn't care; in the back of his already-cluttered mind he was still mad at her. She stared hard at him, her lips tightening into a thin line and her forehead wrinkled in a frown.

"I'll be outside," he said, rising from his chair and walking out the door. "We'll talk when Anthie gets home."

*That man makes me so mad sometimes, I think I could scream,* she thought. *He's so filled with pride and he doesn't even know it.* She went to the counter and started putting the clean dishes up on the shelf. It wasn't long before the tears began to well up in her eyes.

* * *

The sun was still high in the west when Anthie turned onto the road about a mile from the farm. He'd spent most of the trip from Sudie's thinking someday he might marry her, but as he got closer to home, that dream faded and he focused on what he was going to tell his pa. He'd created a list of the important things and thought, *Pa'll be glad I found out all of this. I sure hope he ain't been drinkin'. I don't wanna get hit again if I messed up.*

"Ma, I'm home!" he yelled, walking into the kitchen. The house felt empty as he headed upstairs to his bedroom. John Stanley was still lying on the bed, his covers pushed down to the end.

"Quit yellin', would ya? It hurts my head."

"Where's Pa?"

"I dunno. If he ain't in the house, he must be outside." He looked at his brother for a second and then whispered, "Anthie, thanks for bringin' me back to the house when . . . you know."

"Aw, that's all right," he said, a little embarrassed. "When you gonna get out of bed?"

"Pa said maybe I could tomorrow. I sure hope so, 'cause I'm gettin' tired of layin' around here doin' nothin'."

"Okay then, I'm gonna go find Pa. I got some things to tell him. I'll see you later." He turned and left the room.

Anthie found his pa out back of the barn. Wes was splitting logs; each vicious swing of the ax sent the stove wood flying. Connie was quietly stacking the wood and watched his brother approach. A little afraid, Anthie hesitated before he spoke.

"I'm back, Pa. You need any help?"

Wes stood in silence, clutching the ax tightly in his hand before turning toward Anthie.

"Did you find out anythin' down at Sudie's?" Wes asked,

his voice harsh.

"I sure did. Do you wanna talk about it now?"

"No, I'm almost done here," he said. "You go find your ma right now and tell her we all need to talk. We'll meet you in the kitchen."

"Where is Ma?"

"I don't know!" he yelled. "I ain't seen her for a while." He paused, remembering how she'd looked when he walked away from her. "She might've gone over to see your Aunt Malinda again," he said, his voice edgy. "Look around the house first, and if you can't find her, run over there. Tell her to get back home now. It's important."

As Anthie turned the corner of the barn, he saw his ma coming down the lane from the road. He stopped by the well and waited for her. When she reached him, he scooped up a cup of water in the ladle and handed it to her. She looked up at him, and he could tell she'd been crying. Her blue eyes were dark, cloudy, and her smile was gone.

"Are you all right, Ma? You look—well, you don't look happy."

"I'm fine, son," she said when she finished sipping the water. "Let's go inside."

"Pa says we need to talk about somethin' important. He's out behind the barn with Connie. Should I go get 'em now?"

"No. I wanna talk with you first, and then you can get 'em. Come on inside."

Zora took off her bonnet and set it on the table. She dipped a cloth in the pan of water on the counter and wrung it out. She took a moment to wipe the dust from her face.

"Sit down, son. I wanna ask you somethin' before we talk to your pa and Connie."

She pulled a chair away from the table and sat gently on the edge. Anthie waited while she gathered her thoughts. *Ma looks sad,* he thought, *or maybe even a little mad.* He didn't want to interrupt her, so he remained quiet.

Zora cleared her throat. "Before we talk to your pa about his crop, I need to know how you're thinkin' about him right now. Are you still mad at him?"

Anthie wasn't sure how to respond. His ma had never asked him anything like this before. "The truth is, Ma, I guess I'm still a little mad," he said. "Pa don't seem to be as angry as he was a few days ago, but he ain't said anythin' more to me about last Sunday. I don't even think he remembers what I said to him when I was carryin' John Stanley. I've tried to stay out of his way and do everythin' he's asked."

While Zora listened to her son, she watched his eyes, looking for the truth in his words.

Anthie continued. "I found out some things today that might help him. Or they might make him madder than he was before. I just know that I gotta tell him everythin' I heard, Ma."

"But do you hate him?" she asked, recalling what he'd said earlier in the week.

Anthie looked away from his ma and thought for a moment. Then he turned back to her and said, "I don't know, Ma. I guess I'm still thinkin' about it."

"It'll be all right, Anthie." She touched his face and held him close for a moment. She forced a smile onto her face as she looked at him. "You go out and get your pa and your brother. I'll make some coffee and we can hear what he has to say."

* * *

A light breeze fluttered the curtain hanging over the kitchen window. Wes sat slumped at his spot at the table, his head bowed, searching for the words to start the discussion. Zora watched her husband, but made no attempt to help him. *He's got to say what's on his mind,* she thought, *and I can't do it for him.* She looked across the table and

saw that both Connie and Anthie had turned away from
their pa, as if they were giving him time or space to think.
*That's good, boys,* she thought. *Let him work it out.*

Wes stared for a moment at the blowing curtain and
listened to the distant laughter of his daughters as they
played in the yard. He sat up straighter in the chair, pulled
his shoulders back and turned to look at his wife and sons.
His face was ashen, but his eyes seemed filled with fire.

"Before I tell you what I know and what I think it means
for the family, I want to hear what Anthie learned down at
the Morris farm. There's a lot goin' on, and we all need to
hear it and talk about it before any decision gets made."
Trying to keep his voice calm, he looked at Anthie and nodded slightly. "Go ahead."

Anthie had decided during his ride home that he'd tell
his pa the easy things first. He thought if he told about the
killing his pa would be really mad and that wouldn't be
good., So, he told him that Mr. Morris had asked about their
tobacco and what they were going to do about the Association.

"So I told him you were still thinkin' about what to do
and you hadn't decided yet. He didn't ask me any more
questions about the crop, but he wanted to know about our
family and where we lived."

"Did he say anythin' more about the Association?"

"He didn't say anythin' more to me about it, but Pa, I was
sittin' on their porch by a window, and I heard him talkin'
to Sudie's ma." Anthie squirmed in his chair, his joy at having news for his pa was tempered some by having eaves-
dropped. "I feel bad about listenin' to 'em, but if I'd moved
they mighta heard me."

"It don't matter, son. Now just tell me . . . Tell us what you
heard." His words snapped from his mouth.

"Sudie's pa told her ma that when he was in town he
heard that a farmer up in Christian County was murdered

by the Night Riders."

Zora gasped and reached across the table to touch Anthie's hand. She looked at Wes and started to touch him as well, but his look stopped her.

"Tell us exactly what he said, son, word for word if you can. I gotta know what he heard about Christian County."

"He said that the Riders went to the man's house and whipped him with a thorn branch." Anthie closed his eyes, trying to remember the words he'd heard. "Then they killed him with a shotgun in front of his wife and children. He said that if the Night Riders could do that in Christian County, they might do it in Tennessee."

"What else did he say?" he said quickly. "Try hard to remember."

"He told Sudie's ma that the only safe thing to do was to join the Association. They talked about how they'd done all right with their other crops last year and would be okay without their tobacco money for a while. Sudie's ma was mostly worried about the children and said no crop was worth harm comin' to the family."

Wes looked at Zora and then turned to Anthie. "Is there anythin' more that you can remember, anythin' important?"

Wes watched and waited so he wouldn't interrupt the boy's thoughts.

After a moment, Anthie spoke. "I'm sorry, Pa, but I don't remember any more." He looked across the table at his ma and then added, "But when Sudie's folks were talkin', they were real serious, almost scared."

"Wes, I don't know—"

"—Wait a minute, let me finish thinkin'." Zora frowned at the interruption, but remained quiet, watching her husband ponder the news. When he finally spoke, his words sounded strong, but to Zora the look on his face told her he was angry about something.

"Mark told Art and me the same story this mornin'. We

talked about it and decided we don't know if the man was killed for not joinin' or for some other reason. But I think we all know the real reason. Art's likely gonna join the Association because he's afraid of gettin' raided and what that'd do to Mollie's health. He did say he'd wait until after we go to the meetin' on Wednesday. Then Mark told us about somethin' that happened Thursday night."

Wes looked around the table and saw that the others were focused on him. Then he went on to tell them everything that had happened on Thursday. He talked about who was there and what was said; he left out nothing.

"Does Mark think they believed Jones?" asked Zora.

"He's pretty sure he convinced 'em Jones was lyin' and just tryin' to stir things up. All three of us agreed we still need more information. We're gonna meet at the store for a while on Monday night and talk over everythin' again. Once I tell 'em what Anthie learned, I think Art will definitely choose to join up, but I believe he'll wait 'til after the meetin' to do it."

Wes rose from his chair and paced around the kitchen, circling the table. The others stayed silent, knowing he hadn't finished talking.

"Here's what we'll do. We'll keep standin' watch and takin' care of our crops. I think we have time before I gotta decide what to do, but it won't hurt to be careful. I'll stand guard tonight, and you'll all go to church tomorrow. I'll stay here with John Stanley." He looked at his family. "Connie, I still think you should go over to Maud's tomorrow. Anthie, you did good findin' out what the Morrises' are doin', but I'll need you to take your ma and the girls to church."

Sensing that he was done speaking, the boys rose and walked toward the back of the house. Anthie turned toward his mother as he reached the door and just nodded. Zora waited for Wes to say something else to her. When he stayed silent, she got up and followed the boys.

* * *

While the last minutes of Saturday quietly ticked away, Wes sat on the porch bench, looking out into the dark night. The moon hadn't yet risen, but its glow showed dimly off to the southeast. The stars spread across the blue-black sky like crystal raindrops on a dark coat. The crickets kept up their pleasant sawing, and an occasional night-bird called, but Wes wasn't aware of them; he listened for more ominous sounds. The soft night breeze blowing across the fields did little to cool the nerve-driven sweat that oozed out of his pores. Wes sat quietly, but he wasn't resting. He stared into the night, listening to the sounds in the woods surrounding his farm and struggling with his demons.

Wes was growing weary of wearing his mask of control. He knew that it was necessary, that he had to appear calm and alert if he was going to keep his family's trust. But the battle in his mind was so intense he feared that the mask was slipping away and that Zora and the others could see how angry and bitter he'd become. The things that bothered him—the killing, the raids, the Association, the secrets—gnawed and chewed at every corner of his mind. A few days ago, these things had felt like a pack of wild dogs, but tonight they seemed more like demons, poking and screaming and circling him, looking for a weak spot. *But they ain't gonna get me. I ain't gonna let 'em.* Like a blacksmith pounding on an anvil, the thoughts kept repeating in his head: *It's my farm; nobody's gonna tell me what to do. It's my family; nobody's gonna hurt 'em. It's my decision, my decision, my decision.*

* * *

In the room in the back of the house, Zora was on her knees, her face buried in her hands on the rumpled blanket spread across the bed. The battle in her mind was different than Wes's. She was afraid if she pushed Wes too hard with her words and attitude that she might lose him to madness. But, if she didn't speak up, his pride might lead him to do something rash or worse. Her only help, her only solace had to come from a belief that God wouldn't let them down. So she prayed quietly, undisturbed by the crickets outside.

Alone on the porch, Wes growled like a mad dog, "I hate what this is doin' to all of us."

# Chapter 14
Sunday, May 13

By Sunday morning, Anthie's bruises were gone, but as he lay in his bed, listening to his brothers sleeping, he thought about the question his ma had asked the day before. *Do you still hate him?* she'd said. He listened to the last of the serene night sounds and searched for an answer to the question. *It ain't easy,* he thought, *but a couple of days of bein' nice don't take away the pain of what he done. I know Pa's worryin' about lots of things.* He reached up and touched his cheeks, knowing that the bruises had faded and his broken lip had almost healed. *But it weren't right for him to beat me. I deserved a whuppin', but not like he did.*

He heard the cow's bellowed complaint through the window and sat up on the edge of his bed and whispered, "Time to milk that silly old cow." Anthie pulled on his pants and an old shirt and made his way to the kitchen. Before opening the door, he looked through the window out into the dark morning to see if his pa was still on the porch. *If Pa's sleepin' on the bench,* he thought, *I sure don't wanna wake him.*

He struck a match to light the lantern and spotted his pa standing by the well, looking out toward the road. Wes held the shotgun by the barrel, the butt resting on the ground by his feet. When he heard the porch creak, he turned toward his son.

"Mornin', son," he said.

"Mornin', Pa. I'm gonna milk the cow."

Anthie hesitated, wondering if he should stop and stand with him for a while. But when his pa picked up the gun and walked off toward the tobacco, Anthie headed to the barn. The chatter of the crickets stopped when they sensed his movement, but the cow must have heard him coming because she bawled again. *Hold your horses, I'm comin',* he thought as he reached the barred door. Then he smiled, wondering how a cow could hold its horses. He lifted the bar of gnarly wood from its slot and pulled the heavy door open. Inside, the smell of the mule and the cow reminded him how much he hated this chore. He set the lantern down on the hard-packed dirt and went over to the cow's stall. *I hope you don't give me no trouble this mornin'. I'm tired and I wanna get back to sleep for a while.* He picked up the stool and bucket and opened the gate, pushing the animal against the far wall. The cow bawled once more, and Anthie got to work, filling the bucket with her warm milk.

Wes walked a dozen rows into the tobacco field and stopped. Through the gaps in the green-black tree line, he glimpsed the first rose-colored glow of the sunrise and felt the muted breeze as it tickled the tops of the young tobacco plants and chattered through the corn in the field behind him. The air felt cool against his sweaty forehead. As the sky brightened, he could see the green shoots had already grown a few inches after only a week in the ground. He kicked at the dirt, and a small cloud of dust rose and settled on his boots. Cradling the shotgun in his arms, he stared off toward the woods and spotted the glowing eyes of a coon as it scurried through the weeds at the edge of the field. He lifted the gun, but didn't shoot.

Wes was tired from thinking about the problems that swirled around in his head. There seemed to be no stopping the endless chatter. His head hurt, not from the voices in his head, but the essence of them. Even his eyes burned, and the screeching cricket sound in his ears would not go

away. The few swallows of liquor he'd snuck during the
night had left him with a sharp pain in his stomach and a
sour taste in his mouth. He hawked and spit some of the
nasty-tasting phlegm into the dirt at his feet. The battle
against the snapping dogs in his head had worn him out,
but he couldn't let his mental fatigue keep him from looking strong and in control. *All I need is some time and the
right information. Once I know everything, I can make a
choice, and then all of this trouble will be over.* He looked
down at the shotgun and thought, *Nobody's ever gonna say
I quit like my pa did; never.*

Wes heard Anthie close the barn door and turned to
watch his son carry the milk bucket back to the house. *He's
a good boy. I just wish he wanted to be a farmer.* He shoul-
dered the gun and called for Rufus. The dog ran out from
under the porch and looked around. Wes whistled once and
the dog turned toward the field, spotted Wes and raced toward him. *Rufus is smarter than most people,* thought Wes.
*He knows how to stay between the rows.* The dog followed
Wes until he saw that they were headed into the woods.
Then he bolted ahead, running through the brush, sniffing
the ground. Wes wanted to walk around the perimeter of
his farm to see if anyone had been hanging around where
they shouldn't have been. If there'd been someone in the
woods watching the house, Rufus would know.

By the time Wes walked up to the porch, the sun was
shining over the top of the trees. Rufus stopped and drank
from the tub of water, scratched at a couple of fleas and
crawled back under the porch. The smell of fried bacon
wafting out of the kitchen caused Wes's stomach to growl.

Zora looked at him as he came into the house, but didn't
speak. She focused on the eggs in the cast-iron pan on the
stove. Stirring them, she made sure that they were totally
cooked. She knew Wes would get upset if there were the
slightest bit of runny, uncooked egg on his plate, and she

didn't want him upset this morning. Mary Lula poured a cup of coffee for her pa, picked up Ruthie from the floor and put her in a chair.

"You sit still now," she said. "It's almost time to eat." She smiled at her pa and walked toward the back of the house. At the foot of the stairs, she called up to the rest of the family to get moving or they'd miss out on breakfast.

Zora scooped the fluffy eggs out of the pan into a large bowl and set it on the table. She wiped her hands on a towel and then turned to Wes.

"Did anythin' happen last night?" she asked.

"It was quiet," he said.

"Are you still plannin' to stay home with John Stanley?"

"Yeah, I am. Somebody's gotta do it if all of you're goin' to church. Besides, I'm tired, and I gotta get some sleep."

"I think the boy is well enough to go with us," Zora said, as Connie, Anthie and Irene walked into the kitchen. They sat in their chairs without speaking, not wanting to interrupt the discussion. "I'm gonna go up and check on him."

All of the children tensely watched their pa. He stared down at his empty plate, and as best he could, he forced a smile onto his face and looked up at them. "You all gonna eat or is this all for me?"

Mary Lula filled plates for her ma and John Stanley and set them on the table just as the two of them came into the kitchen. Wes greeted his son as the boy found his seat and sat down to eat. Zora looked at her family and felt the light mood in the air. She glanced at Wes and saw that he was smiling and knew it wasn't real; she could see in his eyes that something was different.

Zora sat down and picked up a slice of bacon. She bit off a piece of the crispy meat and chewed it delicately. "My," she said to no one in particular, a forced grin on her lips, "they certainly have a great cook in this house. The food is delicious."

For a moment, nothing happened, but then the happy sound of the younger children talking drove the tension out of the air. Wes and Zora watched them, but didn't look at each other. They'd each given up something of themselves to make things easier on the family, and they both knew that they were in trouble.

* * *

*We gotta get a horse,* Wes thought as he watched Connie head through the field to George's farm. He stood on the porch, his hands in the pockets of his overalls, wondering when his brother was going to get tired of lending out his horse. *I hate owin' anybody a favor almost as much as owin' money, but a promise is a promise, and Connie ain't seen Maud for more than a week.* He'd thought about Jones's offer throughout his restless night and knew that taking it would be the end of any kind of relationship with his oldest brother—and any other family as well. *If I take his offer, we could buy that horse and maybe find a place in Missouri or Arkansas and start over.* Wes knew it was all just a dream. No one in the family would want to move away from Lynnville. Connie and Maud were probably going to get married soon. Even though no one had been calling on Mary Lula, she was at a marrying age, so it wouldn't be long until she was gone as well. Anthie was only sixteen, but he was spending a lot of time thinking about Sudie.

Wes sat down on the bench and rested his weary head against the wall, glad that everyone was gone. He closed his eyes against the glaring sun and felt the tepid breeze on his sagging cheeks. Somewhere in his head he heard the clicking of the dog's nails as he drifted off to sleep.

* * *

Rufus barked and bounded into the yard when he saw the wagon turn down the lane toward the house. The

racket startled Wes awake from where he'd been lying on
the bench. "What?" he yelled as he rubbed the grit from
his eyes and tried to figure out where he was. When the
dog barked again, Wes stood up and held onto the porch's
corner post. He shaded his eyes from the blinding sun and
watched his family as they got down from the wagon.

Wes walked over to Zora and helped her from the wagon seat. There was sweat on her cheeks, and what little
of her hair showing beneath her bonnet was damp and
curly. When her feet touched the yard, she didn't linger, but
headed into the house without saying a word. *Lord knows
what's got her upset,* Wes thought as he went around to the
back of the wagon to help Mary Lula.

"Thank you, Pa," she said, handing Ruthie to him before
sliding off the wagon bed and onto the ground. "I'm not
sure this little girl is gonna stay awake long enough to eat
dinner, so I'd better get inside and help Ma get it ready."
She smiled at her father and lifted Ruthie up onto the porch
and led her into the kitchen. Mary Lula was beautiful; she
reminded Wes of her ma, and he thought about how much
she looked like Zora when she was younger.

When the wagon started moving, Wes turned to Anthie
and reminded him to wipe down the mule and give it some
oats. He stepped back from the wagon and watched his son.

"I won't forget, Pa," said Anthie back over his shoulder.
He'd seen his pa struggle to get up from the bench and
hoped he wasn't drunk. *If he is,* the boy thought, *this day
ain't gonna be a good day.* Taking the animal by the bridle,
he led it into the stall and set a bucket of oats and fresh
water at its feet. Then he checked the cow to see if she was
ready for her afternoon milking. She wasn't, and he was
glad. When Anthie walked out of the barn after wiping
down the mule, he heard his pa yell.

"Come over here a minute, son." Wes sat down and patted at a spot next to him.

Anthie walked over to his pa, a little anxious, not sure what he wanted. He could see in his pa's eyes that he hadn't been drinking, at least not recently, and when his pa opened his mouth to speak, Anthie couldn't smell liquor.

"What happened at church?" Wes said. "Your ma is awful quiet."

"Church was the same as it always is, Pa. We didn't do much but sing and pray and listen to the preacher. I thought for a while that he was gonna preach through dinnertime all the way up to supper. He must've got tired of listenin' to himself, so he finally quit. It was a good thing, too, because as soon as he was done, everyone ran to the outhouse. It ain't often we see a line to the privy at church."

Wes smiled at Anthie, thinking that he and his son shared the same opinion about church. "But what about your ma. Why's she so quiet?"

"I don't know. She seems the same to me, Pa. Maybe she's still worried about John Stanley. He was pretty quiet this mornin', too."

"I suppose that's it," said Wes. "She gets that way when one of you children gets sick or hurt. My ma was the same way with all of us, especially with me." He turned from Anthie and looked off at the field of tobacco. "I guess we better get washed up and go see if we can help with dinner, although I wager your ma'll kick us out of the kitchen rather than have us under foot."

Anthie went over to the well and washed his hands and face. Wes waited until he finished and then did the same. Once he was alone in the yard, he looked out at his field again. *Somethin' is up with her, but I can't figure out what it is. Maybe she's mad 'cause I didn't go to church, or that I was sleepin' when she got home. If that's it, then there ain't a thing I can do to change her mind. Besides, I still ain't talked to her about talkin' to George.* He wiped his wet hands on his overalls and went into the house.

* * *

By the time Connie got home, it was getting dark. The last rays of the sun had turned the bottoms of the few clouds in the sky to orange and the tree trunks on the western side of the farm to black. There was no breeze, but the air had cooled some since midday, and Wes and Zora were sitting on the porch. They usually shared the bench at times like these, but tonight Zora was sitting in one of the chairs from the kitchen. They'd managed to keep up the pretense of calmness around the children, but since they were all inside cleaning up after supper, the two adults were silent. Each was unwilling to start a conversation that would likely turn into an argument.

Wes had seen Connie ride past the house on his way to George's. When he spotted his son coming across the field from the east he pointed him out to his wife and said, "Here comes Connie. I wonder how his visit with Maud went." He hoped he could break the tension.

"I imagine that he enjoyed gettin' away from here since he ain't seen her for awhile." Zora's words were clipped, guarded and there was little warmth in her voice. "It seems like there ain't much good news around home these days."

Wes watched Zora as she stared off into the yard, adding her coldness to his list of worries. *One thing at a time,* he thought, *I can't take care of everything all at once. Anyway, why's she mad at me? I'm the one who should be mad at her for keeping a secret.*

Connie stopped first at the well to wash his hands and face and walked to the porch. "I'm glad you're both out here," he said, barely controlling his excitement. "I got somethin' to tell you and I gotta tell you now." He was afraid that if he waited, the smile on his face would give him away. "Maud and I are gonna get married."

Zora was stunned, but her dark mood quickly gave way to a wide, genuine smile. "Why Connie Lee, you sure surprised me. I thought you was gonna tell us you'd gone and joined the army," she said as she stepped forward and hugged her son. She'd known that they'd get married someday; she just didn't think it would be so soon. Connie's joy made her happy and took her mind off Wes for the moment.

"Well, well, well," said Wes, "I guess we're gonna have to start makin' plans to find you two a place to live." He wasn't as quick to cover his shock, but only Zora saw the hint of concern flicker in his tired eyes. "I'd sure like to know how her ma and pa are takin' the news." He looked at Zora and then back at his son. "When is all of this gonna happen? Have you two decided on a date?"

"We've been talkin' about gettin' married for quite a while, Pa, but I was scared of tellin' her folks for a long time." He grinned and looked at his father's face. "Her pa's almost as mean as you, and I didn't know if he'd run me out of their house and chase me down the road with a piece of stove wood." He raised his hands in front of his face and feigned a duck and then laughed, "We're gonna wait until all the crops have been harvested, so the wedding'll probably be in October."

"Well I think you'd better get on in the house and tell your brothers and sisters what's goin' on." He put his hand on Connie's shoulder and squeezed it. "You son of a gun, you sure did surprise me." Wes's head throbbed in pain, but he set his own worries aside for Connie's happiness.

Zora knew that Wes wasn't as pleased with the news as he let on, but she was glad he'd somehow managed to bury his worries for the moment. She reached up and put her small hand gently on Connie's other shoulder. "Your pa is right; you better get in there and tell everyone the news. I expect they've been wonderin' when you'd get up the gumption to finally ask her."

Connie bent down and kissed his ma on the cheek and

rushed into the house. Zora knew Wes was struggling and moved over to stand next to him.

"Thank you, Wes."

"For what?" He turned and looked at her, surprised that she'd finally spoken to him.

She turned to him, her eyes glistening. "Thanks for showin' your son that he's important even when you got a lot on your mind." *And don't forget about your other son,* she thought, *because he may not be around much longer.* Without asking if he was coming, she stood and said, "I'm goin' in to see how the cleanin' up is goin'."

Wes knew he should follow her and be a part of the happiness surrounding Connie. He was painfully aware that his absence would send some kind of signal to his son, and worse, to his wife. He took a moment more to get his head together, making sure the mask was in place. Over the next hour or so he laughed with his family, hugged his son and kidded him about the perils of marriage. But inside his head, Connie leaving the farm added fuel to a fire that was growing more dangerous every day.

When the excitement finally settled down and the rest of the family got ready for bed, Wes stepped outside and looked up at the stars wheeling through the sky. There was no breeze, but the night air was cool and dry. He stepped down into the yard and sat on the edge of the porch next to Rufus. He ran his hand along the dog's flank and scratched his ears. *You're the only one who understands, ain't you dog. You know what it means if Connie leaves. He knows farmin' and hard work. He don't complain, and I depend on him. Connie's leavin' ain't gonna be a problem 'til after harvest, but I still gotta deal with it 'cause I'll be losin' my best farm-hand.* "So if you got any ideas," he said aloud, "you better give 'em to me quick, 'cause I can feel more trouble comin', and I need to know what to do."

Wes patted the dog on the head and stood up. He went

over to the well and splashed cold water on his hands and face, hoping to ease the pain, but it held on tightly. *Just one more thing to gnaw on,* he thought.

# Chapter 15
Monday Morning, May 14

In the ditch beside Mark's store, a sandy brown doe stood watch as her spotted fawn grazed on the damp grass that had sprung up following last week's rain. When she heard a dog bark nearby, she led the fawn out of the ditch and down the road to the woods. The sun filtering through the trees speckled the side of the building as the animals disappeared into the trees. The few clouds overhead picked up the glow of the rising sun, and a gentle, puff-like breeze carried a medley of scents through the slowly awakening town. The aromas of cooking side-meat, brewing coffee and dew-covered roses blended with the rank smells of manure, outhouses and the coal fire of the blacksmith shop.

The town was the economic heart of this part of the county and the reservoir of all the information that its citizens needed to carry on with their lives. Spring in the Black Patch could be a wonderful time, and on this particular day it seemed that even the most cynical of its residents would have agreed that life was good. J.D. Hooper, probably the most sardonic man in town, was thinking how good this day was going to be. He and Charley had made their list for Jones and were looking forward to sharing it with him when he came to town. Plodding along slowly, the two farmhands rode side by side in the middle of the road. Neither of them had spoken since leaving the shack. J.D. was enjoying the silence; Charley, as always, was afraid of saying something that would upset his partner and had spent most of the ride thinking they were headed for trouble playing both sides of the tobacco war. So, when J.D. broke the silence, Charley squawked out an unmanly "Huh?"

"I said, how come you're bein' so quiet? This is gonna be a great day. We're gettin' some money from Jones, we're gonna go over to Art West's and find out when he wants us back workin' on his place and then we need to find the captain and see what plans he's got for any night work."

"I know all that," Charley said. "I'm just worried someone's gonna find out we're dealin' with the Trust and with the Association."

"How's anyone gonna find out? We ain't gonna tell anybody. Besides, Jones don't care if we are, and he sure ain't gonna tell either, is he?"

"No, I guess not."

"Then stop worryin'. You're beginnin' to sound like an old woman." J.D. was silent for a moment and then added, "If the worst thing happens and the Association finds out, all we gotta do is get outta here. We've got these horses, and we'll have our money from Jones. Hell, we could be in Arkansas in a few days and they'd never find us."

Charley looked over at J.D., his face pale-gray with shock. "But they'd hang us for stealin' the horses."

"No they wouldn't. They'd probably shoot us for double-dealin' before we ever ended up in court. You know what the Night Riders did over in Christian County. Do you think this bunch would be any different if they knew we'd helped Jones?" J.D. waited while Charley settled down. "So go ahead and fret if you want, but keep it to yourself, and let me do the talkin' and plannin'."

J.D.'s show of confidence did nothing to quench Charley's agony. When they left the shack that morning, he thought he would enjoy the quiet ride, the singing birds and the warmth of the morning sun. But now he felt like he was headed for a funeral. *I just hope it ain't mine.*

As they passed the Lynnville sign, J.D. spoke up, his voice harsh. "Listen, Charley, I don't want your frettin' to mess this up for me. If you want out, then you better do it now. I—we—got a chance to make some money from Jones, from West and maybe even from the Association if they do another raid, and I ain't gonna let you ruin it. So you need to tell me if you're in or out, and you need to tell me now."

Charley stared straight ahead, silent, brooding. J.D. hadn't threatened him, but it sure felt like he had. Sweat ran down his back, chilling him, and he shuddered. He heard his own heart pounding beneath his shirt and then swallowed hard and turned to J.D., his face blank. "I'm in."

* * *

Mollie had just finished clearing the dishes after dinner and found a seat at the table next to Art. He said, "I'm glad you're feelin' better. I've got somethin' I need to tell you."

"What is it, Art?"

He looked at her across the table, one hand holding hers and the other gripping a cup of hot coffee. He paused a moment to listen to the children in the back of the house and said, "It's about us—you and me and the children."

Mollie squeezed his hand and smiled, her soft lips turning up at the edges. Her cheeks had turned a pale rose color, and her irises were blue again, shaded by her lashes. Art returned the squeeze, grateful that she felt better and amazed that she loved him.

"There's been a lot goin' on while you were sick." He went on to tell her everything he could recall—about overhearing J.D. and Charley, about Jones and even about the killing in Christian County. Art also told her that he was working with Wes to gather as much information as they could before they made a decision. "But I can't wait anymore, Mollie, I just can't. The only way I can protect you and the children is to join. If we got raided because I waited too long, I'd never forgive myself. I've got to join up even if Wes doesn't."

"I understand, Art." She looked directly at her husband. "It's hurting you to go against Wes, isn't it?"

Art shook his head in wonder at his wife's insight. "It does hurt, because he's always been my friend and always trusted me." Then he paused, shuddering a little before he spoke again. "I kept something from him, Mollie. I heard something that I should have told him about, but I was afraid to. I thought that he might do something bad if he knew what I did. Now, if I do tell him, he'll wonder why I kept the information from him for so long."

"But he'll understand that you have your reasons, won't he? Isn't he tryin' to do the same for his family?"

"I think so, but some of the things he's talkin' about doin' don't make sense. I don't understand why it's takin' him so long to decide that joinin' up is the only way for him to keep his farm and his family and his friends. I just don't understand."

"Art, if you knew everythin' that was in Wes's head and heart right now, then maybe you'd wait. If you think you owe it to him to wait until after the meetin' on Wednesday, then do it. Honor the friendship and give him the few more days."

They sat quietly, listening to the sounds from the back of the house. Sunlight filtered through the curtains and the colored glass bottles that Mollie had set on the window sill. The breeze carried in the honeysuckle's gift, and its sweetness seemed to cover them like a blanket. Mollie kept holding Art's hand, feeling his strength. "Are you scared of Wes or what he might do?"

Art flinched at the question and turned to face her. "What do you mean?"

"I guess I'm just wonderin' if the way he's actin' scares you."

"I'm not afraid of Wes, and I don't think he'll do anythin' to harm the people he loves. He just ain't himself right now."

Art wanted to tell her that he wasn't afraid of Wes or anything. But in his heart he knew that something was going on with Wes, something that maybe was a bit frightening. Besides, he didn't want Mollie worrying so soon after she'd started feeling better.

"I love you, Mollie, and I'll do everythin' I can to take care of you." He thought for a moment and then added, "I got to think some more on this, but I'll let you know what I'm gonna do before I do it." He pushed the chair back up to the table and stood up. "But now I need to get out into the field to see what needs doin' and then try to get them boys back here to work." He walked to the door, pulled his hat off the peg and shoved it onto his head. Art turned to Mollie, smiled and walked out the door.

* * *

J.D. figured that Jones would come down the main road from Mayfield. When he and Charley finished their business in town, they headed back north and waited in a shady copse of trees about two miles north of Lynnville. They wanted to stay off the road so they wouldn't be seen by any of the Night Riders and near their shack in case Jones wanted some privacy before he started calling on the farmers. The leaves and branches of the trees kept away some of the growing afternoon heat, but the puddles of water left over from the rain made the air soggy. Both men were sweating, and Charley was violently swatting at the young, hungry mosquitoes.

"How long we gotta wait in this god-awful place, J.D.? These bugs are drivin' me crazy." Charley emphasized his discomfort with a loud slap on his forearm. "Damned mosquitoes. It's way too early for 'em to be out. It ain't even June yet."

"Why don't you just shut up? They ain't that bad, and besides, we need to stop Jones before he gets into town."

"I know, but ain't there a better place to wait?"

"I'll tell you what," said J.D., "why don't you go out and stand on the road and put up a sign. Then if any of the Night Riders see you, they can just shoot you without askin' any questions." He paused to slap at a bug and added, "Better yet, don't make a sign; just wait until Jones gets here and then let someone from the Association see you two havin' a sit-down meetin'. Whatta you think?"

"Now, come on, J.D. You know I didn't mean nothin'. I just wanna get this over with and get our money. There ain't no way I wanna be seen with him by anyone from the Association—members or Night Riders."

"Then shut up until he gets here, and if the bugs keep eatin' on you, why don't you just rub on some of that sweet smellin' puddle mud? That'll keep 'em from chewin' on that ugly face of yours."

Charley sat down on the spongy ground and leaned back against an oak tree. He pulled his hat down over his ears and his hands up inside his shirt sleeves. Crossing his arms, he stopped talking and just mumbled. J.D. lit up the stub of a cigar and blew the acrid smoke on his arms and hands. That solved the problem for him, but he didn't think it was necessary to tell Charley about the remedy he'd discovered. For the next hour, Charley slapped, J.D. puffed and they both sweated.

When J.D. finally heard a horse clopping down the road from the north, he peered around the tree he'd been leaning against and spotted Jones. He reached down and picked up a stone and tossed it at Charley. "Here he comes; let's get out there," he whispered and started out of the woods. He waited until Jones was nearly alongside them and then walked out onto the road.

"Mr. Jones," he said, startling the man and his horse,

"Hold up there, we need to talk before you go into town."

Jones pulled back on the reins and kept his horse from galloping down the road. "Damn it, man. Why don't you give a person a warning before you jump out at him like a bandit?"

"Yeah, well, we don't need to be seen by anyone from around here. It wouldn't do you or us a bit of good to get caught talkin' about tobacco out on the road."

"All right, then," Jones grumbled. "Where can we talk in private?"

J.D. stayed at the edge of the tree line and gave him directions to their place, telling Jones that he and Charley would cut across the fields and be at the shack when he got there. Jones verified the directions with J.D. and started down the road. The two men untethered their horses and took off across a fallow field in the direction of Ol' Man Smith's property. J.D. figured it'd take Jones about ten minutes if he followed the instructions he'd given him, and he and Charley could get there in half that time.

The broken-down shack was about fifty yards off a farm road nearly a half mile from the county road. It was hidden by some old oaks and was nearly invisible because of its faded boards. They put their horses in the small pen at the back of the building and waited for Jones. When J.D. saw the tobacco buyer coming down the farm road, he stepped out of the trees and guided him toward the shack.

With controlled sarcasm, Jones said, "This is quite a place you have here." He looked around the yard at the piles of trash and broken farm implements and added, "A regular little cottage in the woods."

"It'll work just fine for the business we gotta do. Tie your horse to that post and come on in," he said, turning away from Jones, bending over and walking into the shack.

Jones hesitated in front of the short doorway. Not sure what he'd find inside, he thought, *Nothing ventured noth-*

*ing gained,* took of his derby and went in.

"Have a seat," said J.D.

Jones looked around the tiny room for a chair, but there were none. The only place open for him was on one of the two pallets that served as beds. He took out his kerchief and dusted off something that looked like mouse droppings, frowned as he sniffed the air and sat down. The two men sat across from him on the other pallet, watching him and waiting for him to speak.

"So, gentlemen, here we are, meeting in your secret hideout, away from the prying eyes of the men you fear." He put his derby on his lap and waited for a response, but all he got was blank stares. "I assume that you have something you'd like to share with me. A list, perhaps?"

J.D. spoke before Charley had a chance to say something stupid. "Look, Mr. Jones, I know this ain't some fancy hotel, but you gotta understand that what we're doin' could get all of us, includin' you, in a lot of trouble. This is the only safe place we know, so why don't we get down to business, and then you can get out of here."

"That sounds like a great plan. What have you got for me?"

J.D. turned to Charley and put his hand out, waiting for the list his partner held crushed in his hand. He took a second to smooth out the wrinkled piece of paper bag and handed it to Jones. While the buyer scanned the poorly written list of names and locations, J.D. told him what they'd discovered in the few days since they last met.

"There's four names on the list, and we've marked down where they live. All four of 'em are pretty desperate and need money to get through this year. We think the one on the bottom of the list is pretty ripe and may be your best chance to make a deal. He's got a bunch of kids, so he could really use the money. All of them fellas are afraid of the Night Riders and maybe they should be." He looked quickly at Charley. "But we figure they'd jump at the chance to sell their crop and wouldn't care if they had to clear out after harvest."

"According to our arrangement, I owe you fifty cents for each of these names. If any of them sells me his crop, then I'll owe you another fifty cents." He reached into the breast pocket of his coat and pulled out a folded leather wallet. "That means I owe you two dollars," he said, handing the paper bills to J.D. "If any of these men decide to work with me, how will I find you to pay the additional money?"

"Don't worry, we'll know and we can find you." J.D. shoved the money into his shirt pocket. "Now, you better take off and get into town. You need to be damned sure that you don't tell anyone where you got those names, 'cause if we get found out, we'll know that you're the only one who could've put our names out there." He looked at Jones, expecting to see fear, but was surprised by the man's lack of it.

"J.D., is it? Well, J.D., I've been doing this type of business for a long time, and I've never revealed one of my . . . informants. I know how to keep a secret, and I always pay what I promise." He folded the list, slipped it into his wallet and returned it to his coat pocket. He looked across the crowded little room at each of them and then said, "I suspect that things would get very difficult for you gentlemen if word got out that you were, shall we say, helping the enemy, so I think it would be wise for each of us to keep our promises and to tell no one of our agreement." Jones paused and said, "Wouldn't you agree?"

"I agree," Charley blurted out.

J.D. looked at Charley, clearly annoyed, and turned to Jones. "Agreed."

"Good. Well then, gentlemen, I need to get on into the metropolis of Lynnville and get started on my work day. If you'll excuse me, I'll leave you to your business." He got up from the pallet, brushed off the back of his pants and ducked out through the door. Putting on his hat, he walked straight to his horse and pulled himself onto the saddle. He tipped his derby to them, spun the large bay around and rode out of the yard.

When Jones was out of sight, J.D. turned to Charley, planning to give him hell for speaking up, but changed his mind. He pulled the money from his pocket and gave one of the dollars to Charley. "Here, just keep your mouth shut and quit acting so scared. If you didn't always look like that, the fear on your face would give us away in a minute. Now get outta here and leave me alone for a while." He went back into the shack and slammed the door. Charley looked at the money in his hand and thought, *thirty pieces of silver,* and rushed off to the outhouse, feeling a sudden pain in his gut.

\* \* \*

As pleased as he was with the corn and wheat crops, when Wes looked at his five acres of tobacco, his thoughts turned not to satisfaction, but to his own deception. He was tired of pretending. The mask was growing heavy, and it added to the host of problems squeezing their way into his thoughts. He yearned for peace, but his brain never rested. Wes had tried as hard as he could to create a visual image of himself as being in control, no longer afraid or confused. He tried to keep his voice softer and less harsh. He smiled rather than frowned, asked rather than told, and most of the family gladly accepted the change. Only Zora and Anthie seemed doubtful when they looked at him.

Even if Wes suspected their caution, he couldn't acknowledge it without revealing the falseness of his act. He had to keep up the charade and hope that his wife and son would begin to believe him. But in his head, like a pack of dogs fighting over a captured rabbit, his thoughts circled, snarled and growled for control of his mind. Each of the dogs was hungry and wanted a piece of him. The possible riches of Jones's offer, the risk of shunning by his friends and the danger posed by the Night Riders kept snapping at him. He couldn't run from them, nor could he hide. Wes had to face them head-on and would, if only he knew how. But for the moment, he just stood in his field and stared into the woods.

# Chapter 16
Monday Evening, May 14

Red Miller had told the Night Rider captains to meet at his place on Monday evening. One by one they came through the great wooden gate at the entrance to the farm and rode down the lane. They passed dozens of acres of dark green tobacco plants spread out on the russet brown dirt; each neat row glowed in the light of the setting sun. Along one side of the lane, three thoroughbred geldings grazed in a lush pasture behind a white rail fence.

After passing the large white house, they dismounted and tied their horses to the post next to the barn and walked into the tool shed. From a hook on a crossbeam, a single lantern glowed, casting strange shadows on the men already gathered around an old plow.

"We've got ourselves a problem," Red said, looking at the men. "Not enough of the farmers around here are joinin' up. Best I can tell is maybe half of 'em have committed, and that clearly ain't enough if we're gonna force the Trust to give us a fair price." He paused, smoothing his bushy mustache. "You fellas have any ideas why they're holdin' back?"

"Only thing I can figure is that Trust buyer, Jones, is stirrin' up some trouble," replied one of the men. "We know he's been out to a bunch of the farms, talkin' prices with some of the hillbillies."

"Anybody heard any numbers?" Red asked.

"Nothin' specific," said another man, "but they've likely been high enough to interest some of the farmers."

"We could maybe cause that tobacco buyer a little trouble, couldn't we Red?" said the first speaker.

"What do you mean?"

"Well, maybe we could get a few fellas together and rough him up a bit. That'd slow him down, wouldn't it?"

Red nodded, and then he paused and lit a cigar. He blew a smoke ring up toward the lantern and said, "Let me think some more on that. In the meantime, we got another problem, but it may not be as bad as it seems. What those fellas did over in Christian County was foolish. I want you to make it clear to all of our Riders that I won't stand for any killin' by any of 'em." He searched each of their faces, looking for agreement. When he was sure that they understood, he continued.

"However, I think we can use the threat of what they did to get more of these hillbillies to quit stallin' and join us. I want a raid early next week to show 'em we mean business, but I'm not sure yet whose place we'll hit. I heard that Wes Wilson's gonna be at our meetin' on Wednesday. If he joins up, then we'll raid someone else. If he doesn't, then we'll hit his farm. He's a strong and ornery son of a bitch, but the farmers sure like him; so if we can convince him to join, then these other fellas'll fall in line. If we can't change his mind, we'll have to make an example of him—teach him a harsh lesson." He shoved his hands into his pockets, clearly thinking about something.

"Just in case, though, we'll need to get a few names together so we have an alternate target if Wilson does join. I was thinkin' that we get some of the Riders to listen around and see if they can find anyone who's thinkin' of sellin' out to the Trust. I'll put up some money, but I can't be seen makin' the deal with 'em."

"I'll do it, Red," said the youngest of the group. "There's a couple of the fellas we've used before who live near me. I think they'd be willin' to do it."

"Good. Here's five dollars for each of 'em. See if you can set this up tonight, but be sure to do it no later than tomorrow. Tell 'em that you need a list before Wednesday night's meetin'."

As the men turned to go, he stopped them. "Be sure to pass the word to the Riders that we'll be doin' somethin' next week, and remind 'em that we won't be killin' any farmers."

Red watched them leave and reached up to pull down the lantern. He lifted up the glass and blew out the flame. Then he walked over to his front porch. Before going in the house, he turned and looked at his vast tobacco fields, thinking that someday he'd defeat the Trust. "Someday soon, I hope," he murmured and walked into the house.

* * *

Charley and J.D. were sitting outside the shack in the growing darkness, listening to the crickets and supplementing their meager meal with occasional sips from the jug they'd bought with the money from Jones.

"I hate beans," said Charley. Using a scrap of bread, he scooped the last few off his tin plate.

"Beans are cheap, Charley, and until you get the inheritance from your rich uncle, you're gonna have to get used to 'em." J.D. was trying to cheer Charley up, but his tone of voice was gruff.

"I ain't got a rich uncle and you know it." Charley threw the plate on the ground. "Why do you always have somethin' mean to say to me? I thought we were partners."

"We're partners, all right. We been through some ugly times together, ain't we?" J.D. said, waiting to see how Charley would respond. "I been thinkin' that we need to clear out of this town in the next couple of weeks. Things're gettin' complicated, and if we're not real careful, we'll find ourselves in jail. After what Jones said today, I trust him even less than I did before. If he lets anyone know we gave him some names, we'll be in more trouble than just bein' locked up."

"We gotta make some more money before we can leave," Charley replied. "And Art West ain't asked us to come back to work on his farm since it rained."

"If some solid work don't come up this week, we'll take what we got and move on." The crickets stopped chirping and J.D. quit talking when he heard a noise. "Rider comin'," he said and reached into his coat for his pistol. The faint sound of hooves on the dirt road faded and then stopped.

"Hello in the house," shouted the rider.

"That's the captain," whispered Charley. "What's he doin' here?"

J.D. shushed him and stood up. Not sure why the man had come to the shack and fearing there might be trouble, he leaned in close to Charley's ear and said, "Wait'll I get around the side of the shack and then tell him to come on in." He crept around the corner of the sagging building and waited.

"Come on in," yelled Charley, trying to sound relaxed.

The captain got down off his horse and walked the animal into the yard in front of the shack. "Evenin', Charley. Where's J.D.? I got some business we need to talk about."

"Right here, Captain," said J.D. as he walked around to the front of the shack. "I was in the outhouse. What's up?" He kept his hand on the pistol in his pocket.

"I wanted to let you know that we're gonna be doin' a raid next week. Don't have a day yet, but you need to be ready for some night work." He moved closer to the two men and added in a softer voice, "But I've got another piece of business I need you to do for me. There's some extra money in it if you're willin' to do the job."

"We can always use money," said J.D. "What do you want us to do?"

For the next five minutes, the Night Rider told them about making the list of farmers talking to Jones and the Wednesday night deadline. When they agreed to do the job, he gave J.D. the ten dollars and reminded both of them of the oath they'd taken. "Nobody knows about this but us three, so you gotta keep it to yourselves."

After he rode off, they sat outside the shack in near darkness. The only light was a lantern's orange glow seeping through the cracks in the walls of the shack. The surrounding trees were black against the early night sky.

"Are you sure you wanna do this?" said Charley.

"What? Of course I wanna do it. With this money and what we'll get after next week's raid, we can get out of Lynnville. If we can get some work with Art West for another couple of days, we'll be able to leave the whole damned state by the end of next week." J.D. was strutting around the yard, energized by the possibilities he saw in the situation. Smiling broadly, he nearly shouted, "We don't even need to do any more work than we've already done. We can just give the captain the same names we gave Jones."

"I don't know, J.D."

"What do you mean you don't know? This is perfect. All we've gotta do is keep quiet. Jones ain't gonna say anythin', and neither will the captain. We'll get the money and pull out of here on them two nags out back. No one'll miss us, Charley."

"But if someone does say somethin', we're not just in trouble, we're dead."

"Didn't you hear what I just said?" he growled. "The two other people who know ain't gonna say a word. If anythin' does get out, I'll make sure that the fella who couldn't keep his damn mouth shut won't ever open it again." He moved over to where Charley was leaning against the shed and shoved him against the wall. He leaned in close, their noses almost touching. Charley tried to back away, but he couldn't move. He could smell the stink of J.D.'s breath and his own sweat, and he flinched when J.D. spoke.

"Just shut up and do what I say," he said, putting his fist against Charley's face.

Charley turned his head aside, away from the faint light of the lantern and J.D.'s terrible, empty eyes. He'd never been afraid of him before, but this time he knew J.D. was serious.

"I understand. Now back off a little, I gotta go to the outhouse."

J.D. stepped back and watched Charley scuttle around the corner of the shack. "You better understand," he mumbled. "You damned better understand and not mess this up for me."

* * *

The crescent moon had crawled low in the sky by the time Wes headed into town for the meeting at Mark's. The faint silvery glow made the ride easier and allowed him more time to think. The mask had become a heavy burden, and he was tired of forcing his smiles. But away from Zora and the children, he could shed the disguise, and the relief was almost physical. Still, he felt smothered by his problems. A knot had formed in his belly, and his guts felt twisted. His head pounded whenever he was awake, and no matter how hard he tried, he couldn't get the dry, gritty, burning feeling out of his eyes. *But I'm a farmer,* he thought, *and farmers ain't got time to be tired or sick.* He nudged the mule with his heel as he rounded the curve in the road and approached the lights of Lynnville.

Lantern light glowed from inside the store on the south end of town. Wes tied the reins to the porch rail and glanced across the road. Off to one side of the door, barely lit by the lights from inside the hotel, a man sat smoking a cigar. *Hunh,* thought Wes, *I wonder what he's doin' in town. Me*

*and him are gonna have to talk about the lies he's been tellin'
and talk about 'em soon—but not tonight.* As Wes turned to
go into the store, Jones tipped his derby at him and drew
deeply on the cigar, the tip flaring and lighting up his face.

"Lock the door, Wes," said Mark from the back of the
store. "Art's already here. You want some coffee?"

Wes slid the bolt toward the door frame and pulled
down the shade. "Yeah, I'll take a cup." He walked between
the shelves of goods toward the stove. "Evenin', cousin," he
said to Art's back.

Art looked over his shoulder and nodded. "Have a seat,
Wes. How was the ride?"

"It was fine." He took a cup from the shelf and wrapped
a rag around the metal handle of the coffeepot. He poured
the cup half full and sat in a chair next to Art and stared
at him for a moment. "You're lookin' pretty ragged, Art. Is
Mollie doin' any better?"

"Actually, she's doin' a lot better, and thanks for the com-
pliment, cousin. I notice you ain't shaved in a week, and you
don't smell real good, but I won't say anythin' since I don't
wanna embarrass you in front of your handsome brother."

"Don't you two get me in the middle of any argument tonight; I got enough on my plate with Gertrude. That woman is gonna drive me to my grave."

Art and Wes exchanged knowing looks. They sipped
their coffees while he settled into the other chair near the
stove. He poured himself some of the hot liquid and looked
at his kin. "What have you fellas decided to do about your
tobacco crops?"

"Slow down a minute, will ya?" said Art. "We just got
here. We have to think about hard work and problems all
the time, so we actually look forward to comin' by here and
hearin' about how happy you are runnin' a store and bein'
married to the love of your life."

"I don't see the humor in that, and I won't have you sayin' anythin' bad about . . . " he hesitated and said with a grin, "my store." It took a moment for the others to catch on, but when they did, all three of them roared with laughter. Making fun of one another was something they'd always done, and Wes, for one, had missed it since the tobacco trouble began. They laughed about Connie and Maud, and Art even joked that maybe Connie would love his wife like Mark loved his store. For the next quarter hour they forgot about their troubles and enjoyed being friends. But the warmth and peace couldn't last while Art was upset by Wes's lies and Wes was angry about Art's Night Rider secret.

"Shall we get down to business, boys?" Mark poured everyone another cup of coffee. "What are you gonna do about your crops?"

Wes's smile faded, and Art's face darkened. They watched each other, neither wanting to speak first. Mark looked at them, knowing they were troubled, but unaware of the secrets they held back from each other.

Wes finally broke the silence. "I still don't know what to do. The Morrises, Anthie's girl's folks, are joinin' the Association. So is George, at least that's what he told me. The killin' has scared 'em both."

"That killin's got me scared, too," said Art. "Mollie's gettin' better every day, but she's still not cured, and I got her and four little kids to think about." He paused a while, his face tense and knotted. "Sometimes it seems like joinin' would be the easiest thing to do. But I'm still willin' to wait until we're sure that it is."

Wes looked at Art and said, "I'm more mad than scared. Them Night Riders got no right to shoot a fella and in front of his family too. They're murderers, that's what they are. If they come around my house, they're gonna get a taste of it, but it'll be them that gets killed."

"Hold on, Wes," Mark interrupted. "That happened in some other county, not here. And we got the word out that you're goin' to the meetin' Wednesday, right? So you shouldn't be worried about the raid no more."

Art said, "Yeah, we're goin', but I don't know what else we'll learn at the meetin'. Survivin' is all I care about, and unless they got a plan for loanin' us money or buyin' our tobacco, a bunch of us're gonna lose a lot."

"Art's right," said Wes. He turned to Art. "I know you got a sick wife and your kids are young. Most of mine are grown up, and Zora's doin' just fine, but I still worry about 'em. It would be easy to just give up and join the Association. It'd be easy to think about havin' lots of money after harvest, too."

Surprised, Mark sat back in his chair. "Joinin' might be the best thing to do, Wes." Mark couldn't believe that Wes would actually consider selling his tobacco.

"It might," he said sitting up straighter in the chair. "But I'll tell you this, and I know you've heard me say it before. I ain't gonna let anybody tell me what to do about my family or my crop. They ain't got the right to force me to do anythin'. If, and I do mean if, I decide to sell my crop to that lyin' son of a bitch Jones, then I'll do it, and anyone who tries to stop me or scare me or hurt my family will pay hard." Wes was trembling, his hands clenched, his lips a straight slash across his face.

Mark thought, *Someday that man's pride is gonna get him hurt real bad.*

Mark stood up, hoping to break the tension. "I know that I ain't got much to add to this since I don't own a farm. But you're both family, and I don't want either of you doin' anythin' that'll get you hurt or run out of town. Promise me you'll both be real careful about what you do and what you say."

Art finally spoke up. "Let's do this: we'll go to the meetin' and find out whatever they got to say about loans or money. If we hear anythin' about the Night Riders between now and then, we get a message to each other." He stopped and looked directly at Wes, waiting until his cousin looked at him. "I promise you this, Wes: even though I'm leanin' toward joinin', I won't make a decision until after Wednesday night."

Wes stared at Art, his slate-gray face rigid, still trembling. "Thanks, Art," was all he could say for a moment. "I'll see you on Wednesday."

"All right," said Art. "In the meantime, let's all stay in touch. We need to know everythin' we can before Wednesday night."

"You both know that I'll do whatever I can to help if you get in trouble," Mark said.

Both Wes and Art nodded and stood up, and the three men shook hands. Wes thanked Mark for letting them meet in the store, and then he and Art walked out the door, mounted up and headed to their farms.

* * *

The moon bathed the farmyard in a silvery blue glow, and the cool wind blowing across the fields brought with it the scents of growing crops to the porch where Wes and Zora sat. Around her shoulders, Zora wore a woolen shawl and clutched it close against her throat. Rufus lay at her feet, his head resting on her shoes. The rhythm of his tail as it swished across the porch wood created an exotic harmony with the breeze.

Wes sat slumped on the edge of the porch, his feet resting in the scrub grass of the yard. His hands clutched the whiskey jug in his lap, while the shotgun lay on the wood next to him. In the hour he'd been home, he hadn't taken a drink. He'd pulled the cork several times and even lifted the jug to his lips once, but he didn't drink from it. He wanted to take a drink; oh Lord he truly wanted to, but he fought it hard. Despite the quietness of the night, his ears buzzed like an army of crickets. His muscles quivered, vibrated, pulsed with some internal, almost painful energy, and his mind would not rest. Everything that he'd worried about and thought about for the past week fought for his attention. The thoughts wouldn't go away, the voices wouldn't shut up and they wouldn't let him rest. From deep below the noise, his voice fought to be heard. It sounded like it came from a child, a weary, hurting child. "I'm so tired," it said. "I don't know what to do. I just wanna rest."

Zora usually enjoyed nights like this when she and Wes could relax after a hard day of working and dealing with the commotion that having six children generated. But on this night, she was not relaxed. She needed to talk to Wes, and even though she knew that pushing him to talk would probably lead to an argument, she decided to take the chance.

"Wes, what did you talk about at Mark's tonight?" Her voice was soft and clear and flat.

Wes didn't speak up right away. He knew where this conversation was heading and what it could do to Zora if he lost his temper. He was worn out from the ride and didn't have the energy to wear the mask and pretend. He just couldn't do it anymore. When he turned to face her and the words finally came, they poured out of him—hot, loud and full of anger. "Damn it, Zora, we talked about tobacco and murder! We talked about sick wives and hurt kids! We talked about how hard it is to make decisions when nothin' seems to make any sense and none of the choices we have are any good. You don't know how hard it is to decide between feedin' your kids or losin' your friends; or decidin' between protectin' your property against Night Riders and then losin' it when you run out of money. All of that's my job, my responsibility and I gotta think about it all of the damn time."

He paused and his voice, though still angry, softened a

little. "And I'm so damned tired, I can't think anymore."

Zora felt pinned to the wall by his angry words. She knew that they were unfair and selfish. She wanted to lash out at him and tell him he was wrong, but didn't want to drive him into doing something like his own father had done. So she swallowed her own bitter anger and, her voice hushed, said, "You're wrong, Wes, about so many things. We're a family, you and me, and we can decide this together."

"No, Zora, we can't," said Wes, his pride taking over. "This is my problem. Only I can choose what to do." He stood up, holding the jug in his left hand, and reached down to pick up the shotgun. "Now go on back into the house and leave me alone."

She watched as he headed across the yard and into the tobacco field, disappearing in the darkness.

* * *

Zora rose quickly from her shattered sleep and sat stunned on the edge of the bed. Thinking that the explosion sounded like a gunshot, she started to rise and then heard footsteps outside the door.

"Ma, what was that? Are you all right?" The urgency in Connie's voice added to her fear. "I'm goin' to the kitchen to see what that was. Pa's out there, ain't he?"

"No, wait son. I'll go with you."

When they got to the kitchen, Zora peeked through the window and saw Wes fumbling in the dark, struggling to load his shotgun. Before she could stop him, Connie opened the door.

"I dropped the damn gun, and it went off," Wes yelled. "Now get on back in the house." When Connie hesitated, he shouted, "Damn it, I said to get back in the house."

Zora heard a whisper from behind her. "Ma?"

She turned and saw Mary Lula standing in the dark hallway, holding the baby. Irene and John Stanley stood beside her, their eyes full of tears. Anthie spoke from behind the children. "It was just some stupid thing Pa did, wasn't it Ma?" Zora didn't respond, so he turned around and stomped upstairs to his room.

"I'll get that bastard next time, I swear I will," grumbled Wes, still fumbling with the shotgun shells.

# Chapter 17
Wednesday, May 16

Wes's brain felt numb as he sat on a stump in the door of the barn, puffing on a cigarette and letting the smoke drift from his nostrils. The smell of his own body blended in with the stink of the pigs and the pungent odor of mule and cow manure. His shirt reeked of the sweat that permeated the cloth, and the mud on his overalls had caked into a hard crust. Above his week-old beard, sores had broken out on the dry, flaky skin of his cheekbones. He scratched and picked at them with his ragged nails, causing them to bleed. Half a dozen flies circled his head, and several more gathered on the crotch of his pants. He'd eaten little food for the past few days, and the only things he'd had to drink were sour whiskey and bitter black coffee. His mouth tasted and smelled bad. He just didn't care. He took one more drag from the cigarette and dropped it on the ground, kicking some of the coarse dirt over it.

All three of the boys were out in the cornfield picking weeds. John Stanley anxiously moved through each row, doing much more than his pa had expected of him. Connie managed to work hard at the task, but he was just too focused on the idea of being married to Maud. Anthie, however, was simply putting in time in the field. His mind was clearly fixed on Sudie and getting away from the farm. *Why can't I get married,* he thought. *I'm sixteen, ain't I? Connie ain't that much older than me, and Ma and Pa got married young, too.* He yanked a corn plant out of the dirt and quickly put it back in the hole. *I'm glad Pa didn't see that,* he cringed, trying to pay closer attention to pulling weeds rather than corn.

Zora was praying in her room at the back of the house, and Mary Lula stood in the hallway outside the closed door, listening to the murmuring and occasional crying. Mary Lula was quiet and observant, and she was worried about her parents. She knew her pa was fretting about something and wasn't sleeping, and her ma had stopped laughing. She had promised her ma she would take care of the family and, wise beyond her eighteen years, she was keeping that promise.

Something fell on the floor upstairs. *I hope that wasn't Ruthie,* she thought. When she opened the door and peeked in, she saw that both girls were asleep on the bed. The wooden bowl that Ruthie'd been playing with lay upside down on the floor, and the dried beans she'd been stirring around inside it were spread in an arc across the hooked rug. Mary Lula smiled at the scene, thankful for her sisters. She stepped back out of the room and pulled the door shut. Sitting down on the top step, she closed her eyes and said a prayer for them, for her brothers and especially for her parents.

* * *

The early afternoon sun was bright on the road, but in the woods the light was speckled by the spring leaves on the trees. It wasn't any cooler there, since the breeze never made it past the first row of trees and scrub. J.D. and Charley waited for the Night Rider captain. They had met him in similar places over the past few months, but always at night, never during the day.

"I hope he gets here soon," Charley said. "I ain't likin' this one bit."

"Just quit your whinin', Charley. He'll get here. We'll give him the list, and then we can lay low until the meetin' tonight."

"You don't think anyone'll see him ridin' off into the woods, do ya? Or maybe just waitin' to see who comes out of the woods after he leaves?" He sucked in a great draught of air. "We're walkin' dead men, that's what we are. We ain't been shot yet, but we're dead just the same."

J.D. leaned against an old ash tree, whittling on a broken branch he'd found in the rotting leaves that covered the ground. When he'd reduced the stick to white flakes of wood, he looked around for another. Charley paced between the trees, mumbling and sighing and regularly looking out to the road. The ring of sweat under his arms was growing darker against his faded shirt, and he kept wiping his face with a torn piece of an old flour sack.

"Will you stop movin' and sit down? 'Cause if you can't, then maybe I'll just shoot you myself."

"All right, all right," he said and sat on a fallen log. His voice had changed pitch and sounded like a squeaky saw cutting through wet wood. "I just wish he'd get here."

For nearly an hour, there was little activity on the road. Charley had about given up when he spotted the captain's horse turning toward the woods. "It's about damned time," Charley whispered so softly that even J.D. couldn't hear him.

"In here, Captain," J.D. said, stepping a short distance into the daylight. The captain just nodded at him. J.D. turned away and disappeared into the trees. The captain got down from his horse, threw the reins over a tree limb and walked to where J.D. stood.

"Before we talk about the list," the captain said, "I wanna let you know that we're gonna raid a farm here in Lynnville. After we look at your list, we'll decide who and when. As soon as I know, I'll find you or get word to you."

The two men nodded, and J.D. handed the slip of paper to the captain. He started to speak but was stopped when the captain held up his hand. He watched the captain scan the names quickly and then read the list again more slowly.

"How sure are you that these fellas are considerin' sellin' their crops?"

"Well, of the four names on there, we're sort of sure about three of 'em," said J.D. "The name at the bottom of the list is one we're real sure about 'cause we heard someone mention his name at the hotel. We also heard from some other fellas that he's been talkin' to that buyer named Jones."

"You're real sure, you say? Sure enough to talk to someone higher up in the Association if necessary?"

"Yes sir, real sure," said J.D. Charley started to say something, but J.D. silenced him with a piercing look.

"Good, then. The fellas in charge are gonna be pleased with the work you've done. I'll be givin' 'em the list tonight at the meetin'." He looked at each of them and said, "It's okay for you two to be at the meetin' place tonight, but don't come inside or let any fellas see you hangin' around. If I need you, I'll step outside the door and give you a whistle. When you hear it, stay in the shadows and slip inside when no one's watchin'."

"All right, Captain. We'll be there. The meetin' starts at seven o'clock, right?"

"Yeah, seven, but don't you worry about bein' on time; it'd probably be better if you came a little later. That way all of the members and any visitors'll already be inside the church." He climbed up on his horse and settled into the saddle. He looked at their sullen faces and then rode out of the woods and headed back toward town.

"Why'd you tell him we're sure about Wes Wilson?" Charley's voice had risen to a girl-like pitch. "We ain't any surer about him than we are of the others. God almighty, J.D., we're gonna end up gettin' killed by the Night Riders, and if they don't do it, Wilson surely will." He started pacing again, and this time he was panting like a hard-ridden horse. "We're dead men," he said again.

"Shut up, Charley. We ain't dead yet. I got a plan that'll maybe get us some more money. I'm still workin' on the details, but by the time we get over to Art West's place, I'll have it figured out. Let's get goin'; I wanna be there before it gets too late."

J.D. got up on his horse and rode the animal out of the woods. Charley pulled his horse by the reins out into the sun. He climbed into the saddle and followed J.D. up the road toward Art's farm.

* * *

Art's corn and wheat fields were in good shape; he'd spent most of yesterday walking the rows and clearing away what few weeds had found a home in the dark dirt. The garden he tended while Mollie healed was also progressing. The sweet corn, snap bean, okra and potato leaves grew larger every day, and the wire fence he'd built around the garden was keeping the rabbits away. He'd even caught a rabbit in one of his traps, and they'd enjoyed it for last night's supper. Yesterday had been a good day, and despite his worries about Wes, he had slept well.

Today wasn't going as well. After milking the cow and feeding the hogs and chickens, he and Clarence went out to the tobacco field and found weeds in most of the rows. The pesky plants weren't taking over, but there were far too many of them for him and his son to clear out by themselves.

"Can we get 'em all, Pa?" With a confident smile, Clarence looked up at his father.

Art stood at the end of one of the worst rows, his hands shoved down in the pockets of his overalls and the brim of his hat drooped over the irritated look on his face. He walked to his right and checked out the next few rows. Taking the same pose and frown as his pa, Clarence followed him, looking at the weeds.

"I wish we could, son, but I think we're gonna need some help. You an' me an' Thressie could probably get a lot of 'em, but we'd have to be out here every day from sunup to sundown. Even then we'd be doin' it for a month and then have to start all over to get the ones growin' up behind us." He shook his head slowly and then moved further along to the right toward the tree line and found those rows were the same. "Yep, son, we're gonna need some help." *I just can't get a break,* he thought.

Art looked down at his son and smiled when he noticed the boy's posture and the innocence that showed through the frown he'd forced on his face. "But standin' here talkin' about weeds don't get 'em out of the ground. So, here's what we're gonna do. Let's go back to the barn and get us a couple of hoes and a pail of drinkin' water. Then we'll get on back out here and see how many of them weeds we can kill before supper. That'll help me figure out how much help we're gonna need. What do you think, son? Does that sound like a good plan?"

Clarence's face wrinkled in a childish frown as he turned from looking at the weeds toward his pa. "I think that's a good plan, Pa."

Art reached down for Clarence's hand and took it in his own. A feeling of pride and comfort nearly brought him to tears as they headed back to the barn, kicking the dirt clods at the edge of the field. Some of the dust clung to their sweaty arms, but without a breeze, most of it just settled back down on the ground. Art thought about how the rain had been welcome a few days ago, how it had drenched the plants with its healing moisture. He knew, though, that it had also watered the weeds that were invading the field.

On the way back to the house, Art's attention was drawn to the road when he saw two riders heading toward the farm. *It's J.D. and Charley,* he thought.

"You go on up to the house and see if you can help your ma," he said to Clarence. "I gotta do somethin.'"

"Okay, Pa," he said and ran off across the barnyard.

As usual, J.D. was riding in front and Charley lagged behind him. The closer they got to him the easier it was to see their faces. Even shadowed by his black felt hat, J.D.'s dark, unshaven face broadcast his smugness, his arrogance. J.D. always made Art feel uncomfortable, but Art got along with Charley and often wondered how two men whose personalities were so different had become partners. As they approached, Art could see that Charley looked troubled, maybe even afraid. His face was gloomy and sallow, and his sunken, bloodshot eyes made Art think about a dead man he'd once seen. *These two are Night Riders, and I don't want 'em anywhere near my family.*

They stopped their horses a few yards short of where he stood. When J.D. spoke, Art could tell that he was keeping his arrogance in check. His feigned courtesy was so out of character that if Art wasn't so afraid of him, he might have laughed; but he didn't.

"Good afternoon, Mr. West."

Art acknowledged him with a nod of his head.

"We were wonderin' if you might have a few days' work for us to do. We ain't been here since late last week and thought maybe you could use our help, your missus bein' sick and all."

"It might be that I could use your help, but you don't need to concern yourself with my wife or any of my family."

"I'm sorry, Mr. West. I meant no disrespect. But we'd surely like to get some work today. We're sort of in a bind and need some money."

J.D.'s words were cordial, but the truth of his feelings, the agony of having to beg, showed in his wrinkled brow and clenched jaw. Art knew that he was dealing with a dangerous man, but he needed help with the weeds in the tobacco, and these fellas could solve that problem.

Art watched Charley fidgeting in his saddle, wiping his face with an old rag.

"We might even be willin' to tell you somethin' important about your family if you'd hire us for the day," said J.D.

Art looked from J.D. to Charley and saw him wince at the words. Charley coughed and wiped his face again.

"I'm not interested in hearin' anythin' you got to say about my family right now, but if you wanna work, I'll pay you." He glared at J.D., using every bit of control he had not to reach into his pocket and pull out the pistol he'd been carrying since he and Wes had met last week. "So, do you wanna work or not?"

J.D. hesitated for a moment, not wanting to seem desperate, and said they'd take the work. Art told them he'd pay them for the rest of the day and the next if they could clear the tobacco field of weeds. There was no handshaking on the deal; the two hired hands just rode on to the barn to pick up the tools. Art followed them down the lane and watched them as they headed out to the field. *At least that chore will be done,* he thought, *and I can be done with those two for good.*

Art waited until he was sure they were working and then walked toward the house, wondering if he should tell Wes the truth about them before the meeting.

* * *

John Stanley looked back over his shoulder at Irene as she followed him off the porch and into the yard. Laughing and whooping like an Indian, he ran around to the far side of the pump, keeping his eyes on her and the broomstick she clutched in her hand. Screeching his name, she jumped off the porch, waving the stick like a saber, and chased him around the well.

"You're mean, John Stanley, you're—" She pulled up

short of the pump and dropped the stick.

"What's the matter? Are you scared of me? Come and get me, c'mon." He stopped his taunting when she didn't move. "What's wrong with you, Irene?"

She looked at her brother and then pointed at the man sitting on a tall horse at the head of the lane. John Stanley stared at her for a moment and then turned toward the road. In the bright afternoon sun, the bay glowed red and stood rigid, like the soldier statues in Mayfield. John Stanley didn't recognize the rider at all. The man wore a funny-looking round hat that made his head look like a newel post on a stair rail. When he saw that the rider was wearing a suit not at all like his own tattered overalls, he realized it was the man who'd given him the coin, the tobacco buyer Mr. Jones.

"Go in the house and find out where Pa is," he said to his sister. When she didn't move right away, he said it again, and she turned and dashed into the house. John Stanley ran toward Jones and stopped a few feet short of the horse.

"Mr. Jones," he said, gasping for air, "I think you oughta wait right there. I ain't sure my pa wants to see you."

"Well good afternoon to you too, young Mr. Wilson." Looking down at the slight boy from the saddle of the tall horse gave Jones a sense of power. "Although you seem quite sure of what your pa might want, I'm certain that he'll want to talk to me." He waited a moment while the boy panted. "Perhaps when you've recovered your breath, you could walk back to the house and get him. I'll even wait here, as you've suggested."

Looking at Jones's face, John Stanley saw the same falseness in the man's eyes he'd seen the week before. He didn't trust Jones and was pretty sure his pa didn't either. He nodded at the man, turned and raced back to the house. Irene had just stepped off the porch, headed for the barn.

"Ma says he's sleepin' in the barn. If he is, I don't wanna

have to wake him up."

"I'll do it," said John Stanley. "You go on back inside and tell Ma that Mr. Jones is back and she and the others oughta stay inside. Tell her that I'll get Pa to talk to him." This time he didn't have to say any more.

John Stanley walked from the sun-filled yard into the darkness of the barn. He spotted his pa sleeping on a pile of straw against the west wall. Both the cow and the mule acknowledged the boy's presence with grunts, but he paid them no attention. He crept toward his pa's makeshift bed and stopped a yard short of him. Wes wasn't moving, and John Stanley could smell the foul odor that seemed to rise from him like steam. His pa's face was pale and dirty, and there was blood on his cheeks. At first, John Stanley was worried; he even thought his pa might be dead. If Wes hadn't snored just then, the boy would probably have groaned and run for his ma.

"Pa," he whispered. He didn't want to have to shake him awake; he'd done that only once before, and he still remembered how his butt hurt after he'd been paddled. "Pa," he said again louder, "Mr. Jones is here, and he wants to talk to you."

"Huh? What's that?" Wes opened his gritty eyes and tried to focus on his son.

"I said Mr. Jones is here to see you. I told him to wait out at the road, but he says he wants to talk to you. Please, Pa."

Wes sat up and leaned back against the barn wall. "Mr. Jones is here?"

"Yeah, Pa. Do you want me to tell him to go away? I can do it, Pa. I don't like him very much."

"No, don't do that, son. It's okay, I'll see him, but I need to wake up." Wes tried to stand up and bumped his elbow against the wall. He winced, but didn't say anything. He looked around the barn, trying to orient himself. Shaking his head to clear the sleep from his brain, he told his son to go on back to the house. "I'll go talk to him. I want you to tell your ma to stay in the house."

"I already told Irene to do that, Pa. Can't I come out there with you?"

"No, son. You done good, but I need to see him alone. You go on now, and I'll see you back at the house in a bit." The mask felt heavy, its agonizing weight dragging him down.

John Stanley was disappointed. Wes could see it in the look on his face and the way his shoulders slumped as he turned and left the barn. Wes loved his son and knew the boy wanted to help, but he didn't want him to see or hear what might happen to Jones.

Rubbing the sore elbow and favoring his numb, buzzing left leg, Wes limped out of the barn, squinting against the glaring sunlight. He glanced left toward the house and saw Zora standing in the doorway with her hand on John Stanley's shoulder. When she turned and drew the boy into the house, Wes headed down the lane toward the road.

He watched Jones dismount the bay and brush the dust from his clothes. Wes wasn't sure what he was going to say or do to Jones. He wondered if he would listen to the man's annoying words or just beat the hell out of him for lying. *I guess I'll know what I'm gonna do when he opens his mouth,* he thought.

By the time he got to the road, Wes had worked the numbness out of his leg. When Jones extended his hand to shake, Wes deliberately ignored the gesture and rubbed his sore elbow instead. Jones deftly kept his hand moving and took off his hat, trying to cover his awkwardness at being ignored.

"Good afternoon, Mr. Wilson. When we spoke last week I promised to visit you again as soon as I returned to town so that we could talk about your tobacco and my company's offer. I must say that it's a fine—"

"Shut the hell up!"

Jones stepped back, bumping into his horse, frightened by the strength and anger in Wes's voice. He felt as if he'd been physically struck and nearly wet himself.

"But sir, I—"

"I said shut the hell up. You need to stop talkin' and do some listenin' if you wanna get away from here without havin' them flappin' lips of yours turned into some kind of shredded meat."

Wes moved close to Jones, forcing him against the flanks of his horse. Jones cowered in front of the taller man and nearly gagged at the fetid smell of Wes's breath. He tried to slide away from the horse, but Wes moved with him, preventing his escape. Wes raised his arms and put his hands against the horse, grabbing onto the saddle and trapping Jones in a frightening, stinking embrace.

"Are you ready to listen?"

Jones whipped his head from side to side, trying to avoid the smell and the terrible closeness of Wes's gnarly face. Not wanting to inhale any more of the foul air than necessary and unable to use his suddenly dry throat, he just nodded. Wes held onto the saddle until he was convinced that Jones was not going to run. Jones's eyes were squeezed closed, and sweat dripped down his face. Wes felt the man trembling and only released him from the trap when he realized that Jones had stopped breathing.

"Look at me, Jones." Wes stepped back a foot or so. "Open your eyes and look at me."

Jones peered out the side of his face, looked with one eye and saw that Wes had moved away from him. He turned toward Wes, keenly aware of the dirt and sores on the farmer's face, the deep furrows in his cheeks. The tight knots of his jaws were more frightening than anything Jones had ever seen. He knew he couldn't fight the man, and any chance of escaping the trap he was in seemed impossible. In that moment, he had only one concern, and it was not his job or Wilson's tobacco or even his own pride. He wanted to survive. So he swallowed hard and said, "Please, Mr. Wilson. Let me speak."

Wes took another step back, giving Jones room enough to move away from his horse. He knew he had his attention, and he wanted him to be afraid. The man was still shaking, and his starched white collar was dark with sweat. Wes leaned in closer to his face, glaring directly into Jones's eyes.

"I'm doin' the talkin' right now. I want you to listen, 'cause I'm gonna ask you a question and I want you to think real hard about your answer." He didn't blink or move away until the man nodded his head. Wes backed away from Jones and reached into his pocket and pulled out his pistol. Jones gasped and bumped into the horse. "Don't worry," Wes said, "I ain't gonna use this on you . . . yet."

Keeping the weapon in sight, but at his side, Wes looked once more at Jones's face and asked, "Why did you tell my brother that I'd made a deal to sell you my tobacco?" He watched as the man's eyes shifted between his face and the gun. Wes could see that Jones was thinking.

Jones stood a little straighter and took a shallow breath. When he finally spoke, his words wheezed out of his fear-squeezed lungs.

"Mr. Wilson, I—" He tried to swallow, but his mouth was dry. "Mr. Wilson, I must confess that I was encouraged by our conversation that day, and I let my enthusiasm get the better of me. Perhaps I was unwise in sharing the information, but I truly believed that we had an agreement."

"No we didn't, and you know it," Wes said, raising the pistol. Jones watched him, glad that Wilson hadn't yet pointed the weapon at him.

"I know it was imprudent of me to break a confidence, and I'm sorry for that. But I was so excited about buying your crop. I wasn't aware at the time that doing something so . . . foolish . . . would mean trouble for you." Jones began to believe his own lie and pushed on. "If I've caused you any difficulties, Mr. Wilson, I'd truly like to make amends." He kept his eyes focused on Wes's face, but was keenly aware of the pistol. "Perhaps you'd be interested in hearing what my company has asked me to do." Wes was silent, so Jones continued.

"I have been authorized to keep the nine cents per pound offer on the table for you alone for at least another week. We've already reduced it to seven cents for any new purchases, but my company would still pay you nine cents a pound for your crop." Jones would be hard-pressed to get his boss to accept the deal, but thought he still might have a chance to convince him if he had a contract in hand.

Jones stopped talking. In the past, he'd have gone on until he'd run out of words. But today, more afraid than he'd ever been, his silence worked in his favor. Wes was intrigued—because the price hadn't dropped and because Jones had apologized.

"Go on."

"Again, sir, I apologize for placing you in a difficult spot. It was surely never my intent. But I hope you understand that this offer is intended as reparation for my lack of sensitivity and, more importantly, because my company wants your tobacco."

Wes slipped the gun into his pocket, and Jones relaxed a bit, watching Wes's eyes. Wes still didn't trust Jones and thought he might be lying. But if he could get the offer in writing, even if he didn't sign the contract until next week, he believed he'd have Jones and the company where he wanted them.

"Okay, Jones. Put that offer in writin' and give me a copy of it. I wanna look at the papers. Maybe I'll sign it next week." He watched Jones's body relax as the man began to breathe again. Jones nodded his head and pulled at the lapels of his coat. Wes put his hand into the pocket with the gun. "But if you say one word about this to anyone, you'll wish you'd been born without a mouth."

"I think you've made the right decision, sir. I'll confer with my office in Lexington and get a copy of the contract to you by tomorrow or Friday. Will that work for you?" Jones extended his right hand, hoping to confirm the agreement with Wilson, but Wes kept his hand on the gun in his pocket.

Jones moved his hand back to his lapel and nodded some more. "Well, then I'll get on my way back to Mayfield. I'm pleased that we've been able to conclude our business successfully, Mr. Wilson, and I promise you that I will keep this to myself. We certainly don't want any more unpleasantness." He looked at Wilson, hoping to see something positive, but all Wes did was nod in agreement, turn around and walk away. Jones said, "I'll see you on Friday, then," and without looking back, Wes headed to the house.

# Chapter 18
Wednesday Evening, May 16

By the time Wes arrived at the Baptist church in Lynnville, the few clouds in the sky picked up the last rays of the sun as it slipped below the tree line. There were more than a dozen wagons and buggies standing in the field and another thirty horses and mules hobbled or tied off to the wagons. Most of the men who'd come for the meeting were still outside, smoking and talking in small groups. The few lanterns hanging on the porch of the church and those lit inside the building cast a glow on the ground, and outside the bright dots of light from the ends of the cigars and cigarettes sparkled like red stars in the growing darkness.

Sitting on his mule at the end of the lane, Wes watched Art loop the reins of his horse over a tree limb at the edge of the church lot. He rode toward him, thankful that his cousin had not yet joined one of the groups.

"Evenin', cousin," he said as he slid down off the mule.

"I see you made it, Wes," Art said, stepping closer to shake his hand.

"Yep, I had to come and find out if these fellas know what they're doin'."

"Damn, Wes. When was the last time you took a bath? You stink like you've been sleepin' with your hogs."

"Never mind how I smell. I been workin' and thinkin' and ain't had time for no bath." Art's words had angered Wes. "Now can we talk about what's important and forget about how I smell?"

"Yeah, as long as you don't mind if I stand back a little."

Art chuckled and moved as close to Wes as he could stand. "So, in your thinkin', did you decide how you feel about the Association?"

"No, I didn't. How about you? Are you still gonna join?"

"I haven't decided yet, for sure, but that's the way I'm leanin'. I thought I'd hear what they have to say tonight, and then we could talk about it afterwards. I wanna get this settled so I can think about my family and my farm."

"Well, I hope they talk about what they're gonna pay and when they're gonna do it if we sign up. But, I don't trust 'em one bit. I don't trust anybody."

"I expect they will." Art coughed; the stink coming out of Wes's mouth was as foul as the rest of him. "I heard that fella Jones is back in town. Have you seen him?"

Wes was caught off guard when Art mentioned the buyer. "No, I ain't seen him." The lie burned his lips as soon as the words left his mouth. "Let's stick together inside and listen close to what these fellas have to say," he said, changing the subject. "I need to get back to workin' like a man's supposed to work. I'm near worn out, and I hope we get enough information tonight so I can get some damned sleep."

The church bell rang once, and the clusters of men ground out their cigars and started moving into the building. Their quiet conversations changed to a droning sound like a fly caught against a window. The two cousins walked toward the building, following behind the crowd, not wanting to get too close to the front in case they chose to leave early.

At the far end of the room, up on the platform where the preacher reigned on Sundays, five chairs were lined up behind the pulpit. On the floor in front of the wooden altar, all the pews were full, and twenty or thirty men stood against the walls. Art, Wes and a few stragglers stood in the back by the door. The droning noise was quieter, but when the door behind the pulpit opened, it stopped altogether as a group of men filed out.

Wes knew most of the men on the platform by sight, but he'd only ever spoken to two of them. He'd never had much need to talk to men whose tobacco fields were ten times the size of his. Besides, he'd always wondered if they'd ever been in their fields to weed or cut creepers or kill the deadly, crop-killing bugs. But these rich men, with their fifty-acre tobacco fields and their big houses and well-dressed families, were in charge of the Association in Lynnville, and their influence over struggling farmers like Wes and Art was huge. Wes hated them for their power, but he was at the meeting to listen and to learn, so he kept his mouth shut and didn't join in with the others who began to applaud the men as they sat down in the chairs. He glanced at Art and saw that he, too, was keeping his hands at his side. *He's a good man,* Wes thought, *a good friend. I hope he makes the right decision. I hope to hell I can.*

When the crowd grew quiet, the man in the center chair rose and walked to the pulpit. For several moments he scanned the crowd, almost willing them to focus on him. When he caught Wes's eyes, it seemed to Wes that the man looked at him longer than he had the others, but he couldn't be sure. Everyone in the building was quiet and still, following the man's progress with their eyes. Other than Art, the men standing near Wes had moved as far away from him as they could in the crowded room, seeking a sweeter atmosphere than that created by his reeking body. Wes didn't notice and clearly didn't care. He just wanted the talk to start so he could learn something about the Association's plans.

"You all listen up," the man at the pulpit said in a deep, rugged voice. "I wanna see the hands of all of the fellas who ain't joined the Planters Protective Association." There was little movement and only two of the men put their hands up. When Art finally raised his hand and Wes put his up as well, another four or five joined them. "Keep 'em up a minute while we take a count." He and the man on the far right of the line of chairs did a finger count of the raised arms and then looked at each other. Evidently they agreed, because they nodded and the speaker said, "Okay, fellas. Thanks." Wes noticed that the seated man who'd done the counting was still writing on his paper. He thought that he might be noting the names of the new men, but he couldn't be sure. He knew that the man, Red Miller, had a big farm and seemed to know a lot about what was going on in the district. Wes had never talked to the man, but he'd heard that he was tough to work with.

The speaker at the pulpit said, "Before we start this meetin', I want you all to know some rules." He paused to make sure everyone was listening. "This here's a house of God, so there'll be no smokin' or spittin' or swearin' inside the buildin'. If you gotta do any of those things, then do 'em outside. If you gotta do anythin' else, you know where the outhouse is." This caused a round of laughter that quickly died when he banged on the pulpit. "If any one of you fellas gets to doin' somethin' unruly or ungodly, then somebody bigger than you'll take you outside and teach you some manners." He looked back at the seated leadership and then said to the crowd, "So settle down, sit if you can find a seat and let's get this meetin' started." He returned to his chair and, during the rustling and murmuring of the men in the church, the tall man seated in the far-left chair rose and stood behind the pulpit.

Wes whispered to Art, "Do you know that fella?"

Art shook his head and said, "No, but I've seen him around the county. He must live up towards Mayfield. But that redheaded fella was at Mark's that night after I left your place."

Despite the cool breeze drifting in through the one open

door at the back, the temperature inside the building was rising. The pews were packed tight and those men who had to stand were crowded shoulder to shoulder. Wes was the only one who had any space around him. When the mumbling and shuffling settled down, the man at the pulpit spoke.

"Most of you have already heard what I'm gonna talk about tonight. But some things are important enough to hear again." His clear, horn-like voice boomed across the room. "Some of you might not see it the way the rest of us do, but we—all of us in this room who grow Black Patch tobacco—are in a war."

A man in the front pew shouted out amen and was quickly shushed by those around him.

"Thank you, brother," said the tall man at the pulpit. "It is a war against treachery and lies, deceit and dishonor. As much as it troubles me to mention him by name in this holy place, our enemy has a name." He waited, watching the faces of the men, timing his words to match their energy. "Our enemy is the man who owns the American Tobacco Company, the Trust, and his name is James B. Duke!"

The crowd shouted and growled. Some men shook their fists in the air, while a few others, including Wes and Art, watched and listened.

"Over the past few years, this man and his company, with their lies and their money, have driven away all the companies we used to sell our crops to. They've made secret agreements with these other companies in order to control the tobacco market in our country."

Like a rousing Sunday sermon, the man's words were often interrupted by the crowd. But instead of amens, the listeners would yell or boo, rise or sit, driven by their emotions. But he'd continue at each pause.

"We have been grievously injured by the Trust. They have stolen food from the mouths of our dear children.

They have forced our loving wives to work their fingers down to stubs. They have done everything they can to take away our rights as American citizens. They might as well have bound us up in chains and called us slaves."

Even Wes and Art joined in the titanic uproar that followed the man's last words.

"This monopoly has only one purpose, and that is the eventual ownership of not only our tobacco, but of our farms and our livelihood. They want to own us and our tobacco so they can grow rich at our expense. They want to feed their children fine food while ours eat slop. They want to have servants wash their clothes while our wives scrub and patch the worn out and tattered rags we wear."

He waited until the noise settled down to a cricket-like buzzing. When he continued, his voice was softer, but no less ardent.

"But this Association in Lynnville is not alone. There are others like it throughout the Black Patch. In nearly two dozen counties here in Kentucky and across the line in Tennessee, men just like you have joined together to fight the enemy. You have struggled for too long and have seen the value of joining with your fellow sufferers in this crusade against the Trust." He paused to drink water from a glass he'd set on the pulpit.

"Since last year, the Trust has offered prices which are lower than it costs us to produce the tobacco they so desperately want. But some of your brothers in other associations have come up with a way to fight back, and I want to tell you how we can do the same here in Graves County."

As Art listened, he also watched his cousin's reaction to the speaker. Wes stood rigid, his fists clenched at times, only occasionally nodding in agreement. Art hoped that he was listening and that he'd ultimately see the wisdom of joining the Association.

"So, gentlemen, here's what they came up with. The

members of these other Associations have agreed to deliver their crops to warehouses that they will secure. The
farmers who put their tobacco in these warehouses will receive certificates that they can turn into cash at their local
bank. The value of the certificates will be sufficient to cover
the cost of production, so the farmers can cover their costs.
When the tobacco ultimately sells at a price they believe
will be higher, the farmers will pay the bank back and keep
the difference."

This caused another, more modest outburst. Most of
the men talked among themselves, quickly calculating
and wondering how this system might work for them.
Wes looked at Art, but he couldn't tell what his cousin was
thinking.

"We've made arrangements with the bank in Mayfield to
use this same method in Graves County. All of the details
haven't been worked out yet, but we should have more
information for you in the next several weeks. That's why
it is vitally important that you join the Association. That's
why it is just as important that you do not sell your crop
to the Trust. You must realize that anyone who does this
is as much an enemy as James B. Duke. We have to stick
together if we're gonna win this war. Talk to your reluctant
neighbors. Persuade them, educate them, encourage them
to join with you." The buzzing sound of the energy in the
room grew. "The Trust won't negotiate with us," his voice
louder, "so they single out hillbilly farmers who think they
need the money more than their neighbors do. What the
trust buyers do is offer high prices that blind the hillbillies
to the suffering of those around them. But these holdouts
are not acting like our friends and neighbors, are they?"

A chorus of hisses and no's broke out in the room. The
man raised his hands for quiet.

"There's one more thing we need to talk about tonight.
There was an unfortunate event last week in Christian

County. You've all heard about it, but you may not know all of the facts. A group of men—call them Night Riders, or the Silent Brigade, if you wish—decided to take the law into their own hands and tried to convince a tobacco farmer to join the local Association. That farmer agreed to do so and when he bent down to pick up the weapon he'd set on his porch at their request, someone accidently shot and killed him. You've heard that he was murdered, but that is not what the facts show. We have it directly from the sheriff in Christian County that the coroner over there has ruled his death an accident. Nevertheless, it is important for you to know that we, the Lynnville PPA, do not condone violence of any kind."

"It was murder," someone yelled, and some in the crowd shouted in support. The man at the pulpit raised his arms and tried to calm the farmers. The noise faded, but the mood in the church had changed.

The lack of a breeze and the nervous sweat of nearly a hundred angry men had given the room a sultry atmosphere. "Gentlemen, if you are already a member of the Association, we thank you and ask you to be patient while we work out the details regarding the certificates with the bank. For those of you who haven't yet joined, we'd like you to come on down front so we can answer any questions you might have."

A number of the men started to move out of the pews and rows when Wes shouted out a question.

"You said the bank ain't worked out the details. Are you sure they'll loan us the money?"

The speaker looked up from his notes, searching the room for who'd spoken up. "What's that you say?" Red Miller and the others in the chairs looked in Wes's direction. Some of them stood, clearly agitated by Wes's challenge. Red wrote something on his paper.

"I said, are you sure the bank will loan the money?" Wes

saw that he had the man's attention and that Red had noticed him as well. Some of the farmers around Wes agreed with him. Most of the others were already filing out the door. Art was shocked that Wes would ask such a question.

The speaker walked over to Red, leaned over to listen to him and then nodded. He looked up at Wes again and said, "Mr. Wilson, if you'll come on down front, we'll tell you what we know."

But Wes wasn't interested in talking to these men. He'd heard all he needed to know about the Association and the bank.

"I'm leavin'," Wes announced. "Come on, Art. We need to talk."

Pulled along by the tide of farmers pouring into the darkness, Art walked across the ground to his horse. He could hear the cottony sound of dozens of voices calling out, but the words were mushy, jumbled together. They only clogged up his already muddied thoughts. He untied the reins from the tree and started to mount his horse, but was stopped by Wes's hand on his shoulder. Art shuddered at his touch, suddenly afraid.

"Where're you goin'?" Wes asked. "We need to talk." He dropped his hand and stood back, unable to see Art's face clearly in the faint light.

"Why'd you say that in there?" Art's voice trembled, the words fighting their way out of his spitless mouth. He slapped the free end of the reins against his leg and whined, "Why did you have to ask that?"

"What're you snappin' at me for? I asked a simple question." Wes snarled and tried to move closer, but Art stepped back. "Damn it, Art. What's wrong with you?

Art sucked in a huge gulp of the cooling night air. His hands shook as he retied the reins to the tree and started back toward the church.

"Wait," said Wes. "We ain't talked about what they said

in there." He followed his cousin and grabbed his shoulder again. This time, Art shook it off and turned to face Wes.

"What I heard in there was that now we have a way of stayin' out of trouble," Art said. "All we gotta do is sign up, put our crops in with theirs and we can get some money from the bank. We won't have to worry about starvin' or hidin' from the Night Riders." He stopped for a moment; his fear had turned to anger. "We've been workin' together to try to get information. That's why we came here tonight. But you show up lookin' and smellin' like some kind of crazy man and then ask a question like a damned troublemaker. I stood there right beside you, heard the same words and walked out with you. Now that bunch up front is gonna think I'm just like you." He paused only a moment and added, "But I ain't."

"Hold on, Art. That's crazy."

"No, Wes. It ain't crazy. We're cousins and friends. Everybody in that room knows we always work together and talk things through. But tonight I don't understand you. I don't even know who you are. I promised to tell you when I'd figured out what I was gonna do. Well, I've decided to join up. I'm gonna protect my family and get enough money to get by until my crop sells." He started to leave and then turned back. "I know you still gotta think about it, Wes, and I hope you make up your mind soon, because what you did in there is just like paintin' a target on your back." He walked across the yard toward the church.

"We still got choices," Wes yelled, loud enough for Art to hear as he walked away. "We don't have to do everythin' they say."

Art heard Wes's voice and felt the arrogance behind his cousin's words. But he went into the church and signed up anyway.

\* \* \*

J.D. and Charley stood in the shadow of the trees not twenty yards from Wes. They'd overheard his encounter with Art and waited until they saw him mount his mule and ride away.

"Well, ain't that somethin'," said J.D., an ugly grin splitting his face. "It appears that Mr. Wilson's got him some choices. I wonder what the captain'll say about that." He took a quick swallow from the whiskey jug in his hand.

"Maybe he ain't gonna join up, and it could be that he ain't gonna do nothin'."

"Oh, he's gonna do somethin'. I can feel it. I'll bet he's got a deal goin' with Jones. Maybe he's already signed a contract. If we tell the captain what we heard right here, that'll make us look real good, seein' that we already put Wilson's name on our list."

Charley shivered and looked around the emptying churchyard to make sure no one was watching them. "If you're gonna tell him that Wilson has a deal with the Trust, you'll be lyin', 'cause you don't know that he does. And if you do tell the captain that, I don't want you tellin' him that we heard it. I don't want any part of that." He walked back into the woods a few paces and then turned back to J.D. "Don't you think if word got back to Wilson that we gave his name to the Night Riders, he'd come after us? And if he did, do you think he'd just yell at us? Hell no he wouldn't. He'd put a bullet in us without even thinkin' twice."

"You ain't got any brains at all, Charley. Do you think I'm stupid enough to say somethin' like that? I'm only gonna tell the captain exactly what I heard tonight. I'll let him figure out what it all means. Either way, we end up lookin' good. He might even throw in a little extra money when we raid Wilson's farm."

"Who said the Riders are gonna hit Wilson's place?"

"Nobody's said it yet, but I'd bet real money that they're gonna do it soon." J.D. walked past Charley deeper into the woods and sat on a stump. He lifted the jug and took two large gulps. "Come on, Charley. Have a drink and relax a little."

Charley walked away from him and stood in the dark. He looked at the church building and wondered how evil things could be talked about in such a place.

The two Night Riders waited another hour before the captain called them over to the church. "We've got another job for you two if you're interested."

"We're always interested, if it means we're gonna get paid," said J.D. "What do we have to do and how much is it worth?"

The captain looked at J.D. in the faint light from the church window and shook his head. "This ain't just makin' a list of names or ridin' with the Night Riders. It's a dangerous job. But if you do what's on this note, you get twenty dollars of gold."

"Twenty dollars—" was all Charley got out before J.D. shut him up.

"Where's this note?" he asked. "What does it say?"

Looking around the empty church lot, the captain said, "It's right here, but you ain't to look at it until you're far away from here. If you do the job, you'll get the gold. It's that simple." Ignoring Charley's pained expression, the captain looked at J.D. "If you decide you wanna do it, you need to let me know before Sunday."

"We'll let you know," said J.D.

When they got back to the shack, J.D. lit the lantern and read the note. He let out a slow, tuneless whistle and told Charlie they'd be leaving town within a week. Charley asked what they needed to do for the money, but J.D. told him not to worry. J.D. lay back on his cot and thought for a while. Before he fell asleep, he already had a plan.

\* \* \*

Connie sat on the porch in the dark, trying to listen past the sawing crickets for sounds of approaching horses. Last week's moon had shrunk to a heavy scythe, but the light was enough to see night creatures scurrying across the road into the fields. He lifted a cup from the porch and sipped the hot coffee his ma had sweetened with a bit of sugar and squinted as the steam fogged his eyes. He'd set the shotgun against the wall in easy reach of his spot on the bench, but hadn't touched it in the hour or so he'd been on watch. There was no light in the kitchen behind him, but he was pretty sure that his ma was sitting at the table in the darkened room, waiting for his pa to get back from town.

He watched a dim light move beyond the trees on the eastern edge of the farm and smiled. *Somebody at Uncle George's is headin' to the outhouse,* he thought. *Must be Aunt Malinda, 'cause none of the others would take a lantern.* He watched as Rufus wandered into the yard from behind the barn and jumped up onto the porch. The dog settled down near Connie's feet and started gnawing on an old hambone. Even with his ma sitting in the kitchen, he was glad for the company.

Rufus dropped his bone and growled, lifting his head and staring off toward the road. Connie looked in the same direction and reached for the shotgun. He and the dog rose at the same time and stepped down into the yard, watching the road and straining to see who was coming in their direction. "Easy Rufus," he said. "Maybe it's Pa." Connie forced his ears to hear what had spooked the dog. Rufus walked a few yards toward the road and then sat on his haunches. He woofed softly and then trotted off in the moonlight. Connie's ears picked up the faint sound of hooves on the dirt road, and he spotted his pa as he rode the mule past the western tree line. He knew his pa would be tired and that he could help him by putting the mule away for the night. He walked through the open barn door and lit a lantern, giving the cavernous building a dusk-like glow. He swung back the gate of the mule's stall and set a half-bucket of oats against the far wall just as his pa led the animal into the barn.

"What're you doin' with the gun, Connie? Has there been any trouble?"

"No, Pa, there ain't been any trouble. I was standin' guard. Me and Anthie talked it over and thought since you were gone we'd keep watch 'til you got back. We decided we'd take turns." Connie walked out of the stall and leaned the gun against the workbench. "Here, Pa, let me take care of the mule. I'll put him up and you can go on up to the house." He took the reins out of his pa's hands and led the mule into the stall. After pulling the bridle from its head and the blanket from its back, he carried the tack out and closed the gate.

Wes stood back and watched, pleased that his son had protected the family and the farm while he was in town. He knew he should say something, but his thoughts were still knotted up like a bag full of snakes, and he couldn't find the words. Connie picked up the lantern and the shotgun and waited at the door for Wes.

"You ready, Pa?"

Wes didn't answer his son; he just followed him out of the barn and they walked to the house. The kitchen lamps were lit, and the warm light spilled out onto the porch. Zora was standing there, quietly waiting for them. Wes could only see her silhouette, her face hidden from him, but he knew she'd want to know everything about the meeting. *Why can't she wait 'til mornin',* he thought. *I don't wanna do this with her now. I wanna be left alone so I can think.*

Zora moved aside as they stepped onto the porch and walked into the house. Wes stood near the stove, his back to Zora, waiting for her to speak first. But instead, she stepped out of the kitchen and walked to the back of the house. Zora noticed the glow of a candle at the top of the stairs.

"Good night, son," she said. "Thanks for watchin' out for us."

"Good night, Ma. See you in the mornin'."

When she returned to the kitchen, Wes was sitting in his chair at the head of the table. He'd poured himself some coffee and cut a chunk off the loaf of bread on the counter. He didn't look up at her until she spoke. Even then, he only threw a quick glance and returned to eating.

"Did you learn anythin' that'll help you decide what you're gonna do about our crop?"

He continued to chew on the bread and sip at the coffee and didn't respond to Zora's questions. She thought about asking him again, but she knew he was ignoring her. After pouring herself some water from the pitcher, she carried the cup to the other end of the table and waited for him to respond. *I'm not leaving this chair until he tells me what he learned and what he's decided, even if I have to sit here all night. Our family needs to know.*

When the bread was gone and the cup empty, Wes looked down the long table at his wife. Somewhere deep inside he knew he owed her an answer. He had to tell her something. *But what am I gonna say to her,* he thought, *when I don't have the answer yet. Right now, I'm tired, my mind's crowded and I don't feel like I have enough energy left to pretend.* But he had no choice. He closed his eyes, and when he finally looked at her from behind his mask, the right words seemed to fall from his mouth. He barely knew what he was saying.

"There was a big bunch of fellas at the meetin'. It was crowded in the church, and we had to wait awhile for the PPA men to show up. When they did, they looked around and counted eight or nine of us who ain't joined up yet." Wes watched Zora, looking for some response, but she just stared at him. "Then one of 'em talked a lot about the Trust and how they was cheatin' all of us by cuttin' the prices on the tobacco. He said that the only way to beat 'em was to put all our tobacco in Association warehouses." He never took his eyes off her. "Then he told us that one of the banks in Mayfield was gonna make loans to any farmer who would hold his tobacco back from the Trust. They'd give us enough to cover our costs until the crop sold, and then we'd get the rest of the money."

Zora sat up a little straighter at the mention of the bank, but then she asked him, "How sure are they that the bank'll loan the money?"

"That's exactly what I asked 'em," he said, surprised that she could even think of something like that. "Then they talked about the killin' and said nothin' like that was gonna happen in our county. They said that the sheriff over there called it an accident. After that, the meetin' ended and we left. Art stuck around and said he was gonna sign up for the Association. Then I came home." He waited just a moment, hoping this would satisfy her.

Zora rose from her chair and poured herself some more water. She turned toward him and said, "So, what are you gonna do with your crop, Wesley?"

"I still don't know," he said, wanting Zora to stop talking and leave him alone. "The choices I have tonight ain't much different than those I had a week ago—join up or sell; go broke or get rich; save the farm or lose our friends—none of 'em are any good."

"Look, Wes. I know you think this whole decision is up to you. Well, maybe it is, but I think I ought to at least get to tell you what I think."

Wes didn't want to hear what she thought, but nodded at her to continue anyway. Now he had to force himself to listen when his head felt numb.

"I think that the only safe thing for you to do, the only

way you can protect the family and the farm, is to join the Association. Even if the bank don't loan the money, all we gotta think about is makin' the mortgage payment. We'll have to tighten our belts a bit and eat a lot of fried dough, but we'll still be alive. We've been through hard times before and survived, and we can do it again. You gotta join up with the others, Wes."

Wes could feel the heat under his mask. Now even Zora was trying to tell him what to do. He had let her have her say, but he was done listening to her; he didn't want to hear any more, not even from Zora. "All I can do is think about what you said. But I'm the one who's gotta decide what to do, and I ain't ready to do it yet. So just go away. Quit chatterin' about the damn tobacco and joinin' and leave me the hell alone. You gotta give me a chance to figure it out by myself."

"Well then figure it out, Wes. You've put this family through enough." Wes's words hit Zora like a slap in the face, just like he'd done to Anthie. He'd sat there and listened to her and then tossed her idea away like a piece of trash. She'd held herself back, trying not to upset him, but it was a wasted effort. She slammed the water cup on the counter and looked at him. Tears pooled in her eyes, but she willed them not to fall.

Keeping her voice down so she didn't wake the children and with as much venom as she could muster, she said, "One more thing, Wesley. Unless you clean up and shave and start talkin' and actin' like a husband and a father again, you ain't gonna have a seat at my table or a place in my bed. You are scarin' your children, and you're offendin' me. So, until you decide to be a man again, I'm done talkin' to you. Now get out of my kitchen and go sleep with the hogs."

Wes watched her back as she left the room, his body trembling, his heart pounding. The mask he'd worn to appear normal was gone, burned away by his angry pride. In his rage he banged his cup on the table, breaking it into tiny pieces. Then he stood up and rushed out the door, slamming it behind him.

\* \* \*

In the room at the back of the church, Red stood across a small table from his three captains, who were talking about the new members and the good news from the bank. He glanced at J.D.'s list of names and waited until their conversation faded before he spoke.

"It's all set. We're goin' after Wes Wilson Sunday night."

# Chapter 19
Thursday, May 17

Through the window of the kitchen, Zora watched Wes standing in the middle of the yard. The rays of the rising sun trickled between the trees, glazing his face. Rufus sat at his side, the dog's fur burnished by the same light. A faint, tentative smile surfaced on Zora's face, and her eyes, weary from the tension, blinked back a few tears. Wes had heard her demand. She folded her hands and prayed that this would be one of the good days.

The door swung open as a troubled Anthie walked in and set the milk pail on the counter.

"Ma," he said, "Pa's just standin' out there starin' at the field. What's he doin'?"

"I don't know, son," she sighed, "I don't know. But you never mind now and get that milk set to cool. I'll have some breakfast ready in a little bit. See if you can get your lazy brothers out of bed and up before your pa starts in on 'em." She wiped her hands on a rag and patted Anthie on the arm. "Go on now, get goin'."

Zora turned back to the window and saw that her husband and his dog were still standing in the sunlight. *Lord, I sure hope some of that warmth finds its way into his heart.* She reached up on the shelf for a large bowl and half-filled it with flour and went about mixing her biscuit dough. A small cloud of flour dust floated around her, settling on her cheeks, softening them and mixing with the remains of her tears. While she worked, she hummed a mindless melody, her hands familiar with the routine of preparing a meal.

Ruthie toddled into the kitchen ahead of Mary Lula and

wrapped her chubby little arms around Zora's leg.

"Momma, Momma," she cooed, reaching up for her mother's arms.

Zora brushed the flour off her hands and picked up her daughter, giving her a big hug, kissing her pudgy cheeks and nibbling on her neck. "How's my baby girl this mornin'?" Ruthie giggled and touched her ma's cheek. "I need to make these biscuits, so you help your big sister to get the table set, all right?"

Wes wasn't quite ready to join the family. During another sleepless night, he'd managed to wash away the filth and sweat from his body and shave away his scruffy whiskers. The gummy sourness had been rinsed from his mouth and his foul-smelling clothes exchanged for fresh ones. But he'd been unable to flush the anger and resentment at Zora's outburst from his mind. Vivid, eyes-open nightmares had plagued him during the hours his family slept. Frantically moving images of his farm being swept away in a firestorm, of his wife and children lost and wandering and of his own body lying dead on a porch had prevented sleep. In those few moments that the tense dreams slipped away from his thoughts, he wrestled with his feelings about Art's deception and his own lies and the nagging thought about his tobacco crop.

When he woke up in the early morning light, Wes had one tiny moment of clarity and realized that he might lose his family forever if he didn't pull himself together. He was determined that his family would see smiles and hear laughter, feel gentle touches and hear calmness in his voice. With the pressure of their fears removed, he might be able to deal with the real problems, but he knew the battle raging inside him was fierce.

Wes shielded his eyes as he stared toward the rising sun, breathing in deep draughts of the morning air. He turned away, dipped the ladle into the water bucket and filled his mouth with cold water, swishing it around before spitting it onto the ground. Bending down, Wes scratched Rufus between his ears and walked across the yard and up the steps into the house.

* * *

Charley had rousted J.D. awake before dawn, and they'd saddled the horses and left for Art's farm eager to finish the job and get paid. The sun had just peeked through the clouds when they carried their hoes out to the far end of the tobacco field.

"I hope West brings us somethin' to eat. I'm starvin'."

"You should've thought of that before we left the shack," said J.D.

"I did think about it, but there weren't nothin' left. We ate the last of the salt pork before we went to the meetin' last night. I see you didn't forget to bring that jug of liquor you got hangin' on your saddle horn."

"Well, at least we won't go thirsty."

They stopped at the tree line and split up. Charley started digging at the weeds in the middle of the row and moved toward the western edge of the field. J.D. took a quick sip from the jug, picked up the hoe and started chopping in the other direction.

* * *

From the kitchen window, Art watched the two farm-hands chop weeds in the tobacco field. They'd put in a good day's work yesterday, and at the rate they were working, he figured they'd be done by dark. He knew if he joined them, the job would get done sooner. But he had something else to do today, and it was important to get it done early.

He sat at the table while Mollie fixed him a plate of bacon and beans. She poured him a cup of coffee and set it on the table next to his plate. Then she eased into a chair across from him.

"Are you sure you want to do this, Art?"

"I've got to, Mollie," he said between bites of the hot food. "Wes is family, and I need to apologize to him for what I said last night. Besides, I gotta try one more time to convince him to join up before somethin' bad happens."

She reached her hand across the table and touched his face. "Aren't you afraid that you'll be pushin' him too much?"

"That's always a risk with Wes. He don't like to be pushed into anythin'. But things are gettin' serious, Mollie." He set down his fork and picked up the coffee cup. "I can't leave things like they are right now; he's been too good to me." Art swallowed some of the dark liquid and put the cup down.

"All right, Art, if you think that's best." She stood up and smiled at him, adding, "Now finish up that food. I won't have you headin' out on the road still hungry."

He pulled the plate back and ate some of the beans. "Send Clarence in here, Mollie. I gotta tell him somethin'."

Mollie walked out onto the porch and saw the boy chasing one of the chickens. She spoke to him briefly, and he rushed into the kitchen.

"You wanted to see me, Pa?" said Clarence as he walked into the room.

"Yeah, I did, son. Come on outside."

Clarence followed his pa out the door and stood beside him on the porch. Art pointed out to the tobacco field and said, "See them two men out there?"

"Yes, Pa. I see 'em."

"I want you to stay out here this mornin' an' keep an eye on 'em. If you see 'em leavin' the field or just standin' around, I want you to tell your ma, okay?"

"Sure, Pa. I can do that." The boy shoved his hands deep into the pockets of his overalls. "I'll watch 'em good."

"I'm countin' on you." He looked down at his son and smiled. "Now get on in there and eat your breakfast. A workin' man can't do a good job on an empty belly." He patted Clarence on the head, and the boy went into the house.

When he pulled the horse out of the barn, Mollie was standing on the porch. He dropped the reins and walked up to her. She looked out at the field and then back to Art.

"Why do you want Clarence to watch those fellas?"

"I'm just bein' cautious," he said. "I wanna make sure they keep workin', so when they're done I can send 'em off for good. I don't want 'em around here anymore after today." He stepped up on the porch and put his hands on her shoulders. "If he comes in and tells you they ain't workin', you sit here on the porch and keep an eye on 'em. I don't think they'll do anythin', but if you don't feel good about 'em, lock yourself and the children in the house." He watched her face grow stern and said, "You know where the gun is and how to use it."

Mollie nodded her head and kissed Art on the lips. He hugged her tightly and walked to the horse. Pulling himself up onto the saddle, he waved at her and rode off to see Wes.

* * *

"Wonder where he's goin'," sneered J.D.

"Ain't none of our business," said Charley. "All we need to do is get rid of these weeds, not talk about the man who's payin' us to do it." He never lifted his eyes from the chore, but chopped at the stringy plants, moving away from J.D.

"Maybe it ain't our business, but until he gets back, I don't plan to work so hard I get sore," said J.D.

Charley stopped in mid-swing and said, "We don't get paid until we're finished, and I wanna get done before dark if we can. So let's keep workin', okay?" He turned back to the task and moved quickly down the row.

J.D. saw the boy on the porch watching them. Then he uttered a curse and got back to work.

"I got an idea," J.D. said when he and Charley met at the next row.

"C'mon, J.D., your ideas usually mean somethin' bad for us. Can't we just keep workin?"

"Just shut up. I'll tell you about it later. You don't even have to be a part of it, but you gotta keep quiet and let me do all the talkin'. I don't want you messin' things up."

Charley glanced quickly at the house and then faced J.D. "That's fine with me; just wait 'til we get paid before you say somethin' to him. Otherwise, your idea might backfire, and we'll end up tired and broke."

"Don't you fret, Miss Charley," he said to Charley's back as his partner walked away down the row and out of hearing. "I'm not stupid enough to throw money away. Don't you worry one little bit."

* * *

While the family ate breakfast, Wes laughed and played with his children. As Zora watched him, she thought he looked like a happy man, and she'd already thanked God for that a dozen times this morning. The younger children had easily warmed up to their pa, but she could tell the two older ones were being cautious. Perhaps they just weren't sure that the change in him was genuine. A quick look at Anthie, however, left her with an uneasy feeling. It was clear by the icy look on his face that he wasn't convinced that his pa had truly changed. *He must still be upset about last week,* she thought. *Wes's change has to be real. If it ain't, we'll know soon enough.*

Wes looked down the table toward the boys and said, "I guess we better get outside and start on our chores. This day ain't gonna get any longer." He stood straight up from his chair. Ruthie was tucked under his left arm like a sack of corn, and Irene hung around his neck. "But first I gotta get rid of these two pretty little girls." They giggled as he walked around the table, dragging his feet and acting like they were a heavy load. When he got to where Mary Lula was sitting, he put Ruthie in his daughter's lap and slipped out of the hold Irene had on his neck. "I'm sorry, girls, but your pa and brothers have got to get to work," he said, smiling and poking at them. Irene started to protest, but a stern look from her ma stopped her.

"You girls let your pa go now," said Zora. She rose and carried her plate to the counter. "Go on, now, get the table cleared and push in your chairs. We got lots of things to do around the house today."

Connie and Anthie left the table and walked out to the porch to wait for their pa. The sun had just cleared the treetops, and the yard filled with light. The front of the faded barn reflected the light like a dusty mirror. Rufus walked across the porch, and Anthie squatted down to scratch the dog's ears while Connie rolled and lit a cigarette. As Wes joined them, Anthie stood up, looking first at Connie and then at his pa.

"Let's take a walk," Wes said. He stepped off the porch, and they followed him out to the tobacco field. When he got to the first row, he turned around and looked at his sons. He started to speak, but afraid of the words that might come from his angry heart, he stopped and thought for a moment. When he finally opened his mouth, his voice was rusty but calm.

"I know things ain't been easy around here for the past few days. There's a lot goin' on that I've had to think about, and I know you two have been workin' hard to keep the family safe." Wes paused, his thoughts grinding against one another. "I think your idea of sharin' the guard duty is good, so I'll watch tonight; Anthie, you get tomorrow night."

"Okay, Pa," he said, his words flat, emotionless as he

kicked at a clump of dirt.

"We'll figure out a new schedule on Saturday," Wes said, looking out at the field of tobacco. The green plants had grown half a foot in the two weeks they'd been in the ground. "These here plants," he said to his sons, "are what keep our family out of the poorhouse. We gotta protect 'em and take care of 'em. You both know there's people out there who'd like to pay us less than it costs to grow 'em. But we ain't gonna let that happen."

He turned back around and looked at them. What should have been easy for a man to say to his sons, Wes had to conjure from out of the jumbled mess of worries and pride that had taken over his mind. From the deepest part of his soul, his spirit groaned in pain as he said, "Thanks for watchin' over things."

As Wes laid out plans for the day's work, Connie puffed on his cigarette and watched his pa. He could tell something was different, but he wasn't sure that anything had really changed. *Just have to wait and see how things go the next few days, I guess.* He dropped the butt on the ground and crushed it with his shoe, anxious to get to work.

Anthie heard the words coming out of his pa's mouth, but he wasn't listening to them. After hearing the sounds of the argument the night before, he'd not slept well and he was tired. Trying to hold back a yawn, he turned his head back and forth, feeling the bones of his neck crack. *Nothin's changed,* he thought. He watched a flock of birds soar low over the field and then turned back to the conversation, watching his pa through sallow eyes.

"I guess we've done enough talkin'," Wes said, "so let's get to work." They walked in silence toward the barn, feeling the sun on their backs. As they reached the water pump, Anthie spotted Art turning off the road onto the lane.

"Pa, Cousin Art's comin'."

Wes looked up, surprised to see Art, wondering why

he'd come. "You boys get started. I'll go see what he wants." Wes turned away from the open barn door and walked up the lane toward his cousin.

"Mornin', Wes," Art said as he dismounted, pleased to see that Wes had cleaned up since they last met.

"Good mornin' to you, cousin. What're you doin' all the way over here so early?"

"I've got a couple things to say about last night. Let me water the horse first, and then let's find a place to talk." They walked down to the well, and Art threw the end of the reins over the pump handle. Wes watched as he filled the bucket with water and set it in front of the animal.

"Might as well sit up on the porch," Wes said. "You want some coffee? I think there's still some left from breakfast."

"Sure, I'll take a cup of coffee, but can we go somewhere private?"

Wes stepped into the kitchen and returned in a minute with two cups of tepid coffee. They walked around the corner of the house, past the barn and out to the cornfield. Wes stopped at the first row of young plants and turned to Art.

"This is about as private as we're gonna get around here," he said. "What's goin' on?"

Art knew what he had to say to Wes. He'd spent the entire trip thinking about how to say it, but now, standing in front of his cousin, the words didn't come easily. He sipped the barely warm coffee, grateful for the wetness in his throat.

Wes watched Art struggle for words, wondering what he'd hear.

"First thing I wanna say is that I'm sorry for the way I acted last night. I know I shouldn't have just rushed off when you weren't finished talkin'." Art took a shallow breath and continued. "I was afraid I'd say somethin' wrong, so I just went inside and signed up. I had to for my family's sake."

Wes nodded, lifted the half-empty cup to his lips and took a drink. He wasn't surprised that Art had joined the Association, but the apology was unexpected. Wes mentally adjusted his mask. "It's all right, Art. I probably deserved it anyway. It ain't my business to tell you what to do with your family. If you joined up to protect 'em, you did what a man's supposed to do." But deep down, Wes was angry with his cousin.

Art looked into his cup, poured the dregs on the ground and sighed. *Now comes the hard part,* he thought. He looked at Wes and said, "There's somethin' else you need to know." He felt the beads of sweat start to run through his thick hair and down the back of his neck. He regretted pouring out the last of the coffee because he could sure use it now for his suddenly dry throat.

"I been thinkin' about what you said in the meetin' last night—especially the question you asked about the bank and the money." Art could see a shadow growing on Wes's face.

"What about it?" Wes said, feeling the millstone weight of the mask, fearing it would crumble away.

Art could hardly breathe as he tried to say the words he knew would get Wes stirred up. "I heard what them fellas who were standin' next to us said, how they thought you might be onto somethin'. I also watched the Association men. It was pretty clear they didn't like what you said, and I seen 'em writin' on their papers. It looked like they was real unhappy that you'd asked the question and even madder that you might've got some other folks thinkin' the same way." He waited to see what Wes would do, but his cousin's face was empty. "I'm scared, Wes. I think they might decide to get word to the Night Riders and send 'em after you if you don't join."

Wes nodded, but the dip of his head was almost invisible, like a heavy leaf nudged by a gentle breeze. Wes's body didn't move—no clenching jaws, no quivering lips, no tightening muscles. Art had expected more of a reaction and wondered if Wes had even heard the words. When his cousin finally spoke, Art was stunned.

"Have you heard somethin'?"

"No," he said, the lie flying out of his mouth. "I ain't heard nothin'," the pain of his untruth squeezing his heart like a vise.

"It don't make sense they'd send the Night Riders out here just because I asked a simple question," Wes said, but the malice he was feeling was still there. Barely able to say the words, knowing that Art was keeping something from him, he added, "But thanks for lookin' out for me. What'd they make you sign?" he asked, not even aware he'd spoken.

Glad that Wes had changed the subject, Art said, "It was a pretty simple thing to do. All I did was agree to not sell my crop to the company and to support any other farmer who did the same thing."

Neither of the men spoke for a while. They looked out over the tops of the corn toward the trees. The damp morning air was beginning to warm up, and Art's thoughts started gnawing at the crust of an idea. *What if Wes has already made a deal with Jones? Maybe that's why he ain't joined up. But if he has made a deal, then why won't he tell me?*

"We could stand out here all day," Art said, "but I need to go home and get to weedin' my tobacco." He looked at Wes. "I ain't gonna bother you with this anymore, but I sure wish you'd consider doin' what I did. You won't get rich joinin' up, but bein' a part of the Association will be one sure way to keep the Riders from destroyin' your field."

"That fella in Christian County was ready to join too, and look what it got him," his words were bitter. Wes felt like someone had fired up a lantern in the dark corners of his brain. *Why's he pushin' me so hard?* he said to himself. *Does he think I've made a deal with Jones? Why else would he be wonderin' about my choices?* "I'll be makin' a decision soon, probably by next week. But I gotta ask you one more time. Are you sure you ain't heard anythin' new from anybody about them raidin' my farm?"

"I'm sure," he said, and once again he felt the gripping pain of lying to his best friend. "I gotta get goin', Wes. I left Mollie and the kids alone at the house, and I got them two farmhands workin' the weeds. I don't wanna be gone too long." Neither of them spoke as they walked back across the yard to the pump. Art pulled himself up onto the saddle and set his feet in the stirrups. "I hope you join up, but whatever you do, you know that I'm still family and I always will be. I'll see you later, cousin. Maybe Saturday at Mark's."

"All right, you be careful and give our best to Mollie." He waved at Art as he rode down the lane and turned toward home. This thought—that Art might know about his dealings with Jones—just added another rabid beast to the pack of circling, snarling demon dogs that fought for control of his mind.

* * *

When Art turned his horse off the road, J.D. and Charley were still working the field, and Clarence was proudly standing lookout on the porch. Art smiled when he saw the pile of throwing-rocks at his son's feet. "Hey, boy," he said. "Is everythin' all right?"

"Yes sir, Pa. Everythin's fine. I been watchin' them two, and they ain't stopped workin' since you left." He stepped down to stand by Art as he slid out of the saddle. "Ma came outside a little while ago and brought me some water. I told her that I was keepin' watch and she should get on back in the house 'cause that's what you wanted." The boy's steely voice and grim face were youthful, but serious. Art thanked him, man to man, for keeping watch.

"I think we should both go in now and check on your ma and the children, don't you?"

"Yeah, Pa. We're done out here for now." He kicked the rocks off the porch and picked up the empty water cup.

"After we eat some of your ma's good cookin', I'll head on out there and help 'em chop weeds. And since you've been standin' watch all mornin', I want you to have some fun this afternoon. How's that sound?" Clarence smiled at his pa and said he thought it was a good idea. Art lifted his son and threw him over his shoulder. Then he carried the laughing, squirming boy into the house.

* * *

J.D. leaned on his hoe, a nasty smirk on his face as he watched Art and his boy. "You bastard," he muttered, and yanked his hat from his head, looking around for Charley. He spotted him working a row near the far end of the field, chopping at the weeds, creating clouds of dust that caked in the dark rings of sweat on his work shirt. *Damned fool's workin' too hard for the little bit of money that farmer pays us,* he thought. *And I need a drink.*

He dropped his hoe and walked between the plants, crossing the rows they'd already finished to where the horses grazed in the grass. He found his jug under their coats next to a tree and took a quick, bitter sip. The sun was heating up the late morning sky, and the shade should have felt good, but J.D. found little pleasure in it. He just wanted to sit in the grass and sip from his jug. He would have let Charley do all the work, but he saw West come out onto the porch. *Damn farmer never lets us rest,* he thought as he put his jug away and went back to work.

Art grabbed another hoe and walked across the yard. He joined the two farmhands in the tobacco field, handed each of them a ham sandwich and said, "Go ahead and take a couple minutes to eat. I'll get started down at the first row 'cause I wanna be done with this by dark." He walked away and started chopping at the near side of the field, clearing one row for every two of theirs.

They worked another three hours and finished the entire field. The warm morning air had given way to an intense heat as the day headed toward dusk.

After taking a drink of water from his pail, Art gave it to Charley and then reached into his overall pocket, pulled out some coins and handed them to J.D.

"Here's your money," he said. "I'm glad you finished today." He waited a minute and then added, "I won't be needin' your help anytime soon."

J.D. counted the money in his open hand and looked up at Art. Charley thanked Art for the money, noticed J.D.'s frown, and walked toward the horses.

"Are you sayin' you ain't gonna use us no more?" asked J.D.

"That's what I'm sayin'. If you need to find more work, you'll have to look someplace else." Art tried to keep his voice calm, afraid that if he spoke too harshly, J.D. and Charley might convince the Night Riders to raid his farm. "I just don't need any more help right now, that's all."

J.D. watched Charley mount his horse and said, "I guess we'll be movin' on then." He put the money in his pocket and glared at Art. "There's somethin' I been wantin' to tell you, and now that you don't need us, I guess I can say it 'cause it don't matter what you think." A menacing grin broke out on his ruddy face. "Your cousin is a dead man, or he might as well be, 'cause the Night Riders are gonna hit him next week. They know what he's plannin' to do with his crop, and they know that too many folks'll wanna do what he does. So he's gonna get hit." He paused to let the news sink in, his face now red and his eyes burning in their sockets. "Now, you can warn him if you want, but if he's waitin' for us when we get there, we'll know you told him, and we'll come after you and your family. Get it?"

The threat made Art's blood turn to ice and his heart hammer in his chest. He was afraid of J.D., but he refused to show it. He inhaled slowly and spoke, his words strong. "You've got one minute to get off my farm and out of my sight, and if you and your friends do anythin' to my cousin or any of his family, then I'll be comin' after you first. Do you understand what I'm tellin' you J.D.?"

J.D. was surprised by the farmer's resolve, but he had never backed down from a fight. "You think I'm afraid of you? Why, you ain't tough enough to kick me off this farm." He started to reach for the gun in his pocket, but paused to measure the effect of his words. When he opened his mouth to speak again, Art slipped the pistol from his own pocket, keeping it at his side.

"You got anythin' more to say, you better say it from your horse, 'cause your minute has about run out."

Charley kicked his horse in the flanks and raced to the road, not waiting for J.D. Walking quickly toward his horse, J.D. thought: *One of these days I'll find a way to make you sorry you ever pulled that gun on me.* He didn't look back as he followed Charley down the road.

Art watched them until they rode out of sight beyond the trees, and then he began trembling. The small reserve of strength he'd drawn on to face-down J.D. rushed out of him like a flash flood. He felt his stomach churn and fought back the urge to vomit. Art slipped the gun back into his pocket and bent over, spitting the rusty taste of fear into the dirt at his feet.

When he finally caught his breath, he stood up straight and walked like a drunk across the ground toward the house. *I gotta tell Wes,* he thought, *but not today. That Night Rider bastard said next week, so I got at least 'til Sunday.* He took a drink straight from the bucket at the pump and then dunked his head into the water. He kept it under, holding his breath and hoping to drown his fear of J.D. and the Night Riders. When his lungs could wait no longer, he stood up, the water streaming down his face and from his hair, drenching his sweat-stained shirt. He sucked in great gulps of air and felt tears pouring from his eyes, mixing with the cold water. *That was close. I could've killed him. But that wouldn't have helped Wes or me.*

* * *

A rind of moon cast a dim blue glow on the porch as Wes stood guard late Thursday. The night breeze felt good on his skin, but did little to cool the furnace that was burning in his head.

He knew what the risks were if he chose to take the money from Jones or if he decided to join the Association. *But why do I need to make a choice?* he thought. *What happens if I do nothin' until my crop's in the dryin' barn?* This seemed to calm him, and he noticed the peaceful sound of the crickets. He relaxed a little and set the shotgun against the wall, breathing slowly, letting the darkness in the shadow of the porch roof cover him like one of his ma's quilts. *Three choices,* he thought. He felt good, better than he had in a long time. He closed his eyes for just a moment, but they popped open when he heard footsteps on the kitchen floor.

Wes sat up straight on the bench and turned toward the sound. He waited and saw Anthie peek through the opening door.

"Pa," he said," I gotta talk to you. I remember the name I heard the Night Riders say last week."

Wes rose up, his body rigid and his ears ready to listen.

"The name was Charley."

# Chapter 20
Friday, May 18

The air was damp and cool, and the light from the barely risen sun was out of focus, blurred by the thin, gray clouds spread across the sky. Wes slept on the porch bench, bundled up in a blanket; the shotgun lay across his legs. Lying on the porch next to him, Rufus appeared lost in another world as he licked at his paws, occasionally lifting his head to watch the birds flitting into the yard and landing softly in the dust.

The stillness seemed to engulf Wes, to wrap itself around him like another blanket, yet he was not at peace. He'd dreamed that his body was burning up from the inside. Even now, the demons played with his sanity as the thoughts smoldered in his brain, each lick of flame flaring out the name "Charley." When Anthie had given him the name of the Night Rider, all of his thoughts about choices became dim coals, cast aside into distant corners of his mind. Throughout the night, he'd grappled with the thoughts that Art must have known he'd hired a Night Rider and that Charley was the source of the threat.

For an instant, when the barn door creaked, he thought his son was one of the raiders and nearly lifted the gun toward him. He caught himself before pulling the trigger, but the incident shocked him. Anthie set the milk pail down and shut the door. *I could've shot him,* Wes thought. The heat inside his head didn't go away, but his heart slowed down as he took deeper breaths. *I gotta get things under control.*

Wes stood up and stepped off the porch, holding the gun by the barrel. He just didn't feel good. His head throbbed, and his back was sore. The gentle sigh of the breeze washing across his face brought some relief, but it wasn't enough. He went over to the pump and drank some of the cold water, pouring the rest of it on his head, relishing the iciness of it as it ran down his neck and onto his shoulders. He looked over toward the barn. Then he picked up the gun and walked out to the cornfield. Looking up at the gray, cotton sky, he thought it would probably rain.

Standing near the rows of young plants, Wes shivered as the breeze blew across his wet shoulders. He watched Rufus run off toward the edge of the field and disappear into the woods. Wes stretched his back, feeling the bones grind against each other. He heard the dog bark and figured he was chasin' after a rabbit or a coon. *Sometimes I wish I was a dog,* he thought. *They don't have to worry about protectin' their farm, or sellin' their crop either. And they don't have to wonder if their cousin's been lyin' to 'em about hirin' a damned Night Rider.* This last thought flared like an ember in the wind. *Why wouldn't he tell me?* Then the ember turned into a flame. He had to know. *What else hasn't he told me?*

Wes stood, rigid as a fence post, staring at the woods, disconnected from anything but his thoughts. A whisper of cool air brushed his ear, but he fought it off, unwilling to turn from the burning questions. A second soft ripple of wind interrupted his thoughts about Art, reminding him he was losing control. His thoughts were not his own. He sighed deeply and looked up at the gray sky again, searching for the safety of his mask. "I can't think," he mumbled. "I wish it would just all go away."

He turned back toward the house and noticed the faint ribbon of smoke from the chimney disappearing into the grayness of the morning. He looked toward the east and could barely see the sun, lost as it was in the ever-thickening blanket of clouds. *I think I'm ready to face 'em now.*

From the barn, Anthie watched his pa. *I'm glad he's not on the porch. Now I won't have to talk to him 'cause somethin's wrong with him, and I'm gonna stay as far away as I can.* He walked back to the house, wishing he could become invisible.

* * *

Well before mid-morning, Wes had barely recovered from his fiery night. The demon dogs were quiet, but they were still there. He could feel them and knew they were just waiting. As far as his family could tell, he looked as normal as he had on Thursday. He'd teased his younger children at breakfast again and kept his anger and confusion hidden from Zora and the older ones. Connie and Mary Lula seemed unconcerned; they went about their chores as they always had, and Wes appreciated their indifference. He could tell Zora was being cautious with her words and her interactions with him. She spoke little and watched him a lot. But Wes thought that Anthie knew he was covering something. The boy hadn't looked at him during breakfast, and he'd left the table to start his chores as soon as his plate was clean. Wes felt his son's doubt and anger and knew he should do something about it. But now, as he stood looking out the kitchen window, he thought, *I don't have time to deal with him. I gotta figure out why Art is lyin' to me. And I gotta meet with Jones, get the papers from him and keep him the hell away from the farm in case some of the Night Riders are around. And then I gotta...* His thoughts finally gave way to weakness while another flaring ember—one of hate and mistrust—loomed somewhere in his head.

After dinner, Wes headed out to the barn to get the mule. He wanted to find Jones before he got to the farm. *I don't need anyone seein' him at my place,* he thought, *especially*

*Zora; and I ain't ready to talk about this with her yet.* But when he led the animal out of the barn, she was standing on the porch.

"Where you headed?" she said.

"I need to go into town," he said, keeping his voice calm. "I wanna talk to Mark about somethin'." This second lie rattled the chain that was keeping the dogs at bay.

Zora stared at him, searching his eyes for the truth, and saw only the lines and grooves in his tired, empty face. Wes stood in front of the mule, looking at her through vacant eyes. She started to say something about being careful, but instead just shook her head, turned away and walked into the house.

Wes pulled himself up onto the mule's back and rode up the lane. The lies lay heavily on his shoulders, his eyes constantly scanning the horizon. He'd only been riding a short time when he spotted Jones on his bay. Wes stopped, afraid of being seen, and waited for him in the shade of some trees. When Jones drew close, Wes called out, "Over here," and led him into the glade.

Wes slid down from the mule's back and dropped the reins, letting the animal chew at the grass. Jones dismounted his horse. "I was just headed to your place, Mr. Wilson. I didn't expect to meet you on the road." He held onto the reins, not sure what Wes intended to do.

"I wanted to keep our meetin' private," Wes said. "People might be watchin', and there ain't no need for anyone else to know what we're doin'."

"Okay, Mr. Wilson," he said, reaching into his pocket, still watching Wes.

"You said you'd bring the papers today. You got 'em?"

"I do, sir," Jones said, handing the papers to Wes. "They're all in order, of course. I've discussed the details with my headquarters, and they are quite pleased that you . . . " Jones paused, cautious. "May I say they are anxious to conclude an arrangement with you," he said as Wes lit a cigarette and took a deep drag.

"Like I said last time, I'm gonna need to look these papers over. I ain't gonna be ready to sign nothin' 'til next week. Is this all there is?" he said, glancing at the two sheets of paper.

"Yes sir, Mr. Wilson. Our company tries to keep things simple. You'll see that we've committed to buy your entire crop when delivered to our warehouse at the end of the harvest. We'll pay you nine cents a pound at that time." Jones paused, a little afraid of what Wilson might do when he heard the next condition. "There is one more thing, however."

Wes looked up from the contract and glared at Jones. "What one more thing?"

"Well, sir, this offer is only good until next Monday, May 21st. If the agreement isn't signed by that date, then the offer will be rescinded."

Wes continued glaring at the man, holding back his anger. He folded the sheets in half and then in half again and shoved them into his pocket. "I'll let you know on Monday. Will you still be in town then, or will you have to ride in from Mayfield?"

"Oh, I'm staying in Lynnville this weekend, so I'll be able to come out here on Monday morning."

"No!" yelled Wes. "Don't do that, I don't want you anywhere near my farm. I'll come find you if I decide to sign your papers. If you don't see me Monday by noon, then you can head back to Mayfield or Lexington or wherever you came from, 'cause that'll mean I ain't signin' anythin'." Wes waited to see how Jones would react and was surprised at the man's calmness. Jones started to reply, but Wes kept talking. "One more thing, Mr. Jones. What we talked about last time, about you keepin' your mouth shut, still holds. If any word of this gets out now or later, even if I sign the papers, I'm comin' after you. Do you understand that?"

"I do, Mr. Wilson," his voice trembling. "I certainly do."

The two men stood in the wet, knee-high grass, each waiting for the other to speak. Jones broke the silence. "Of course, if you signed today, we would be very pleased and would of course continue to keep our arrangement confidential. Nevertheless, Monday is the deadline."

"It won't be any sooner than Monday, Jones," said Wes. He walked over to where the mule was grazing and pulled himself up onto its back. "If you don't see me by noon, don't come lookin' for me." With that, he rode out of the glade and headed home.

\* \* \*

Anthie walked out of the kitchen onto the porch. The rain had changed from a drifting mist to a steady shower, enshrouding the house and yard in a curtain of water. The sun no longer peeked through the western tree line. *If the moon was going to rise tonight,* Anthie thought, *I wouldn't be able to see it, let alone any Night Riders on a raid.* He rested the barrel of the shotgun in the crook of his arm and walked to the edge of the porch, gazing out into the rain in the direction of the tobacco. "Why would any raiders wanna be out tonight?" he said to himself.

Pulling the collar of his coat up around his neck, he sat down and stretched his long legs out in front of him. He could hear his sisters talking in the kitchen as they washed up the supper dishes and was glad that he didn't have to do that chore. *But I'd sure trade with 'em if they ever wanted to milk that dumb cow before sunrise,* he thought.

He knew he should stay alert while he was on guard, but with the noise of the rain and the blinding darkness, that was not an easy task. Soon his thoughts turned to Sudie. He hadn't seen her in a week; he'd dreamed about her when he slept and thought about her when he was awake. But thoughts and dreams couldn't take the place of holding her hand or seeing the sparkle in her eyes. His heart felt warm, and he thought, *Someday I'm gonna marry that girl.* Even the clattering of the rain on the roof couldn't interrupt his musing, but when his pa stepped out onto the porch, the sweet thoughts disappeared.

"How's everythin' out here, son?"

"There ain't nothin' happenin', Pa. It's too dark and too wet." Anthie spoke without emotion, wishing his pa would just go back into the house and leave him alone so he could recover his Sudie dream.

Wes looked out into the rain, trying to see through the darkness. *Ain't gonna be any raid tonight,* he thought. *Still need to keep watch, though.* He walked to the end of the porch, stood for a moment and then turned to his son.

"Stay out here for a couple more hours. If the rain don't stop by then, come on back into the house and get some sleep. If it lets up even a little bit, though, you'll need to be out here watchin'." Anthie didn't move from the bench. "You got any questions?"

"No, Pa," he said, his voice quiet, dull.

"You come wake me if you see anythin', you hear?"

Anthie nodded, not wanting to say any more, but thought better of it and added, "Okay, Pa. I will."

After his pa left, Anthie sucked in a deep draught of air and held it in his lungs. Then he let it run out like a slow leak in a pail of water. His mind went searching for Sudie, but he couldn't find her. He kept tripping over thoughts of his pa. *It ain't just the tobacco or the Night Riders,* he thought. *There's somethin' else.* He covered his ears and squeezed his eyes shut, trying to block out the drumming on the roof. *There must be somethin' goin' on between him and Ma. Things don't look right between 'em. If there is a problem, it's gotta be Pa's fault. If he don't change, then I don't wanna be around him. Sometimes I wish he'd just go away, leave for a while, but that ain't gonna happen. No matter what, I ain't ever gonna be like him. Ever.*

Anthie finally wore himself out thinking about his pa. He'd even started to drift off to sleep, but the wind picked up and the rain came down harder and kept him awake. He pulled his collar up again and wrapped his coat tighter around his chest. Pulling his hat down around his ears, Anthie settled in for what would turn out to be a long, wet night.

# Chapter 21
Saturday, May 19

Booming thunder quickly followed a silver flash of lightning, and a howling wind beat against the wooden walls of the house as Zora tried to sleep. Lying in bed next to her, Wes barely stirred. When the second bolt came a moment later, she looked at the face on the old wind-up clock next to the bed; it showed nearly four o'clock. The rain slashed against the milky glass window, diffusing the light and painting odd shimmering shadow-creatures on the walls.

Zora was certainly tired enough to sleep, and it wasn't the pealing thunder that kept her awake. She was worried about Anthie. Her other children had found ways to cope with their pa's behavior over the past two weeks. In some ways, this surprised her. Little children, like Ruthie, often sensed trouble but didn't know how to deal with it, so they cried. The other youngsters could recognize trouble and find ways to hide from it. She figured that the two oldest were grown up enough to recognize that difficulty came with being an adult, and they learned how to handle it.

But Anthie, even though he was sixteen, was caught between the crying and the coping. *What can I do to help him,* she thought as she watched the wind-swirled water on the glass. *He thinks he's a man, but in so many ways he's still my little boy.* Another round of thunder interrupted her for a moment, and she paused to whisper a prayer for her son. When the rumbling stopped, the gusts of wind against the house sounded peaceful in comparison. *Anthie's bruises are long gone, and his broken lip is healed,* she thought, *but there's no peace in his heart.*

Zora looked over at Wes's face exposed by the flashes of lightning and saw the creases in his brow and the wrinkles that gathered at the edges of his eyes and lips. He muttered something, but the sounds were just dream words. She crept down the hall to the kitchen. Anthie was standing at the window, staring out into the storm. When he turned and reached for the coffeepot on the stove, he saw her.

"Ma, what're you doin' up?" His voice was raw, but muted.

"The thunder was so loud I couldn't sleep," she lied. "I thought I'd come see how you were doin'." She walked over and stood next to him.

"You didn't need to do that. I'm doin' fine."

"I know you are, son."

"There ain't been nobody on the road all night, Ma. I ain't even seen any critters out there except for Rufus, and that was a couple hours ago."

"Anthie, you could've spent the night in bed sleepin', you know."

"No, Ma, I couldn't. Pa told me to stand guard, and that's exactly what I been doin'."

Zora looked at his face. She saw a tired little boy with the same wrinkle lines she'd seen on Wes's face. "But I don't think he expected you to stay up all night when the whole county is holed up in their houses hidin' from the rain."

"It don't matter, Ma." He took a drink of cold coffee from his cup and paused to fill it with a hot portion from the pot he still held. "You want some, Ma?"

"No thanks, son."

He turned back to the window just as another bolt of lightning lit up the yard.

Zora continued to stare at her son. "Last week you said you hated your Pa. Do you still feel that way?"

"No, I guess not. But it still don't matter. He's mean, and he don't let me forget that I'm not a man yet." He clenched his jaws tight and cleared his throat. "I ain't a child anymore, Ma. I ain't, and he don't care."

Zora knew when to be still and let a man roll words around in his head before he said them out loud. *It is more than the creases and wrinkles that made Anthie like his pa,* she thought. *He's got his pa's looks and stubbornness and pride. He is a sixteen-year-old version of Wes.* For a brief moment, a memory of the first time she saw Wes flashed in her mind, and a tear dripped out of her eye and ran down the side of her face.

"Son, I can't tell you what to think or how to feel. You're too grown up to want to hear what your ma has to say, but I want you to listen to me." She turned him toward her and looked softly into his face. "Your pa loves you. He just don't know how to show it, especially when he's troubled about so many things." Anthie started to pull away from her, but she dropped her hands from his shoulders and held onto his arms. "I will only say this once, and I pray that you hear me. Your pa and I both love you. We always will no matter what you do or where you go or what you become." When she finished, she turned away from him and walked back down the hall to her bedroom.

Anthie waited until he could no longer hear his ma's footsteps. Then he looked out into the rain again and fought the urge to cry, failing miserably.

* * *

By daylight, the thunder and lightning had moved off toward the east. The rain continued to blow in torrents, creating small ponds in the low areas of the yard. The streams of water pouring off the roof looked like crystal curtains. Anthie braved his way to the barn and back, setting the full pail of fresh milk just inside the kitchen door. He was soaked from the rain and didn't want to drip all over the floor because his ma had enough work to do without cleaning up his mess. Anthie trusted and loved his ma and liked pleasing her.

Wes stepped out onto the porch and looked at his son. "You been out here all night?" He spoke quietly, but there was a raw edge to his words.

"Most of it," said Anthie. "I didn't see anybody, just a lot of rain and lightnin'."

"I told you if it kept rainin' you could go to bed. Why'd you stay out here?"

"I couldn't have slept with all the noise anyway, so I figured I'd just stand guard." He got up from the bench and stood next to Wes. "I'm goin' in now, Pa. I'm tired and need some sleep." He took off his wet clothes, squeezed the water out of them and walked into the house. Wes wanted to say more, but Connie came out before the door shut.

"Guess we better go see what kind of a mess we got, Pa," he said. "I think we're gonna get wet, though."

"You don't have to go out with me."

"Sure I do, Pa. Two of us can take a look, and we'll only get a little wet." He smiled at his pa and pulled his hat down over his ears. "I'll take the sty, the coop and the west side and meet you back here." He stepped off the porch and ran toward the chicken coop, nearly disappearing in the rain.

Wes shook his head, surprised at Connie's enthusiasm and pleased that at least one of his sons was going to be a farmer. *If only that was all I had to worry about.* Making sure his coat was buttoned up, he held onto his hat, stepped off the porch and headed out to the tobacco field.

Working different sides of the farm, he and Connie trudged through the sticky mud and driving rain, focusing on the damage. They noted the flooded areas, which would have to be drained, and the flattened wheat, which may or may not recover. Some of the tobacco looked trampled, but

Wes judged that they'd been blown over by the wind. In less than an hour, they'd surveyed the whole farm and met back at the barn.

"What'd you see out there, Pa?" said Connie, greeting Wes as he stepped into the shelter of the barn.

"Lots of water. We'll have some drainin' to do, and we might lose a little tobacco, but I think we'll be okay if the storm ends soon."

"There's some wheat down, but it don't look busted," said Connie, "and the corn is fine." He took off his felt hat and wrung it out, the water making a puddle on the dirt floor. "Won't be able to wear this hat to church no more," he said, trying to hold back a laugh. "I'm so wet I think I'm turnin' into a fish."

In some deep part of himself, Wes saw how hard Connie was trying to cheer him up. "We'd better get into the house and dry off. Besides, I'm hungry, and I bet your ma has breakfast ready." He put his hand on Connie's shoulder and squeezed it, the gesture earning him another smile from his son.

They ran through the rain to the house, getting wet all over again. Both men shed their coats and kicked off their boots, stripping down to their long johns on the porch. They shivered while they twisted the overalls and shirts, wringing the rain out of the cloth. Stepping around the water on the porch, they carried the wet bundles into the warm kitchen. As they stood next to the stove, steam rose from their bodies like fog, and the laughter of the youngsters filled the crowded room.

* * *

Wes could feel the darkness of Art's lie consume his thoughts again. He paced in front of the window, looking out at the ceaseless rain, listening to the rumbling thunder coming in from the west, looking for an out, a place to go where he could be alone. Even though it was after noon, the sky was dark, dusk-like. Zora walked into the kitchen, carrying one of her glass-globed lamps, and set it on the table. She lit it with a match and watched Wes, feeling his nervous energy.

"Another storm comin' in?" she asked.

"Or it's more of the same one." Wes stopped and looked at her briefly. Then he turned back to the window. "The ponds and the creek are already full, and some of the fields're flooded. If it keeps up longer than today, we're gonna have more water than we need."

"If it's still rainin' tomorrow, we'll likely miss the foot-washin' at church," Zora said, her voice revealing sadness. "I hope it quits soon, 'cause I'd really like us to go." She waited for a response from Wes, but he was silent. She reached over and touched his arm and walked away, leaving him alone, knowing that he was still worried about his crop.

A loud clap of thunder shook the house and rattled the window glass. He watched as the wind blew the rain across the yard. Behind his watchful eyes, though, his mind continued to struggle with Anthie's revelation about Charley. Like the thunder from the storm, the man's name would suddenly rumble through his mind and drench him with thoughts of Art's secret. He was wading through the dark hole of one of these mental squalls when Irene screeched as she came running into the kitchen, chased by John Stanley.

Jolted by Irene's screams, Wes turned to his children, enraged. "What the hell?" he roared. At once his mask crumbled, and the snarling dogs of anger pushed their way onto his face. He glared at his children, his heart pounding, his fists clenched. He started to say more, but saw the fear in their eyes. Disappointed in himself, he turned and ran out the door through the driving rain all the way to the barn. He slipped in the mud, struggling to keep his footing as he worked the door open and stepped inside. Wes bent over trying to catch his breath, water dripping from his hair onto the floor. He stood up, slamming the door shut and punching his fist into the wall, angry with himself for frightening his children and at Art for lying to him. The rain fell harder outside the barn as a loud crack of lightning hit the ground near the road. Wes was caught in the middle of two storms: the one outside and the one in his crowded mind. He couldn't get away from either of them.

* * *

North of Lynnville, J.D. and Charley were holed up in the leaky shack. The single room was damp; rain dripped on the canvas mattress bags, and the small puddles that formed between the cots leaked through the cracks in the floorboards. Charley listened to J.D.'s raspy snoring, which filled the gaps between the claps of thunder and the howling wind. The concert of noises and the sogginess of his clothes and cot kept him from sleeping. There was nothing else to do but think and plan.

What little money they'd managed to keep was his. J.D. squandered the rest of his money on another jug of whiskey after they'd been kicked off Art West's farm. Then he'd spent the last two days drinking, and his pockets were as empty as the hollow jug on the floor. During his conscious moments, J.D. had spoken about little but revenge against Art and his cousin and rambled on about plans to carry out his rage against the two. They still had the work with the Night Riders ahead of them, and J.D. thought that the raid money and the twenty dollars for the other job would be enough for the two of them to finally clear out. *But what is the other job,* Charley wondered. Not knowing where the money was coming from scared him.

*Half the money's mine,* thought Charley, *and clearin' out sounds good to me. But I ain't goin' along with him.*

*The things he says and does are evil, and I don't wanna be caught up in doin' any of 'em. Even if I tell the law that I had no part in it, they'd arrest me just for bein' with him, and I ain't goin' to jail again.* Charley's stomach growled, and he glanced around the room looking for something to eat. A soggy bread crust lying in the water-filled bottom of a tin plate became his dinner.

J.D. snorted and gagged. Then he rolled over in his bed. The huge drops of water coming through the roof fell on his shapeless hat and the burlap sack he'd pulled over his shoulders. Charley cupped his hands over his ears, trying to block out the noise so he could think. *Maybe I should just forget about the money, keep what I have and clear out right now. He won't know which way I've gone, and if I leave on foot, he won't even have a trail to follow.* Charley stood quietly and picked up the sack holding his few possessions, hoping the wind muted the floor's creaking. He looked down at J.D., glad that he didn't have to explain what he was doing and knowing that J.D. would find a way to make him change his mind. *But I ain't gonna change my mind.* He waited for the next thunder clap, and when it rattled the walls of the shack, he opened the door and slipped out into the storm.

* * *

J.D. leaned over the edge of his bed and threw up on the wet, cluttered floor of the shack.

"Charley!" he yelled. "Where the hell are you?"

He swung his legs off the cot and sat up, leaning back against the wall. "Charley, get in here!" J.D. searched around for his jug and spotted it on the floor. Charley still hadn't answered him, so he yelled again. He shook his head, trying to clear the whiskey mud from his brain, and then he rubbed his eyes with the heels of his hands and looked across at Charley's pallet. *Somethin's missin',* he thought. Even in his muddled state, he noticed that his partner's bag, the one that held his personal things, was not hanging on the rusty nail above his bed.

"What've you done now, you sorry son of a bitch," he muttered. J.D. tried to stand up but fell back. Then he tried again and managed to stay upright, bracing himself against the wall. Kicking the empty jug out of his way, he stomped to the door and pushed it open. A fresh blast of windblown rain hit him in the face, and he wiped it away, trying to see into the dark night. When a flash of distant lightning lit up the bottom of the clouds, he saw both of the horses tied off on the rail. He yelled again for Charley.

J.D. walked into the rain and circled the shack and out-house, calling out his name. Wet and cold, he went back inside and kicked the jug again. "Well I guess he's gone," he snarled. "Ran out on me like a damned coward."

Near midnight, J.D. threw a bedroll over the back of the best horse and pulled himself up into the saddle. The rain had lightened to a steady shower as he rode out of the yard and onto the road. He'd made up his mind that he didn't need Charley's help to carry out the captain's instructions. *Now I won't have to share the twenty dollars,* he thought, *and after gettin' paid for the raid I'll have enough to get away from here.* The thought seemed to comfort him, and a crooked grin grew on his face. *Maybe I'll just take a ride over to Wes Wilson's and take a look.* Hunched over the sad-dle, he rode the miserable horse south, past Lynnville.

Standing in a copse of trees across the road from the farmhouse, J.D. hid behind the trunk of an old oak tree. There were no lights showing from the house, but he saw that the barn door was ajar. Off to the right, the leaves of the tobacco plants rustled in the wind and an owl hooted.

Whispering to himself, J.D. said, "I'm gonna enjoy torchin' this place, and maybe even roughin' up his wife and kids. Then we'll see how tough he is." He sucked in one last time on his cigar, the tip glowing hotly, and dropped the stub into the mud. "Maybe the last thing I'll do is put a bullet in his head."

\* \* \*

Wes willed his heavy eyelids open as he stood in the open door of his barn. The rain and wind had let up a bit, but the cloudy sky blocked out the moonlight. He yawned deeply and tried again to keep his eyes open, but he couldn't. Struggling to stay awake, he slid to his knees and leaned against the door. He thought he saw a red glow across the road in the trees just as he passed out.

# Chapter 22
Sunday Morning, May 20

Even though the thunderstorms were moving off to the east, the storm in Wes's head raged out of control, blowing with such force that he knew it would all end soon; it had to. After only a few hours of dreamless sleep, he'd been jolted awake by the pounding thought of what to do. The money Jones had offered was very tempting. If he took the deal, he could buy a horse and provide much more for his family, and that would make him feel like a man. On the surface, the bank offer seemed solid as well. But no one had seen anything in writing to ensure the farmers, and he was not going to trust that group of men at the meeting. Finally, as the last peal of thunder faded away, Wes reached a decision about his tobacco. The painful tension of the past weeks seemed to flow from his body like wind through a knothole. His shoulders sagged, his cheeks softened and his once-racing thoughts slowed down as he closed his eyes and fell asleep on a pile of hay.

When he woke up, he felt calm, as if surrounded by a peaceful cloud. He didn't know what would happen next because of his decision, but he felt ready to face whatever lay ahead. When he heard the cow rustling in her stall, he picked up the pail and opened the gate. Pulling on her udders, he leaned his head into her side and relaxed as the pail filled. When he finished, he carried the pail to the porch and sat on the bench. From the doorway, Anthie stared at his pa.

"Let me have it, Pa," he said, taking the pail from Wes

and silently returning to the kitchen. *Why is he milkin' the cow? Nothin' makes sense anymore when it comes to Pa.*

After he'd washed up, Wes sat on the bench. He gazed at the glow of the rising sun on the dwindling clouds and leaned back against the wall. For now, even though he felt the heat of Art's lies, a great burden had been lifted from his shoulders, and all the other worries would have to wait. Yet he knew he still needed to get at the root of the lies and find out the truth about the Night Riders. *Can't do anythin' about that until church,* he thought. Almost surprised by his own calmness, he relaxed and watched a few birds fly into the yard as Rufus crawled out from under the house.

Zora had waited up for Wes all night. She'd checked on him a few times, but he never came in from the barn. Taking the milk pail from Anthie, she looked out the kitchen window onto the porch and could just see Wes's stretched-out legs. She pulled a big mug down from the shelf and filled it with coffee, wrapped a shawl around her shoulders and carried the cup out to the porch. She approached him cautiously, and he turned toward her as she pulled the door closed.

"I thought you might like some of this." He took the mug in his hands, feeling the heat of it, and realized that it had been a long time since he'd felt anything other than confusion and anger.

Wes scooted over to make room for Zora on the bench and patted the empty spot at his side. She sat down quickly, not wanting to miss the opportunity to be close. He shook his head when she asked if he was cold, yet she could feel the chill coming off his arm as he draped it around her shoulder. He turned to her, and she looked into his blue eyes and saw that much of the redness was gone. His face was softer, more relaxed, and she could see that something was different. Zora felt a fluttering in her chest and a tenderness toward Wes that had been absent for over a week.

The hard feelings she'd carried began to fade like fog drifting away in the morning sun. She wanted to cry with joy; instead, she turned her face into his chest, reveling in the smell of him. They stayed that way on the bench for a while, silently watching the sunrise. Then, as the first rays of the sun peeked over the trees and flooded the porch with light, he said, "I've made up my mind about the crop."

* * *

On the way to church that morning, Zora drank in the warmth of the sun and of her husband's strength as she gazed down the long, muddy road ahead. The azure sky, unblemished by clouds, was clear, the fresh air warm and damp. A riot of birds, glad to be away from the cover of trees, flew across the road over the soggy fields and the damp, velvet-like grass at the edge of the fields. In the back of the wagon, Mary Lula told the younger children a Bible story, the one about Noah and the flood, while Connie and Anthie sat quietly at the rear of the wagon, their feet hanging just above the gooey road.

The mud-muted sounds of the mule pulling the wagon and the soothing sound of Mary Lula's voice calmed Wes, but in some silent corner of his mind, the names Art and Charley had found root and were gaining strength. *How could he keep this from me,* pounded in his head over and over. His heart ached for peace with his cousin, but his mind told him he might never find it again. They'd been close forever, but now the gulf between them was growing wider and deeper.

Even though they'd arrived early, the muddy churchyard was already crowded with horses and buggies. Some of the wagons were lined up to drop off families at the church porch.

"Wes, you don't need to drop us off," said Zora. "We can walk from the field."

"No need for you and the girls to get muddy," he said, trying to block the chatter in his head. "I'll take you up there and then try to find a place for the wagon on the grass out back." He clucked at the mule and slapped the reins as the wagon in front moved up. Clearly distracted, Wes looked around the growing crowd, trying to see if Art had shown up. *What'll he say when I ask about Charley?*

"I'll stay with you, Pa," said John Stanley as he stood behind Wes. "I don't mind walkin' in the mud."

"Oh no you won't, young man," Zora said softly. You're comin' inside with me. I want you sittin' right next to me when I thank the Lord for takin' care of you after you got hurt."

"But, Ma, I'm better now."

"That's true, and you're gonna stay better without gettin' muddy," she laughed. "I don't want you slippin' and fallin' and bumpin' your head again. It's only been a week or so, and I'd like you to stay clean for a little while today."

Wes drove up to the porch, set the brake and jumped to the ground. He walked around to Zora's side of the wagon, where Anthie was already standing by his ma's side.

"I'll help you, Ma," said Anthie, reaching up to help her down.

"I'll do it," said Wes, pushing himself in front of Anthie, forcing his son to take a step back.

Anthie moved out of the way, slipping in the mud. He glared at the back of his pa's head for a moment. Then he turned and stalked away. Without looking back, Anthie wound his way between some wagons and disappeared into the woods at the edge of the churchyard. *He ain't nothin' but a mean ol' selfish son of a bitch,* he thought as he stopped and leaned back against a tree. He couldn't hold back the hot tears that streamed down his cheeks.

Unaware of Anthie's reaction, Wes set Zora on the porch and went around to the back of the wagon to help Connie finish unloading the rest of the family. Both Mary Lula and Zora had seen the look on Anthie's face and knew that he wouldn't be coming into the service. Zora didn't know why Wes cut Anthie off or why the boy had taken it so hard, but it troubled her deeply that the two of them were still fighting.

Wes climbed onto the wagon, reached under the seat and picked up his pistol. Slipping it into his pocket, he drove around to the field behind the church and stopped near the back tree line. He'd just set the brake and slid down from the seat when Art walked up behind him.

"Mornin', Wes," he said.

Surprised and unprepared, Wes turned and looked into the smiling face of his cousin. At the sight of him, Wes felt the heat of his anger spreading over his entire body. *How can he stand there smilin',* he thought, *when he's keepin' the truth from me?* Wes forced a smile, but the mask felt thin. He walked around to the front of the mule, trying to collect his thoughts, to get control of the situation. Art followed him and put a hobble on his horse. Then he stood waiting as Wes fussed with the mule's bridle.

"You goin' inside this mornin'?" asked Art.

Walking around the wagon, Wes tried again to put some distance between them, but Art followed closely. "Didn't plan on it," he finally said. "I got a lot to think about. Besides, I ain't interested in gettin' my feet washed by that yappy ol' preacher."

"Ain't that the truth." Art said and then changed the subject. "How'd you do with the storm?"

"Got some wheat down and a bit of floodin', but we'll be okay." Wes was forcing the words out, aching to have some time to deal with the jumbled mess going on in his head.

The air seemed heavy, the conversation flat as Art continued. "I got some damage too. Pretty much the same as you did. I'm gonna be busy for a while drainin' off the water, but I'll get it done." Keenly aware of Wes's coldness, he added, "There's gonna be a lot of work for me and my boy since I let J.D. and Charley go."

At the mention of the farmhands' names, a fire rose in Wes's belly. He was speechless, stunned by Art's news. He mumbled a few senseless words while his thoughts raced. He forced a cough to cover his confusion and then asked, "Why'd you fire 'em?"

"Clarence is old enough to start doin' a little more work around the farm, so when I went to pay them two for the work they'd done, I said I didn't need 'em anymore. Then J.D. started gettin' all mouthy, swearin' and threatenin' like, so I told him to get off my farm." Art was quiet for a moment. "I had to pull my gun on J.D. to show him I meant business." Art touched the pistol in his pocket. "Those two are up to somethin', and it ain't anythin' good." He hoped that would be enough for now, but he knew that Wes would need to hear about the raid planned for his farm as soon as they were away from the church.

Wes watched Art's face as he spoke, looking for something, anything that would tell him if his cousin was lying. But Art's dark eyes seemed only to show real anger at the two men and nothing more. Wes noticed that most of the women and children had gone inside the building and that a small crowd of men was gathering at the edge of the field. "We gotta talk some more about J.D. and Charley, and it can't wait 'til after church."

Art really didn't want to have the conversation at all. He just wanted to warn Wes about the raid and leave it at that. If he said anything else then Wes would know he'd been holding back information. *And that can't happen,* Art thought. *It might mean the end of our friendship.*

"You're right, we do need to talk about them," said Art, "but I don't know how much more I can add."

*That's another lie,* Wes thought. *I can't believe a damn*

*word he says. There's a whole lot more he can add, and I intend to find out the truth.*

*Ask him now,* his mind screamed. He looked away, confused, not ready to confront Art. Drawing a breath through his nose, he said, "Why don't we join them fellas and see what they know. We need to talk more, but not now." They wandered toward the other edge of the church field. "But we better do more listenin' than talkin' 'cause you never know, some of 'em could be Night Riders."

At the mention of the raiders, Art felt his guts clenching. As they walked together, he fought to remain calm and keep his emotions under control. *That's all I'm gonna do is listen,* he thought. *I don't know what to say anymore. Nothin' good's gonna happen if I open my mouth.*

The mid-morning sun was beginning to heat up the damp air as they walked through the grass toward the other men. They heard the singing starting up inside the church, but it was nothing more than background noise to their thoughts. Not a word passed between them as they neared the tree line, and neither of them saw Anthie watching from his hiding spot in the woods.

\* \* \*

Inside the clapboard church, Zora was staring into an open hymnal, but, unlike the rest of the crowd, she wasn't singing. The smile she'd brought into the building had faded. The vacant spaces to her left and right should have been occupied by her husband and son, but both of them were still outside, and she was not happy. She glanced down the pew and caught Mary Lula looking back in her direction. Her daughter wasn't singing either, and after a moment the girl gently shrugged her shoulders and turned back to the front. Despite the change she'd seen in Wes that morning, Zora knew he would have nothing to do with the foot washing. She remained hopeful. Some things just take time.

The rumbling of people sitting down in the pews shook Zora from her thoughts, and she sat down with a thump. John Stanley started to giggle, but a light tap on the back of his head from Connie squelched the laughter. Zora glanced over at the window, willing her husband to come inside and be with her, but her senses told her otherwise. Up on the platform, one of the deacons stood behind the pulpit and asked the congregation if there were any prayer requests. A few raised their hands. Zora bowed h*er head and prayed while the preacher droned on and on. That man is in love with his own voice,* she thought. *I wonder if the Lord don't get tired of him sometimes. God'll take care of all them needs, just like he'll take care of ours.*

She took a moment to clear her mind of the preacher's voice and focus on her missing son. *I gotta be doin' more for Anthie,* she prayed. *I've tried talkin' to him. But he don't wanna listen to me anymore. He can be a sweet boy sometimes, but right now he just seems to be lookin' at all the bad things goin' on, and he acts hurt and mean. I don't know how to turn him around.*

She paused and looked down the row at her children, and her mind eased a bit. All of them except the baby were doing what she'd taught them—sitting quietly, their heads bowed, their eyes closed. Connie sat at the end of the pew, and Zora sighed as she realized that right now he was the man of the family. Ruthie was resting in Mary Lula's arms, holding the small rag doll Connie had made for her. *She's lucky,* Zora thought. *She ain't got nothin' to worry about like us grown-ups do.* She heard the preacher's voice as he headed toward the end of his prayer. Finished with her own prayer, Zora looked toward the window again, wishing she could help Anthie and Wes. But an uneasy feeling filled her heart.

The hot sun in the late morning sky glared through the few windows on the east side of the room, and some of the older ladies fanned themselves as the air grew warmer. One of the deacons stood and walked to the other side of the room and opened a window. A light breeze wafted across the folks in the pews, and an almost imperceptible sigh drifted along with it. When he was certain he had their attention again, the preacher said, "Pay attention to the reading of God's holy word."

Zora didn't need to open her Bible. She knew the words told how Jesus had washed his disciples' feet, humbling himself to them. Zora knew all about pride and how it can destroy; she saw it in Wes and feared it in herself. In the past two weeks, she'd stood up to Wes when he'd been wrong. She'd thought it was important that he realized what he was doing to the family. But in the days following her outbursts, she worried that she'd gone too far and made things worse. Perhaps it was her own pride that had created the tension in her family. She gripped the edges of the book in front of her, not seeing the words, but hoping that their message could be squeezed into her hands and from there into her heart. Then, quietly and tearlessly, she wept.

* * *

Anthie stood hidden among the trees and out of the sun, where the air was cooler. His shoes were muddy, and the cuffs of his pants were soiled, but he didn't care. He felt only a growing anger as he watched his pa and cousin walk over to the men and boys gathered at the edge of the woods. He took off his hat and hooked it on a broken tree limb. Then he wiped his drenched brow with the back of his hand. As he stared through the trees, he found a comfortable position and listened to the buzzing conversations of the farmers. He knew it wouldn't be long before a jug of whiskey appeared in the crowd. *Someone always brings a jug*, he thought, *and when Pa takes a drink, I'll know he ain't the fine, gentle father everyone thinks he is. He's nothin' but a liar and a drunk.*

\* \* \*

Wes stopped short of the clearing and away from the other men, still wanting to confront Art about the Night Riders, urgently hoping that his cousin would tell the truth. Art kept walking toward the center of the clearing, where most of the men stood around talking about the rain and their crops. He knew that in a crowd Wes couldn't force him into a discussion that would probably be difficult. Then someone behind them mentioned Jones, and both Art and Wes turned around to listen.

"I heard that damned tobacco buyer is still in town," said Slim, a tall, skinny farmer they both knew. Some of the men nodded in assent, but one of them shook his head.

"That ain't what I heard," Albert said, taking his pipe from his mouth and spitting into the grass at his feet. "Word is that Jones already made some deals and headed back to Lexington." This caught Wes's attention, and he took a step forward.

There was some shuffling and mumbling in the group. "So who'd he make a deal with?" Slim asked.

"I don't know that, Slim, but that's what I heard."

"Well then, who'd you hear it from?" Slim demanded. "Maybe they know who's talkin' to the damned trust buyer."

"Listen, Slim, I told you I don't know who he's made a deal with. I don't know that he's even made a deal. All I know is that I heard that he's dealin' and that he left town. That's all I'm gonna say."

Wes waited for the bickering to settle down and said, "Maybe this fella Jones is talkin' to a lot of folks. Maybe he's just tryin' to stir things up." He paused, thinking carefully about what to say next. "We know he's been ridin' around the district for the past few weeks, so he's likely talked to a lot of fellas. That don't mean any of 'em have made deals, and even if they have, they ain't likely to tell anyone, are they? Everybody knows that makin' a deal with the Trust means they'd likely get raided by the Night Riders."

Art felt lightheaded, almost sick. He knew that Wes had been talking to Jones, but he never believed that his cousin would make a deal. But now, listening to Wes defend Jones and with his own knowledge of the planned raid, Art was positive that Wes had already sold his tobacco to the Trust and was keeping it from him. The hard truth of these thoughts made him take a step back from Wes. Several of the men began talking among themselves, but Art didn't join in. He was watching Wes and thinking back to what both he and Mark had done a week ago. He remembered covering for Wes in front of the fellas from the Association. *Wes was lyin' to us the whole time.*

A roar of laughter from the far corner of the church lot drew everyone's attention, and most of the men wandered over to see what was going on. Wes held back, anxiously wanting to talk with Art, but his cousin seemed to avoid him as he joined the others in their trek toward the laughter. Wes followed Art, wandering along behind the crowd toward the edge of the field. *Maybe I can get him alone now, and we can get this out in the open.* His face hardened as he thought, *I can't trust him no more.*

* * *

Leaving her shoes under the pew, Zora rose from her spot and walked slowly up the aisle toward the platform. She took a seat in the chair placed in front of a pan of warm water, but she couldn't focus. On the other side of the pan, the preacher was kneeling, facing her, quietly praying to himself. As he had done several dozen times in the past hour, he spoke of humility and service while he quietly rubbed her bare feet with the water and then dried them with a towel. All the while, Zora prayed—not for the preacher or the deacons, not for the church, not even for herself. Just as the preacher set her dry feet on the floor, a feeling of urgency overwhelmed her. The sermon and the foot washing had brought her no comfort, and she sensed that something terrible was going on outside. She was afraid and couldn't hold back the tears as they flowed from her eyes and rained down her cheeks. She stood and walked to the window and looked for both Anthie and Wes. She spotted her husband just as he put the whiskey jug to his lips.

* * *

Anthie was right about one thing: someone had brought a jug of liquor. From his hiding place, he watched as it was passed around among some men he didn't know. The talking and laughter grew louder with each swig of the whiskey.

In a matter of minutes, the crowd had grown to several dozen, and a few more jugs appeared. Anthie watched intensely as Art and his pa joined in the drinking. He glanced over in the direction of the church and saw that the door was still closed. *Must still be washin' feet,* he thought. *They'll be done soon enough, and this drinkin' will be over.* He turned back to the men and watched his pa take a long drink out of someone's jug and then hand it to Art. Anthie lifted his hat off the limb, turned away from the hiding place and headed over to the wagon. *He makes me sick. He's nothin' but a drunk. I wish he wasn't my pa.*

While the drinking and laughter continued, Wes stayed close to his cousin, all the while hoping to get Art drunk enough that he could get him to admit his deceit. But Art still wasn't paying attention to Wes, ignoring him as he listened to the jokes and drank the liquor. The jug came to Wes again, and he took another drink, the amber liquid burning his throat. He welcomed the fire in his belly.

*You've ignored me long enough,* he thought as he turned and moved toward his cousin.

Art was seething. *Wes not only lied to me, he lied to his own brother. We could be in real trouble with the Association because we stood up for him.* These thoughts boiled in his chest as he moved to the middle of the crowd where a fight had erupted.

Two of the farmers were shoving each other around. There was a lot of swinging and swearing as each fighter tried to gain an advantage. The brawl might have gone on longer, but the sheriff pushed his way through the bystanders and pulled the men apart just as the doors of the church burst open and dozens of children ran out of the building and into the field. Most of them ran directly to where the men circled the fight. Not far behind the children came the women. At first, they tried to gather up the youngsters, but when they saw that the men had been drinking and some had been fighting, they let the children go and tried to gather up their husbands. Had the sheriff not been there to stop the fight, the two farmers might have killed each other. As it turned out, they both needed medical attention, and the crowd of men—now joined by women and children—laughed as he loaded them in his wagon and headed off to Lynnville to find a doctor and to lock them up.

When Zora saw the large group of men and heard the noise of the fight, she was afraid. Scanning the crowd, she looked for Anthie but saw only Wes standing with Art well away from the action. She headed in his direction, hoping that he knew where Anthie might be, but when she saw her son sitting on the back of the wagon, away from the fight, she relaxed. Turning in mid-stride, she walked toward him, glad that he was safe.

As Zora approached the rear of the wagon, Anthie didn't look up until she spoke to him. "Are you all right, son?"

"No, Ma. I wanna go home."

"I'll go get your pa and the others. You get the wagon ready. I don't wanna stay around this trouble any longer than we have to." Putting her hand on his leg, she patted him and smiled, then turned and walked back to the other end of the field.

"Okay, Ma, I'll meet you over by the church," he said as she walked away. He went around to get the mule ready. Then he climbed up onto the bench seat, clucked to the mule and drove the rig toward the empty church building. Mary Lula and the three youngsters were still on the porch. Anthie couldn't see Connie, but suspected that his brother was somewhere in the crowd of people milling around at the edge of the field. He thought about leaving the wagon near the porch and heading home on foot, but decided that would only upset his ma more than she already was. *Better just sit here and wait for her. Pa's gonna be in real trouble with her, so he won't have time to pick on me.* Anthie pulled the brake on the wagon and jumped down so he could help the others into the wagon box. He didn't respond when John Stanley asked him about the fight, nor when Mary Lula put her hand on his cheek and turned his face to hers. He gently brushed her hand away and sat down on the back of the wagon away from everyone.

# Chapter 23
Sunday, Afternoon May 20

Wes reined the mule to a stop on the east side of Mark's store. After setting the brake, he looked back and told Connie to get a bucket of water for the mule and sent Anthie to get his Uncle Mark. Both boys slid down from the wagon and headed off. A quiet Art got out of the wagon, glad the bumpy ride was finally over. He wasn't feeling well because of the liquor, and he was still upset about Wes and Jones. John Stanley had already untied Art's horse from the back of the wagon and stood proudly waiting.

"Thanks for lettin' me ride your horse, Cousin Art," said the boy. "That was fun. I'm gonna have me a horse just like this someday."

"You're welcome, young man," Art said. He coiled the reins and started to pull himself up into the saddle when Wes's words stopped him.

"Wait, Art. We need to talk with Mark."

"I gotta get back home to Mollie and the kids," he grumbled. "Can't this wait 'til tomorrow or Tuesday?"

"We need to clear up some things," Wes said, struggling to keep his voice calm. "It shouldn't take too long." *You can't ignore me anymore,* he thought.

Even though he didn't want to get into a difficult conversation with Wes, Art finally agreed. He stepped back to the ground and tied the reins to the wooden pillar holding up the store's roof.

"Thanks," Wes said. "Give me a minute to get my family

headed home." He turned to Zora, put his arm around her shoulder, pulled her close to him and leaned in to whisper in her ear. Holding her cheek close to his, he said, "Everythin's gonna be all right, Zora. Everythin'."

Her hair had come undone, and the loose strands tickled his nose as he spoke. Zora reached up to Wes's hand where it lay on her face. She patted it gently and turned to him. Despite the smell of whiskey on his lips, she smiled and kissed him gently. Her heart raced with love for Wes.

"Thank you, Wes."

Her reverie was interrupted when Mark came out of the house.

"What're you all doin' in town on Sunday afternoon?" Mark said as he walked up to the wagon. Gertrude waddled along behind him, breathing heavily as she tried to keep up with her husband. She walked around to the side of the wagon to speak to Zora just as Wes got down from the seat. Mark shook Wes's hand and reached into the back of the wagon to pat Ruthie on her cheek and rub Irene's head. "And how are you two sweet girls? I ain't seen you in a while. You keep gettin' bigger all the time." The girls giggled and tugged on their uncle's ears. He let out a familiar howl, and they giggled some more.

"How about me, Uncle Mark? Ain't I gettin' big too?"

"You sure are, John Stanley. Pretty soon I'll be lookin' up at you. Why, you'll be taller than my store before you know it." He turned toward Mary Lula and just shook his head, smiling at her until she blushed and turned away.

"Anthie said you needed to see me, and it sounded important," said Mark. He waited for Wes to reply and then shook Art's hand as he came up to where they stood. "It must be important if you fellas couldn't wait 'til Monday."

"Not sure what it's about, Mark. But Wes says I need to stay." Art crossed his arms on his chest, frowning.

Wes paid no attention to Anthie, who returned to the

back of the wagon. He waited while Connie finished watering the mule and then called him over to his side. "You take the family home, son. I'll be along in a couple of hours."

"Okay, Pa," Connie said. "I'll take care of everythin'." He climbed into the seat and sat tall next to his mother. Then he looked around to make sure everyone was settled. Satisfied, he flicked the reins on the mule's back and said, "Come on, mule. Let's get." The wagon creaked as the animal pulled against the leather harness and started moving forward. Zora looked at Wes and returned his smile. She waved at Gertrude and looked down the road toward home.

"Bye, Pa," yelled John Stanley, waving wildly. "See you soon!" Mary Lula quickly pulled him down into the wagon box, and Wes watched as she scolded him and Irene punched him in the shoulder. He saw the sullen look on Anthie's face and waved at his son, but the boy just turned away.

"Do you think we could sit in the store for a while?" asked Wes. "We need to talk about some things, and I don't wanna get interrupted by any of the folks who might be walkin' around town." He looked over at Art, but his cousin stood silently staring at the ground, thinking, *I don't wanna have this discussion. I just wanna get away from him to do my own thinkin'.*

"Rather than hang around here, I got a better idea," said Mark. "Let's take my wagon out for a while. My horse is gettin' lazy and could use some exercise." At this, Gertrude put her fists on her hips and glared at Mark.

"It's Sunday, Mark."

When he didn't respond to her obvious displeasure, she spun around as nimbly as she could and then trudged off in the direction of the house.

"That's the real reason," he said and watched until she closed the door. "I'll be in some measure of trouble later, but I don't care." He paused and said, "I'll be right back."

Wes and Art faced each other, neither one speaking.

Mark disappeared around the back of the store and returned in a few minutes leading the horse and wagon. He asked Art to check the harness and ran into the store. Returning quickly with a bundle under his arm, he glanced toward the house. When he saw the curtains close quickly, he laughed and said, "Yep, I'll be in a heap of trouble tonight." He put the bundle in the back of the wagon and climbed up into the seat. He waited while Wes and Art got in, and then he flicked the reins along the horse's back. The animal pulled at the wagon, and the three friends started down the road toward Dresden.

"What's in the bundle, Mark?" Art pulled at the layers of cloth and discovered two full jugs of whiskey. Some of his tension faded as he lifted them up. "Why, Cousin Mark, I do believe that you intend to lead us down a path of unrighteousness this Sunday afternoon."

"That may be the result, Art. But it's not my intention. It seems to me, if we got important things to discuss, we might as well be comfortable." He laughed out loud and snapped the reins again. The horse picked up the pace as they made the first sweeping turn on the southbound road. Wes heard the humor in his brother's voice, but didn't share it. The discussion that lay ahead was going to be difficult, and he wasn't sure if his friendship with Art would survive it.

\* \* \*

The sky had turned a dark gray under a gathering blanket of clouds, and the warm air seemed heavy with rain. Mark drove the wagon at a leisurely pace down the road. Each of the men had shed his coat and rolled up the sleeves of his white Sunday shirt as though preparing for a fight. The silver disc of the sun behind the clouds had warmed them, and a goodly portion of the first jug of whiskey was working to do the same. For the first mile, a silence engulfed the cousins, as neither Wes nor Art spoke. The quiet forced Mark to carry the conversation by himself, but all of his tales did nothing to stir them.

"Should I be sorry I missed the foot-washin' up at Cuba church?" he said, glancing back at his brother and cousin, noticing that Wes still looked uneasy.

Art pulled the cork from the jug, took a quick draught and passed it to Mark. "We didn't go inside the church," slurred Art. "All the men had gathered out by the trees, and there was lots of talkin' and drinkin' goin' on, which led to a fight between two fellas. Then church let out, and the whole place was covered with women and children. The sheriff finally broke up the whole mess." Art rested his elbows on his knees and stared at Wes. He could almost feel the weight of what was bothering him. *Whatever it is, he'll have his say soon enough. He always does.*

Mark laughed out loud and nearly dropped the jug, but caught it just before it slipped off his lap. He pulled back on the reins and stopped the wagon in the middle of the road, then turned around to face the others. "We never have that kind of fun at our church. Hell, we never have any kind of fun at our church. I think if a fight broke out, Gertrude would have a faintin' spell and I'd have to drag her all the way home. That ain't somethin' I'd wanna do." He smiled and started to hand the jug to Wes again, but his brother wasn't paying attention. "You'd better hang on to this, Wes. I'm likely to spill it, and then what would we do for a drink?"

Wes was waiting for his chance to bring up the Night Riders—the only thing he wanted to talk about—and all this chatter only added to the pressure building up inside him. *Just tell me about the damn Night Riders,* Wes thought. As Mark handed him the jug, Wes glared at Art.

"We still got this other jug," said Art. "That should be plenty enough to get us all the way back to town."

Art looked at Wes, then said to Mark, "There was also considerable discussion about that fella Jones. Lots of fellas was wonderin' if he'd made a deal with somebody." He stared at Wes, but got no reaction and continued, hoping to push his cousin to start talking. "Your brother here seemed to know a lot about him and said maybe he's just out stirrin' things up. Ain't that what you said, Wes?"

Wes turned to Art and scowled. "All I said was that he's probably met with a lot of fellas and if anybody made a deal they wouldn't talk about it." He lifted the jug and took a swallow. "Besides," he said, raising his whiskey-choked voice, "if word got out that Jones bought someone's tobacco, don't you think the Night Riders would be plannin' a raid on him?" Art frowned and looked away. The thought that it could happen echoed in Art's mind, and the unspoken truth bounced around the wagon, waiting to be heard.

Mark was desperate to keep the peace between his brother and cousin. "We better get movin' before someone comes along and crashes into the back of this wagon." He snapped the reins and the horse started pulling the rig. Wes wished that his brother would shut up so he could say what he had to say to Art. He looked off to the east, and as they passed the Cook farm—the place where Zora had been raised by her grandparents—he thought about her for a moment, missing her and her quiet love, wishing all of this was over. When the wagon hit a hole in the road, he lost the image of Zora and took another drink from the jug.

"Either of you fellas wanna go down to Dresden?" said Mark. "If not, I'm gonna turn on the Boydsville Road." When neither of them responded, Mark took their silence for agreement and continued to the crossroad.

"You know, Art," Wes said as he looked around, "this is probably the place where Anthie saw them Night Riders a couple of weeks ago." He looked up at Mark and added, "Have you heard anythin' about 'em since last week?"

Mark shook his head. "There ain't been any news since the shootin'."

Wes glanced at Art and realized that this was the opening he'd been waiting for. "How about you, Art? Have you heard anythin' about the Night Riders?" Wes watched his cousin's eyes and face, silently urging him to react, hoping he'd see something that would confirm Art knew his farmhand was a Night Rider.

Art took a long swallow of the liquor, afraid of the fire in Wes's eyes. He wiped his lips with the back of his hand and pushed the cork into the opening of the jug. *I can't tell him now,* he thought, afraid of what might happen. He cleared his throat, turned to his cousin and said, "Why would I know anythin' about Night Riders, Wes?" The lie came easy, but he saw that Wes didn't believe him. "Just because I joined the Association don't mean I know what the Riders are doin' or who they are." Suddenly afraid, he folded his arms across his chest and turned away.

"Are you sure?" The words rushed from Wes's throat and his face turned red.

Mark feared the worst. "Hey fellas, pass me that jug," he said, feeling the heavy tension in the wagon. "I need another drink before I get to the turn." Mark felt helpless. *This has gone too far,* he thought.

Wes continued to stare at Art, but his cousin just gazed at the trees. Mark made the turn onto Boydsville Road and flicked the reins along the flanks of the horse. The wagon's steel wheels created a pounding noise as they bounced in the ruts left over from yesterday's rain. The harsh light of the sun behind the steel gray clouds was still well above the tree line as they rode toward the west. Mark slowed the horse when they neared the next turn.

"Pull up, Mark," Art said and waited for the wagon to slow down. He pointed over to one of the farmhouses and turned to Wes. "See that big red bay tied to the fence? Ain't that the one Jones rides, Wes? I wonder what he's doin' at Alderdice's farm?"

"I don't know if that's his horse," said Wes, his voice hard. "You think there's only one red bay in Western Kentucky?"

"That's his horse, all right," said Art, ignoring Wes's tone. "There ain't no red bay that tall in these parts."

"Even if it does belong to Jones, what's that got to do with me?"

"I don't know, Wes. You tell me. We all know that he's been to your place, 'cause you told us so. You been sayin' that you didn't make a deal with him. But Jones has been tellin' everybody that he made one with you." Art waited, his heart pounding. The question came hard and fast to his lips, "How much did he offer you, Wes?"

"If he offered me a price, and I ain't sayin' he did, it ain't none of your damn business."

Art's body shook, his voice scratchy. "I thought we were friends and told each other everythin'."

"So did I, Art." Wes glared at his cousin. "Have you told me everythin' about the Night Riders?"

Mark whipped the horse's rear with the reins, throwing both men off balance. *I gotta get them to the store and try to calm 'em down before they get into a fight.* He kept the wagon going and didn't look back. The empty jug rolled around, bouncing off the sideboards, sounding like a bomb each time it hit. Both men sitting in the back of the wagon held on tight, unable to speak.

When the he reached the road that headed back into Lynnville, Mark turned the horse east and kept the wagon moving all the way into town. The sun was going down behind them as he pulled up to the front porch and set the brake. Before Mark could say anything, he heard his name called from the other side of the road. He looked over at the hotel and saw Jon McCuen and Joe Paige, two of his better customers, walking toward the store.

"Evenin', Mark," said Paige. "You gonna open up for business? I need to get a few things, and they can't wait 'til tomorrow mornin'."

Mark knew this wasn't a good time for business and that he needed to get Art and his brother calmed down. He looked back and watched as they climbed out of the wagon, each staggering and carrying an empty liquor jug. "Let's all go inside," Mark said, unlocking the door and walking into the store. "I can put on a fresh pot of coffee. What do you say?"

The two farmers smiled and grunted their agreement, but Wes and Art didn't say a word, still seething from the words that had passed between them.

While Mark fixed the coffee and set the pot on the woodstove, Art wandered down the side aisles to the back of the store, and Wes stayed up front by the window. The two farmers headed to the middle of the building and pawed around in a box of hardware. Mark shoved some wood into the stove, not taking his eyes off Wes and Art.

"Are you findin' what you need?" Mark asked, wanting the visitors to leave. "If not, I've got more in the back."

"Looks like you got what I need," said Paige. "Been wantin' to fix that gate on my pigsty, and these hinges oughta do the trick."

Suddenly, Mark wasn't in a hurry for the visitors to leave. If he could keep them around and get enough coffee into Wes and Art, maybe it would help diffuse the tension between the two good friends. Mark knew he was the only one sober enough to help them both.

"Why don't you fellas stay for a minute and have some coffee?"

The visitors obliged and joined Mark by the woodstove.

"You wanna pay for the hinges now, Joe, or should I put 'em on your account?" He waited while the men sat down.

"It don't really matter. Go ahead and put 'em in the ledger, I guess." Paige sipped at the coffee and leaned the chair so it rested on its back legs. "What you fellas been doin' this afternoon?"

"Mostly just rode around and talked," Mark said.

"Judgin' by the empty jugs, it looks like the three of you also had a drink or two," said McCuen, smiling as he settled down in his chair and glanced at Wes. "Must've been some powerful talkin' goin' on."

Wes looked back over his shoulder in the direction of the men seated by the stove. His eyes were dark and foreboding. Mark hoped Wes could control his temper long enough for the farmers to finish their coffee and head out.

"We mostly talked about family business," Mark replied, and that ended the conversation. The two men grew quiet, and then Paige set the half-empty cup next to the stove and rose from his chair.

"I guess I'd better get on home," he said, signaling to Mc-Cuen with his eyes.

"Me too, I suppose. I don't wanna miss out on supper."

McCuen got out of his chair, and the visitors went with Mark to the front door. He thanked them for their business and locked the door after they walked outside.

"I need to sit down," Mark said as he slumped into one of the chairs by the stove. He buried his face in his sweaty hands, his energy drained by the nearly physical tension in the room.

Lost in thought, Art looked up from where he stood and saw Wes in the front of the store. Art had found the last derby hat on the shelf and was holding it by the brim. Glancing over at Mark, he said, "I gotta get home. Mollie's probably wonderin' where I am." Rolling his neck to work out the kinks, he put the hat on the top of the shelf and staggered toward the door, only stopping when Wes spoke up.

"We're not done here, Art." Wes's words were mushy.

"I said I need to get home. I'm leavin' now."

"Not yet, you ain't," said Wes. "There's somethin' I need to find out. Somethin' you need to tell me."

"I don't know what you're talkin' about, Wes," said Art. He reached for the door handle, but Wes grabbed his arm.

"Hold it. I wanna know why you lied to me."

Art shook Wes's hand off and stepped away, looking to Mark for help. "When did I lie to you?" But Art knew the answer, and it pained him to ask the question. He burped up sour whiskey and spit it onto the floor.

"You lied to me about Charley Randall," Wes yelled. "You knew that he was a Night Rider, and you didn't tell me. You hired him and J.D., and you knew all the time that they was Night Riders and are gonna raid my farm." Wes held onto the edge of the counter, trying to steady himself.

"You don't know what you're talkin' about, Wes," he said, staggering away from his cousin. "Whoever told you they're Night Riders is a liar."

"It was Anthie who told me, and my son don't lie to me." Wes's rage was growing, and he felt the throbbing behind his eyes.

"Well maybe he didn't lie. Maybe he's just wrong." Art paused, his own lie growing beyond his control. "It don't matter, Wes. What matters is that you've been lyin' all along about makin' a deal with Jones. Mark and I know that you met with him. We both stood up for you and told the Association that you would never make a deal with the Trust. But now you've made us look like damn fools." Beads of moisture flew from his mouth.

"I ain't lyin' to you," Wes yelled. "I did not make a deal with Jones." He turned away from his cousin and walked a few steps down the center aisle of the store. He took the pistol out of his pocket, looked at Mark and set it on the top of the counter. Swaying a little, Wes spun around and leaned against the counter, staring at Art, his bloodshot eyes glaring, his jaws rigid.

"Wait a minute, you two," pleaded Mark as he rose from his chair. "You fellas need to calm down a little. There ain't no reason for you to be fightin'."

"We ain't fightin', Mark. We're just speakin' our minds, ain't we, Wes. Your brother thinks he's always right and that the rest of us are stupid." Art's voice was thick, his words unclear. He stood up as straight as he could and looked directly at Wes. "Well, you ain't right this time, Wes, 'cause the Night Riders *are* gonna raid your farm."

Wes's hands trembled as he pushed himself away from the counter. He took a step toward Art and yelled, "You know what your problem is, Art? You're afraid. You're afraid of bein' a man and standin' up for yourself. Maybe you oughta go home and sit with your sick wife. Maybe she'll tell you what to do."

"You son of a bitch," slurred Art, as he reached into his pocket for his gun. Pulling it out, he aimed it straight at Wes. "I've had enough of your ugly mouth. You're a dead man."

"No, Art, no!" yelled Mark as he reached over and grabbed Wes's gun from the counter, his hand shaking, his mind blurred. He aimed the pistol toward Art and pulled the trigger; several wild shots pierced the air, one ripping a huge hole in the center of Wes's body. As he fell, a flood of dark red blood spread across the floor. In the confusion Art fired back, one bullet tearing through Mark's heart, the other grazing the derby hat. The last two shots from Mark's gun shredded Art's chest.

In seconds, both guns were empty. All that remained was thick smoke, the acrid smell of gunpowder and the sound of the explosions as they bounced around the room. The windowpanes shook, and the echoes searched for a place to hide. There was no pride or arrogance in the lifeless bodies on the floor as the last of their heartbeats faded.

Soon, the air was as dead as the three friends.

# Chapter 24
Monday, May 21

The headline on Monday's paper read:

**Triple Killing at Lynnville**
**Bloody Tragedy Occurred Sunday Evening in**
**Mark Wilson's Store**

Lynnville was a town in shock. No anvil-pounding sounds rang out from the blacksmith's shop, no shoppers filled the boardwalks and, except for three wagons parked in front of Mark Wilson's house, the roads were empty. From the hotel's second floor, Edwin T. Jones shook his head in disappointment as he looked through the window of his room at the wagons and thought about the effects that last night's shooting had on his business. He let go of the curtain and turned away to finish packing his bag.

Inside Mark's home, the bodies of the three friends were laid out on makeshift wooden biers. They'd been cleaned and examined by the doctor and dressed for the final time by their wives. In a few hours, they would be placed in their coffins and carried to the cemeteries. Mark was going to be buried less than a mile from his store. The funerals for Wes and Art would take place later in the day about six miles southeast of town at the Beech Grove Cemetery. Zora and Mollie insisted that the two best friends be buried side by side.

\* \* \*

A single mule pulled the wagon carrying Wes's casket. Connie held the reins tightly in his hands while his ma sat silently, her Bible resting in her lap. In the wagon with Art's casket, Anthie sat on the seat next to Mollie. Behind them, a long procession moved slowly up and down the hilly roads between the tall oaks and beeches and past field after field of fresh, green tobacco.

Leaving the wagons at the road, the two families followed their friends and the men carrying the caskets up the slight incline to the west. The fresh-turned red dirt of the two holes stood in stark contrast to the rich green grass on the crest of the small hill. Each of the holes was six feet deep and just ten feet apart.

The mourners stood quietly in the dappled shade, listening to the gently stirring crickets. There was no preacher in attendance. Instead, some of the folks shared fond memories of the two men. Zora stood in front of the graves, her arm around Mollie, as the pallbearers lowered the boxes into the ground. Each of the women was surrounded by her children. Mary Lula cradled Art's youngest in her arms while Irene and Thressie held tightly to each other. Little Ruthie sat quietly in the grass, her rag doll squeezed to her chest.

Standing tall and silent, Zora looked around at each of her children, letting her eyes fill up with the beauty of them. When her gaze reached Anthie's face, her heart quickened. She saw his sadness, his loneliness, the numbness in his features and the blankness in his eyes. She felt a deep longing to hold him and to tell him everything would be all right. He's a good boy, and he'll have some good days and some bad days ahead. *Maybe tomorrow will be one of the good days,* she thought, as a tear caressed her cheek.

# Epilogue

In the days following the funeral, in a fallow field not far from Ol' Man Smith's place, a saddled red bay was spotted wandering by itself. Most everyone the sheriff and Cleary talked to agreed that the horse belonged to the tobacco buyer, Jones, but no one had seen the man since Saturday. When Cleary asked around town if anybody knew who Jones might have been with, he learned from the hotel clerk that J.D. and Charley had talked to the buyer. Unable to find either of the farmhands, Cleary put the horse up at the stable and decided to wait for Jones to claim the animal.

On Friday, Gertrude received a check for five thousand dollars from a life insurance company in Louisville. Unable to get over her husband's death, she left the store closed for nearly a month. When some of the farmers asked about buying supplies, she tried to meet their needs, but could never keep the money straight. In the end, she sold the store, its contents, its debts and its accounts.

Not long after the shooting, in Princeton, Kentucky, two hundred Night Riders burned a warehouse full of Trust tobacco, completely destroying the building and all of its contents. A year later, a slightly larger group of Night Riders raided Hopkinsville, Kentucky, and torched three more tobacco warehouses. Over the next few years, Night Riders burned tobacco in other towns and other counties. By 1910, most of the violence had ceased, and the farmers began to receive reasonable prices for their tobacco. In 1911, the US Supreme Court determined that the American Tobacco Company had violated the Sherman Anti-Trust Act, and the Black Patch War came to an end.

A few months after his pa died, Connie married Maude Wilkins and stayed on the farm to help his ma. Years later, he finally gave up farming and opened a general store and gas station in Lynnville. Connie died in 1957.

Anthie and Sudie got married in the spring of 1907. After their first son died in infancy, they separated for four years. In 1912 they reunited and had six more sons, four of whom reached adulthood. Anthie never became a farmer. Instead, using a skill he had learned in the army, he became an itinerant barber, moving his growing family every few years through Tennessee, Oklahoma and Missouri and eventually ending up in Michigan. Both Anthie and Sudie died in the late 1960s in California.

Zora eventually married a Lynnville farmer and outlived him as well. She died in 1964 and was buried next to Wes in the Beech Grove Cemetery.

# Author's Note:

My father was a storyteller. On those occasions when he wasn't out in the garage working on one of our old cars or starting another of his destined-to-remain-unfinished projects, my brothers, sisters and I would gather around our dad and ask him to tell us a story. We didn't care that we had heard all of them before; we reveled in our familiarity with them and liked hearing about our father as a kid. One particular story became legendary because it was mysterious and, perhaps, because it was never embellished. My father would only say that one of our ancestors had been killed in a shoot-out in the back of a saloon. He never told us who it was or where or when it happened. He left it to us to use our own imaginations to fill in those details. In time we outgrew our need for these stories, but never forgot them. Years after my father died, I began searching for answers to my questions about the legendary shoot-out.

In 2006, I wanted to see the place where my grandparents—Anthie and Sudie—had been born, so my wife, Mary, and I went to Lynnville. In the course of our time there, we met some elderly gentlemen in a gas station at the crossroads who said they had heard of a shoot-out that took place across the road in what was now a small market and café. Although they didn't have any details—other than a brief comment that the three men had fought over a derby hat—they felt certain that an elderly woman in the rest home in Mayfield could provide more information. We met this woman and learned that her father had purchased the Wilson General Store from Mark Wilson's widow. She thought we could find out more specific information at the Mayfield library. Later that day, we went to the library and began searching through old records. Another couple overheard us talking about the shoot-out, and the man, Bill Foy (whom I discovered was my fifth cousin), led me to the microfilm archives and showed me the front page of the *Daily Messenger* of May 21, 1906. The headline read, "A Triple Killing at Lynnville." The story took up nearly half the page and provided the few details that were known about the mysterious deaths of my great-grandfather Wes his brother Mark and cousin Art.

Over the next eight years I thought about the story often, but it wasn't until I listened to a novelist at a book festival in 2014 that I decided to tell the story about my grandfather Wes and the Black Patch War.

The full text of the front-page story about the shooting can be found on my website, BruceWilsonWrites.com.